STRANGE COMPANY

NICK COLE

Strange Company
Copyright © 2021 by Nick Cole
All rights reserved.

This is a work of fiction. Any similarity to real persons, living or dead, is coincidental and not intended by the author.

No part of this publication may be reproduced, stored in a retrieval system, or transmitted in any form or by any means electronic, mechanical, photocopying, recording, or otherwise without the prior written permission of the publisher and copyright owner.

Edited by David Gatewood
Cover Art: Pascale Blanche

Website: NickColeBooks.com

Wherever in the universe one happens to find them, an old battlefield, a forgotten glade, buried deep in the rubble of a dead and beam-ravaged world, the graves of Strange Company are often marked such:

Strangers to the Universe, Brothers to the End.

STRANGE COMPANY LOG KEEPER'S NOTE.

I'm cutting this out of the main log files and setting it for upload in the event of my death. Our story of what happened is long, and of course, very strange. We are mercenaries, private military contractors, formed long ago into a company at the earliest moments of stellar exploration. There have been eighteen log keepers before my current duty shift as the keeper of our collective history. The teller of Strange Company's deeds. We've been there, done that, and left the dead to prove it. We've seen terrible things, and incredibly beautiful things. The Rings of Corus burning in the vastness of space at the siege on Zero Station beyond the shattered world of Far Reach. The big G-Ships engaging in beam combat over the Cimarron Desert in the last hours of the Fall of Ae-Phaerax. The living machines of Psionica coming out to do battle like the waves of a cruel ocean that would crush everything. But the company allying with the Seeker, a rogue Monarch, is a critical event in the company's very strange history. And possibly… the reason for its bad ending. And so, it must be noted as such. If only so someone might know what became of us. The tragedy of Strange Company. And who we once were.

These events began in 2645 MR…

CHAPTER ONE

That day, our first op planetside, was his show to run. We didn't even see the captain and the initial op order. And of course, we got the frago from the old drunk Stinkeye himself when he waddled into our barracks that hot morning and told us to get our lazy carcasses in gear. The war was on whether the other side believed it or not. We had an opportunity to make some trouble and he was "in a mood to." We'd just finished morning PT and the day was already hot and sweaty, but still you could smell the reek of Stinkeye's gutter liquor on his rank breath as he came into the bay and squinted at us through his one good eye. Both eyes work. Or at least I think they do. It's just that he only ever uses the one to glare around at everybody, wishing the galaxy nothing but bad. As is his way. Always weaving slightly as he studies whose soul he might steal today. His voice a hypnotic broken screen door as he promises unholy death and destruction on anyone who dares dispute or mock him.

But these are hard men. They've faced worse. Been low on ammo and hip-deep in trouble. They don't scare easily. Even if Stinkeye is the closest thing to a witch the galaxy has to offer.

I think male witches are called warlocks. For the record. And this is a record.

Stinkeye's gear and fatigues are old. Old from wars that ended hundreds of years ago and to which some of the older log files give reference. I mean like really old. I don't recognize the camo pattern from any conflict I've ever been in. In fact, there's no real pattern left in them, they're so blown out with wear and tear. They're just olive drab now, and somehow so washed and faded they match his tired old dark skin. Like he's some kind of walking ghost of all the soldiers that ever humped rucks on foreign worlds. I think he's what the original Earthers used to call *Asian*. So either he's from the Constellations of Pan, or he's actually Asian from way back on Earth and whatever place exactly constituted *Asia* on the mysterious home world of mankind's birth. Except his skin is black like a sunburn that took twenty years to earn and decided to hang on for what remained of the life inside. Like a scar. A badge. Or a memory.

Stinkeye is technically a Strange Company warrant officer. He mutters under his breath and growls ominously when he isn't insulting everyone right to their face. Never talks. Just mutters oaths and curses, or shouts like the F Class starport drunk on payday night. It's all part of his "space war wizard" act. He once told me, when I found myself accidentally drinking with him and wondering how fast I could pound and get out, that he likes to cultivate "the mystery of himself." Which is fine. Origin stories inside the Strange Company are sacred and often linked to crimes and bounties on other worlds best left undiscovered. All of us are wanted somewhere. A few even for reasons that aren't actually crimes. Best to keep the truth hidden by a body of lies, unless… you feel the grim astronaut of death coming for you on the next op. Then… settle your soul as best you can remember and try to expend as much brass as possible before you go down. Your brothers in the Strange Company appreciate your last efforts on their behalf.

"Up with yer carcasses, we gotta go make some big, big trouble for these little commies." He swore, spat, and took a pull from a dented hip flask as he glared around at us. "You remember, you little whelps… only good commie is a dead commie," he mutters to himself. I have no idea what a "commie" is. And I've never seen the mangy old flask empty. There's a superstition in the company that if it ever is, then it means the old soldier we call Stinkeye is probably dead somewhere. And despite his bad behavior, it means we're probably in a lot of trouble. That perhaps our luck has run out. Good, or bad. The galaxy has had it with our collective troublemaking.

Stinkeye is the literal walking, living, breathing, meaning of *Necessary Evil*.

But as we say in the Strange, "He's *our* evil."

Technically all the freaks in Voodoo Platoon of Strange Company are counted as warrant officers. Which means they outrank everyone except the Old Man as company commander, and they don't have to answer to anyone, or show up anywhere, for anything. But of course, that's always been true of all warrant officers in all armies everywhere. Always has been. Always will be until the heat death of the universe.

Or at least that's what I suppose.

"We ain't had chow yet," I told the old wreck. One of our little enlisted jabs back at the warrant freaks of Voodoo is that we don't stand on ceremony. No one in any of the other platoons would ever call Stinkeye "*sir*."

Stinkeye hit the flask again and held it out to me. I declined. Punch walked by, coming from the shower, grabbed the flask, hit it, winced, and exhaled as he handed it back. Then my assistant platoon leader started wiggling into his tactical equipment carrier over the top of his striker pants and t-shirt.

The t-shirt told everyone to have a nice day.

Stinkeye laughed. More to himself than anyone. And it wasn't a pleasant laugh. Punch continued to shudder from the gutter liquor and even looked like he was gonna hurl at one point as he laced up his boots. Still he kept right on getting into his battle rattle because whether we liked it or not it was time to get it on.

Time for this war to get going and make something of itself. Even if we had to jumpstart the beast.

Drunk or poisoned you're gonna soldier in the Strange Company. That's a fact, Jack.

"Might not want to eat much on this one, Sergeant Orion," Stinkeye whispered confidentially, leaning in. "Gonna be a lotta bodies out in the sun by noon. Smell real bad. Especially if there's gutshot in some of 'em. That's the worst."

He muttered like a ragged tent flap on a windy night with a bad case of having just swallowed weapons cleaner solvent. Again, the "space war wizard" character on display in the play of himself.

I cast the side-eye at the old chief as I shrugged into my plate carrier. It hadn't been shot to pieces yet in that war where we made a dark alliance with one of the masters of the universe, as they think of themselves. The Monarchs. But that was coming. Out on the horizon like a bad storm you were driving into. Looking back, that's how it was. You were stupid if you couldn't taste, smell, or touch it. Like the first few minutes when you think the Sikhan street tacos aren't gonna sit so hot and you start looking for a shot of Ginquil to maybe kill the bacteria where it's breeding in your gut before you start sweating, shaking, vomiting, and exploding all at once.

Most of our equipment was, if not the best, at least still in good condition at the beginning of this mess on Crash. Sometimes you mark your time by the condition of your gear. It makes you feel old and lucky at the same time. Which is a good thing to be when you're a soldier. Both old and lucky. And without too much metal left in you.

"What're you gonna do?" I asked Stinkeye. "Make 'em all sick when the shooting starts?" He'd done that before. Caused equilibrium imbalances resulting in massive waves of nausea as we attacked an enemy position. You almost felt bad for a guy with a load in his fatigues who couldn't stand up as you shot him down. And his friends too. It's awful to die bad. Embarrassed to death as you go. Trust me, I've seen enough of that. But then you remember they were probably going to do something equally horrible to you and it's best to get it done to someone else first before they do it to you.

Rules to live by in the Strange Company.

"Somethin' like that," muttered the malevolent old warrant officer as he gave everyone the evil eye again. "Trucks leave in twenty. Be on 'em, Orion. You… and your men."

He was right. We shouldn't have eaten that day. But we did, all of us grabbing breakfast burritos from the cantina that served as our chow hall inside the developing FOB near Sa'Farm City. We ate until we linked up with Ghost, who'd secured our actual transportation elements into the area of operations that day.

The "battlefield."

Four technicals that could have been any boomba rancher's utility truck. Enclosed cab. High-performance engines. Big fat all-terrain traction balls. Open flatbed with sides. Ghost Platoon had located the type of vehicles they'd want for this op since they'd be the ones doing the shooting. They're the snipers and scouts of Strange Company. Shooters every one of 'em. Our job, Reapers, was just to provide three-sixty security, for the snipers to do their business.

The four snipers from Ghost working this op, and their spotters, would lie down in the back of the truck beds. We'd cover them with tarps and drive the trucks down into the capital area the kids calling themselves whatever passed for "loyalist" on this mess of a world were currently rioting and looting in. Pretending to be an army as news networks reported they'd "liberated" the capital and were intent on seeking a full return to the Bright Worlds Federation. The best status any world can hope for... that isn't the home of the Monarchs. Or Earth, as it has always been known. That's their home. And its status occupies the top of the food chain. Pride of place. The envy of all other worlds.

In the hierarchy of worlds, it starts with Earth, then Bright Worlds a few rungs down on the ladder, then the Frontier, and finally the Undiscovered down below that. Astralon, or Crash as it was known, is a Frontier world. Above the Undiscovered but barely on the ladder.

Apparently, we all once came from Earth. But now you have to be a Monarch to live there. That's their world. A no-go zone for the rest of us.

And Stinkeye wildly claims, when he's especially drunk and playing Cheks and he's lost every hand and telling you horrible stories of the Dark Labs that officially don't exist, that he's actually from there. From back on Earth. And that he's as old as the first colony vessel to reach Centa... some old ship no one ever heard of called *Enterprise*.

That sounds made up. Stinkeye lies more than he tells the truth. If he ever tells the truth at all.

Monarch warships have names like *Medusa, Centaur, Ogre*... and such.

If you believe that fairy tale and all, of any normal space rat coming from anywhere near Earth, I have a free trader with a low parsec count on the jump engines that'll get you all the way out to Lonesome Star.

Trust me. Not.

So, that hot sweaty first morning of operations we drive out into the Heights, the old neighborhoods the second wave of colonists to arrive on Crash set up long ago near the downtown area. What Stinkeye's little operations order, if you can call it that, refers to as the "operational area." From the Heights our hidden snipers in the back of the trucks have a good sight picture of the main protest "army" rampaging across the capital mall, which is a large, beautifully landscaped area, over the old first landing site.

We arrive at our phase line, and to see it from here, it's almost like you're watching some summer street festival of fun and love down there on the old First Landing Mall. All the kids down there seem to be having a really great time despite the collapsing government and the impending arrival of Monarch forces to support the new government and a restoration to the Bright Worlds Federation. And to their credit, none of them, none of those kids down there playing soldier, are firing their brand-new weapons like so many alien tribal species do upon first receiving such lethal gifts from some off-world outfit looking to curry favor for larger political means. Some corporation that needs the locals to pull a genocide on the other difficult tribes so that surveyed deep core minerals can be extracted by the big strip lifters that will hit that world and do seventy years work in six months. Weapons will clear the areas to be strip-mined one firefight at a time.

Don't worry. The galaxy's a big place. There's room to spare. That's the line. Officially. That's what they tell those who take the time and energy to get upset about other people's problems.

Hey, everyone's got problems. But that doesn't mean you need to get involved.

Unless you're getting paid to.

The kids down there who are our enemies and don't know it yet, have gotten enough training to keep their fingers off their brand-new triggers, loaded mags in, and rifles slung. But I'm betting no one has a chambered round to deal with the hate that's about to be laid on them. Fifty-fifty that the safety is off when it's supposed to be on for at least seventy-five percent of them. The taking of the capital was mostly nonviolent. But they, the Loyalist Youth for Tomorrow, as they are called by themselves, treat it like they just liberated Gonga during the Sindo forty years back. When in fact all they really did was throw a temper tantrum for two months until law and order completely broke down. Of course they had operators from among the Monarchs' guard dogs to show them how to do it. Now they have guns, and it appears for all intents and purposes they've just won some battle though they haven't fired a single shot in anger. There's been some revenge, but that's mainly been the street gangs doing business under cover of the counter-revolution.

They've set up a few machine-gun positions at the entrance to the big greensward below. It's really quite impressive, if you have no clue. Some arty, comm, and maybe a low-grade laser designator for my combat lens and I could ruin this "army" in about three minutes or less.

My inquiries into local history say this area, this First Landing Mall, really is where the first colony drop took place over eight hundred years ago. One of the huge Sisyphus haulers pushing out here at sub-light to drop a load of determined, hard-as-nails, desperate for a shake at something new, world builders. Eight hundred years later and it's still a frontier world. That's ninety percent of the problem right there.

I'm in team four riding in the TC position on our technical. I have four guys in each vehicle team. Even as I write this down, I think of the three that won't be with us within two weeks when the heavy fighting starts between actual trained military units. But that first day, compared to the last six months, is nothing but a picnic as I remember it.

Officially it'll be called a massacre.

The kids don't even know we're operational. That PMCs have been hired to come in and fight for Astralon, which doesn't want to be called Crash anymore and wants to be free of Monarch influence. They'd freak if they knew Stinkeye had been thinking this one up. Even just the sight of the old war toad would have had them running if they knew what was good for them. A lot of people like to pretend they've been there and done that. Well, our ancient space war wizard or whatever you want to call Stinkeye, has. And the things he's seen and done are only found in the darkest parts of the galaxy. I heard someone once tell him, after he'd lost a game of Cheks, getting completely trounced by three trolls, that Stinkeye was the galaxy's very own Heart of Darkness.

The old little man nodded soberly, waving one scarred finger back and forth at the speaker as he stared at his bad hand.

"I ain't dat, little soldier," he replied, drunkenly slurring his words. His eyes bleary. His head weaving. "But I seen it once. And it wasn't a thing I wanna see 'gain, tell you so."

We ate the breakfast burritos and drove to the kill that hot sweaty morning the war started. Hot and getting hotter. Looking like laborers wearing work coats over our tactical rigs. Rifles down and out of sight.

Maybe, sometimes I think, that's what got them killed. Those three brothers of Strange Company who didn't make it a couple of weeks into this show we call the War on Crash. It was too easy at first, and it felt like the whole world was just gonna flip because Stinkeye said *boo* that day. But I coulda told them, our three dead of Strange Company, and there would be others, that it's always the same. You start every contract with momentum like you're really gonna do something… and then end up running for your life, swearing you'll never merc again and that you're gonna quit the company as soon as we reach the first decent major port world.

But you never do. You never quit. You just buy it one day and your time in the rotation of the galactic lens is done. Your hash settled. Grave marked.

As a sergeant I could have told them that. The three dead who were riding in the technical on Stinkeye's mission to "make some trouble" that day. As their sergeant I *should've* told them that. Warned them about what was inevitably coming.

And they wouldn't have listened. They never do.

No one thinks they're really going to die.

I once spent a weekend with a Falmorian party girl. She sang softly as we lay there in the dark. Exhausted and watching the fan on the ceiling turn. Counting the hours until the game was over. It was a song about not having regrets. In French. She sang it in French, and I thought that was so odd because the native Falmorian are part eel, which is why everyone wants a party girl from that world. At least once in their life. Falmoria was an early colony world for the French after they left Earth.

"What do you think," she buzzed, and stroked my chest with her long and slender hand. Electricity coursed through my body like some drug that made you sleepy and happy all at the same time.

"About what?" I asked her, dreaming of better things than what I'd seen out there in the dark along the frontier worlds.

"About zee song," she purred softly, her deep voice like electric velvet. "Iz it true?"

She was cobalt-colored. Her eyes big and luminous in the dark. Watching me. Her curves like liquid darkness.

"Can you have no regrets, my *estrangier*? In zis life? Are zhere none?"

She called me that. *Estrangier*. Stranger. I never asked why. Just guessed it was because she knew who I worked for. Just another mercenary with the Strange Company. But since then I've wondered if it was for another reason.

"It's a nice sentiment," I murmured to her and the twirling ceiling fan above us. Falling into sleep for a little while. Falling into a better universe not this one. "But it ain't true…"

I don't know if I said *But I wish it was*. Or I dreamed that I did. I still don't know now, when I think back to that night with her.

Private military contracting is the best casino in the galaxy. You always win, until you lose. Then you lose big time. You lose everything in fact. So, who cares. Because your life got lost along the way too.

If you're going to lose… think about it, then really lose. Lose… everything.

We lost three within two weeks. But on that first day of operations we were a whole company just starting out on a new contract on a new world that thought it was ready to try the Big War Show. Hardrop, Crisp, and Twopeat would get killed in the future beyond that day. But not that day as we drive through the streets of the Heights, ready to do war. None of 'em told me their stories before they went. I guess they weren't expecting to die on the days they actually did die on.

Death is ironically surprising like that when you're a private military contractor. Every day you're expecting to die. Buy it in some hellhole going from bad to worse not just by the second, but by the bullet, and the air is thick with them in that unexpected moment, and then the day you do you're completely surprised it actually happened to you.

Trust me. I've seen the look when guys first get hit. Fatally. It's completely unexpected. But what did we think would happen? Then you do your best to wrap your mind around it. Or at least that's what I think.

All four technicals fanned out that morning to different streets with vantage points over the mall in the bowl of the capital below. We'd parted ways with Stinkeye on the way in. We pulled up to the curb as kids in their new gear and carrying shiny new weapons and protest signs streamed past us. Heading to the party. Heading to the mall. Stinkeye, our Voodoo asset for the mission, looking like the galaxy's mangiest warrant officer who'd never make private in any real army, hobbled off down into the crowd-swollen mall. His bandy-legged stride wobbling his squat frame back and forth as he waded into the press of the young bright-eyed warriors who would return this world to the Monarchs. Hell, in their minds they already had.

They had no idea.

Chiefs Stinkeye and Cook utterly hate each other. That's pretty much the only thing generally known about the inner workings of Voodoo Platoon. Those two would do each other in if they weren't so damn afraid of the captain.

We call Stinkeye *Chief*. But we'd never call him *sir*.

"What if we hit you while you're down there?" asks Sergeant Slick, Ghost's platoon leader, as our chief warrant officer leaves us to go make his particular brand of mayhem among the locals down there playing soldier. Making it on our behalf down along the mall as the operation begins.

"You won't even see me," croaks Stinkeye over his shoulder, and as we watch him walk down the trash-littered dusty street on that hot summer morning as a war kicks off its opening day on this dying world even though it doesn't know it's dying yet, he begins to waver and fade from our view right before our eyes. Like some heat mirage that was never really there all along.

The warrants in Voodoo are pure freaks.

One has to wonder what the big super brains of the Monarchs did to him in those Dark Labs. What a super-genius-level AI can think up. And what was the price of the "gift" they gave Stinkeye. His ability to do Psyonix.

And what would it be like if there really were no regrets.

We mount up and move to our first shooting positions once we part ways with Stinkeye.

It's an hour later and all four technicals are blocks away from each other when we get his signal to engage targets. It's hot and the sun is directly overhead. We pull back the dusty old tarps for the snipers so they can shoot, and they start firing according to Stinkeye's instructions. All the technicals are divided into two groups. West Group and East Group. All of us are on the extreme edges of the massed "army" we're looking down on. Hiding in the streets above the mall. Watching the Loyalist kids frolic as they play conquering hero on this eternal morning. Snapping pictures with their devices as they pose in front of the guns and reflection pool past generations long gone and much forgotten put up to be remembered by. Silly history… don't you know you're just a plaything for would-be tyrants? Smoking joints and cavorting around growing drum circles as slogans they think they've actually come up with on their own are chanted and reverberate. The Loyalists have won the war before it even ever got started. Huzzah!

That's how easy it is.

It really does feel like a festival as our snipers begin to shoot them.

Ten rounds and we shift to a new shooting position.

The silencers are huge and the noise suppression is luxurious. The shots really sound like mere mouse farts. Whispers of ghost breaths. And of course, the snipers are covered by the tarp except for their rifles. Just a couple of workers standing around a truck is all anyone sees. The expended brass is just staying in the bed of the truck as it drizzles away from the ejector ports of the big rifles in steady-slow streams. I run three-sixty for my technical and listen to the shots *puff* and *hiss* as the big fat silencers deal with the noise suppression. No one is interested in us up here. But our rifles are out and we will engage.

Down below no one is screaming. Not yet.

At least not for the first five shots. It's on shot six I hear some girl down there start to scream bloody murder as her friend's head just magically comes apart in front of her. I don't even see this, but I hear Soups, the spotter for Wulf, say just that.

"Got 'em in the head, Wulfy. Nice shot."

I chance a glance down to the mall and iris in with my combat lens dialed in for daytime combat. I scan and spot. Edges of the crowd on our side. Out near the boundaries of the greensward that is the mall. I count three corpses down in the grass and I see the screaming girl, some chubby chick, university age with red-dyed "super hair" as they like to call it, on her knees and crawling away from the guy she was just standing next to. She probably dyed the hair red with an expensive nano-wash to support the movement that morning or at some other recent time. The guy Wulf just blew the head off of doesn't care anymore about supporting hair.

Four more shots and we shift position. The other technicals are beginning to engage as we move to our next loc.

Down below, the protestor-resistor-looter-justice army doesn't quite get what's going on now. Collectively. Why? Because they've been trained to only operate collectively. To take their orders and participate in groups when they attack others, destroy property, and generally make a nuisance of themselves without any kind of actual resistance. They're like jackals. Suddenly forming a mob and going after the law-abiding to demand more change. But things are different today. Right now, they have no clue they're today's victims. Prey. Hunted. Collectively. Individually they just know some of their own have suddenly been shot dead. And in the few cases of exceptionally good shooting, watched heads turned to bone spray and red mist on the hot summer air.

There are gut shots because of course.

Clearly this was not what was planned for *Conquering Hero Victory Day*. Months of the easy victories of smashing glass and fighting the powers that be with endless slogans, chants, and marches in the streets, and full media support, are collapsing as the realization settles in that war is something completely different than one ever imagines it to be. And that it is starting today, whether you like it or not.

None of them realize they're just pawns being used by the Monarchs to show that the Resistance, Strange Company's employers, are nothing but murderers of children.

Everyone must play their part. And yes, there are regrets. It was just a dream I once had that there weren't any.

We know what's happening down there. And this isn't even the Stinkeye magic of Psyonix outlined in his self-aggrandizing drunken op order back at the FOB. Chief Cook making sarcastic remarks from the back of the briefing room and saying things like, "You call that a plan, you old lush?"

Stinkeye barking at Chief Cook that he'd turn the psyops specialist into a junkie who craved nothing but tales of the outer dark until he was little more than a gibbering mass unrecognizable to his own mother. If he even had one. Chief Cook laughed and waved Stinkeye off, all very theatrically. "I read that stuff for fun already, you old fraud. Your feeble powers are nothing more than cons to pull on weak minds. Admit it, Stink. You couldn't suggest your way out of a paper bag, even with a hull torch in one hand, you ridiculous old carnie. You know nothing of how to really break minds and bend hearts."

This last part was pure sinister.

Trust me, we're all brothers in the Strange Company. We really are. But that doesn't mean we're friends.

So, we know the plan even though the horrified kids down there on the mall don't. They're just sitting around like the children they really are, stunned and crying, as the horror that they are under attack begins to spread like an out-of-control grease fire across the milling crowd. Us in the technicals, Reaper and Ghost, we're shifting to new positions to shoot some more. Playing our part in this opening scene of the tragedy we've all come to act out today for the galactic stage. Adjusting to how the crowd is now trying to develop its response. Some of the leaders down there are trying to explain that everyone needs to go to their fighting positions. That they are under attack. The street festival is definitely over today. It's time to play war, gang.

The kids would like law enforcement and the adults to take over now that there are *owies*. Someone's not playing fair and that isn't right. *Didn't you hear our slogans about equality and justice when we smashed your stuff and looted your businesses?* You can almost hear them think this silliness about the universe and how it really works.

We make our next position, for us in team four it's a three-story parking garage. We hit the shadowy darkness of level two, which is open and guarded only by flex wire along the open edges. The lot is empty. Since the riots, no one has been coming into downtown much. The children have gotten dangerous. Tarp back, weapons ready, the snipers begin to do their work again. This time shooting down more of the enemy along the edges of the mass of angry and frightened "soldiers" who'd just won the "war" before it even started. Driving them to panic and run for the center of the mob now.

Only now do they realize the war is just beginning. And that they are the enemy.

What happens next is terrible to behold. At least it is for me. Some of the Strange find it funny. If only because distance lends perspective and we're able to watch the terrorized and terrible children who are in it suddenly react out of utter mindless fear. They have no training to speak of. They are not actually soldiers, like we are, and no amount of sloganeering is going to do that for them. They've merely been dressed up for war to play war. Now they are really in it. War. People, friends, their comrades, are dying along the edges of their "army" and the kids at the edges want to be anywhere but where they see people dying all around them.

So of course they run toward the center seeking help.

Both edges of the same army down there do this at once.

And for some unexplainable reason, they just start shooting each other. And this has to be pure Stinkeye mind-voodoo down there. Within seconds, using his mental powers no doubt, he has confused enough of them to mistake comrades for sudden predators amid smoke, heat, and blood spray. Or what some call the Fog of War. A series of accidental firefights break out as both sides try to get away from the edges. Must get away from the edges. Must own the center.

A girl who had been a Molotov thrower, probably targeting spike shops and banks in the early days of the liberation as she thought of it, unslings her rifle and dumps a whole mag into her compatriots coming straight at her. Un-aimed and wild she does credible damage for an amateur. She's screaming and telling them something as she spends all her ammo and gets a dry click at the end of the party, no doubt. All we can see from up here is her mouth and lips moving in an angry snarl that suggests she would kill more if there were unlimited bullets. She has more mags, but swapping out for a full one doesn't even seem to occur to her. A moment later some guy, a good-looking dude with wire-rimmed virtu-specs who was probably just there for the chicks and had learned to talk a good game about the literature of Early Sauvagan, blows her brains out. And in seconds both sides of the same team are tearing away at each other viciously, shooting anyone they can, and running for their lives straight at those trying to do the same in that terrible-to-behold moment.

It is everyone for themselves down there. Get back to the Mom and Dad you turned your back on and called *stupid* and *old-fashioned* in the lead-up to when all this liberation craziness began. Falling for Monarch propaganda is bad. Dying for it's worse. Even ridiculous.

A minute later and it's a sea of corpses at the center down there.

Then one of the light machine guns, a plaything and picture set piece for their social media blasts moments earlier, turns and opens up on the crowd for no sane or rational reason. I honestly can't believe it's happening. And trust me, I'm the guy who'll tell you he's seen just about everything. Guess not. Its suddenness is horrible because I know what those weapons systems can do to crowds. They're made for them in fact. Traverse and squeeze is a machine gunner's dream. Drums from the drum circle cease but trumpets still blare like that should be a call to remind each other that today was supposed to be a celebration. A festival. A moment of triumph and unity for them all. The conquerors who beat the old guard with nothing but love and peace and all the broken glass that could be smashed at the expense of the status quo.

This was their day.

Sadly, it's not. It's time to get real, children. And that's what happens when private military contracting companies show up planetside. They smell money to be made like sharks smell blood in the waters of every world we've ever found them on. Things get real whether you like it or not. We are not hired out for anything else other than to ruin people's days.

It's what we do best.

Each team shifts positions one more time to take out some of the leaders trying to get things under control and then Stinkeye orders a withdrawal via comm. I get a location tag for team four to pick him up down close to the action, and we divert a few streets over.

In the distance ambulances and emergency personnel are coming, but they've halted blocks away from the massacre. They've been attacked before by the "army" they're coming to save over the last two months. More than a few times. They're not eager to go in and help now that there's been shooting. The local police aren't responding at all. In fact, many of them are now Resistance Army units geared up and ready to do battle on our side.

We pull our technical over and try to look normal as the mob runs through the streets, eyes wild and screaming in horror at what has been done down there back at the First Landing Mall on a world called Crash. The snipers are in the back, resting under the tarp. Kids, bloody, bruised, and dying, come streaming past us, crying and shouting bloody murder at what has been done by the unseen death squads.

Us. In fact. We did it. We are the death squad. Technically though, one of Dog's platoons is called Death Squad. And for good reason. But these kids running past us for their lives have no clue. Just some shady dudes sitting in a truck watching it all go down. That's all we are.

War is hard.

It's amazing what you miss when you're the self-absorbed star of your own reality show. That's the piece of advice I'd give the children, my enemies, running for their lives past our technical.

They're just figuring that out now. Which is late in the game to know such. I should feel bad for them. But I don't. Where did they think this was all going?

That's the thing. You can't just start playing a game and decide to stop when it gets rough. They should have known. It was always going here. It was always going to go badly. For someone.

And if Strange Company shows up, it's gone real bad.

But then again, they've never been on the other ruined worlds of war I've seen. If they had, or if they'd read their histories even though *if they are not official then they're illegal*, well then, they would have known this was where it was all going. They would have known that all the drum circles and broken glass lead here, to this moment, all along. And that when the free guns and uniforms were handed out… they weren't actually free. They came with a price. There's always a price to be paid.

They were going to do the paying now, and for a while to come.

The wind already smells like a hot bag of diarrhea as the kids pass by our technical sitting along the street and loaded with dudes who look like more trouble they don't want. Stinkeye was right. Breakfast burritos were a big mistake as the wind turns hot and awful in the afternoon.

Nothing is easy. Nothing is free.

Stinkeye slides into the cab and he reeks of sweat and blood and alcohol. And maybe even weed. He's not smoking and he merely grunts, "RTB."

I nod to the driver and watch our Voodoo asset in the rearview mirror as we pull away from the curb, the driver delicately pushing us through the fleeing hordes as we return to base. Stinkeye's faded fatigues and open tactical equipment carrier are covered in blood spray turning rust-red. That meant he was down in it. Close to where the snipers fired? Using his powers to alter the perceptions of the already anxious kids? Fear and elation aren't that far apart. Ask any soldier who's almost been overrun on some hellhole. He'll tell you that. He'll tell you the line between those things is thin. Real thin in fact.

Stinkeye wears this necklace that dangles down across his open carrier. It's got teeth in it. And other things. Charms. Totems. Idols. Memories. I watch him in the rearview mirror, his lips moving silently, chanting some old song like an incantation, his dark skin weathered and ancient, his eyes roving and watching the seen and the unseen. The galaxy's Heart of Darkness.

I seen it once. And it wasn't a thing I wanna see 'gain, tell you so.

He said that to me. I don't know what he's chanting now in the back of the cab. But I know what I'm thinking as we drive through the foul smell of the first day of the war that will ruin this world. The dead back down there on the grass. Never believe in anything, Sergeant Orion. It'll just get you killed.

CHAPTER TWO

The loss on Astralon, or Crash, was ignominious.

It's been six months since Stinkeye's First Landing Mall Massacre kicked this whole mess off. "Astralon" was what the new upstart micro-empire paying us for our services wanted to tag their world, after they rebranded themselves and threw off the yoke of the Monarchs, ditching the name "Crash" that had been marked on the stellar maps for more than eight hundred years. The company took a brutal beating there, on Astralon, or Crash, as did all the other private military contractors fighting that loser of a war. But of course, that's what we get paid to do. Fight for the losers when no one else wants to. On the last day, or so we thought it might be but it wasn't, when the pols were hammering out some kind of cease-fire that was really just a surrender, and while we, all the merc companies, were being thrown under the bus in hopes of avoiding payment of services, we were fighting to hold the evac LZ at Syro so we could get all the NGOs and Astralonian Resistance units off-world to wherever it was they thought they could run to and hide from the Monarchs.

It had been implied that we, the merc companies, were somehow going to get a ride off-world too. *Implied* being the active word. File that under *Hopes and Dreams* and, trust me on this one, have I got a deal for you.

But sometimes all you got is hope and so you keep playing your part as though there's actually a good outcome besides the one you know you're gonna have to pay for. Dreams are what you tell yourself you once had before you became a private military contractor. A mercenary.

I knew we were getting close to something when the First Sergeant came into the burned-out building Reaper was holding, with a new recruit for the company.

Some local kid, I thought. Just like every local kid who ever ended up being a part of Strange Company. New. Frightened. And just trying to look hard because somehow he thought he was a pro now that he'd signed up to merc with an off-world company. Just like we all once looked. Even me.

You have to be honest about those things. Especially about yourself. There's something in all of us that we see in the people we have casual contempt for. Even ourselves.

"Sergeant Orion!" shouted the First Sergeant grandly. Everyone in the company loved him because there was just no other choice but to. "Got you a new one, Sar'nt Orion. Kid's as hard as nails and twice as tough. Never seen another like him 'cept maybe myself back when I was a cold-blooded killer with the batts and all. Trust me. Hells o' Suth, if he don't remind me of myself when I was tough as anyone you ever met. He's new to the company and I thought he'd be a good fit for your platoon. Put him with the best so he learns the company right and all, Sar'nt Orion."

All that was just advertising for the kid's sake.

Every new recruit to the company, on every world we managed to end up dying on, started out in the Reapers. SOP. Standard Operating Procedure. Just like I did, once and a long time ago. Just like everyone else did once and also long ago. The fun was when they realized it was always so. It usually took about two weeks. Everyone started in Reaper. Reaper was the bastard child of Strange Company.

Eventually they all realize that. If they live long enough to do so. But by then it's too late.

We called my platoon Reapers because it made the new ones think they'd ended up in something elite right from the get-go. How else were you gonna get someone to sign the contract that would land them with a bunch of mangy war dogs that did all the dirty that needed doing? *Reaper* just makes it sound cool. You can almost see the old First Sergeant rubbing his chin during the intake interview as he smooths his bone-white handlebar mustache, studying the kid now standing here in front of me. Giving the new recruit a look that indicates he sees something extra-special in this one.

Joke's on them. They are far from special. They're just new. And new is nothing in warfare. Now *old*... old is something to measure twice and cut once on. You meet an old guy in battle rattle out on the field one day and you best be careful. This ain't a business you grow old in. Unless you're good at it. And that means you're deadly.

Reapers are the intake platoon, and we're used for all the worst jobs. That's the other reason it's called Reaper, because most new intakes don't survive past here. If they do, given a campaign or two, or sometimes even just one nasty firefight, then they're pushed out into the other platoons who've taken casualties.

Ghosts. Good for them. Nice outfit.

Dogs. Whoops. You really are unlucky, buddy.

Or if they're particularly jacked up in the head... but got some special skill—read "weird" for special—then *Voodoo*. Which is just the unluckiest kind of luck to draw if you ask me for comment. It's like you can't play Cheks at all.

"He's all kitted with the basic setup, Sergeant Orion," continued the First Sergeant as though he were delivering a speech at some awards ceremony instead of a very hot war zone that had seen brutal fighting within the hour. "So take good care of him and show him the ropes, won'tcha, Sar'nt?" The old man in his ever-pristine battle rattle slapped the kid on the dingy OD-green shoulder armor the kid had been issued and banged his dented helmet with one assault-gloved hand.

"You'll do just fine here. I expect great things outta you, kid. Sergeant Orion'll show you how we operate here in the Strange Company and get you up to speed and all. Welcome to the company."

And then the old NCO was off with his ever-tired driver in tow, headed out through the rubble at the back of the old bank we'd withstood three days of shelling and enemy attacks in. Not to mention a battalion-sized push from the enemy rebels who'd just left their dead down the street we called our sector.

The rest of Reaper, in their improvised fighting positions across the ruins of the bank, noted the new kid and went on with their business. Cleaning their weapons, grabbing some chow out of their rucks, or changing socks.

Changing socks. Changing socks is my big thing. They know. They've learned. Most of Reaper has been together for the campaign on this world. Other than the four that got killed here. Sergeant Orion is big on changing your socks. Every one of them will tell you that about me.

"Prior?" I ask the kid, leading him over to the vault and the shot-to-hell teller's console I've been using as a command post.

"What?" he whispers. Low and unsure of himself now that he's been left alone among trained killers.

"Prior service?"

I'm looking at the kid's gear and know the answer already. I also know this kid's a dead man. I'm super optimistic that way of course. The First Sergeant has kitted him with our standard company gear draw. Polymer camouflage OD-green chest armor where I can see some other now-dead guy's name has been laser-etched off by Biggs who runs the company's mobile supply crawler. Ballistic shoulder pauldrons. Slightly used TEC. Tactical equipment carrier. Of course, bloodstained, but Biggs got that out with some harsh solvent and bleach. And probably a lot of swearing as his fat lips worked his ever-present chopped cigar. Thigh and shin guards that don't do squat against most modern ammo types. Brand-new combat boots because the First Sergeant, like me, is a fiend for proper foot care. A helmet with a ceramic patch where someone took one right in the brainpan. Combat tanto to make the kid feel hardcore and all. I doubt he knows how to even fight with it. A very worn ruck to carry everything else one can call their own in.

And an S-16. The all-purpose battle rifle everyone gets issued unless they're pros from other services who've managed to defect with their own personal and preferred weapon systems. Or bought some really slick high-speed gear at some weapons bazaar hauler we've docked alongside when we're slowly crawling between worlds in the *Spider*.

The S-16.

We call it "the Bastard" because it fights like one and no one wants it. It's not heavy. Burns through ammo rough and dirty. It'll shoot dirty too, waterlogged or even recently used as a club at close quarters in a sticky situation that suddenly got outta hand. This tells me one of two things.

If a new guy shows up and Biggs and the First Sergeant have stuck him with one of the seemingly endless supply of S-16 combat rifles we have on hand, rifles the Old Man got paid in surplus for on some pacification gig that went down just before I joined up, this tells me the guy is probably on the run and has no money for a good weapon system to fight for his life with. Most likely he's wanted for murder or something similar. The other possibility—he's just some new kid with no prior service in anyone's military and he wants to get off-world and go kill strange people in exciting new places.

"Prior service?" I ask the kid again as I get him to drop his ruck and sit down at my makeshift little desk for our first interview and welcome presentation to my platoon. "Who'd you serve with?"

The blank stare tells me everything.

No one, and nobody.

I sigh and hand him a protein bar.

"Eat this. No hot chow for the foreseeable future. You murder anyone?"

The kid takes it and doesn't open the pack. He's probably ready to vomit from fear because you can hear enemy mobile artillery pounding the hell out of the outskirts of the city. Again. Trying to go for the Astralonian Resistance units doing their best to get to the LZ and off-world quick. In other places, just blocks away, firefights are underway with no sign of letting up until everyone on one side is good and dead.

Any illusions this kid had about what war is really like are being quickly dispelled by the second. I can see it in his eyes. Right now, instead of burning ammo and throwing grenades at close enemies to die gloriously and prove to everyone you've left behind that you were actually a real live hero, instead you get to experience what real combat feels like for much of the time you're in it. Sitting around waiting to get killed by random artillery you can do nothing about. Or suddenly cut to pieces by a hurricane of gunfire stealthily applied your way and which you had no clue about in the last seconds of your very short life.

What he doesn't know is… we're fine here right now. The enemy probed an hour ago and we murdered them flat-out. Wasn't even a fight. They won't be trying this street until someone figures out that a missing platoon is overdue for check-in. Tries their comm or whatever they're using for traffic and finds out no one is answering 'cause they're all dead in the dark and rubble-strewn street out there.

Sucks to be stupid.

But it sucks worse to be dead. Better them than us.

And they were stupid. Walked right into our kill zone, and I just whispered, "Light 'em up."

And Reaper lit 'em up good.

Ten seconds later a bunch of loyalist guerilla fighters were dead or bleeding out on the street in the night as the moon disappeared behind the skeletal remains of skyscrapers to the west. I bet they'd wanted to die gloriously just like this kid sitting in front of me wanted to when he decided to try PMC'ing. Instead they made the mistake of running into us one dark and arty night. We waited for a few minutes and then sent Choker and Punch in to finish everyone off and get a unit ID for the bounty.

The company can turn the body count in for cash. But I have a gut feeling we'll be lucky to get off this world alive much less get paid in any kind of stellar currency. Fat chance on seeing actual hard mem.

Last time I checked, the Coreward Currency Market was trading Astralonian baht at seventy-thousand to one against CoreBit. One mem is worth a thousand CoreBit.

A case of six-point-five for the Bastard costs twenty CoreBit on the black market.

But CoreBits are hard to come by and beggars can't be choosers when it comes to hard mem. And that's the thing no one ever tells you about being a merc. Yeah, you got freedom. But freedom's just another word for nothing left to spend on something that might save your life when everything goes spinward.

So you're kind of always begging. Especially if you're not too proud. And merc'in and pride do not, I repeat, do not go hand in hand. There's no pride in running when the contract's dead and the LZ's getting shelled. The locals who you've been defending want your blood, and the hoochies you promised were gonna end up on the right side of the conflict are now wondering why you're running and not fighting like they thought you would when they gave away their goods for free.

Nothing's free. Nothing. Is. Free. That can be read and believed both ways.

Nah, pride's just a slick dress uniform and a cheap lie that'll get you killed when the people you're fighting for, who aren't doing any of the actual fighting, start selling you out and making their best deal… for themselves and themselves alone.

So, chuck that. You don't need pride. Not here. Not in the company. Full mags, working weapons, and some dudes who got your back. That's what you need if you're gonna see the other side of this. That's what makes us brothers. Whether we like it or not. It's the galaxy against us and the sooner you realize that the better.

"I'm Sergeant Orion," I tell the kid. "First rule in Reaper is you do everything I tell you. Got that, Kid?"

He doesn't realize it but for the foreseeable future *Kid* is his new name.

The Kid, holding the protein bar and staring wide-eyed at me who looks like he's going to vomit and who has not eaten the bar as I asked him to, just stares at me, unsure what to do… not just next… but at all.

"So…" I tell him, real patiently. "Eat your bar. You're going to need calories and I don't need you getting all weak in the middle of a fight should we find ourselves in such later tonight. Which is probably going to happen sooner than later. Sorry about that."

Still he doesn't do anything. He just stares at me. I'm pretty sure he's figuring out he's just made the biggest mistake of his life in joining Strange Company. If the last two hours with the First Sergeant and his non-stop litany of death and injury life lessons he likes to salt indocs with haven't freaked this kid out, then the energy tower that just exploded on the other side of the city, with close air support ripping the street and skies apart to boot, has done the trick for sure. Death is out there on the streets tonight. And there are darker things than just night on the prowl.

"First rule," I say slowly like I'm talking to a child, or an imbecile. "Do. Everything. I. Say. Kid."

Kid nods. Barely.

"Eat. The. Protein. Bar. I. Gave. You. Kid."

The Kid looks at it. Nods again and begins to tear it open listlessly. If I wanted to double all my useless Astralonian Bhat I'd bet someone close by he's going to hurl in the next two minutes. I don't have very good leadership skills. But I've found betting against myself makes me play harder. So, call pessimism a survival tool.

"I'm gonna teach you how to survive this, okay?" I tell him.

Kid takes a bite and the taste of the bar does something to him. It settles him down. He chews slow at first. Then faster. There's things in the bar that do that. Put you in the zone to get it on for the fight that's coming our way. That's why I make him eat one.

"Do everything I say and you might survive and get pushed to one of the other platoons. Got that? For now, you're in the Reapers. We do all the worst jobs. We do those really well. You will learn to do so and either Ghost or Dogs will fight for your body to add to their squads. Or no one will and you'll stay here and die doing something stupid. But doing it anyway. I'm pretty sure you got no medical training, otherwise you wouldn't be here as both Ghost and Dogs lost medics this week. Tough business being a doc on this one. I'll say that. Plus, Cutter's a real crab and believe me you do not want to work for that man directly."

Cutter's the company doc. He's also a mean drunk. But he's pretty good at meatball surgery. Which, he tells everyone who has to get him out of trouble, is why he drinks. I'm pretty sure he drinks because he's just a miserable human being and miserable human beings need excuses for why they're miserable human beings instead of just owning that they choose to be miserable human beings.

See what I did there.

"And Voodoo... word of advice, Kid, just stay away from them and don't even get interested when they come around. Trust me on that one. You'll be a lot happier with all your marbles for as long as you can keep them."

I pause and make a motion for him to hand me his Bastard.

He seems surprised to see that he's even carrying the sturdy company S-16 combat rifle he was issued back at the supply crawler. He hands it over.

I run a systems check and find out Biggs has given him one of the good ones. I hand it back.

"Okay," I say, indicating the weapon he's holding. "Now go ahead and load that. You're in combat now. If you see the enemy, then you're gonna wanna shoot 'em. And having the weapon loaded makes the process a whole lot easier."

I don't add a pedantic *Okay* like Player does over in Dogs. Because that would be pedantic and people would think I'm a jerk. Everyone thinks Player is a jerk.

Now, if Biggs has done his job, the Kid will pull a mag out of his carrier and load the S-16. Biggs keeps recruits for two days and shows them how to use their gear. He also downloads all kinds of myths that have nothing to do with actual combat, as Biggs, as far as I know, has never engaged in light infantry warfare of any kind. The drone guns mounted all over his supply crawler take care of most enemy interest in his continued well-being.

The Kid pulls a magazine from his carrier, slaps it in, pulls the charging handle back, and a round is in the chamber and ready. I note the Kid checks the safety.

The S-16 is a beautiful weapon system that's probably as old as humanity's interest in modern warfare. Way back in the primeval of Earth, a place I've never been but who has, the original design was called the *Stoner* weapon system for reasons I have yet to discover. It's been improved on over the years and there are variants like the shorty some carry.

"Let's leave that safety on until we got someone to shoot at," I tell the Kid as mobile artillery begins to level a block to our west. "If we get hit, don't panic. Keep thinking and shoot back when you can. The rest of us would appreciate that. Also, it has a tendency to discourage the enemy as far as their initial intentions are concerned. Makes 'em nervous. And we can use that to our advantage. Welcome to Reapers, Kid. Welcome to the Strange."

CHAPTER THREE

I'm half-listening to the squad comm that's always in my ear when Junkboy shows up after I asked him to report to my little command post at the center of the artillery-shell-ruined bank. I'm going to assign Junkboy care and handling of the new recruit who will simply be called "Kid" for the foreseeable future until he does something stupid enough to earn the tag he will come to live with for what will most likely be the rest of his life. In Strange Company.

Junkboy's tag, for instance, was acquired thusly. He has been with the company in So-So's squad for six months. Joined up at Ryan's Cross and managed to convince the First Sergeant and Biggs that he was drug-free and hadn't been kicked out of the Monarchs' own Expeditionary Snipers on a failed drug test. It took him all of two weeks to teach us that was a big old lie. Go figure: drug addicts lie. Amirite? One night we caught him railed to the gills and shooting prisoners of war from a tower three blocks west of the prison camp the people we were working for were running.

To be fair the people we were working for were not treating the people inside all that well and there were already a lot of dead bodies lying around due to starvation and various rage beatings by the new victors in this mean-spirited little conflict on that world. To be further fair, the people who were prisoners had been earning that particular reward for about twenty years while in control of the planet by running a totalitarian overstate in which ninety-five percent of the population were openly considered slaves.

They were really into this old Earth philosopher called Nietzsche or something.

So Junkboy was up there with a .308 Marcotti that Sleeper used for infiltration. Canned and all, so his shots were going unnoticed for the most part. He was mainly shooting down prisoners who were grubbing for grubs in the bloody dirt where their own had recently been beaten to death...

Yeah, it was really that bad and the general consensus in Strange Company was that we didn't like the gig and were looking for the first dropship that could get us all back up to the *Spider*.

Sleeper shows up looking for his rifle because it's missing, and Junkboy, who we were close to calling "Shiny" because he was always so up and ready to pull any op at all hours of the day or night, had been interested in said missing rifle hours earlier. Intensely interested. It caused note among the normally taciturn mercenaries we'd all become during the darkness of that gig. Sleeper checked the duty roster and saw that Junkboy was pulling twelve to two on the OP tower that guarded our little ad hoc barracks. And there our preeminent sniper, he is basically the rock star of Ghost, finds his weapon being employed in the commission of some serious war crimes.

War crimes we will have to pay for. If we're lucky they just come out of our company bonuses. If we're not, and we're caught, the Adjudicators could have us spaced just above planetary orbit.

Yeah, war crimes don't mean much out here on the rim of human space, but given the right circumstances and some government types from Central out here on a fact-finding do-good mission, heads might just roll. Or burn up in atmo.

Or our paymasters could use it as an excuse to cheat and/or extort us. Trust me, it's heads-up ball all the time being a private military contractor company.

So, two things happen. One, we get that weasel Junkboy sober. Within the week he was off the junk and headed toward a really annoying sobriety that bothered all of us coffee-drinkers of late. Long story short... we just PT'd him to death until he was very clean, and very clear that we would not tolerate his habit any longer. Two-hour smoke sessions on the hour. Every hour. Or at least that's how Strange Company corrective PT was supposed to feel. Spoiler: it felt worse. Every sergeant had to go through it to know how it felt, and how it worked. Fun, huh? And two, Junkboy got assigned to Ghost because even though he'd committed war crimes, he'd committed them really well. Sleeper acknowledged that Junkboy possessed a certain unrefined affinity for the sniper trade which could be brightened and honed to Sleeper's standards.

Junkboy did most of this conflict on Astralon and did it well with Ghost as a scout-sniper. Not a hint of drug use. So much so that he was placed back into Reapers as an assistant squad leader so he could train the indocs to serve as squad-designated marksmen and select for talent in sniping.

Sleeper is too valuable in Ghost to be bothered with training indocs. And like I said he's a bonified rock star. So why would he ever want to leave his little kingdom in the Ghost?

Only an idiot like me would want to stay in Reapers forever. But I have my reasons.

So, as I was saying, I was just about to turn the new kid over to Junkboy right there in the abandoned bank we're operating out of inside the big apartment block we took away from the now-defunct Grau Skull and covering the approach to the starport, when Junkboy takes one right in the head. The enemy snipers had been crawling in close to take shots. Half his skull came away and painted the new kid and me in brains and bone matter as we talked. But I was already bloody and dirty from close to thirty-six hours of fighting for that section of the small city.

The enemy now knows we're going for the starport. So of course, they've tried to counterattack for the last three days.

I told myself I'd take a good two-day coma once we got off this whack world. If we got off.

If Junkboy had been wearing his helmet, like he should have been, he might have lived. But hanging with Sleeper and the snipers had convinced him of the folly of such life-saving measures. So now he was dead. And dead was dead as far as the company was concerned.

Now the whole CP was under fire.

The bank was along the outer wall of the massive structure. A great place for snipers to shoot into and assault teams to try to take. So of course, Reaper got it.

The sound of distant artillery mechs moving through the streets three blocks west to the LZ was the only sound just seconds before the sudden cacophonic firefight broke out as once again the enemy tried to storm the bank.

I swore and tackled the Kid, dragging him to the ruined floor and pulling my weapon with me while Junkboy's corpse just lay there and twitched. In the company you always know where your weapon is. You could find it blind in the dark at midnight. Why? Because you have to, otherwise you're dead.

"Snipers!" someone shouts out lamely from the fighting positions along the northern ruin of the wall as an enemy heavy machine gun firing AP and mixed tracer opens up on what remains of the bank's glassy facade. A moment later, the massive shattered windows that faced east and probably allowed the golden sunlight of this world in and onto the marble and bronze of this place, conveying a sense of wealth, propriety, and stability, come apart as suppressive fire rakes that side of the building.

I tap the comm and tell the Old Man we got incoming at Reaper.

"Acknowledged," he says. The reply is characteristically terse in his tired smoke-stained voice. But it's calm and not at all worked up about the situation. Which is exactly what you want in your leaders. Imagine asking for support from some guy who's as freaked out as you are once you start getting pushed by the enemy. The captain's orders always reassure me when the incoming starts incoming. I guess that's why he's in command of the company and why everyone just calls him the Old Man even though every company commander has had that title for hundreds of years of the history of our little outfit as near as I can find in the deep logs.

"Stay close to me," I tell the Kid lying on the floor next to me. Tracer rounds are streaking through the building above our heads and I hear most of Reaper open up in reply. If we have wounded, the best way to treat them in the middle of a firefight is to return fire.

That's good.

"Got movement in the streets!" It's Punch. He's my best squad leader and he generally works well with me to hold the platoon together. All the squad leaders have served in other platoons and they've either been identified as teachers who can help me get the indocs up to speed, or as problems no one wants in the other platoons. Punch is a teacher. He's excellent at battle management and tactics. Combatives and shooting skills, too. One time he flanked an ambush back on Golus and pushed them off their axis of attack all by himself with just his rifle, a bandolier of grenades, and seriously bad intentions. He read the battle right that day and tonight he's reading it and I hope it's right.

"We're pinned from the north by sniper fire coming from ruins across the street, Sar'nt Orion. Suppressive from the east. My guess is they're sending in an assault team from the north."

I'm low-crawling across the grit of the floor and getting cut to shreds by glass and debris. But at least I have my assault gloves on. I'm also spiking hard on adrenaline, so it doesn't matter. I hope the Kid's following because it would be a real waste for the First Sergeant and Biggs to have done all that work only to have the Kid get killed without contributing in the least.

"Orion to Chungo..." I wait for the comm AI to redirect to the indirect squad leader in Voodoo.

"Go for Chungo, Orion. Sounds like you're in the stew."

"Copy. Yeah we're in it for sure. Need you to drop something across TPs one through six I marked out for you. Got anything that'll do the job?"

Pause. Maybe he says something smart, I don't know. I'm close to Hoser who's managed to get a small space in the rubble of the bank with which to engage the snipers' teams to the north. Hoser's Pig makes a lot of noise and burns a lot of brass. But it does tend to keep heads down.

"Whatchu facin', Orion? Say again... Whatchu—" It's Chungo over the comm.

"We got assault teams coming out across the kill zone," I reply. "Anything anti-personnel would be *mucho appreciado* at this time!"

I crawl up right behind Hoser and the assistant gunner, Hustle.

Hoser is laughing his butt off because he's cutting Front Loyalist irregulars to shreds within his small window of traversing fire death. Problem is the rest of the squad is telling me the irregulars are all across the section and the Pig can't hit 'em. Still, the heavy gunner is having the time of his life shooting whoever he can whenever he can. It's almost obscene. But I've never been one to spite a man for his passions. No matter how simple they are. We all have 'em. I'm sure mine would be just as weird to them.

"Shot out," mumbles Chungo over the comm.

The volume of incoming is so heavy there's no way I'm chancing a look to see where anything lands. I've already got wounded. If what he has doesn't work… we're fixed for up-close and personal battle.

What happens next sounds like a thousand angels screaming from far away to suddenly close. And then there's like two thousand thumps. Yeah, my ears aren't that accurate, it was later when I got the ordnance specs that I can add the numbers to the account. But the thousand screaming angels are indirect fire from a one-shot anti-personnel system Chungo had been holding back for just such a special occasion. The one thousand thumps were the munitions splitting in half just before impact.

A second later the entire battlefield lit up like a camera flash. Comms went down and it was clear there'd been some sort of EMP disruption effect in the mix. If they were running night-fighting gear, they were now blind out there. But these were irregulars, and chances were they'd gotten their rifles, NVGs, and a bowl of rice before the attack. So they were really just armed civilians with lots of guns being funneled straight at us to try and do something about our refusal to die. They were still dangerous, I'm not saying that. The Front Loyalist pros were running sniper ops and watching from the heavies suppressing on our right flank, looking to exploit a breakthrough with probably more reserves. They were going to overrun our line inside the bank and break us up for a moment. Then they'd send in a freight train of irregular troops to exploit our momentary weakness.

We got lucky—the freight train arrived a little early while we could still kill it. The Voodoo indirect team came through for us.

But back to Chungo's special.

The first segment of the air-deployed munition was similar to a flashbang grenade. Irregulars who'd probably been taught to crawl and rush in teams, rudimentary movement to contact, were suddenly deaf and blind out in the open and their ears were probably bleeding. They'd even be having trouble standing up.

Even trained pros do the thing you shouldn't do at this point if they're suffering from these effects. Which is lie there and let your senses come back online. Some of them just start shooting wildly, probably hitting their own more than getting anywhere near us. Others stand up and scream something in the local dialect to the effect of, "I can't see!" convinced they've been horribly wounded.

That's when the second phase of munitions went off. A variation on the time-honored mine system as old as human history, the claymore. Except this phase is run by a one-shot AI that's scanned the strike area, determined the targets, and commanded all the munitions be feather-dropped via small drone batteries before activating their smaller grav batteries to readjust their kill arcs for maximum efficiency across the front of our line.

The AI has about a minute and forty-five seconds of runtime. It's more like an expendable AI battery charge.

Then, and this is where Chungo, whose fat and muscle contrive to make him look like a stubby large bull, figure that one out, laughed so hard I thought he was going to have an embolism when he told me later that about sixty-four thousand steel BBs exploded in perfect max kill arcs and destroyed the entire assault force in half a second. A sudden brutal overkill ripping through the night in front of the ruined bank.

He was right about that.

There wasn't much left of anyone.

"Expeditionary Logistics developed that but had problems, so I got a few on sale when we hit that bazaar on Noaa," laughed the immense Chungo. Strange's indirect specialist. A maestro of death from above and the steel rain falling down on your enemies. "It's really a beautiful system though," he said softly after he stopped laughing. Almost reverently wiping a tear from his swollen red face. Almost a holy whisper at the end. "It's only got one problem the Expeditionary couldn't live with, Orion."

What was the problem, I asked him.

"Oh, that." He snickered, and I was sure he was going to go for that embolism again. His face turning red. Him bending over his swollen girth. "It has a tendency to target friendlies."

"Tendency?" I said.

"Above seventy percent of the time." And then he died laughing as he walked back to the CP, when the attack had been stopped and the rest of the night was promising to be a long and tense unquiet.

I hate everyone in Voodoo.

But more about that later.

CHAPTER FOUR

On some date no one will ever care much about, somewhere out along the leading edge of the Stretch, two mercenary companies went to war on one another one dark and rainy night after the defense of LZ Syro—the bank where Junkboy bought it—and the resumption of offensive combat ops by the Resistance. Us. We were back on the move, peace talks dead though some said they were just stalled. Enough mem must have arrived planetside to keep the war going for a few more weeks. Someone somewhere still thought they had a chance to flip the tables. And we were going for it. All this happened during the wide-ranging, and very much lost cause, battle for a world called Crash. Or Astralon depending on who you asked.

The Stretch is a string of stars out along the farthest edge of human expansion. Crash, or Astralon, resides in a bright little cluster of frontier worlds. You could almost call it a micro-capital.

Crash was a very mean little war. That year's mean little war in a long list of small, dirty wars getting longer, and meaner, all the time. One of many, as some like to say. One of many for many, many years since the Monarchs had gotten interested in the galaxy again.

Like I said, no one would ever care much about the date, much less the war. And certainly no one cared about the junkyard dogfight that broke out between Strange Company and Grau Skull Resolutions on a world some long-dead scout had gotten the honor of designating as Crash on the universal stellar charts for all time to come.

Getting one on the USC is something if you're a scout. It's like getting into the Baseball Hall of Fame. Like if you're interested in that sort of thing it makes you a big deal. Kinda.

Who knows, maybe he, that long-ago scout, wasn't dead. Maybe the Monarchs had paid him off in longevity and all the mem he could do way back after this world had been found and colonized. Or maybe that scout was in extended coffin sleep, hyper-headed somewhere no one had gone yet. Looking to hack another world for the maps way out beyond the ever-expanding frontier. Name another planet that would one day become a colony and maybe get big enough to go to war on. Get a note in the histories if he, that scout, was on the right side of things. More stats in the Scout Hall of Fame even though I don't think there actually is one.

The Monarchs like to keep a tight control on history. It allows them to keep a tight control on everything else. Tell the official story and you can tell any story you want. Especially the one where you're always on the right side. Where you're always the hero. That's how the Monarchs like to run the show. And it is their show to run.

But out here on this dark and soggy night, as the drops brought us in a few klicks into this week's No One's Land and the gunships pulled back to protect the transports with standoffs while the dropships blew mud in every direction and howled off and away into the darkness, it was just us. Strange Company was here for the hit. And of course, the poor scumbags who'd signed the dotted line on a contract to be our enemies over at the Skull this time. They were the victim tonight.

They just didn't know it yet.

Grau Skull Resolutions. Like they were, note the usage of past tense, some high-speed security conglomerate with offices on Bright Star and Rigel. Made mercs run by suits wearing the best of suits and sporting cybermodel escorts with six trillion follows. Doing high-tech security contracts with state-of-the-art death merchandise for the slugs in Grau Skull to actually go forth and do said mayhem.

If you've got to be in the PMC biz, being a suit running the contracts ain't a bad life. It's all show and dough with none of the hardships like violent death, disease, and more violent death.

They weren't all that. Grau Skull was just like us when you got right down to it. Mean and desperate. Crash, or Astralon, had reduced us all down to our original binary. We were back to being what we really were after six months of fighting. Just code and no fancy plug-ins. Getting paid to do some pretty shady stuff in this mean little dogfight for all the marbles out here on Crash. Or Astralon. A war no one knew about, or even cared much about, back on glittery Bright Star. This was over on the Eastern Corridor Front after Syro LZ. We were part of the big push for the capital now that the Resistance had gotten financed by a new infusion of mem. Crash City was the goal. The wide vast sprawl of brutalist apartment blocks that went on for featureless kilometer after kilometer. Built back during the techsplosion at the turn of some century. Back when this world looked like it was going to turn itself into something respectable, and the Monarchs were thinking about setting up vacation estates to oversee their holdings. Back when the frontier was here and not fifty parsecs farther out toward the dark and crazy of the rim. Where it gets all weird and scout service ships go missing all the time if you believe the fakes. Back when bucketloads of mems could be made by the fistful if you were willing to haul anything labeled "essential cargo" out here to the boomtown worlds so they could get going and uplink with the big river of mem that feeds Earth day and night.

That's all history now. No one in either of the two merc companies about to shoot it out tonight for some meaningless target reference point on the map cares for the *back when* or even the *why*.

We deal in body counts.

To a private military contractor, the past is not prologue. The past is someone else's problem. Oftentimes you're just the solution to that problem. Kill who you get paid to kill and collect your mems. Blow the world on the next ride outta there and let someone else figure it all out for the official histories. The details tend to bother a little too much if you take the time to think about them.

The human rucksack is only so big. Take care what you stuff in it, because you'll carry all of it all the way to your grave.

But of course I don't do this. The stories are my jam. Officially I'm the company log keeper. Details, pay, supply, deaths, actions, intel. I got the job because the Old Man found out I collect forbidden histories whenever I can find them. He also knows that everyone doesn't have much of a problem telling me their darkest and innermost secrets. I guess I'm just a good listener.

Like I said, none of that matters now as the skies turn dark and gray with night rain and Strange Company gets ready to make her attack against an old cyclopean chunk of industrial living progress that still stands out here in the No One's Land. None of that matters to us. The eastern front of the war on Crash isn't the sexy front. To be sure. If it was, we wouldn't be here. It's nothing but occasional sociopathic ground battles with arcane objectives and more often savage raids against rando enemy positions as everything shapes up for the real big show we've been promised next week, or maybe in two.

The starport that serves Crash City is the big show. It's practically running movie trailers on our brains when we close our eyes for a few hours' sleep.

No one's calling in strike fighters or air cav for us tonight. Only the Strange Company has been dropped off and sent in on foot to dislodge Grau Skull from their mighty FOB inside No One's Land. High Command back in Tolois, a strange little town thirty kilometers behind the line, won't be watching the outcome tonight. They'll get the details in the morning brief as the hungover generals drink coffee from small delicate porcelain cups and murmur over reports from the night before. Rumor is the generals redirected one of the cyborg circuses into the MDA, the main deployment area, and they're getting first crack at the honeys before the line units.

Rank has its privileges. Mercs not so much.

So tonight, both Strange and Grau Skull are going to fight it out with automatic weapons, high-ex, and whatever else they can bring to the dogfight. Fighting over one of the last remaining block-living structures in that sector of ruin on the final approach to the starport. If we're successful, High Command for the rebels, which just happens to be the legitimate government of Crash, will be able to oversee the battle for the port of entry to the west. That is if we win and don't die on the objective. If not… they'll throw another down-and-out company against Grau to make it happen. They'll burn troops until it gets done, never mind the pay. Dead mercenaries have a way of not needing to get paid. Everyone knows that. It's win-win for the generals if we buy it. Then the Big Contest in maybe two weeks' time.

Tonight's target is Objective House Party. House Party is a block-living edifice that once housed thousands of workers during the boom. Again, it will be very important in about a week, or two. Maybe. Unless plans change to attack the starport.

But not tonight.

Tonight, it's just a junkyard dog fight between two down-and-out companies that have seen much better days. Hell, Strange and Grau Skull fought together on the same side in other messes not this one.

But not tonight. Tonight, it's just business we tell ourselves as we sneak toward the kill in a long, winding patrol column with Ghost Platoon out front and scouting. One of us, Strange or Grau, needs to see dawn and be in control of the last remaining structures at the far edge of the ever-shifting No One's Land. Most everything in No One's Land west of our position got wiped out in a heavy D-beam strike from orbit three months ago. Both sides have just been fighting over the mess that's been left behind. Fast attack force raids in and out to hit, destabilize, and ruin further the enemy's position along the approach to the starport. Nothing personal, just business. The business of war. Next week we do the main port of entry for Crash.

The big show we all can't stop imagining.

I keep saying that. I know. It's on my mind. I have a bad feeling about that one. Guys have been telling me their stories. That's a bad sign too. It means they can feel it. They can feel the Grim Reaper Astronaut sharpening his scythe for that one. There will be casualties.

Soft rain begins just after twilight. It's miserable, wet, and dirty by the time we advance on the objective. We caught some rain hanging off the dropships while coming in. I was riding on the portside cargo deck. Open to the night and the wind. Mist and sudden squalls washing over the patched and well-used drops, relics from some other conflict, as we all sat there in the darkness, blocking out the engines and constant chatter from the flight crews. It felt good, and washed some of the day, hot and dusty, off of me. And my gear.

Rain doesn't bother me. I was zoned for the mission. A gun sensei I once trained with told me a little meditation before a shootout didn't hurt no one. Especially... if you knew the fight was coming.

That's always the hard part, ain't it. Knowing when the fight is gonna happen. So I guess you just sit around on the edge of a fight, just left of bang, and wait for it to go down.

Then you get it on and hope you get to see the other side of it. Which can last anywhere from seven seconds to four days according to my general experience.

Like I said. No arty prep from High Command. No precision D-beam strike to boil the defenders inside the block structure from orbit before the building exploded and left a thirty-meter-deep scar in the world's surface. A brief sudden violent blue death beam of superheated plasma straight down out of the heavens like something from an age of fantasy and myth. Cutting a wide scar into the dark mud and literally slicing the massive structure in half as it ruined the defenses and cooked those within a three-kilometer radius alive. Problem was, the rebels lost the ship that could do that, the *Beowulf*, to sub-orbital fighter raids a week after the strike, during the truce talks that fell apart as soon as the *Beowulf* took multiple internals and lost her main drive and had to limp away off to the system's edge. Or face a core melt, so the official story goes.

So, now we're just going in to take them out. Those guys defending the last structure in No One's Land. Grau Skull. Guys who could have just as easily been us if the contracts had fallen differently when this all kicked off and the suits were signing deals before lunch with some beauty in a bright chrome-and-glass palace of dining gentility. We'd fought alongside Grau Skull back on Blue out in the jungle highlands campaign five years ago. Pacification. Hearts and minds against the Gobies. A mega-corp wanted the mining rights inside what someone said the Gobies considered "most very sacred mountains."

Now, here on Crash, High Command needs that structure intact for the big show in a week or two at the starport. No doubt another circus will be redirected for the generals while we go in and spill each other's blood all over the tarmac around the green terminal ring at the stellar port of entry.

On the ground and working dark, Ghost Platoon, Strange's scouts, make their way toward the objective and we listen to the zero chatter they generate over the net as they take out a Grau Skull LP/OP a hundred meters out. Ghost is pro. Slick trains them relentlessly even though there's a lot of freedom within the understrength recon platoon to do what needs to get done. Everybody runs the weapon systems and gear they know best in the recon platoon. In Ghost you do your job and the rest is just noise, as they like to say. Don't do your job and you're up for grabs... that is if anyone else wants you. But why would they? You're just broke, and why would any of the other platoon sergeants in Strange Company want you at all if you couldn't cut it in Ghost?

That's how people end up back in Reaper again. Because if no one wants you, I get you.

With the LP/OP eliminated, the Ghost platoon sergeant is thinking we have about fifteen minutes before Grau Skull figures out we just did their guys and moves to a guns-up posture, knowing things are about to get real imminent and intimate in the next few.

Surprise blown.

Ghost does their job again as one of the snipers whacks a spotter on the roof of the blocky structure we're about to assault from our angle of attack. Like I said, Ghost is pro. Suppressed shot at medium range in the rain and dark isn't easy even if you are running a Kang-Mueller acquisition and targeting scope on a Volk Predator sniper rifle firing dependable 7.62.

I know the sniper and I know his old rifle. Sleeper is in the house. I also know the job was important enough that Sergeant Slick would rely on just that guy to get the job done for us.

But anyone in Ghost could have made that shot. Everyone in Ghost is high-speed-laid-back all the way. They're so pro it seems like they don't care much. In other words, they don't get bothered when things get focused.

Seems is the important word in that sentence.

Being a PMC is ninety-percent actor. I'm not saying you're not pro at private mercenary work. That's gratis if you're going to stick around. But so much about what we do is attitude. Outnumbered, unwanted, and desperately needed, your acting skills go a long way in convincing allies, enemies, and predators regarding your intentions.

It also helps when you're low on ammo and running out of options.

Or at least that's how I view it. Your parsecs may vary.

So, if you don't cut it there, in Ghosts, then you'll end up in the Reapers getting all the whack jobs no else wants to die getting done. Stuff that needs to get done never mind the odds. When new guys come into Reaper they think it's super-cool because we've got a nice patch with, of course, the iconic Grim Reaper Astronaut straight out of all the ancient myths of star travel and legends like NASA, Mars Command, and SPEC. A symbol as old as time itself. Something that's stood for death in vacuum, plague, and general stellar exploration danger zones to be very careful of time immemorial. A warning turned into a tattoo worn proudly. Either chalked on a bulkhead inside a busted hull, or flashing on some still-active terminal deep inside a rock where someone found something they shouldn't have. You get into Reaper and think you're super-cool on the basis of no evidence whatsoever. Later you realize Reaper is just where the First Sergeant sticks you until someone figures out a name and a skill set and picks you up thus making you legit instead of the lost little sheep you really are. Until then you got to survive all the whack things Reaper gets assigned by the captain.

In Reaper you either die or get made. Those are the only two ways out. *Strange rules for a Strange Company,* as the senior-most still like to say. And until you get made you do all the worst stuff with the highest level of promised mortality. It's really easier for everyone that way. Trust us. If you're gonna die, then why take the time to come up with a tag to call you by. Tags are a lotta work. Things have to be considered. It's a waste when they get wasted 'cause you got dead.

There's only one guy stupid enough to stay in Reaper full-time. Supervise the whack ops and run the miscreants and lost orphans. And that guy would be me. Reaper is my platoon. I'm the guy stupid enough to stick around.

Hey, someone's gotta do it.

"Slick to Orion…" The leader of Ghost Platoon comes at me over the comms. "Phase Delta. All quiet. Assault teams clear to move on House Party."

Reaper's cue to get the hustle on and move into place for the assault against our objective has been given. Tonight's Strange Company op is a game we like to play called *Breaking and Entering*.

Breaking and Entering is really just a surprise attack on a fixed position. Surprise being the operative word. If you were in any kind of formal human military unit you learned this there. Whether you learned it in the Saturn Nine Foreign Legions that support the Ultra Marines on occasion, or out in one of the local militaries like the Astralonian Armored Heavy Cav that's supposed to be fighting this war for the Rebel High Command instead of the dozen merc companies who've been hired to defend their sovereignty. The heavy cav and their other famous units are getting held back for the important, and hopefully glorious, work of actually winning the war.

A certainty that seems to change not just day to day, but hour to hour sometimes.

Reaper and Dog are on assault duty tonight. We do the entering. Ghost and Voodoo do the breaking. This is how we do war. This is how we do *B and E*.

Like I said it's raining and dark and gray where it isn't midnight. Everyone is running some sort of night vision, but target lasers and illuminators won't go live until the captain signals the attack. The Old Man is with Dog Platoon. Dog is straight line infantry and they run it just like they came straight out of the ever-loving true believers of the Monarchs' Ultra Marines. All *hooo-ahhh* and dress right dress. Lifetaker and heartbreaker tats underneath combat armor that just isn't available to the rest of us. Everyone over in Dog carries the same rifle and gear like they're auditioning for a supporting role in the Monarchs' guard dog cult.

The Ultra Marines.

We just call 'em Ultras like it's a dirty word you wouldn't actually use in their presence. Which is easy. Because if you happen to be in their presence, they've most likely come to kill you. And you are most assuredly going to die.

It's best to be honest with yourself even if you're lying to the rest of the galaxy. No one fights the Ultras. There's tough, sure. And then there's Ultras. They're just plain homicidally insane. And very well-trained along with fanatical levels of discipline. Best to just run.

Rumor is that the Old Man, Strange Company's current commander, captain is his official rank, was once Ultra Marine in some long-lost life not this one. But that's just a rumor of course because everyone knows no one leaves the Ultra Marines alive. They have that tattooed on their bodies first day of Ultra Basic. *No One Gets Out Alive.* And that's true. I know that for a fact. The only way you get out of that warped little death cult is on your shield on some world you got sent in to annihilate. So, it's probably just a rumor. About the captain having once been in. But one the Old Man neither cares to discourage, nor encourage.

He's an enigma. The Old Man.

But the captain runs Dog, his favorite platoon, like they're natural-born killers. Because they are. Reaper secures the old lev station, or what remains of it, from which we'll be attacking across open ground, and I give the signal to Hannibal, Dog Platoon's sergeant and my personal chief villain in this waking life, to come up along the ruins of the old maglev rail and get in position for the attack. Reaper on the left flank. Dogs on the right.

Jingo, a scout from Ghost, directs our positioning. Crouching in the dark, made into some evil hunchback by the rain-slick poncho that covers his ruck. We move past the scout and fan out into our combat wedges.

"Party time, Orion," Jingo whispers as I pass close by. I ignore him and knife-hand my men to their positions muttering Strange's standard SOP response to greetings. "Get it on."

Dog comes in like pros. Sweeping to the right and moving swiftly to get where they need to be for the attack. Heads on a swivel. Assaulters and weapons teams taking a knee or going prone in the dark mud and broken concrete along the trashed remains of the station. Moving like they're Ultra Marine Scout Recon come to do everyone in sight.

Gone, inside the skeleton of the lev-rail station, with its fantastic curving metallic loops and bright sweeping angles long-dead societal architects must've once thought the very future of Crash would look like as it became a major sector capital in the Stretch. Breaking away from the Monarchs. Taking the reins of a minor stellar empire. A hundred years ago before all their plans went up in apocalyptic D-beam strikes.

Apparently, things didn't work out so well for these people, I think as I stare at the ruin and devastation that remains here.

The night mist has stopped and the place looks like a forgotten cemetery. Quiet and dead.

Now it's just a dark and creepy disremembered place and even Strange Company, whose bad luck in recent contracts has forced us to make do with less so that we've become really good at getting things done by surprise, illusion, and outright stealth, some call it cheating but that's ridiculous—there's no cheating in war—but even us doing our best creep can't avoid the crunch of dirty broken glass that is everywhere in the once-fantastic station made of such materials. Shattered glass and twisted steel. The scarecrow remains of the roof and those fantastic loops that composed the dreamed-of future the long-ago dead had wanted instead of the one they'd get. The metal is twisted and the glass is crushed, broken, and fused into weird shapes no doubt courtesy of the D-beam strike a few weeks back.

They call that strange little feature of the D-beam strike, blackened fused glass twisted into almost malevolent shapes and scattered across the ruin, *Apocalypse Glass*.

"Don't cack this one up, Sar'nt Orion," mutters Sergeant Hannibal as we interface on Phase Delta. He's a looming hulk of muscle and simmering rage in the darkness. A brute of a soldier. A thug of a warrior. Nightmare in human form. *In the darkness* can be used in conjunction with him at all times. Even brightest noon. Reaper rarely messes anything up by the way. But that never stops Sergeant Hannibal, the only guy who uses what may be his real name in the company, from blaming us for everything he can think of.

Yeah, we fight with each other in Strange Company, but we all know we're brothers. We're all we've got in the universe. You end up here, you ended up here for a bad reason. We're brothers. That's the rule. We got each other's ruck. Hannibal… of course he's the exception to the rule.

I say nothing for a second and watch my guys get ready.

But because both of us are headed straight at each other, I have to hit Sergeant Hannibal back with something. Those are the rules. Even though they aren't written down anywhere. Those are the rules of soldiers since forever.

"Yeah. Try and keep the war crimes down on this one, Amarcus. Company ain't been paid yet."

Sergeant Amarcus Hannibal. I used his first name to hit harder. The war crimes part is just a love tap. He's just some good old boy, built like a bull who learned to soldier somewhere violent and ended up in the Strange Company for reasons no one knows. Rumors abound of course. But that's standard for everyone. Rumors abounding. Only I ever get to know the real stories eventually. And then sometimes not even. Only if they want it known. Only if they think they're about to die.

'Cause that's the only headstone you get in Strange. It, whatever it is you did that caused you to end up here, who you really are, your story as it were, it goes down in the company log. And I keep the log. Another of the whack jobs for Reaper.

A minor whack job in a sea of many whack jobs for the platoon sergeant of Reaper. But I like it even though I tell people I don't mind it. I like history. I like stories. The stars are filled with 'em. And… histories are weird since they aren't official. Monarchs like it that way. They don't like competition. Especially for the narrative of history.

So, history is like my little act of rebellion against the galaxy.

I've seen people strung up in colony squares for trying to do history. Especially if it's not the right history.

Sergeant Hannibal spits a stream of dip and snorts like he's trying to show how little I've hurt him with my feeble jabs. In the dark and the gray and the rain, some distant searchlights scan the eastern front and sweep close enough to the dirty rain-covered ruined lev-rail station for me to see him glaring pure murder in the dark between the rain droplets that separate us. I like that. The murder glare means I scored a hit. That's all that matters to me. I'm dumb enough to play for the small mean victories. His skin has that always sunburnt appearance even though he's tanned. He tans red. I also see the wicked white scar that runs from ear to ear where someone tried to slit his throat. And the one where he took a round in the mouth and it ruined his teeth and perpetual sneer, turning it into a weird sort of half grin that has given him a knowing leer. Like he knows all the secrets of the outer dark along the galaxy's rim.

You'd think that'd make him a freak. But not in Strange. Everyone is ruined in Strange to some extent. Puckered bullet wounds. Jagged scars. Rope burns. Jingo's got scars from where he was whipped by someone somewhere sometime before the company. I don't know the story yet. He ain't been close enough to death to feel like it needs to be told to the company log keeper. That's how I know this op against Grau Skull ain't got anyone worried. No one got the premonition and came to me to download their tale of awful and woe. Tell me their real name instead of the tag they've lived with since the day they signed on with the Strange Company.

Tonight, it's just business as usual.

I have no idea where Sergeant Hannibal got the Capellan Necktie. The white, livid, jagged cut that encircles his neck. Rumor is somewhere with the Saturnian Regiments. Rumors abound in Strange Company as I have said because everyone has some kind of past they never talk about. Unless they feel death stalking. Still, stellar warrants and bounty hunters trying to collect on those pasts abound in plenty, just as the rumors do. But a Capellan Necktie doesn't make one a freak in the Strange Company. And bounty hunters, or jealous husbands, who come looking, get everyone in Strange Company's attention with all the ammo we can provide. Debt settlers get settled. That's the reason we become brothers. It's us against the universe. Regardless of whether we're getting paid.

Even the freaks in Voodoo need that protection. And in fact, they probably need it the most if you believe the conspiracies about the Dark Labs. Freaks spend their lives looking over their shoulders. Watching for hunters sent by the Labs.

We've got those. The real freaks are in Voodoo Platoon. Measure twice, cut once, as I warned the Kid. And every "Kid" before him.

But the enemy round that gave Sergeant Hannibal the grin-sneer and reveals him to be the true monster I know him to be for all to see, he got that one on our last gig.

I still count it one of the best days of my life.

For about twelve hours as he got medevacked back to the rear, I was sure Sergeant Hannibal was a dead man and that my life was much improved. Even Chief Cutter confessed he didn't have high hopes for anything other than a traumatic brain injury for my enemy. Our company physician was busy throwing up before morning sick call when I went to ask him if my luck was gonna hold. He waved me away and continued hurling up last night's bottles of rum. Five days later Amarcus shows up like a monster that can't be killed so easily, takes his platoon back out into the bush, and wipes out that village he got wounded near, from off the face of that world.

Burned it to the ground and didn't leave anyone inside alive. Company got docked fifty thousand mem by the War Crimes Tribunal. Client had to pay it out for us. Then they got shy about the rest of our pay. We convinced them otherwise eventually. Voodoo gave their CEO nightmares and gray hair. In the end we got half of what was owed us.

That was on Mira. Mira was a living nightmare. A. Real. Living. Nightmare. Burning down a village of "officially" neutrals was the least of all the wrong that went down on that particular nightmare of a smoldering little genocide.

It was told to me that Sergeant Hannibal was rumored to have muttered, "'*Sides*," to Cheater, one of his toady squad leaders, "*ain't no neutrals in war*." He said that as he watched the whole village that no longer was burn down and bloom like an oil refinery on sudden fire. The just-dead still lying in the long dry keffgrass with their throats cut.

Tonight, between two sergeants who'd murder each other if we could, in the dark near us, the captain, wearing nothing but his standard worn brown leather trench coat with old surplus fatigues underneath, and some carrying harness I've never gotten a good look at, comes onto the lev-rail platform. His worn boots dark and muddy. He keeps low and studies our positions for the attack. He's got his 'nocs out and he's scanning the whole of the objective and checking to make sure all Strange elements are in place.

If Amarcus and I were going to duke it out right now, and it always feels like a summer storm is about to light up right between us, then the captain's presence shuts all that nonsense down immediately. It's company business now. Company time. Even Amarcus Hannibal is afraid of the captain. Because he's smart. Evil, but smart. It shows by how much he tries to pretend he respects the Old Man as a combat soldier. And hates him at the same time when he thinks the Old Man isn't looking.

You can't see that. But you can feel it.

Stinkeye confirmed it one time. "That one," he said of Amarcus Hannibal. "He wouldn't know the galaxy's heart of darkness if he found it. Because it'd just feel like Tuesday to that chile. Know what I mean, Little King?"

He calls me *Little King*. Says that's what the name Orion really means back on Earth. Says it's something called Irish. And spelled different. But spellings changed once we left. And so maybe Stinkeye's right even though he lies all the time.

Amarcus doesn't respect anyone. He's nothing more than a cold-blooded killer looking for his next vic. It's just a good thing he found the profession of mercenary, because if not, I guarantee you he would've become a mob boss, serial killer, or crooked cop on some tiny world or station he'd made all his own. A place that would have been, for all intents and purposes, a kind of hell for those who lived there. And he would have been their King Satan.

Having said all that, all these terrible truths about my fellow Strange Company brother, Amarcus is actually an excellent soldier. And combat leader. He may run his platoon on a pure one-eighty-proof fear that he will kill them all and bury their bodies where no one will ever find them, but he won't let any of his men get killed easily by anyone dumb enough to call him an enemy. So basically, they worship Sergeant Amarcus Hannibal in Dog Platoon. It's a cult. A cult of fear. And that's exactly the way Hannibal wants it.

Of course, half of them are probably wanted for murder themselves on some world somewhere. I ask myself why I'm dumb enough to make Amarcus Hannibal an enemy.

And there's no answer I've ever found that explains it.

I just do.

CHAPTER FIVE

We're sitting there in the mud and the rain of the ruined lev station, waiting for the captain to give the signal to attack tonight's House Party. We always keep operational objective tags the same. We're getting rigid in our old ways. What's next, senility? This is not, repeat *not*, the bright age of the company's history. You should've seen us back when we were really something. Now we're getting old, tired, and maybe even a bit rusty. Or maybe just the last three months on the losing side of this conflict has me feeling that way about us. About me. About the universe in general.

It was getting hard to tell which.

I looked up and down the line of my platoon in the dark blue of the night and ruin. Drifting mist where once there had been rain. Squads and teams, grimly staring forward into the rainy darkness we will soon assault through. Watching the ruin of the No One's Land we'd cross, a hundred meters of relatively open ground, to break and enter into the hulking monolith at the center. Grau Skull had cleared what they could to create this open ground. A kill zone to kill us within.

Chances were... some of us would die out there. Or at least get hit in the process. But like I said no one had come and confessed all their sins to me lately, so maybe it was just me and me alone that felt uneasy about the battlefield tonight. Maybe everyone else felt just the right amount of Strange Company *get it on*. Which, for the Strange Company, was just a little bit too much extreme violence. That was the best way to feel our unit greeting and reply. A little too much. Enough to feel *just* invincible. Too much, and you got crazy. Too little, and you felt weak and vulnerable against what the universe and others with guns were going to do to you. Like the dice were against you somehow.

Just enough and you had an advantage. Like you were just crazy enough to get up to some real trouble. Like… you were the living embodiment of the fact that the enemy had no idea what was coming for them. They were the fishing junk… and you were the typhoon. That's the best way to put it.

I felt the funnel coming on. Dialing in on the ultra-violence I'd need in the next few minutes. Managing that and the ability to think, lead, shoot, move, and communicate through the next few.

Still we waited for the captain to give the signal to attack. He usually just whispered it in the ether of our comms. His dry and smoky voice always tired and a mix of irritation and impatience, go figure that. *"Go. Go now."* That's how he'd give the order to attack. That's how he always gave the order to attack. As if saying, *Go and take some lives now*. That's how he always gave it.

That's how we always did it.

I was rehearsing all that in the moments before the attack because I needed to get into that headspace and I needed to gin up the motivation to do to others what I'd been paid to do. I was approaching *Bang*, and when the order was given I didn't want to be left of it. The right side of the ladder of fun and violence was *Get it on*. Right of *Bang* and both parties were in it whether anyone liked it or not. Best to be there first.

And I needed to be there now.

He'll say this and then we'll do that, I was telling myself. Then Hauser slid into the line silently, near me. Moving from space to space among the squads. Hauser's next in command of Reapers if I get it. Puncher stays where he is. They don't need Hauser much and he basically just plays utility for the other three squads while running Third as his own.

"Do you know what we're waiting for?"

That's such a Hauser question. His voice isn't totally flat and monotone like the old first-generation hunter-killers. There's almost a quiet calm they added into his speech patterns that I find comforting. His model got that upgrade and gave him the hint of a German accent. He told me that one time, when he was reviewing his protocols. Then he told me what German was and spoke some of it. It seemed like a harsh and angry language and I'd never heard anything like it in all my travels. Strange that they gave it to him, the hints of the accent, to make him more relatable to the humans they planned on him working with.

But the question is so Hauser. *What are we waiting for?* No impatience. Just a sincere desire to know. Trying to figure out humanity, and the vagaries of war, at the same time. He's an Eight Series combat-model cyborg with a four-year life span that got hacked after he ran away from whatever hell the corporations had him locked away in. He doesn't understand that the captain may be waiting for some moment only the human can sense out there in the night. Trying to balance the plan against the smell of the darkness and what he finds in it. Watching the shadows of the brutalist block of authoritarian mixed-use space we're about to get involved in. Wondering about snipers and gunners that could be waiting in there, for us. Waiting for the perfect moment to try and cross as much open ground as possible in order to avoid as many early casualties as possible.

War is art.

You gotta feel it.

I reject the science. Even though there is some of that in it too. And magic also. It's best just to call it an art. It can be measured. But then again, it can't. And that's where the science fails. Magic. Hell, sometimes it seems nothin' but.

"He's waitin' on Nether," says Jingo, who's come up to add his two mem, since he'll be attacking with us and interfacing with the scouts for designated fire should we identify targets going into the structure on our way in.

"Oh," says Hauser the Cyborg in melancholic monotone. Like I said, his voice, and towering stature, calm me. Hauser doesn't not like Nether. Everyone else doesn't like Nether. But only because they're afraid of him. What he does… what he can do… that bothers people. Except Nether is actually a really nice guy. Especially for the freaks of Voodoo Platoon. He's just, how do you say… misunderstood.

As if on cue the rain stops and the mist rises. Lots of it after a long minute, floating up from the mud and ruin of No One's Land out there. The hundred meters we need to cross.

"Guy gives me the creeps..." whispers Jingo, and we both know who he's talking about. Nether. "But it is cool and all, Orion. It's cool what that freak can do."

Nether's played this game before. It ain't just mist rising out there between us and them. It's a kind of dense electromagnetic fog. But it ain't that either. What it really is... is a tear in the universe. That's what bothers people about one of our asymmetrical specialists from the ever-weird Voodoo Platoon. Of the three main ones that can do weird stuff in Voodoo, stuff that gives a down-and-out mercenary company an advantage over most normal opponents in combat operations, it's what the weird unexplainable Nether can do that disturbs them in ways they can't understand, but know nonetheless. Not like The Little Girl and her friend. They like her. Her friend though will getcha killed. Seriously. But Nether, they just think he's creepy because of the way he looks. A freak ruined by Monarch super-science in some unknown Dark Lab out on some comet somewhere that's been officially deleted from the stellar charts. You run into them, super-voodoo science freaks, rarely along the rim. If they exist, they work for the Monarchs exclusively. And by *work for* I mean are basically paid and kept slaves. If they aren't working for the Monarchs, well then, they're in hiding from the Monarchs. Nether hides with us, as does Stinkeye and the Little Girl. Maybe. No one has figured out her story. She just showed up one day, and stayed. Chief Cook, who knows?

But Nether, he's one of us too. Even though he bothers everyone on some deeply disturbing level they can't quite put their assault-gloved finger on. He's one of us and he performs his tricks on our behalf. And we are grateful, never mind bothered. His voodoo has made the difference on occasion. If the dead we've made could talk, they would tell you so.

I look around as the fog turns to swirling mist and the last of the sporadic rain stops. I don't see Nether. But I know he's somewhere out there in the darkness making all this happen for us. And it's getting thick, the fog that isn't fog, the tear in the universe that's something else. It's getting so thick and dense that I couldn't see him anyway even if he were right nearby.

"Go. Go now," says the captain over comms. Like he always does when it's time to get it on.

I don't need to say anything. The three squad leaders who run my platoon have everyone in enough shape to know it's time to get it on. Standing, hunched in the silence, we move forward as roughly one. I check in audibly and hear that everyone's battle rattle is mostly secure. Which is a real plus one for me. Our gear is worn, beat to hell, and cobbled together from a lot of pickups and personal choices. Getting it at least silent for an attack on a fixed position has been a goal of mine for quite some time. It is accomplished tonight and I am at least happy about that.

My element is little more than a ragged line of what look to be homeless vagrants moving hungrily toward some night kitchen on the edge of a vast planetside shipyard where low freighters offload.

Of course, Dog is moving in small wedges like apex predators hunting in packs. Ready to tacti-cool and execute with extreme prejudice and all that high-speed jazz Sergeant Hannibal runs them on. I feel sorry for everyone in Grau, on the left flank of our attack, who's about to meet Amarcus's boys. There will be no mercy there. Amarcus wouldn't tolerate it. Mercy is weakness and he's beaten it out of them. Dog wasn't always that way. But Sergeant Stix, Dog's old platoon sergeant, died badly on Mira, and Hannibal got the platoon after that. Against everyone's objections.

We cross open ground and Grau Skull's gunners do not open up and murder us all to death. I keep waiting for them to, but they don't, and the suspense almost kills me. I'm sure at any moment the unreal silence one finds inside the tear in the universe that masquerades as Nether's fog, because that's all the mind's willing to accept it as, will be broken by short bursts of staccato enemy gunfire from medium and light machine guns exchanging murder with one another. I remember Grau always had an abundance of Z450s they got surplus from the Sindo Wars. Old. But incredibly reliable. Ultra death squads used them effectively back when they were state-of-the-art. High-cycle with nano-conductor-cooled barrels that could burn all day and night and not need a barrel change. The death squads would leave every battle a killing field full of ruined corpses mangled by high output with those beasts.

One long burst right about now and we'd all be dead in our worn-out boots. That's what a good platoon sergeant thinks about as his men cross open ground toward a sweaty madhouse of soon-to-be CQB. All the easy ways everyone can die there.

Both platoons cross and reach the target building, hugging wall to stack for entry… and then the gunfire starts. Short bursts as Dog catches sentries by surprise. Closing suddenly out of the thick fog and firing at ten meters or less. And then Dog, and my own, professionally murder our old buddies at their guard posts.

It's on now.

Get it on. It's what we mean in the Strange Company when we say it.

Everyone in all four of my squads knows what to do next. It's breach and clear and CQB to the inner courtyard and central well of the massive building we've tagged tonight's objective House Party.

The plan is on automatic now. My main job is I've gotta fight First Squad. And I've got to make sure they, and I, come out of this alive. For selfish, and unselfish, reasons.

My two breachers go to work on the entrance we've been assigned to hit. Building schematics, pulled from Crash City's building and planning commission's ruined server, indicate this was once a large apartment back in the day. Water charges are placed along an iron door made from scrap someone welded onto the frame that isn't so stable anymore. Second breacher comes in and swings a sonic ram, and the door is down.

Funnel time.

Of course, I lead the way.

The night-vision lenses along the surfaces of my tired eyes switch over to low light and we're in and ready to kill everyone. Room was unguarded. Grau thought a welded door was "good enough." They thought wrong, and it'll cost them tonight. We clear the room fast and proceed to the main access corridor beyond the inner door. I go right, and So-So, First Squad leader and gunner, swings left and opens up immediately on three Grau Skullers caught in the hall and responding to the multiple breaches across this level. The Stuka 42 So-So carries for a light machine gun blurs and just ruins them. A tornado of invisible fire races from the barrel of his weapon just as I turn left and shoot one of their leaders talking on his comm, hand up to his throat mic and probably sitrepping a bad situation getting worse. For them. I shoot him three times. Twice in the body and then once in the head as he slides down the wall. He gets it in the face as blood spatter paints the wall leading away from his wall-sliding corpse.

I should have shot him in the face first. That's always a bad call, but I should've done it if just to shut down the comm he had with high-ups. Usually you want center mass and then you Mozambique the head for the kill. In the funnel and working, breathing hard and trying to get all that under control, and run my squad, and platoon, I was doing the best I could. I'd expected the killing to start in the last room. And somehow my mind must've dialed back a second. So when I fired, I nailed him center mass just to be safe. I wanted him down and dead now. I dotted his body twice and then blew off his face underneath his combat helmet. Then he was dead.

And so was the sitrep.

When I turned back to So-So smoke drifted through the hall where the sudden gunfight had broken our way. The 42 has ruined the three Grau Skull responders. Flashbangs are going off in other locations as is more gunfire across the first floor of the structure. Maybe I recognize it's mostly our weapons.

Maybe I'm just hoping it is.

A huge explosion goes off in Dog's lanes and rocks the building's foundations underneath our boots. Over the comm I hear the captain order Ghost to enter and shift for the roof as we blast our way through ground level. All my squads are in and up. Next line of defenses is to take the rooms on the far side of the corridor. Doors get kicked and we enter shooting. No resistance survives. Still some gunfire here and there. Once again, the breachers come forward and place our biggest charges along the inner well walls of the central core. Blasting these will give us access to the interior of the building where we expect their command and supply to be located. A once-opulent—according to online brochures we found from fifty years ago—shopping arcade where the latest goods and highest-quality services could be had by the dwellers in this state-of-the-art living adventure, awaits us. We theorize that Grau's command and control are located here.

Crush the head and the serpent dies. After that it's just cleanup.

The brilliance of the captain's plan is that we hit them from a direction they hadn't oriented most of their defenses toward. The dropship put us in behind their line and we'd hit at an angle that wasn't considered the front door. Now we were inside and they were having to shift their defenses to respond to our sudden incursion.

We backed out of the room that abutted the inner well and detonated the heavy charges placed on the inner wall. Again the building rocked, creaked, and groaned, and Jingo swore as he linked up with us.

"She's gonna come down on us, Orion!" he shouted, looking at the crumbling roof in the dark and shadowy room of the once-opulent "living adventure." I could hear the fear in his voice. I waved him back and moved my assaulters into position. Guns up and stacked, I had my count on personnel. No one was down or even hit. I saw the Kid in the back. His eyes were wide, but he was in the game. Smoke and dust drifted from the room where the explosives had just gone off, and yeah, bits of ceiling rained down on us out here in the corridor. I could hear gunfire coming from the courtyard well. Dog was engaged.

"Move."

We entered, So-So picking up the left once more with his team, me on the right, selecting targets and shooting them down.

The next three minutes were solid gunfight.

We took some casualties. But we'd made sure everyone at least had ceramic plates on their chest carriers. No fatalities for us. Instead we gave out a lot more than we got. No one was sure if we got their command at first when a hurricane of lead got exchanged in a crossfire between us and a group fortified behind a long dry elaborate water feature made of concrete blocks that must've once reminded the residents how fortunate they were to live in such a tranquil place. In the end, Sergeant Hannibal ordered up one of our ATs on the fortified position at the center that must have once been some kind of building security position in that long-ago opulence. Glass and concrete exploded in every direction a second after the missile streaked in, smoking through the shadows of the dark and ruined place, and found its mark. Afterward, there wasn't much left of anyone inside.

The worst moment for me came later. Within the hour we had the building. Once Ghost gained the roof and started shooting down into the central well at the defenders, it was ours. A firefight between both sides of the building had broken out as those in Grau with nowhere to run decided to shoot it out and bargain at the same time.

"Hey," a croaky voice called out in a brief lull in which we'd all been reloading or shifting positions. The Old Man was busy identifying concentrations of the enemy and assigning teams to go in and root them out on the upper levels. "Hey!" shouted the croaky voice. Bouncing off ruined concrete corridors and shattered doors and walls.

"You guys Strange Company?"

I was with First and Second Squads now. We were stacked at the entrance to a long hall of apartments high up in the structure. It led deeper into the far side of the ruined building. Shattered plaster and savaged wall art hung grimly in the darkness up there. The captain had sent us in to take them out. We were not taking prisoners tonight.

Yeah, I know…

I knew that voice. Couldn't remember the name. But I knew it from back on Blue. I felt bad hearing it as the guy called out to us in the reloading silence. The guy knew he was on the wrong end of this whole thing. I could tell that from here in the hall, stacked and waiting to murder him and his buddies. But he was still playing his cards like he'd been there before and walked away from it.

"Yeah. It's us," I said and eyed my squads, directing them with hand signals. Making last-second adjustments before we went in, blazing. Automatic leader stuff you don't even think about as you get it done.

Silence.

Maybe the guy just wanted to know who we were that had come to kill him and his brothers. And maybe the knowing was enough. Or maybe he was trying to buy some time to pull a trick. Get some directional magnetic mines in place and stall our assault with about ten thousand steel mini-balls moving at a couple thousand kilometers a second inside a tight corridor.

A real damper on our day.

"Orion, is that you?" said the croak-voice down the dark and ruined corridor after a moment.

Jingo shot me a smile. Like this was fun for him now that we were winning. Having the upper hand instead of the fear I'd seen in his eyes just after the breach when it felt like the building was going to come down on us. His emotional outlook swung like a pendulum that way. He was like that.

"Yeah. It's me. Who's that?" I shouted down the hall, wiping sweat from my throat.

"It's me... Steadly. 'Member we did patrol together that night during Certain End? Ended up in that firefight till dawn near Red Circle Temple Complex that got hit three days later or so? Remember, Orion?"

I remembered.

"Yeah."

"That was somethin', wasn't it?" he said after a long moment of silence.

It had been. We'd fought for our lives together. Blue was a beautiful world. It was the war that ruined it. Best night sky you ever saw. Full of stars like someone broke an expensive chandelier all just for you to look at.

"Yeah. It was," I admitted and thought about some way out of this for the both of us.

What was I supposed to say? How have things been, Stead? Doesn't look too good for you. What? I held up my hand to my squads. But I didn't know why at the time. Now I realize it was my body taking over. Saying, *Don't kill this guy. I know him. We were once in it together. In it really deep one long and very dark night when neither of us thought we were gonna make it to see a sunrise.*

And that was it. That was all he said. He didn't ask for a way out. Didn't try to surrender. Thinking back on it, as we secured the building later and waited for the new day, I heard his voice, replaying it in my head. Not grim fatalism. But a kind of practical, well, this is it, isn't it?

"You guys comin' in?" Steadly asked finally.

I hesitated for a long moment and then I must've mumbled or not shouted loud enough down the corridor where we were. That we had to.

"What?" he yelled back.

"Yeah," I told him. "We're comin' in. Got to, Stead. You know how it is."

I was sorry about that. But I couldn't tell him.

You become a paid private military contractor, this is how it shakes out sometimes. You know that going in. You know that all along. We weren't here to take prisoners. We needed to own this loc for the next two weeks. Until the big show.

"Figured," he said back down the hall.

"How many you got in there?" I asked. But why? Why did I ask? Like if he gave the right number was I gonna dare call it into the captain and say *Hey we couldn't kill twelve guys we once knew on another contract*? Or did I do it because I was just desperate to survive a fight? This was a fight and maybe I needed to know how many he had in there. If I could trick him into giving me a number, using sentimentality like maybe that might humanize the defenders a little more and buy them some mercy, then I'd do it. I'd use it to kill him so I could stay alive one minute longer.

But we were both pros. And we both knew it.

You have to be honest about these things.

"Guess you'll have to come in here and find out, Orion," said Steadly in the silence that followed.

And so we did.

CHAPTER SIX

The attack on the Astralon port of stellar entry was two days later than the two weeks I'd expected it to happen by. And what was supposed to have been an oh-dark-murder didn't kick off until the sun was mid-morning high and no one was in the mood to cross open ground to get their kill on.

The Resistance generals, again the actual legitimate authority of the world known as Crash on the official stellar charts, had dithered over a massive artillery strike on our behalf, finally releasing the big guns to fire at dawn. Great. I love artillery. Let the gun bunnies do all the work. Instead they did *some* work and then we were ordered forward into the day at the edge of the kilometers-wide starport of entry. The whole line was. This was the big one we'd all been waiting for.

The Resistance generals were going for all the marbles. I mean, they weren't here. *They* weren't actually going for it. It would be *us* going for all those marbles across all that wide concrete ring, artillery-savaged starships still on the ground, docking and boarding terminals on fire and burning. But that's why we get paid the big bucks. Right?

Eight months of fighting on this world had boiled down to today. Whoever owned the starport owned traffic in and out of Crash and the rest of the system. Crash, like many of the rim worlds out here along the frontier, just needed a win to throw in with the actual rebellion against the Monarchs.

Something that wasn't officially happening, according to the networks.

Maybe it's time for some big-picture stuff. Since I'm slicing this account out of the main logs, and who knows what will happen to it, if all I can do is get it onto a cargo light hauler doing less than sub-light for the next forty years before it can get to the company's lawyers and someone useful, then maybe I need to explain the whole galactic situation. Chances are it's changed by the time someone reads this account.

Listen, you have to be realistic about these things. The galaxy's a big place and stellar travel is an iffy proposition on a good day for most of the ships making the long dark haul between worlds.

Sorry to infodump. When I got this job, the job of the keeper of the official company log from Jojo No-Toes, before he got medical'd out on Surrant... Listen, there's only so many limbs you can lose and still fight on without cybernetics, and the company hasn't had cybernetic augments mem in ages. At least five contracts. But when I got this job, I said I'd do my best. So here it is. Here's my best to get it all down on how we got involved with the Seeker.

A real live actual Monarch.

Listen, you didn't catch us at our best. You should have seen us back in the day. Or so the old company logs seem to indicate about the mercenary outfit known as the Strange Company.

We ended up on Crash because it was just another contract. We have no dog in this fight between the rim worlds and the Monarchs. We've fought on both sides in a dozen different brushfire conflicts since the Sindo. That was the last big conflagration to sweep the galactic scene.

It's just work. We try not to get caught up in the reasons for it. Therein lies belief, and as has been illustrated, belief will get you killed, right?

Crash, or Astralon as it likes to call itself, is the same story you'll find on every one of those other worlds that are now either smoking piles of irradiated ruin, because a Monarch *Avenger*-class Battle Spire showed up and did it to death twenty-six different ways including G-beam strikes operating in the six gigawatt range per beam strike... or are under total Monarch control with a new outlook on life courtesy of orbital re-education rings, cyber-racks, and the locals always reminding one another it was "a good thing" the Ultras showed up. Like culties chanting out the orders that must be repeated and repeated if one is ever to earn some kind of reward in this life.

There are worlds forever ruined by a Battle Spire crew. Forever. Skeletal cities. Blackened landscape. Mutated freaks crawling the ravaged wasteland looking for a morsel to eat and maybe a dirty irradiated puddle to drink from. Starving masses ruled by the warlords left behind who managed to hold on to the military-grade weapons that survived the conflict.

No one goes to those worlds ever again.

Crash, or Astralon, isn't there yet. It's still in what I like to call DeathCon Three. Three is where you get to have a war because you think you're actually gonna get free of the Monarchs' tight grasp on human expansion and end up like some modern-day Juan of Mars. That you'll fight a battle, or a series of battles, and carve out a nation-state among the stars that the Monarchs, enigmatic though they may be, will have to live with. If they could do it in the home system, then hey… why not out here along the dark rim and so far away.

Except that's all a big lie. Juan and his Ranger buddies died badly a hundred years after they got their taste of temporary freedom. And every minor potentate, or newly formed Independence Committee, on all these rim worlds out here thinks they can do it differently than old Juan did. So, they train up their militaries and maybe the local generals with combat service to the Monarchs, and convince them that yes, given enough supply from the haulers moving between worlds they can break away from the Monarchs and be "free."

What did someone once say "freedom" was?

Anyway, they go for it. The corporations are all pushing for it because everyone knows they're playing both sides, and of course for their own.

That's Phase Three. Or rather DeathCon Three. War. Let's do it, guys!

That's when we mercenaries generally start showing up because we smell easy mem. Companies directed by their lawyers, like ours, back on Bright and Central, made worlds, sign the digital and we redirect from wherever it is we are. The only question is *Who are we fighting for on this one?* Sometimes we're working for the Monarchs. Sometimes we were working for the losers.

See what I did there?

But just because you're working for the losers don't mean there ain't profit in it. There is. And if you play it right, time it right, and do it right, working for the losers is actually where the real *big* money can be found.

See, the losers are often willing to throw an entire planet's economy at you for the win. They have no other choice. If they lose, believe me, they really lose. The Monarchs don't look kindly on failed upstarts, and for the civilian populace, a two-hundred-year light hauler sleep to a reeducation ring and who knows what after that, is convincing enough to fight hard and throw everything you have at the mercs you hired to win you some "freedom."

So we fight, take all the dangerous money, and hopefully get off-world before the Battle Spires show up in Phase Five. Or rather DeathCon Five.

What's DeathCon Four, you ask?

Honestly that's the worst phase for a mercenary company. It means the Ultras, the Ultra Marines, show up with all their deadly toys. Toys courtesy of Monarch super-science. On one hand Ultras are good for the locals. Ultra Marines, if you survive their first pass over the battlefield, are more than likely to send you to the rear to seek adjudication and payment for your sins via the Adjudicators' Guild. Survive that and maybe you just lost your life savings and you get to start over somewhere else. The lucky ones get to move off-world and try again. The unlucky get to stay here and hope Phase Five doesn't go down between both sides.

The Ultras pull a ruin while the Battle Spires fly in over atmo and start targeting solutions for their G-beams.

That's DeathCon Five. Or... the end of the world. Skeletal cities, irradiated water puddles, warlords of the wasteland. Living death.

But for us mercs... the Ultras are pure death sentence. Anyone bearing arms on a world where the Ultras show up is fair game to them. Best to make for the ships and get off-world.

That is not just merc *thinking*. That is mercenary holy writ. You don't want to be around when the Ultras show up.

So, this account is a slice from the main log and I have to get down an important point right here in it to show how we ended up in league with a rogue Monarch known as the Seeker.

Our ship, the *Spider*, can no longer make planetary landings and her jump drive is down until major overhaul and replacement of the quantum compressor array. Right now, she's down to sub-light flight only. I've been in planning sessions with the command team of Strange Company—that means the platoon sergeants, the First Sergeant, the wizards of Voodoo, Chief Cutter, the XO, and the Old Man. We know that no jump drive overhaul is possible here, and that has us prepping for the big sleep and a twenty-five-year trek to the nearest world, Blackrock, where we might, emphasis on *might*, get one.

Blackrock. Sounds like a fun place don't it? Well we'll find out in twenty-five years after we get off this dog of a world.

But, there is a Class Delta starport on Blackrock and maybe we can get our jump drive repaired if we have the mem from this job.

Currently, we do not have the mem from this job.

So, the contract. Crash, or Astralon, decided they could become a stellar empire all on their own like some of the farthest-out rim worlds and the myth of Mars that never really did. They hired mercenaries to supplement their military forces and here we have been. Supplementing. Which means doing all the dirty work that needs to be done regardless of politics.

At first the war went extremely well for the Resistance. We were fighting Loyalist units that appeared out of the populace. Guys and gals who saw the winds of change coming, even though that breeze came from the Monarchs themselves and from their lofty blue jewel once known as Earth to us all. But the kids never seem to care where the winds of change are really coming from. And the Monarchs… well, that dissent and unrest, and grand ideas, fomenting on Crash, didn't seem to bother them much.

Until it does.

It's always that way. The Monarchs never seem interested until they're very interested. Then you got problems.

So at first Crash, or Astralon, was easy. Once we were off the *Spider* and planetside, we started operating. We took two weeks to get acclimatized and get as much gear and ammunition as we could from the locals.

Cook in Voodoo, our intel and psyops specialist, developed the situation and briefed command nightly. The Resistance, which was what the legal government as duly elected by the people of Crash had called themselves, weren't that many. And this too is almost always the same story on every world. Among the

Resistance, or whatever they choose to call themselves on the world we happen to get hired to fight on, are usually people from the middle classes and definitely from the old early star pioneer stock. The ones who want freedom and the chance to either win bigly, or lose bigly. And gloriously.

They're always on about *gravitas* and destiny. I've found those things, like dignity, too often are a needless luxury. Especially if you can't afford them.

They just want to make all the big calls like their ancestors did since the planet came online and got discovered. Back when the real big fortunes were made. The Loyalists, on the other hand, loyal to the Monarchs that is, usually want things to stay the same. Which means letting the Monarchs have more and more control of your lives. They love the Monarchs. The Monarchs give and provide and as long as you accept your lot in life, in that the sky's the limit as long as you don't want to be a Monarch, then life is all gravy if you're willing to bend the knee and wear the leash.

Some people want to be *Chiefs* though. No matter what. And the Monarchs only want *Indians*. So it goes. Enter mercenaries…

I guess the Resisters are a little jealous. Jealous of all that unlimited power the Monarchs have. Hey, I don't judge. I just show up and get paid to fight for whoever. If I seem hard and callous, that's totally by design. I got schooled a couple of times early on about getting caught up in that week's cause. Now I know the realities and I measure everything twice, so I can cut once.

It's best to just keep your pod face on and collect the pay from whoever's paying you to kill. *Believing in one side or another has a tendency to get you killed.*

Think that's just hardboy, fatalist mercenary with the tat that says, *Kill 'Em All and Let the Universe Sort*? Well I don't have that particular ink. But every morning I get up and tell myself the same thing. Whether it's in some mud hut, the actual mud, or even a five-star shot-to-hell hotel we commandeered for our base of operations on a world slowly going fever-mad, I look in the shaving mirror and say to myself, *Believing in one side or another has a tendency to get you killed, Sergeant Orion.*

So, don't.

Example...

Our first op planetside. Here's what belief has to do with getting you killed.

We were on the ground for about two weeks after getting shuttled down by sub-orbital drop-off from the *Spider*. Getting acclimatized. Geared up. Ready to go. Assessing the actual situation on the ground as opposed to what we were being told by our employers. That's important in our line of work and we try as best as we can to get our own due diligence done so we can know the score before we start pulling the trigger.

When this conflict started, like I said it was one faction, probably the faction in charge, deciding it wanted to be free of the Monarchs back on Earth. Why share the take when you can keep it all local? So of course, they started all the independence rhetoric that gets everyone killed, eventually. Big speeches. Pride in planet. Spirit of the original colonists. That whole thing.

And of course, the Monarchs have their agents. Always watching. Always reporting back. It may seem like the Monarchs, mankind's elitist of the elite, may do nothing and are only ever concerned with their fantastic-beyond-imagining lifestyle and schemes. But I know different. When they're not using the fist, they're in the shadows watching and waiting. Counting and calculating. Pulling the strings.

The indifference is just for show.

The Monarchs run everything and it's best just to accept that if you wanna have a nice life. In a galaxy full of have-nots, they are the haves and this cannot be disputed. And they have no intention of having it any other way.

So the "loyal opposition" to the Resistance arose, and as ever with the Monarchs it rose within the mass of angry and disgruntled youth who wanted to be more like the Bright Worlds. Monarch Poster-Child Worlds is what they really should be called. *Blah blah blah*. Whatever. The Loyalists are just playthings of the Monarchs' psyops division. Creations by master puppetmasters. They fell for it. They always do. Agitated. Made a nuisance of themselves to the Resistance and the undecided silent majority. And then one day found themselves in possession of lots of off-world weapons. They, the Loyalists, were dumb. If they would've looked closer they'd have seen the bloodstains on their weapons from the last group on another world the Monarchs ruined who thought they wanted to freedom-fight by serving the masters of the universe without knowing they were doing so.

It gets complicated because it's murky and byzantine and the Monarchs are involved. To put it so it's easily understood:

If you don't want to accept the truth that the Monarchs rule everything then you are Resistance. Especially if you'd like to be the one ruling at least your little slice of everything.

If you're local pop, and you envy the Bright Worlds that are the poster children of the Monarchs and you'd like to live your best life courtesy of the stellar state, then you are Loyalists. You're usually dumb, young, badly though extensively educated, and have very little work ethic. You think the people in charge are doing a pretty great job with what seems to be a tedious task and you'd prefer for the local greedheads not muck it up because they want to be "free."

And here's one more wring on the shammy to make it easier. Both sides want power and don't like each other much. Or at all. They hire mercenaries to settle the constant disputes.

The Resistance—which, as I have pointed out is the legitimate government of this world—hired their mercenaries, rogue navy, and started training their own people up to liberate themselves from the shackles of oppression and maintain their sizeable business holdings. Meanwhile the kids decided to go *a'rampaging* in order to maintain the status quo. And now that they, the Loyalists, those kids, had weapons and uniforms and even cool red berets courtesy of the Monarchs even though they didn't know it, they thought they were an actual military.

Reaper and Ghost got assigned the first mission planetside. The Massacre. Dog was still digging in our first FOB and filling industrial-sized sandbags for our little fort. Of course, Voodoo was in the mix. But you never know if it's gonna be Nether, Cook, or one of the other freaks. No one knows how they, Voodoo Platoon, interface with the Old Man and decide what tricks they're gonna play on the enemy on our behalf. That first op planetside, it was Stinkeye dealing the cards from the bottom of the deck.

Stinkeye does magic. Stinkeye does fear. Maybe he can do other stuff. But maybe because he's such a miserable old alcoholic, the fear is what he knows and what he can do best drunk. It ain't really magic. But it might as well be. Whatever Monarch Super-Voodoo science lab cooked his brain and turned the dial to do what they call Psyonix, might as well have called it magic as far as I'm concerned. I've seen him pull some crazy tricks.

That was the situation as we started the battle for the starport, on the day we'd meet the Seeker. And after that… well, that's what this is all about.

CHAPTER SEVEN

That was how things on Crash, or Astralon, kicked off. How a disagreement about the future of a world turned into a snipers' shooting gallery and a total bloodbath, and then a war both sides needed someone else to finish. But hey, that's how it's always been, hasn't it?

Someone picks a fight for two other guys who'll do the fighting. Same as it ever was.

Now, we were being told, this was how things ended once and for all on Astralon or Crash, as we moved on the starport. Winner take all. Resistance elements in this sector attacking the starport from half the points on the compass. The winner would decide the future once there were enough dead to make it clear who'd actually won. And the Strange Company had certainly stacked their share of bodies in this little conflict. But that was what we did. Now we'd take the port of entry for Astralon, or Crash, or whatever it was being called this week, and then the Resistance would control the re-entry beacons to the system and therefore stellar trade and navigation.

In a galaxy full of all kinds of starflight—jump, hyper, decades-long dumb-thrust hovering just under sub-light, and of course the rumors of other darker weirder things in development, or for private use by the Monarchs only—those navigation systems inherent to every populated star system were still very important. And whoever controlled them got to determine what was important.

Whoever controlled them was definitely the winner at this stage of the conflict.

That's why the port of entry had remained relatively untouched by the other side. Destroyed, it was utterly useless to everyone. For a long time during the course of the war it had been held by the Loyalists and was used as the main Monarch-paid resupply base for most of their war effort.

Stinkeye had once hissed at me in passing, "Whoever controls the spice, controls the galaxy, Little King." He was drunk and laughing to himself while I was out checking the night watch one hot summer night. We were about a week away from the big fight at the Hooper Reservoir. "Know what that means, Little King?"

When Stinkeye is really drunk he calls me that. Like it's an insult, which it is. And I know you'll think this is strange, but I'm one of the few people Stinkeye talks to when he's *not* drunk. Which is something. Sober he's still crazy, but you get some fascinating tales. So I don't mind it. Stinkeye is half legend and half unwanted old relative. He commands a certain amount of respect in the company just by virtue of having been around for longer than anyone can remember. He's been here longer than the Old Man has been commanding. There are logs hundreds of years old that mention him, or someone a lot like him using different tags.

I had no idea what *Whoever controls the spice controls the galaxy* meant. Half of what Stinkeye mutters is chalked up to nothing more than just drunken nonsense.

"Book back on old Earth," he slurred. "Read it when I was a kid and there was still such a thing called NASA. Can't remember the name… Little King, can't remember it… no more. Can't remember. But it was a thing that was. And that used to mean something, Little King. It really did."

He took a long hot pull of the jet fuel he called *hooch*.

Waved it at me.

I declined. Because of course I wanna live. And that stuff will kill ya unless you're actually Stinkeye.

"It means, *Little King*, that when… when… you control the thing that allows transportation between these little islands we call… the stars… well then, boy, it means you control the stars themselves. Trust ol' Stinkeye. Always trust me, Little King. It's truth straight from the deep dark well o' the universe. Cold water, whether you like it or not, eh?"

Depriving our enemies in this war of the base that was the port of entry would be a major, if not final, blow in this six-months-long struggle for the supremacy and control of the main habitable planet in system.

This was for the entire bag of marbles.

For us in the Strange Company, it was like we could see daylight to getting paid off on this dog of a contract. There were problems though, of course. There are always problems. There were rumors running through all the platoons that the Resistance generals weren't putting mem in our accounts like they were supposed to. And of course, each platoon's barracks lawyer had it all figured out down to the bit. Stinkeye was the main prophet of this heresy, and the First Sergeant had barked at the chief to "shut his damn drunken mouth about stuff he didn't know nothin' about."

Stinkeye promised he'd peel back the senior-most NCO's sanity like a banana and show him the true nature of what he muttered was, *"da dark side."*

But the rumors about short and no pay were actually true.

Payments to our lawyers on Bright had stopped six weeks ago. Our current account rep, Astacia Esquival, had advised the captain to conduct no further operations until some of our back pay was settled up. She'd even advised him to withdraw us off-world for our next contract and let the lawyers figure the aftermath of the struggle with whoever ended up in control of the planetary assets.

Oftentimes the Monarchs' reps would do just that.

There were two problems to this though. The *Spider* could no longer make planetary landings, besides being no longer jump-capable. We needed a starport with extra-orbital transport to effect the eighteen-hour flight for link-up with our ship and to get off-world to our next contract. And with no mem on hand we couldn't hire orbital transport. That was problem one, and it was a big one.

The Resistance was paying all the merc dropships in mem by the bucketloads for excessive contracts. The only transport we had was wheeled. And no matter how much of Stinkeye's hooch you ran it on, no high-speed battle goat was going to ever achieve escape velocity beyond a few meters of height on the bad roads between everywhere we needed to go.

Problem two was there were only three starports on Crash. One was currently a giant smoking crater, the result of a tac-nuke early on down in the southern hemisphere. That was a denial-of-service attack being that the port was away from the main action and therefore capable of operating as a major supply hub for our enemies. The Resistance generals hit it just to make their case for the main port of entry being critical. That main port was the one we were trying to take this unseasonably hot morning. And the third starport was five hundred miles out in the desert wastes and dead seas west of our position. The Crash Wastes, as it's officially known. Near the famous landmark that gave this world its name. The Crash. That starport was nothing more than a dry lakebed and a lonely old terminal with a small settlement built up around it. But, big valuable *but*, it ran its own tracking beacons and could be used to make system entry and planetary landing. That made it extremely valuable once the main starport went down.

The only caveat was that any ship setting down there had better be able to get itself off the planet otherwise it was stuck forever. No services out there.

It was a smuggler's port. Every world had them. And it was amazing how they defied destruction even in the worst of conflicts. Probably because the leaders of both sides were using them to line their coffers with smuggled contraband in the event of either a win or a loss.

It pays to play it both ways sometimes.

All that was the big-picture strategic view of what we were trying to do, and what needed to be done, as we got the order to move on the starport along with almost every other ground unit the Resistance had in our sector to throw at the Loyalists.

First the Wraiths came in before dark. Stealth bombers shaped like flying crescents that hummed on evil notes in the predawn overcast skies that were already hot and expectant with the day's heat and battle. They were like the black blades of Death's scythe flying through the darkness to hit their targets. These were actual Astralonian air power assets. Astralon had once had a carrier group but the Monarchs sent it in with the first wave at Mistral Bay and of course we all know what happened there.

That was a bad day for everyone. Including the Monarchs.

Since then the Astralonians had developed a great planetary air force but had shied away from carrier production, preferring to transport their aircraft off-world via bulk carrier and deploy them planetside on whatever world they'd been ordered to fight on for the Monarchs.

So the Wraiths, jet-black and moaning like drowning ghosts in the night skies, swept in and hit a lot of targets to the southwest of our staging positions. Deep in the rear of the front lines of the Loyalist units. Probably nailing supply columns and staged units that would react to our impending assault. Now they were blown to bits, covered in burning fuel, and trying to scramble out of meters-deep craters along the main MSR at two hours before morning light.

Hot chow was most likely canceled.

Dawn came up hot and steamy within the misty gloom. The day felt tense and sweaty just as the long night had. Reaper had spent the darkness in a culvert located along the main aqueduct that supplied this district. A large and impressive engineering feat worthy of any of the Bright Worlds. Water was a big thing on Astralon. In some places it was everywhere. In others it was nowhere to be found. Sometimes the dividing line was so clear it was unnatural. It made you uneasy to see a desert scar and a tropical forest divided by a rushing boulder-strewn river that seemed like a tear in the world. Many people chalked this up to the actual crash site itself. Saying that somehow the crust of the planet had been fractured long ago and therefore the water tables, moisture, and weather patterns of this world were all ruined from that long-ago impact with something the expansion of humanity couldn't yet wrap its mind around.

But the planet had reached a strange kind of equilibrium with the early colonists building these huge continent-spanning aqueducts that would have needed to be hit by at least hundred-megaton warheads to destroy. And even then, the water would have just found its way past the irradiated lake that had formed in the hundred-megaton crater.

The giant structure of the aqueduct feed we slept in that night, or didn't sleep in in the case of some of us, made you feel insignificant. I spent a lot of time outside the feed to the culvert where everyone rolled out, smoking and watching the stars and the big concrete colonist-made riverbed that was currently dry.

The Loyalists had control of a dam upcountry and they'd been cutting off the water supply to this sector in prep for our attack.

Its vastness made you feel insignificant, like I said. Like it was some temple where you just contemplated truths, pushing away Stinkeye's drunken mutterings, and tried to find what the stars knew. Or what they cared about.

Spoiler: They don't care. They're just giant balls of burning gas. If anything, they're amused. But only slightly. Or at least that's what I tell myself when I spot Betelgeuse thundering across the night dark. Betelgeuse don't care. Betelgeuse gonna Betelgeuse as they say on a frozen world called Horn.

The starport was hit with a lot of artillery in the first hours of morning light as we waited to commence the assault. We watched from the far lip of the aqueduct we'd moved into the night before, studying the terrain we'd cross in the next few hours. We were assaulting from the northeast section of the giant landing field and our first objective was to take the main terminal in the outer green ring of the port. Which was the outermost ring and where some of the largest ground-capable starships came in to transfer cargo. The big lifters, inter-system cargo, and some of the heavier independent operators docked and offloaded cargo or passengers in better times there. Smaller ships and the main passenger liners came in at the central terminal a few kilometers further in at the blue and gold terminal rings. That was where the underground tube led into the main city.

We watched as ghostly artillery shells began to fall through the hot morning mist out there toward the positions the enemy had chosen to defend, and which had been identified by nightcrawler scout recon spotters in the days leading up to the battle. Of course, the main cargo stacks got hit hard out in the storage areas of the vast sprawl at the port's edge. We knew the Loyalist troopers would be emplaced with infantry heavy machine gun teams there, and main arty gave a lot of attention to the cargo area and distribution centers. Several explosions rocked that facility as secondaries went up after the high-impact anti-personnel munitions started getting used in effect.

The sounds were crazy as starship loading cranes bent and immense mobile crawlers groaned and twisted and fell into the stacks like distant tiny models of such giant things represented in miniature scale. War shows you how temporary everything is. Strange, almost science-fiction sounds screeched out across the sky as the exploding munitions rattled through the heavy metal cargo containers. Ricochets and sudden ringing notes like ominous noises rumored to be heard in the vast wastes of lonely edge worlds. And even then, in their most remote places where few seldom dared go.

Legend and myth were legion regarding those noises and their sources. Hearing them now made you uneasy about the day ahead. Like they were something unseen and close by that was going to ruin everything. Including your neatly packaged view of the universe you were currently so certain about and carrying around like it was something that could be exchanged at a bank for meaningful credit. And your sanity. Something large and relentless and bigger than you was stomping around at the edges of the universe. I could hear Reaper muttering about that, getting quieter with each titanic strike out there across the fields we'd cross.

A sergeant has to listen to the battle, and his men, at the same time. Knowing his men are only listening to the battle. Trying to get ready for what they might find within it… so that once they're in it, they might survive it.

The thinking of the enemy defensive planners was to create bunkers out of the cargo containers filled with off-world goods. Our planners had decided high-impact artillery rounds with AP munitions should do the trick to ruin their defense in that sector off on our flank. Maybe it did. But something hit something, as they like to say, and an unexpected series of utterly huge explosions suddenly rocked the distant facility we were most likely going to have to sweep through to reach our assault lane. Gargantuan masses of bent steel flew away, end over end, in every direction across the morning sky as the main admin terminal for the cargo facility blew its lid like some reactor going suddenly and unbelievably redline. And then some.

Chief Cook came up behind us in the unreal quiet that followed, hands in pockets and smiling, as all of us wondered if someone's gun back in main arty had just hit a local on-site reactor no one knew about.

Would black sand graphite come raining down through the white fog? Dosing us all with lethal levels that would start as sunburns and then melt our flesh off over the next two weeks?

Fun.

"Nah," said smiling Chief Cook. He's always smiling. His teeth are spaced far apart, and it gives him an almost skeletal grin that makes you think he's genuinely happy except that you suspect he isn't really and it's all just an act. And that bothers you. He's thin, medium height, and incredibly tanned. Wiry is what people would call him. He dresses like a Monarch spec ops advisor, pressed jungle patterned-gray fatigues, tight pistol belt with sidearm, bloused boots, and a black beret, because he was one. His specialty before he parted ways with the government was psyops. Now he does it on our behalf and because he does it so well, he's a CW3 with the freaks in Voodoo. Chief Warrant Officer Three.

Most Strange Company feel very nervous around him. He has this way of making you feel like he knows a lot more than he's letting on. A lot about stuff that isn't supposed to be known. And maybe he knows so much he even knows why and how you ended up in the company. Men keep conversations with him short. And it always seems, when I observe these interchanges from a distance, that he's sad to see these *one-sided knowing* conversations end. He likes to talk politics and he'd love to go on. But he lets you go and watches you for a long time after you've left. Studying you. Like he's completing some note in a mental file he keeps on everyone. I've seen this. I've watched him do this. Studying them as they go. And he's seen me seeing him. Then he smiles at me, waves, and moves off like he's had someplace to be all along.

I chalk all this up to being a specialist in psyops. They're masters of the human psyche. They know what makes people tick. And more importantly they know how to freak you out and get you to do the thing their commander wants you to do, tactically, so you can get killed by his men.

Think about that. I tell myself that every time I deal with Chief Cook. Whom I actually like. Our politics aren't dissimilar. In fact, he thinks, or has convinced me to think, that we both share the same nihilistic view of galactic culture. And that we both know how it will really end. Which is very badly. For everyone.

That's not even politics. That's just watching the news and reading between the lines.

It's just reading the road map and seeing what lies ahead whether anyone likes it or not.

Most Strange Company don't get that deep on subjects of the way things are going. It's too sober.

But Chief Cook usually just says to me, "You know, Orion." Gives me a wink and keeps on moving. I've taken to pretending I do know. But who knows? Sometimes it pays to play both sides. Know what I mean?

As far as we can tell, Chief Cook is uncannily good at what he does. Which is mess with people's, the enemy especially but sometimes randos and even us, he messes with their heads on a grand scale. As has been noted, he hates Stinkeye. Utterly. And the hate is reciprocated in full, if not more so. If the company is ever overrun and given the order to die in place, once all the brass is expended and we're pulling into our last positions calling out "last mag" to meet our bad end, I fully expect to see those two going at it with knives. Two lunatics who thought the enemy was really just practice for the real villain they saw in each other.

Getting down to the business of settling scores with what little time remains.

But then I remember Sergeant Amarcus and I don't think too badly of them. Everyone's got a villain. Or, in someone else's story… you are someone's villain. You're the bad guy.

I try to keep everything in perspective. It makes the mental sight picture work much better. And, as an old sergeant once told me, "Front sight forward isn't a bad way to live when you think about it, Orion."

I test it out all the time to see if it's still true. So far it has been.

"No worries," Chief Cook's telling me and the rest of Reaper as we watch the cargo terminal off to our left begin to gush clouds of black smoke, each of us praying we're not suddenly going to get graphite rained-on in the next few minutes. The black billowing smoke looks like a demon's chest heaving and getting larger by the second as the fires over there consume and combust more material. "They were storing some illegal munitions that came in last week on the *Archon of Delago*," mutters the warrant officer behind us. Chief Cook. He's a big mutterer. A low talker. Sometimes you can't even tell what he's saying and you miss half of it at that. "Big freighter. Torpedoed by our bombers as she tried to make the jump. So..."

Chief Cook paused and exhaled, whistling through his wide-spaced teeth as he did so. Studying the local apocalypse we were all watching, and wondering if we had to go fight in shortly. Honestly, it looked to be devoid of enemy even now. Who could've survived? But uncontained radiation does have a tendency to freak one out. Especially if you have to go mucking about in it, looking for a fight.

"So... what you're looking at there..." lectured Chief Cook like he was some instructor back at EOD school, "is about five tons of high-ex munitions that got hit somewhere in south shipping will-call, as far as I can tell. We knew it was there. Inside man tipped us off. Well, he's probably dead too now. We were gonna take it. Guess not. That's the way things break, kids."

I can't tell if Reaper actually believes our psyops spook, but they sit back down in the culvert and return to getting their gear ready for the attack. Deciding what's too heavy to carry for the rest of the day across all the kilometers we're going to need to fight our way through to reach the main terminal in green ring. And deciding what's necessary to do that fighting.

The worst thing is to be in a firefight and need what you don't have. Then you have to get real creative, or real violent.

I stood there scanning the morning's destruction. It was zero-seven-forty local. The day was promising to be a big mess. I could feel that. I knew from the op order that we wouldn't be going into that mess to clear. That was Dog's job. But we were supposed to transit to keep our profile low on the approach to the main objective. Now I was getting an updated feed on our order. Our job now, as of the update in my combat lens, was to move through the tall dead grass surrounding the port and reach the first landing apron's edge in the thin morning shadow of the main terminal for green ring. I was worried about that. The tall dead grass catching fire from the nearby explosions, while we were out there in it. That could happen if that storage facility kept burning like it was and exploding like it was doing. Then we'd be at the landing apron, a wide half-kilometer circular highway that encompassed the entire green terminal ring where the big ships set down. And it would be quite a view for the defenders watching from the smaller terminals and the docks we would be approaching.

So, let's just call that the kill zone. There was no way to cross that without taking a lot of incoming. Hence Reaper was getting the job.

As you can see... I was worried about those areas. Not so much about the fighting until the terminal, but a lot of open ground to get shot at in.

Which, let me tell you, is actually no fun. I was now thinking better of carrying a ruck full of supply ammo. I'd need to move fast. But then again the new guys, especially that Kid, had a tendency to burn mags. Being dry inside the terminal wasn't going to do anything for anyone, except the enemy.

I looked at Chief Cook and wondered what he was doing down here, down with Reaper. The freaks from Voodoo rarely get involved in CQB. Off to the right I could see Dog ready and waiting to go forward. Like they wanted to. What a bunch of... they actually liked this. I kinda wouldn't have minded just throwing up. Except I had nothing to throw up. I told myself to eat a protein bar so I could throw it up before the attack. Each of Amarcus's people had their entire ruck stuffed with all the weapons and ammo they could do. They were going in heavy. Amarcus had them carrying all the AT he could get his hands on. I knew secretly he had this fear of getting hit by fast-attack armored cavalry. An infantryman's worst nightmare if you were on open ground and on foot and got caught in a sudden raid.

The AT weapons were for that. Though he'd use them on entrenched defenders if he needed to. "Fire in the hole" was Dog's most commonly used phrase. Or as Duster, one of the EOD guys over in Dog told me once, *"Why try when you got explosives, Orion."*

"What're you doing here?" I barked at Chief Cook. My voice sounded dry, like I was spitting clipped words. I sounded bitter and irritated. I never slept well before a battle. If only because there was no time. And any time you had was another minute to get ready for whatever it was you were gonna face the next day. Whatever it was that was gonna try and kill you in that day.

"Came down to give you a little good news, Sergeant Orion," said the warrant officer crisply.

I doubted it would be good news.

I picked up my ruck and put it on. I wasn't making most of Reaper carry one. It was going to be a long hot day with a lot of crawling. Under fire I wanted them to move fast. Not tired. The supply crawler could bring our gear up later. I'd carry as much spare ammo as I could. For everyone. I've learned that fear of getting shot will get me moving fast enough if I need to. No matter how loaded down I am. Incoming has a tendency to motivate.

"And what's that good news?" Like anyone in Strange I was expecting the "good news" to actually be bad news. Chief Cook was smiling, his teeth white and big and gapped. Theatrically he raised his giant steel watch, probably very expensive, and noted the time. Then he executed a perfect left face and studied the distant terminal that was our objective.

"See that Clipper berthed below the big thirty-nine on the OBJ, Orion?"

I did. There was a beautiful Clipper-class starship berthed alongside the main terminal. Our objective.

Yeah. It was a standard Star Clipper. Long command neck and hammerhead bridge, wide-disc graceful main hab, huge engines and thrusters erupting from the engineering stack at the aft section of the vessel. But every line spoke of distant tropical worlds untouched by us. Natives and enterprise. Adventure. Maybe even lost alien ruins undiscovered and guarding some of the secrets of the universe. Every kid's fantasy of such places. We'd all grown up on *Stewart Young of the Starship Horizon* streams.

"That was," said Cook, continuing to study his watch, "the *Neptune Clipper*, just in from the Sweet Worlds. Commissioned six years ago at the Martian shipyards in the actual vicinity of Earth. Owned by the Pan-Stellar Starways line. Captain—"

"Was...?" I asked, interrupting him to note the obvious use of incorrect tense. You know like soldiers do and all?

His eyes went wide as though he'd suddenly been jolted by some random wandering bolt of electricity. He looked up from his watch and then very theatrically turned around, like some teenage boy playing tricks and miming dumb at the same time. That was the thing about Chief Cook. His age was indeterminate.

Some days I would have sworn he had to be younger than me. Like some kid who'd just gotten out of university and needed to pay off his loans with a little military service. And then there were other times you'd come upon him in the dead of a late-night op, catching him unawares with his mind intently working some problem in the thin ghostly light of a battlemap, seeing some horror he never spoke of, and then, it was at those times that he looked older. Much older than me. And I look pretty wrecked, in my opinion, for a guy just turned thirty-six standard years. Technically, I'd been rode hard.

Coffin-sleep flight time has made me much older, also technically. But really, I've only had thirty-six years of actual non-cryo waking life. Still, I look every kilometer of it, and some.

The Falmorian party girl thought I was handsome though. "You are like zee avenger from one of za early romantic novels written by Luc Desaix," she said in her pidgin French with the Falmorian buzz of the humanoid eels. "A man withs many scars zhat make him zo attractive to ze woman who zeeks a competent and daring man who has done ze zhings normal men are too afraid to do. Walked ze night unafraid. To fight… when others will not. To pay back wrongs zat must be answered, my *estrangier*. You look like such a man."

My *estrangier*.

I think about her a lot. Still do. I wrote her one time.

But that's a common side effect of Falmorian party girls. Ask any penniless mercenary.

So back to Chief Cook's little playlet.

"Was…?" I'd asked as he recited the vitals of the big beautiful Clipper docked out there on the green ring near Gate 39. Even from this distance it was huge, rising high into the morning fog, heedless and serene as artillery rained down on the terminal off to the west. Ships were considered off-limits by the powerful Commercial Nav Guild. Too important to be wasted on petty conflicts. For the most part, both sides abided and didn't target. Of course, there were accidents and those got decided in Stellar Appeals Judiciary. One downed ship could wipe out a company like Strange and force us into bankruptcy, or piracy.

Whichever paid better.

He'd executed that perfect left face and raised his hand to his tanned tight forehead to shield his brown eyes from the morning sun burning through the gauze overcast. Except now I noted he had his mirrored aviator shades on. As trademark a part of him as the spec ops beret and shiny black boots he polished alone at night, listening to acid jam from forty years ago, big during the desperate years of the Sindo, muttering to himself and finding certain things funny. As though telling himself jokes he'd never heard before again. Jokes only he found funny. Jokes he'd never tell another living soul. Secrets too.

Then I saw a downpour of smoking artillery out there, more ghostly-ghastly shells arcing through the sky to rain down on the area near Gate 39 and all over the serene *Neptune Clipper* waiting to lift and heave off to those worlds we all dreamed of.

Someone swore back in the culvert as it went down. They saw it too. Shells smashed into the shining white-and-blue upper hull of the beautifully graceful starship getting ready to take on high-paying evacuees no doubt. Those who'd realized the game was over on Crash, or Astralon, or whatever.

Engineering was hit first. One massive round straight through the superstructure. One of the wings portside took three shells and lost her landing gears as the indirect rounds went straight through, tearing dark maintenance decks and components like lifters and inertial stabilizers to pieces. An explosion in the outboard thruster tanks sent hull plating into the shattered glass at the back of the terminal. Huge sheets of the stuff cascaded down in great waterfalls. But we heard nothing at this distance. Only saw its slow-fall destruction. Compartmentalized, as all starships are for that kind of damage, the ship simply and unceremoniously collapsed along her port side onto the tarmac and landing apron, listing like a drunk who couldn't find his way home after a night's binge. Other rounds struck the beautiful Clipper but none caused destruction so fantastic as the damage to her portside wing.

One round went wide... on purpose possibly... and nailed the nearby APU pylon that powered the ship while she was docked. Fuel cells went up, and there must've been flammables for refueling nearby along the tarmac. Now black billowing smoke was coming from that area and also the portside wing array of the Clipper.

Chief Cook turned back to me, smiling that wide, skeletal, almost perpetually psychotically happy-trip grin.

"*Was*," he stated officiously.

I studied the scene for a moment. It was right in our lane. We'd have to go through that.

"Why?" I asked.

"Figured you'd need cover, Sergeant Orion. Generals up at High Command don't want to hit that section of the terminal because some of them have, how shall we say, recalcitrant cousins among the defenders. So I noted that the artillery plots were going to make sure that section of the terminal didn't get hit at all. Then they could murder you on the approach. And... oh boy oh boy, Sergeant Orion, I don't need to tell you how much weaponry they've got in there to repel, but it's a lot if the long-range observers are right. So I figured we'd hit the ship, get you a smokescreen going, and if you move your men just right you can keep the smoke of the ship, and in fact use the ship, to hit the terminal without taking too much incoming. Black oily smoke and flaming starships have a tendency to obscure the field of battle. That's straight out of the Ultra Marine field manual, Sergeant. Trust me. Top secret stuff. I'd have to kill you if you told anyone."

I thought about that for a second. I could see the merits of what he was saying. Using the ship as cover to hit the terminal might work.

"But the ship's on fire."

"It is, Sergeant Orion. It is indeed. Once you reach her engineering stack you should be able to use the main spine inside the ship to get up to the hab docking arm and infiltrate through to the terminal. No one will expect an attack through a burning starship. That's crazy, Sergeant Orion. Right? Gonna be a big surprise for them when it actually does happen. You and your boys pop out. Bam. Pow. There you are right inside their line. Pretty cool, huh? It was partly the Old Man's idea. You could say I'm here to officially change your orders and have you assault through the *Neptune Clipper* to breach the enemy line. Once you're in, the rest of the line is going to hit the terminal on cue in this sector. So, we'd better get going, Orion."

"We...?" I asked the warrant. I didn't like this. Voodoo had priorities that didn't often match up with those of keeping my men alive and completing the mission. Half the time it seemed like they just *wanted to do some darkness* as Punch once put it. *That's whack, Sarge.*

Again, the theatrics of surprise from the chief. Behind us, coming down the aqueduct, I could see a mammoth fuel hauler with twelve massive big ball-wheels, low and flat, smoking and belching as it came up shifting through its gears in the morning mist never mind the distant explosions and flames. I recognized it as old war surplus from the Monarchs' military supply units. Soldiers who knew it, and there were very few left who'd seen this kind of vehicle in active service, called it the Land Whale. It was used to fuel supply guppy dropships back in the Sindo.

Cook cleared his throat.

"Uh, yes, Sergeant Orion. I will be following you in with the," he turned to indicate the Land Whale, "HMWVFT 195 as you can see. I call it the... uh... Ice Cream Truck. For purposes of the operation henceforth." Then he laughed mischievously to himself because this was all very funny to him.

Of course, I had to ask.

"And why do you call it that, Chief Cook?"

"Well, Orion," he said grandly, holding up one tanned long finger I could see small white scars on. "It's loaded with near-deadly, and almost certainly deadly in oversaturated doses like those currently contained within the HMWVFT 195, psychotropic gases. Real, real crazy stuff, Orion. We used this back in the Call-Galli in sixty-nine when things started to go pear-shaped big-time. Highly effective. Extremely deadly in high doses. And... critical to Strange Company's mission objective to take the main terminal in green ring. We're gonna drive this pig in there and gas 'em until they can't distinguish between reality and the Nine Hells of Qua."

CHAPTER EIGHT

I asked Chief Cook if we needed to mask up before the assault on the port of entry green ring main terminal. Chemical warfare was not unheard of in the world of private military contracting along the outer worlds. In fact, it was expected. Especially if you accepted the soldier's evergreen maxim that *if you ain't cheatin', you ain't tryin'*. All soldiers and mercenaries live by that wisdom. The Stellar Judiciary might have strong feelings on the subject of chemical warfare, but we'd go chemical on someone just as fast as they would on us. That was the way it got played if you were playing to win. And we were always playing to win.

There are no second places in war. In it to win it is the only way to play.

Winning meant you got to fight another day. Or, it just meant you survived.

Chemical's a hassle, but it beats gettin' shot by a... well, it beats getting shot by a long shot. If anyone ever told you war was fair, or that it was supposed to be, they were lying to you because they wanted to do some very unfair things to you by surprise.

Bullets are quick, but gas'll do the trick, I once heard a merc say when we hit an entrenched bunker with nerve agents. The bunker was so deep and well-built, it had survived all our AT and arty. We'd cracked the front door and lost two squads on the threshold. Just like that. Fifteen seconds of full-auto sentry-gun murder. So we regrouped and gassed 'em and then went in later after they were all dead.

Either way they were gonna end up dead. The only difference is, there were just less of us dead when the equation solved for the same outcome. Breach, or Gas. Either way it's gonna get done.

Still, the thought of going to an advanced protective posture to keep us safe from chemical agents was going to add to the suck of an already long day getting longer, and hotter by the second. Jingo walked by sweating and proclaimed that the weather analysis for the battle was all off. It was supposed to be cool and foggy. Instead it was hot, humid, muggy, and foggy. And it felt like the sun was going to burn off all that cover any second. Then it'd just get hotter. Lotsa fun in full-assault battle rattle. But I complain too much. Back to the hassle of using chemical agents in warfare. First off everyone would have to get a lot of extra gear out of their personal supply. Or Sergeant Biggs, *Go Biggs or Go Home* as our supply sergeant likes to say every time over initiated comm, for no clear reason, would have to come forward with the crawler for an additional personal gear draw.

All kinds of problems with that. Not the least of which was it would give our position away to enemy observers watching our line and waiting for the attack out there. Then they'd have a pretty good idea of where to drop some artillery rounds once we were out in the open.

"Nah," laughed Chief Cook in that quick friendly-psycho machine-gun bark-mutter of his. Waving his hand as though dismissing an offer of more cake at a lady's high tea. "I got some retro-agent doses for you and the boys that are going to shift the effects on you for a bit. Not saying it's going to be pleasant, but… at least the nerve agent won't be lethal if you don't get a full dose. Theoretically. I tried the stuff on myself last night. And a little this morning to be honest. It's fun and I feel great. Seeing the connections in the universe and the big-picture stuff if you know what I mean, Sergeant Orion. Worked for me. Real trip though. Ever try pharmaceutical-grade acid, Sar'nt?"

I had not.

"Of course you haven't. Stuff doesn't exist if you believe Monarch Psyops. Well," he said, heading off to the truck in a business-like manner and waving at unseen insects, I supposed, "you're in for some fun. Damn bats are everywhere today!"

He opened the truck and I saw the Little Girl in there. When he came back with an OD-green medical bag and started rummaging around for our retro-agent doses I asked him about her.

"What's she doing in there, Cook?" I whispered because I didn't want her to hear us talking about her.

He made a *Who?* face, looking up from the bag and seemingly perplexed at my perfectly logical question. I couldn't tell if this response was genuine or not. He was starting to act strange. Which was saying something even for him.

"Natalie," I hissed, not wanting her to hear me. "You know who I'm talking about!"

I was angry and it came through. I was just hoping the fear didn't also.

He looked back at the dark Little Girl sitting in the passenger seat of the big chemical transport crawler. Seemingly unconcerned with us. Which was a good thing. She scared the hell out of me. She was small. Even for ten years old. She looked like any other refugee from all the worlds where wars got fought and no one cared much about the victims. Even the least and most vulnerable. Which she was not. She was pale. But olive-skinned. Wide dark eyes. Dark short hair. Big green coat someone in Strange had given her. Little more than a shift for a dress underneath. A black potato sack. But who makes potato sacks in black, amirite? Large oversized combat boots she painted happy faces on with white breaching marker. She'd been with us since the contract on Blue.

Her name was Natalie. But we called her The Little Girl.

She was a freak too. But too freaky even for Voodoo. Even Stinkeye got all quiet around her when she silently appeared, muttering, "Little *Brujita*" and making mystical and religious signs with his leathered old hands dangling with prayer beads as he did his best to shuffle on out of her presence.

"Oh, her," said the psyops chief. He returned to rummaging in his medical bag. "Thought she and her… friend… might be useful out there today. You never know… but I have a feeling it's gonna get hairy, Sergeant Orion. Just a feeling, mind you. I've learned to trust them and I'll tell you, Orion, I got it this time. And that's not just the acid talking… I mean retro-agent. It's not that." He waved at the bats again and muttered at them to "Stay back!"

Okay, I said to myself.

"Listen," began Chief Cook anew. "I didn't have to be here with you and Reaper. But I got that feeling back at the TOC when the Old Man was studying the battle. Told him, 'Sir, that right there is gonna be the lynchpin to this whole operation. Where Reaper is going, and I need to be out there with Reaper when it happens. Right in the mud and blood and guts, sir.' He just stared at me that way he does, y'know how he does, and then nodded that I could go do my thing. So I brought her, Orion, and myself, down here to help you and Reaper not get killed. Today. And before you go getting all weepy thinking I'm some kind of noble spectacuthriller hero... I ain't, Sergeant. Three of your guys owe me sizeable gambling debts. I can collect if they're alive. If they're dead... well, you know how it goes. Gambling debts get paid last in Strange. Even if they're inside the company. So I'm here purely for financial interests. Purely. This is business, Sergeant Orion. I can't do this much longer. I have this idea to start a multi-world conglomerate specializing in buying high and selling low. Don't ask me how it works... it just works.

"Here, take these tabs. Hand them out to your men and when I give the signal, put them on your tongues and hold on to your butts 'cause it's gonna get real weird real fast. Also kill everyone you think might be the enemy. Even if they look weird. I'm not gonna use the psychotropic gas until we're on the objective. Then I need you to keep them off me until I can find a main AC conduit and flood the terminal's external intakes with this stuff. Then we dose up and go in, guns blazing, Sergeant Orion. Guns. Blazing. And kill 'em all and let the universe sort. Did I tell you it was gonna be freaky?"

He did.

"Good," he muttered, nodding to himself. "Told myself last night to really make that point to you, Orion. Seemed pretty important when the walls started melting. A little."

Twenty minutes later Reaper was on the move, combat wedge with all four squads and the big chemical transport half a click behind us and waiting for the signal to move on to the objective. The drifting smoke was thick, and we were getting good cover from it. There was some incoming, but we kept our alignment and formation, tracking a good course through the tall dead grass as we made for the landing apron in the mist and haze of late morning.

None of the other units were moving yet. And I won't lie to you, we felt real naked out there. Someone had to start shooting at someone first. And usually that was the first bunch to appear on the battlefield. Surprise, it's us. I could almost feel some sniper out there watching our skulls and thinking who to nail first. Or some LT getting all excited about dropping arty all over us. Life is fun for an NCO that way.

"We're out front, Sar'nt?" asked Choker in disbelief as we waded through the tall dead grass that hadn't been seen to in eight months of fighting. "Ain't anyone else moving? Man... I gotta get out of this platoon, Sar'nt. I wanna be a Ghost. I wanna be unseen."

"Tip of the spear, Choke," answered Punch for me as we moved forward ready to deal some death. "Tip o' the spear."

First Squad was the top of the wedge. Second and Third to my right. Fourth Squad to my left. We moved into the battlespace, ready to do as much harm as we could, and stay alive while doing it.

Mercenaries don't die for causes. Other people do. True believers. We kill people for money. That's what we do.

The black smoke really kicked up from the fire at the loading docks and the burning starship and for a moment we couldn't see anything ahead of us. Not even each other. It was like darkness had fallen over the world in judgment and we'd never ever see again. Or like someone had opened a portal into some hell that specialized in burn pits and we'd just blindly gone on in, doomed to wander for all eternity for sins we had a pretty good idea we'd committed.

You could smell bodies burning on the hot morning wind and that made the moment feel darker than it already did. The defenders at the cargo admin were roasting. I reminded myself to eat a power bar so I could throw up. I hadn't. And I forgot to as one of my boots landed on the concrete apron of the starport's LZ. We were in their kill zone now, even though they couldn't see us through the hot black smoke boiling up into the schmazy day.

My combat lens had been tracking the route and suddenly both eyes updated the data feed and corrected for our location. They'd been doing that lately. Either because of the efforts of enemy jamming assets, or because my gear was whack. I didn't know.

This war had been hard on personal gear, among other things. Some were like that. Others not so much. Every conflict was its own personal thing with an identity you could almost talk about like it was a real person. The problems came when it started talking back. But that's another story.

The black smoke cleared for a second and I could see the rest of Reaper from my position at the tip of the spear. We emerged from the dark drifting banks of black smoke like killers in the business of making trouble for others. I felt just a moment of pride as I studied my platoon on the move. Observed them. Watched their homicidal swagger and predator's caution. First was led by Punch as the squad leader. Choker in the medic slot. Hoser in the gunner position. Hustle as the AG. Boom Boom in the squad designated marksman position. Then Firsty, then New Guys One, Two, and Three, and finally the Kid.

The "New Guy" designation for the three in Reaper First Squad was the first step after getting called "Kid." You got "New Guy" and a number, especially in Reaper because we always had two or three floating around. New Guy Two was about to get tagged as Farts for obvious reasons. Apparently, a lot of our chow disagreed with him. Badly. He didn't mind and he was known to hang tough in a firefight. The other two New Guys were indistinguishable so far. The Kid was still the Kid and it was best not to get attached to him until he proved he wasn't gonna get waxed right off the bat.

So far he had not. But you never knew. Today seemed like one of those days where someone was gonna buy it. So why not him?

And as I always told myself, *And why not you, Orion. Sergeants get killed too.*

It's best to be honest about these things. Trust me. Don't lie to yourself about the bad things you're facing in life. It could happen to you. And a lotta the times they, the dead, don't just go away.

"All right Reaper," I said over the platoon comm. "Get it on."

What I saw before me was a good three hundred meters of open hot concrete apron where we should have been completely murdered by enemy marksmen if it weren't for Chief Cook making sure the docked starship in front of us was billowing burning starship fuel from her portside tanks and obscuring our approach to the objective. Flames were spreading across the tarmac, igniting support vehicles and engulfing offloaded cargo around the ship. If it were a normal day of starport operations, this would be a real mess complete with evacuation and screaming sirens and even emergency assistance vehicles. For us it was just today's mission.

For Strange Company it was just another day on the job.

And like I said, I was glad for that burning starship, otherwise all the enemy defenders currently holding the main terminal up there in the green ring would have started shooting at us down here on the runway.

We were nothing but out in the open and vulnerable to traversing fire.

As if on cue, artillery strikes crossing over our heads, indirect shells screaming through the smoky atmosphere above, fell and savaged the ornate roof of the terminal. If there had been enemy snipers up there they would be dead now. Blown to shreds in every direction.

I checked the rest of Reaper as we came out of the smoke, making sure both ends of the wedge were clear. Some were ducking. Incoming artillery could make you feel like it. Even if it was yours. It wasn't like dumb shells fired using physics discriminated about who they landed on. But mainly my guys were moving forward through drifting black smoke and falling shrap. And that was good. Shrapnel had a tendency to get your mind working about the thousand ways to die. And that made you harder to kill. Not impossible. But at least harder. This war had turned Reaper into killers. The New Guys and problem children had had their major malfunctions corrected and were starting to soldier the Strange Company way. Realizing that their brothers in the Strange needed them to do their jobs if everyone was going to make it through this one and get paid. That had made better fighters out of most of them.

Chances were, I was gonna get cleaned out of New Guys to resupply the other platoons that had taken losses, and would take losses today. And believe me, I'm fine with that. Each of my soldiers was ready to serve in the other platoons and that was the gold standard for the sergeant who ran Reaper. Sort and select the ones that would go deeper into the mysteries of the Strange Company. Weed and wait for death for those that wouldn't, or couldn't, cut it.

Like I said… it's best to be honest about these things.

Hauser, the Third Squad leader, gave me the thumbs-up that we had everyone and hadn't left anyone in the smoke. I got us moving with an "All right Reaper. At the double. Move to the engines."

I blinked in my combat lens field of view and my retina tagged the shadowy area beneath the Clipper's massive main starship engines where I wanted us to concentrate. Not everyone had combat lens capability, but the squad leaders did and Hauser didn't need it. He was a cyborg after all. His brain was a giant supercomputer. And a very advanced one at that.

We were on the double and the air was hot and acrid with chemicals and smoke. Choking us and making our lungs burn. You could taste the burning chemicals in your mouth and nose. If I sounded out of breath when I contacted Chief Cook to check his progress, it was due to that. And the fear too. As we crossed that three hundred meters, I was just waiting for a symphony of medium to heavy machine-gun fire to open up and end Reaper as it was known that day.

"Holding in the smoke," smiled Chief Cook pleasantly over the static of the comm. I could hear the onboard AC whirring heavily in the driver's cab. There was melodic and almost hypnotic music chanting in the background of our communication. "Once you've secured the starship, I'll bring the whale in and we'll begin the breach, Sergeant Orion."

Unbelievably, the defenders had actually sent armed men down to attempt to stop the flames and assist terminal personnel in assessing the damage to the beautiful and fantastic docked starship currently ruined and burning along her port side. I'm sure they were concerned damage to its reactor might be a little problem for everyone within a ten-mile radius.

I saw them, the enemy riflemen, watching the maintenance personnel work and try to minimize the cascading damage. One guy was spraying white billowy foam on the wing tanks and no one was waiting for an impending enemy ground attack. Burning starships had a tendency to draw the eye.

"Do not open fire," I whispered into my comm, hoping everyone in Reaper had their ears on. I wanted to cross as much of the sweltering runway as we could before a firefight broke out. At one hundred meters the dream of surprise attack intersected with the enemy's sudden awareness of our presence.

"First," I called out over the comm, "engage and keep moving forward. Second and Fourth, secure right. Third get ready to assault through. Get it on, Reaper!"

There was at least a small enemy squad there near the massive blast-blackened starship engines watching the maintenance people do practically nothing to stop the spreading and out-of-control flames licking at the central hull. At least a small enemy squad was what I could see as we approached. First brought their primaries up and slowed to a fast walk, continuing forward motion, and began to fire at the enemy troopers. Of course, Boom Boom painted the first dude right off the bat with his rifle. I saw that one take a solid hit, body armor or no body armor, and go spinning away into a luggage cart that was on fire nearby. A gaping hole from Boom Boom's Tesseract Archer Rifle. The .308 Magnums he fired didn't care about modern plate armor. Now flaming luggage was falling all over that dead guy.

Wisely, Hoser and his AG kept moving, keeping pace with the wedge, and scanning for what we in Reaper liked to call "The Other Guys." The ones you never see until you open fire. The gunner would suppress while everyone else did the singles in the initial target group.

It's a personal thing for me. There's always another shooter nearby, and best to train that way. Even if you're engaging an enemy group, all carrying, most likely there's someone you don't see. Bad guys always travel in pairs. Even if those pairs are groups.

The New Guys, and Choker and Punch, along with the Kid, did the rest of the enemy squad, who were caught flatfooted and watching maintenance guys who themselves weren't too keen about the safety of the situation as they tried to figure out if everyone was about to get nuked by a sudden core melt from the starship's onboard reactor.

Everyone who's not engineering on a starship has an inherent fear of the onboard reactor. Bad things can happen and the fear is neither superstitious nor unwarranted.

Second and Third fanned to their tagged positions to get under the starboard wing and react to any ground forces coming out of the terminal docking bays. Covered by the wing they should be safe, I told myself.

Fourth came up on First and I told Punch to tell the maintenance techs to scatter and get lost. They were more than happy to.

Choker finished a couple of the downed enemy troopers with double taps to the skull and remarked on the poor shooting of the new guys in not getting kills in the first pass. "Make sure dead guys are really dead, guys!" he shouted pedantically, considering the middle of a battle to be a teachable moment as he stood there on the hot burning tarmac beneath a starship's main engines. He's right though. Fights teach you in ways training never can. You just have to live long enough to learn the lesson they're trying to drive into your thick skull. Choker's only the squad medic because our company physician, Chief Cutter, gave him a first aid class once. Before that he was the AG until Klutz got killed at Tebibi Field three weeks ago. Ironically, it wasn't Klutz's fault. For once.

We lost the last medic there too. Bad day.

Klutz just stepped on a jolt mine connector and got an eighty-thousand-volt burst through his central nervous system. That could happen to anyone. Trust me. Jolts are real hard to spot. It's a good thing they're expensive otherwise there'd be a lot more of them lying around for us to step on.

And like I said, it was a good thing our gunners, Hoser and Hustle, scanned and waited to engage the second group we hadn't spotted. They were ready to go and had most of a belt to use up when the first of the enemy troopers came pouring out of the rear landing ramp just below the burning ship's main engine nozzles. So of course... Hoser hosed. Opening up with the IG-M89 medium man-portable rapid defense gun. A beauty made by Colt-Horakawa, it dumps over five hundred rounds a minute. Nano-cooled barrel means no barrel changes. Cybernetic assist harness means "the Pig," as we call it, can be hauled around by one man as long as he's got an AG with him to keep feeding the thing belts of ammo. Which it devours. Hoser opened up with a judicious burst of 7.62 AP and tore the first Loyalist troopers to shreds. These were their regular units, not the guerrillas we'd been facing in the first few weeks. And not mercs. These were enlisted and officers with formal military training on what they felt was the right side of the war. Crash's military, except for a few high-speed units and the heavy combat forces, had defected to the Loyalists, sensing an upgrade in pay if the Monarchs had a firmer grip on the situation. That was a smart play. That was usually a Monarch first step. Reward the military for all the brutality it was about to be asked to do now that regime change had begun. Plus, it had a tendency to teach everyone fear and respect.

Which, spoiler, and sorry if you watch the news feeds or believe the propaganda, fear and respect are the basis of the entire Monarch empire.

It works. Trust me.

Hoser's Pig tore the reacting troopers, probably part of some detachment that had been sent in to check on the ship's internal reactor, to shreds. Like I said. The Pig also tore through the boarding ramp because I insisted it be supplied and fed by high-grain load AP. When I ordered the Pig deployed, I wanted it to make its point effectively. Regardless of cover. And it did. Very much so in fact.

It just ruined stuff in a cone of outgoing lead-death.

Enemy fire came from the terminal after that. They didn't have great angles, but they knew they needed to get something done. New Guy Two took a round right through the thigh and started limping around swearing before he fell to one side. Choker was quick and grabbed him by the drag handle to get him under the engines and out of the line of enemy fire.

I had two jobs to do right here and right now. We'd secured the point of entry. The plan was to board the wrecked and burning starship and make our way forward, and up a few decks of course, and then we could drop into the terminal directly through the hard connect boarding ramp.

What if they've got it mined or rigged with explosives I only now wondered in the middle of the plan and battle because that's what kind of tactical genius I am.

Job one was to get the breach underway. I ordered Third in to assault and clear a path through Engineering to the ship's transport system along the main spine. Then I ordered Second to pull back to the aft engine boarding ramp and support the assault there. First I got organized on the perimeter and ready for an enemy QRF to come and ruin our day.

Fourth was going to help here.

Sitrep to the First Sergeant who was with the captain and ran ops control for the company.

"Good work, Sar'nt Orion. Casualties?" bellowed the First Sergeant too loudly over the hectic comm.

I almost said "none" and then remembered New Guy Number Two had taken a round through the thigh. I tapped the comm for hold and asked Choker for an update on Farts's medical status.

If you got hit, we usually advanced you to getting your earned tag. Kinda like a motivation to stay alive.

"He good, Sar'nt," shouted Choker over the incoming and outgoing gunfire. "Went through the meat. Anti-coag in effect. Medi-sealant attached. Two pops of morphidol."

Two was a lot.

"I don't want him drooling, Choke!"

"He good, Sar'nt." Then off comm, "You in the game, right, Farts?"

Farts nodded and his eyes rolled back in his head for a second.

"Hitting him with Quick now, Sar'nt. He'll be good to go, trust me."

Quick is our medical amphetamine and combat enhancer. It tends to make one extremely violent. But I couldn't see how that would hurt for what we had ahead of us.

Choker hauled the man to his feet and had him walk a few steps. Farts swore and made it with difficulty.

Choker told him to quit complaining.

I tapped for the First Sergeant.

"We got one hit but he's still effective."

The First Sergeant would make the call as to whether we had him return to the rear or wait for the main body to catch up. Sometimes our senior-most NCO would just drive out in his Mule and pick the wounded man up. Regaling the casualty with horror stories of gruesome wounds the First Sergeant had received, seen, or handed out.

You weren't really Strange Company until you got that experience. Or so some of the company old guys like to say. And yes, I'd had the pleasure.

"Good," said the First Sergeant over the comm. "Make a man out of him. Captain says we're moving forward now. Punch us a hole, Sergeant Orion."

I switched over for Chief Cook and had him bring the crawler in, warning him we were taking fire from the terminal.

"Hammer down, Orion!" shouted Chief Cook with a giddy war whoop that seemed out of place. Above the gunfire and flames, I could hear the chemical transport's big engines spool up and begin to howl through the drifting smoke that surrounded the besieged starport out there like some wounded beast.

I wondered what would happen if the thin-skinned crawler did actually take a round in its supply tanks as it came in. Leaking deadly hallucinogenic gas would be a problem for those of us on the ground outside the terminal but not so much for those inside, entrenched, and defending. Against us.

"Fourth and First, covering fire on the terminal!" I shouted to be heard. "Engage any targets and give the crawler time to get close to the ship!"

Now I needed to identify an AC conduit that led into the terminal. Chief Cook had given me three locations to spot, and I toggled the combat lens with my watch controls to assess and scan. I found the closest one that wasn't too far away from the back of the starship and ran for it, hearing rounds chasing me across the burning cement.

"Punch, you're in charge until I get back!"

I ran for the massive AC condenser and inductor stack and made it fifteen seconds later. I pulled open the service admin panel and checked that the unit was operational. It wasn't. I went through the root commands and switched it over to manual flow. There was no port connector for the crawler's hose feeds, just ground air getting sucked into the terminal. There was no way to just rig the intake.

And then I remembered this was Chief Cook's operation and he'd have to take responsibility for that. Responsibility for hallucinating my men to death inside a firefight. I wasn't comforted by the lack of accountability and personal responsibility, but I understood that there was math in a battle. Math I wasn't always good with. Math that made me uneasy. A battle is five percent planning, ninety percent skill, and five percent weird and undefinable magic. There're some other subcategories in there but that's what it felt like right now. Don't canonize that. It's not Orion's Law. I have other laws I want to be remembered by for posterity. This one's not ready for prime time yet. It still needs to be refined.

But right now, it would do.

Seconds later the wide, flat, and gigantic crawler rumbled through the black smoke and thundered straight toward the back of the wrecked starship at top speed. I popped purple smoke and waved it at Chief Cook behind the wheel. He mashed the accelerator and I chanced a look at the AC inductors. They were sucking the signal smoke in greedily.

So that was... mostly good.

For a second it seemed Chief Cook was just going to run me over. At the last moment, he yanked the gargantuan wheel and the crawler came alongside the AC inductor stack, braking hard. He hopped out, mindless of the fire we were taking, and went to work getting the main hose detached from the crawler in a very businesslike fashion. As though he'd only recently studied and memorized the primary maintenance orders so he could perform this operation. Saying things like "I think this is how it goes" and "Well this is all wrong" and finally, "Let's give a whirl and see if we can win us a purty girl, Orion."

Again, he was heedless of the shooters in the terminal that were actually trying to kill us. But to his credit he was wiry and agile, and he moved like a spider monkey on pure Quick. I assisted his passive defense by trying to spot the shooters and return fire, if just to keep their heads down. Wisely, I did this from the cover and concealment of the tall AC stack.

One round smashed into the hauler near my defensive position and instantly a jet of necrotic bluish gas began to hiss forth from the crawler's large tanks and dissipate into the air I was breathing. I had the feeling that it hadn't actually dissipated. That it had just micro-atomized and was even now overwhelming my sanity via my nose, eyes, and mouth. Still, I shot back at the enemy.

Keep the main thing the main thing. And killing the enemy is always the main thing in these kinda situations, as the First Sergeant likes to say.

Chief Cook saw the sudden puncture and ran for it, his run almost comic and over-exaggerated as he pumped his arms and fists. He had a roll of high-speed tape out of his starched fatigues cargo pocket, ripped a strip, tore it with his gappy teeth, and smothered the bullet hole in the tank.

Then he looked at me.

"Might wanna dose up now, Orion."

Ulp, I thought to myself and placed a tab on my tongue. I'd issued one to everyone and a few extra to Choker.

Cook looked at me and smiled psychotically.

"Aren't you gonna take one?" I asked Strange Company's psychological warfare specialist.

He laughed maniacally.

"One? Already took three, Orion. Get it on, Sar'nt. Get. It. On. Man."

CHAPTER NINE

We left the chemical hauler full of psychotropic toxins pumping its poison into the green ring's main terminal AC system and made for the back of the ruined starship that had been making the run between the home world and Crash, or Astralon, before it got permanently ruined by friendly artillery. The enigmatic Chief Cook, our attack's Voodoo asset, seemingly oblivious to, and unhittable by, incoming enemy fire from the terminal, went back once we were halfway across the burning tarmac and heading for the cover of the aft bulk of the grounded starship. He called out over his shoulder as he comically ran, "Forgot something!"

If he wanted to get killed by tempting exposure to incoming lead hornets, that was his business. Mine was to get the platoon fighting. It was Reaper's job to breach and clear the access points into the main terminal as the show kicked off up and down the line for the main body of the attack. Already, out there across the northeastern edge of the starport, Resistance infantry units were underway, sweeping out in wedges in front of the low and menacing Raider tanks and Javelin light-walker mechs. The Raiders had been doing really well with their menacing 140mm recoilless main guns and not so much with their AA pods. The medium armored tanks were brought out because we currently had air superiority and could take the chance to gain some ground as long as the enemy didn't go for some early close air support.

As if to make Resistance Tac Plan a liar, two Warbird fighters, Loyalist versions of the vaunted F-705 the Monarchs once armed their ring carriers with, small forward wings swept back for control along the sleek rocket-shaped needle fuselage and aft wings fanned out for max lift at slow flight, rolled in out of the milky morning sun and shot up a Raider tank in the vast sprawl of dead grass just before the terminal apron. Both of the streaking fighters unloaded thousands of rounds of depleted uranium ball and tracer against one of the incoming Raiders there to support our attack. The low ominous *BRRRRRRRTTTT* of their attack resounded across the early moments of the main attack.

Enemy close air support had been pulling this kind of attack lately. Coming in slow and low, raking the tanks from above. Raiders were lightly armored along the top of their angular hulls, and the AA pods were hasty installs that had yet to do anything other than badly attempt to acquire targeting data, throw up a cone of fire, and miss as both fighters went to full thrusters after the kill and roared off into the clearing morning mists, leaving a burning tank on the ground. You could tell both streaking fighters had reset their control surfaces for supersonic flight an instant later as sudden twin booms tore through the sky above the rattle of gunfire and the *thump* and *whump* of distant arty coming to play.

I made for the rear maintenance ramp that led up into the wounded Clipper's engineering decks. It lay below the silent thruster nozzles, giant and looming, massive and circular at the back of the ship. They would probably never fire up again. This state-of-the-art Clipper, part of the lifeblood of humanity's continuing outward expansion through the stars, was probably destined for scrap now. As much of this world would be once we were finished with deciding who got to own what was left of the pile of rubble on the other side of this conflict.

I linked up with Punch, who told me Third was inside and securing Main Engineering. Engineers had been sent in by the enemy to make sure the ship's reactor was offline and cooling. No one wanted an exploding starship to get in the way of anyone's plans to kill everyone else. They'd had a security detail courtesy of the enemy along for the shutdown. Detail was dead and engineers were in zip ties, thanks to Third Herd.

Later I'd wonder if the engineers had been sent in to either det the starbird or melt its core, in case the Loyalists started losing. Yet one more time I would figure out how the enemy had had a chance to kill me that I hadn't known at the time. It was a fun game I couldn't help playing in the few quiet hours between midnight and dawn I seldom got to myself. Why sleep peacefully when you can think up a thousand new ways to die behind your closed eyelids?

Since Farts was walkie-talkie, up and moving, I detailed him to watch the prisoners until we secured the ship. Chief Cook came in, towing the Little Girl that'd freaked me out. She was the something he'd "forgotten" back at the chem hauler the enemy was busy shooting at. And he'd gone back for her.

I had to force myself to remember that was what you were supposed to do for little orphan girls in wars. Keep them safe. Especially in combat zones. Technically she was one. And yes. This was a war for all intents and purposes. But what she was doing here would hurt your morals if you thought too hard, or too much, about it.

So I didn't.

Plus, she was very dangerous. And not just to the enemy. Technically she counted as a company secret weapon. An ace in the hole. But friendlies had died just as easily as enemies when she did her trick. And so it was not a decision made lightly to use her when things got dicey.

You read the old logs of the Strange Company, and you'll see we fought some straight-up no-holds-barred battles on all kinds of worlds in all kinds of environments. We had what at the time were considered great weapons and solid gear. The best. There was a time when the Strange Company was equivalent to saying "the galactic boogieman." But that was way before my time. Back during the early days of outward expansion along the old frontiers and established shipping routes to the outer worlds. We were the something you threatened people with so they'd behave. Little children were told to eat their hyper-peas and carrotini, or *"Strange Company'll get ya."* First Sergeant said to me one time, "Shoulda seen us back then, Orion. We were mean motor scooters if you believe all the old books. Killers every one of 'em. Lifetakers. Heartbreakers. You know…"

Now we do tricks. Aces in holes. We cavort with the unclean of the galaxy for mere survival just to get to the next gig. The freaks. We need 'em in lieu of state-of-the-art weapons and bad reputation. What thousands of years ago some would have called *sorcerers* or *wizards*. Or carnies and hucksters. We cheat. We lie. And yes, we occasionally steal. Our gear sucks and our weapons are third-rate at best. There's better out there to be had. But what makes us still dangerous… what shows we have a few teeth still left… is that we're real good with what we got, and we pull dirty tricks on our enemies thanks to the freaks in Voodoo. There really isn't any trick too low for us that we won't try it to get the win. At least once.

Believe me, we're not proud anymore. Pride died a long time before any one of us ever signed the company contract.

They, the freaks in Voodoo, are like a drug we can't shake. One we need real bad at the same time as we hate ourselves and what we once were before them. I think the same goes for them too.

"You shoulda seen us back then, Orion. Forty thousand enemy KIA at Crow's Hill on Cet Moon. Slaves and tribute taken to cease hostilities," says the First Sergeant when the night watch is late and we sit having stale coffee, listening to the nothing on the comm late in the dark. Imagining history whispers in the ether.

Main Engineering for the *Neptune Clipper* was all matte-black rubberized floor and hulking drive reactor in the emergency damage control red-lit darkness. Gray panels and screaming systems were also all in the red. Panels were broadcasting system failures through the big ship's navigational and drive systems. Huge holographic illuminations in nether-ghost green crossed the floor making sure everyone here was very aware fuel cells portside three through fourteen were compromised and that atmo flight was not possible at this time. A matronly female ship's automated voice warned us the hull was compromised at several points and emergency damage control parties had not reported in with status checks at this time.

"Reported fires on decks sixteen through twenty," she said cautiously, as though warning us not to go swimming so soon after eating a tuna sandwich by the side of the lake on a hot summer day that was the opposite of all this. *"All personnel are authorized to evacuate this starship as soon as possible."*

It was clear she was concerned, though motherly. And then, almost brightly…

"The All Worlds Corporation, a subsidiary of Neuf-Badtmueller Stellar, apologizes for this inconvenience and thanks you for your continued compliance with emergency personnel."

Chief Cook tilted his head toward the zip-tied enemy three-man engineering team and gave me a quizzical, almost angry look. Like, *C'mon Orion, why aren't they dead already.* I was busy getting ready to take Reaper through the aft crew deck up to sixteen and crack the spinal transport, or just use the tube, to get into the main passenger decks that connected with the hard dock into green ring's main terminal. Hauser was busy having his way with the onboard system map, making sure we had all bulkheads opened along our route through the starship. Everything along our flanks locked down.

"What're you gonna do with them?" whispered Chief Cook as he eyed the prisoners. His tone the same as if he wanted to sell me a stolen trans-cycle with a severely illegal modified boost capacitor. The kind capable of 420KMP in less than six seconds. Pressure suit required to ride.

I indicated that Farts would stay and watch 'em.

"Nah..." Cook hissed. He took a small clamshell out and was shooting them up with something from a three-injector hypo a moment later. The first one watched in stunned disbelief and when the other two saw the first one's eyes abruptly roll back in his skull as the man passed out, or died, who knew... they started to struggle for their lives.

Chief Cook muttered, "Come here... cowards," like he was wrestling defenseless babies, and he grabbed hold of another one, a lock of hair falling across his sweaty forehead as he worked to shoot them up. He injected both and they were out seconds later. Or at least I hoped they were just out.

"They're just out, right?" I asked.

"Sure," Chief Cook said like the liar I knew him to be, wiping sweat from his forehead as the Little Girl watched us. Especially when we played Cheks, that's when he really lied. "Sure," he said again, as if to himself only. Trying to convince himself more than anyone, like he was sure he'd gotten the right injector. Straightening the tunic of his fatigues and making sure his pistol belt was aligned once more, he stowed his clamshell back on his pistol belt. There had been other injectors inside. Each color-coded differently. I was sure there were all different kinds of "fun."

"What do you think I am?" whined Cook as he got himself ready. "Some kind of monster?"

Yeah. I did. But weren't we all, these days? I used to tell myself lies that some of us, me mostly, weren't all monsters. But I'd given that up in my time with the Strange Company. We were hired to fight monsters. And if you don't have a knight in shining armor handy standing around to do just that, fight and kill monsters, then what you're left with isn't pretty. What you do is hire other monsters to go fight your monsters in order to get the job done. Because the job has got to get done. Monsters gotta die, and of course, someone's gotta do it.

And that was where Strange Company came in.

The lie I kept telling myself that week was that some monsters weren't as bad as other monsters. Right? The lie of *good monsters* I had been telling myself the week before, had died when I watched us use a flamethrower on an enemy convoy refueling point on the outskirts of the city while we were defending LZ Syro. Listen, it was just Reaper who did that. The First Sergeant said, "Here, Orion, you'll need this," as he handed me the old Sindo surplus Ultra Marine banned weapon Biggs had stowed away in the crawler, acquired somewhere in our long haul across the stars. "Rather than shoot it out, you just hit and run with this thing and let the flames do the all the work, young sar'nt." And when we got there, and I assessed the tactical situation… yeah, it was a lot easier to just start a firefight we had no intention of winning while Choker and I hit one of the fuelers with a jet of flame from a nearby alley. I still don't have half of one of my eyebrows, and we roasted two enemy companies at the refueling point. At least. So I needed some new architecture for my crumbling philosophies. *The Good Monsters Theory* hadn't survived that night.

I was adrift and getting fatally honest with myself about what we were doing. There ain't any shining knights out in the dark parts of space where we find ourselves today. Out here at the limit of human knowledge, out here along the perimeter, it's just us monsters. Out here in the dark it's just us killing each other.

And brother, it's gettin' darker all the time.

Second Squad went in first and made it to the Clipper's aft stores before they got into a firefight with Loyalist troopers sent in to respond to our boarding incursion. I listened to the sitrep coming in from Sergeant Jacks, Second Squad leader. We used Second as we ran First. Straight rifle squads made up of two fire teams, a squad designated marksman, and a medic to support. I ran through the squad in my mind as I tapped comm and went down on one knee, listening to the enemy strength report from Jacks. Ro-Ro, Dip Weasel, Killer Joe, Mass, Too Much, Red, Snorts, Shoots in the SDM position, and Patches as medic were in a clearing the next section.

All good. No "New Guys" and they wouldn't have a "Kid." Only I got those in First. Last New Guy they had was Snorts. He'd earned that nickname because he snorted after he ate. As though somehow he'd eaten so fast he inhaled some of his barely chewed food into his nose and needed to get it out by snorting like an elephant in the throes of intense intestinal distress. He'd sit there and snort and ignore, or was oblivious to, all the murder looks he was getting from the rest of his squad after chow. Especially if we had some downtime and everyone crashed out in a patrol circle. If we weren't on mission, that is. Then he'd just snort and bother everyone. One day the weirdest thing happened. Once we'd tagged him Snorts, and he'd shrugged his shoulders and embraced it, him snorting after chow didn't bother anyone else anymore. Snorts. *That's what he does, man.* It was like that. Once we'd tagged him, classified him, it was then we understood him and after that it was all copacetic.

The minor rules of the universe are arcane and mysterious in the Strange. So it was. So it be.

But Second was in good shape for combat. They'd pinned the enemy with fire from Killer Joe's Pig. Everyone had concealment and more important, good cover according to the sitrep from Sergeant Jacks. The enemy was stacking at two to one and looking like they were gonna push any second.

"Feels like an augmented squad, Orion!" shouted Jacks over the outgoing blur of high cycle from Killer Joe's Pig. He musta been nearby, pinned behind a bulkhead and trying to assess the tactical situation. He'd done boarding ops before he linked up with Strange. He knew behind a thick ceramic-forged bulkhead was the best place to be in a firefight inside a starship.

Killer Joe, the Pig gunner for Second, looked like the kind of rough customer from the block who would have slit your throat just for lunch money to spend on smokes. He looked like that horror-movie monster Cyberstein, but with more scars. And uglier. That's how he got the nickname. Someone had said he looked like "Joe Killer" from a serial comic book that was big back in the day. Some hitman who works for the Alta Mob on Suaguar and plays both sides against the middle. Eventually we just settled on calling him Killer Joe.

Truth was, his looks were unfortunate. They didn't match the person. You couldn't have met a nicer guy. And when we got let loose on some town, it was Killer Joe who was the guy that made sure no one messed with us and that we got home no matter how sloppy we got. Even if home was just a bombed-out warehouse with cardboard for bedding and a helmet for your head. Joe didn't drink. But he liked to watch others have a good time. That made him laugh and it was then he wasn't so ugly.

Killer Joe also cleaned us out at pool, which was his thing and which he was an actual absolute serial killer about. Watching Killer Joe play pool was like watching a Monarch ment-savant decode the secrets of quantum distance travel aboard one of the big Spires. State-of-the-art dark magic engine science. Crossing the big distances in an instant. Defying all the written laws because there were unknowns not available to the rest of the heaving slob-mass of stellar humanity surging for the farthest reaches.

Us and our dumb ships trying our "real bestest" to go real fast to get somewhere we could call our own. Even jump drive was lame compared to that stuff the Spires and their navigator ment-savants could do.

"Hause!" I yelled to the cyborg squad leader who ran Third Herd. "Need a way to come at them from the flank while Two pins. What's the ship's map say we can do about this?"

The blare of outgoing and incoming fire was making comms almost unintelligible deep within the tight quarters of the lower engineering decks of the starship.

Hauser, with no emotion and utter calm, ran his fingers over the touchscreen and found our map. He airdropped it onto my combat lens and I ran through it quickly. We'd go into aft crew, hang a left at the first junction, and take off into crew hab. Run crew hab for a hundred meters and cut back through the galley to come out with an angle on stores that might change the course of events for Second Squad in a firefight.

"First up. Hauser take Third and stage behind Second. Once we attack from the left, bounding overwatch to move through stores and put fire on them as you close. Watch for friendlies here…" I said, highlighting a ping on our map to show where I thought First and Hauser's combined element might get close enough to start shooting each other.

"Copy, Platoon Leader." It was hard to break Hauser of his rigid military coding from his time with the Ultras. It was wired deep and hard into his cyber DNA. I always found the story of his escape, and awakening, amazing. And I knew I could count on him to make sure we got no friendly fire as we noosed the enemy and went for the kill.

Yeah, a C-985 Infiltration Cyborg optimized for terror and urban combat protocols with a heavy warfare chassis wasn't a thing you wanted to run into out there in the dark when the lines of combat were good and blurred. Especially the Eight Series Heavy Combat models. But having one such cyborg have your back, that was actually a great sense of comfort not to be underestimated.

I liked Hauser, if only because he gave me courage. I'd read that somewhere and I couldn't remember where. But when I thought of Hauser, who once innocently asked me if he had a soul, I thought of that line and I thought of him.

Somehow the universe made a little more sense after that. Or indicated there was a trail of bread crumbs that might lead to where the answers were hidden. It just took an awakened combat-model cyborg to ask the question.

And the other cool thing about Hauser was he could carry the Pig and a couple of other weapons. Third had two Pig gunners, one being Hauser, and that made them our heavy weapons squad. He turned, almost mechanically, away from me. The motion was not quite natural human movement, and then he led both squads off through Engineering to reach the main entrance to the aft crew sections.

"First on me."

I gave them the rough sketch of how we were gonna hit the enemy element that had Second pinned in stores as we moved.

They all listened, nodding, making adjustments to their gear. Getting magazines loosened in pouches for easy pulls and reloads. I noticed the Little Girl staring at me. Her face passive. Her eyes judging me. Trying to find out what kind of man I actually was. That was her thing. She stared at you like she was seeing everything you'd ever done, and sifting it. And trust me... you didn't want to be the wrong kind of man with her. She could do real bad things when she wanted to.

"All right," said Chief Cook a little too gustily. What the Little Girl was doing with him, and why she didn't adjudicate him in the "wrong kind of man" category, I had no idea. The gap-toothed warrant officer checked his watch and then pulled his sidearm to chamber a round in the silver-plated 1911 .45 with Grim Reaper Astronaut handle grips. Pearl ivory. Black as night Grim Reaper Astronaut embossed at the center. "Let's do this, Sergeant Orion. Fun's about to start. It's good and *get it on* time, children."

CHAPTER TEN

We hit the enemy inside the permanently grounded Neptune Clipper from the sides, shooting into their flank deep within the ship's stores. A quick hustle through the near-pristine crew quarters, First constantly remarking on the quiet and unoccupied luxury digs we were passing by, and then we were in position to open up and try to scratch the enemy in a deadly crossfire. The crew quarters of the Neptune Clipper were indeed immaculate, and state-of-the-art compared to the habs on our old bubble-gum-and-baling-wire destroyer turned mercenary troopship. The Spider was a five-hundred-year-old Newmax warship that hadn't seen better days for most of that time. Rumor was she was a Ceti Alliance destroyer from back during the early years of space flight. After the civil war with Centaur and the establishment of the Monarchy, she'd been sold off as surplus. Modifications had made her, if not fast, then very dangerous in a gunfight. She'd pulled us out of more scrapes through sheer firepower and determination than anything else. And honestly, they didn't make hull armor that thick anymore on modern warships. She could lay the hate, and she could take it too. And that was one of the reasons we called her home when we were on the ground in some war for pay. The goal was always to get through the whack and make it back to the Spider. But the living quarters aboard the Spider were extremely spartan. Not that it mattered. We had an onboard MMO and the coffins were all slaved into it. A forty-year haul between worlds wasn't so bad actually. You could live whole lifetimes in there. Or just switch off and go Deep Sleep.

No combat wedge formation as we pushed through the crew sections of the Clipper. Now we were using the standard starship boarding column, checking blind angles and dead passages for the enemy attempting to do exactly what we were about to do to them as we pushed deeper into the belly of the ship. Stacking at intersections and bulkheads and running scans to see if we'd find any unfriendly IEDs, or ship's security systems running on backup reserve, before they found us. If it had been another merc company we were going to hit, like the now most-likely-defunct Grau Skull, then there would've at least been sentries or another fire team coming at our main body to pull the same stunt. You don't get to hang around being a named private military contractor by being dumb enough not to put at least a few sentries out on your flanks.

But true believers, like the Monarchs' Loyalist Brigades, they thought war was all stand up and fight. Slogans, chants, and good intentions. And of course, their cause was right. Ask 'em. They'd been told they were on the right side. Ah, the blind belief that you couldn't be defeated because you'd believed all the lies about the superior side. And that somehow meant something in the big dice roll of who was gonna win, and who was gone get dead in the next few.

These guys were dumb. The dice were with us. But of course we only ever played with loaded dice as much as possible. Even then sometimes the dice come up snake eyes. Even for the Strange Company. Attend and know Murphy's Wisdom, as the First Sergeant liked to lecture over one of our recently dead.

Stacked and racked down-passage, we saw them in control of Central Supply Conduit 06, as the ship tagged their location. They were all wearing new "space marine" gear the Monarchs would ship out when the war started to heat up to there being a need for formal military organization. Good stuff. Lots of gadgets, and armor that would stand up to our sidearms if we didn't shoot them too many times. Technically it was supposed to stand up to rifle grain loads. But of course, PMCs never use standard grain loads. Go high power or go home in a body bag, as Biggs liked to bark during ammo draws. In private military contracting, you ain't cheatin', you ain't tryin'.

But I've said that before and excuse me if I say it again. If only just to remind myself what the truth is. Some truths must be repeated if only because it's fatal to forget them.

We had no intention of using our sidearms, or standard grain loads.

The rule of thumb is this.

Sidearms put a hole in you.

Battle rifles put a hole through you.

And combat shotguns just remove nice big chunks of who you used to be.

There were already several enemy dead on the matte-gray rubberized decking inside Central Supply Conduit 06. In starships like this the crew decks are always utilitarian. Clean, cool, and dark. Which was perfect for boarding ops even if the ship was grounded and burning. Dark and rigged for low-noise impact combined with a good breakdown of the ship's internal layout made the work easier. Note, I didn't say easy. Just easier. The other side rolled the dice too, and sometimes they got the snake eyes. Sometimes boxcars.

Speaking of which, now that the ship was powered down and ventilation wasn't operational, I was starting to smell the drift of burning chemicals come along in brief hot drafts from the passages that led off to the port side of the ship. Where the burning fuel cells were spreading through other compartments, defying the vain attempts of the ship's automatic fire control and suppression systems.

It's insane to board a burning starship and engage in a firefight. The only thing you should ever do in a burning starship is hit the escape pods and lifeboats and get off. But of course, this was not my first burning starship firefight.

We needed to do these dudes and get up-ship before the lower decks were fully engulfed in fire. Which would happen sooner than later. Getting caught down here in a runaway and out-of-control compartment fire could be real bad. What about the engineers in zip ties, my mind whispered? Oblivious to the fact that I was on the stalk, running four squads, trying to keep the New Guys from dying and teach the Kid how to soldier before he died too.

Time to kill, I said to me. Centering myself and keeping the main thing the main thing. All that other stuff would just have to take care of itself until the other side of this.

Lots on my mind. I raised my slung Bastard and dropped the first trooper in "space marine" gear hoping he was their on-site combat leader. Probably a guerilla vet who'd proved himself and gotten a commission on the side of the "winners" even though he, and they for that matter, hadn't won. Yet.

It was dark and shadowy down there in the ship's passages, and even my enhanced vision couldn't tag where I got my hits for a couple of seconds as the combat feed updated. It wasn't until the guy was down on the deck and not being helped, boots and legs doing the kickin' chicken, that one of the *heroes* who would one day earn the impossible love of the Monarch overlords, or so that guy and possibly all of them thought, came out to help his downed leader, and my HUD, inside my combat lens, updated with assessed damage and wounds.

I got...

Hit. Armor penetration. Upper chest cavity. Possible collapsed lung.

Hit Lower abdomen. Damage unclear. Possible bleed out and excessive damage to the lower intestines.

I'd fired three rounds from my tricked-out Bastard, trying to tag his helmet on the last as he went down. Apparently... I hadn't. But two hits were good enough to draw another target. That guy, the wounded man on the ground, was having a bad day and getting worse.

Then *Hero* popped out and I shot him quickly. His helmet cracked, flying apart in two directions as he turned, raising one gloved hand to the back of his skull as if to brush away where I'd tagged him with a six-point-five-millimeter round. People do funny things when they're dying. I pulled smooth and fast, shooting him again and glad for good hearing protection as I absorbed the recoil of the Bastard in my shoulder. I didn't have a lot of high-speed gear for my workplace, but I made sure some of my mem went to protecting my ears. All three shots ruined that guy regardless of the fancy-worthless armor he'd been issued and shown, in what was in essence a propaganda film, how to use and how effective it was supposed to be against the enemies of Law and Order. The enemies of the Monarchs.

It wasn't.

Six-point-five ruined that guy all day long.

Now I had them pinned down in Central Supply Conduit 06 in crew stores deep in the belly of the dying-burning *Neptune Clipper*. Whoever was in charge tried to get their reaction force to lead the others into the battle. Let's call them troopers loyal to the Monarchs, who were stacked and supporting their heavy gun that was pinning down Second. They got ruined as First opened up, our Pig throwing a hot hail of deadly AP right through their commander who was trying to get everyone to react to the new threat on their flank.

Their heavy went silent and I knew their team was reorienting to deal with this new attack. Us. I keyed Hauser's attack as Second shifted, or stopped, and Third and then Fourth, moving through stores that hadn't been offloaded, looming like the eternal blocks of ancient lost monuments skinned in shipping graphite, slipped through and into the enemy positions.

A couple of the enemy troopers tried to re-establish a second line at the exit to aft stores, fighting from either side of a security bulkhead that would not close. Hauser had seen to that, ruining those with his Pig, red targeting laser revealed in the smoke and burnt cordite of all the gunfire in the tight passages. The cyborg advanced like a real live relentless Cyberstein monster from the Age of Technohorror. Even his fake mechanical eyes glowed demonically in the shadows as the powerful targeting laser at the front of the ruthless Pig cut them all down as he advanced through outgoing fire.

We didn't even use flashbangs or grenades in the end. They were doing the pop and spray, feeling very action-hero-last-stand as they alternated from cover and dumped fire on us.

Over the squad comm I heard Boom Boom's smoky whisper telling me the squad designated marksman was ready to play ball. "Got this, Sarge."

He fired once and turned the first guy into a corpse with nothing but red mist expanding away on a heat draft for a head, standing there for a moment perfectly silhouetted by the access bulkhead's open and well-lit space. The next section of the ship was guest-accessed and therefore had the pleasant gold-and-white lighting of some of the finer starships. *Stellar Spa,* I'd once heard the theme called.

Incredible. Even with the dead guy with no head falling over into a clump, Chungo Number Two thought it was time to hold at all costs. My hearing protection, augmented to detect sounds below thirty decibels, even heard the guy bellow, "Let's give 'em something to think about, boys!"

Boom Boom landed one of his giant rounds right in that guy's upper chest. I got the tag as my combat lens recorded the hit.

"Nice shooting, Boom," I whispered as all four of my squads basically watched the clown show of untrained troopers thinking they were making a difference for the galaxy.

Boom Boom shot down four more and then we heard them pull back. Which is a nice way of saying they ran away.

We were sweeping the deck where they'd made their brave stand, making sure everyone was good and dead, when all the colors, and there weren't a lot, suddenly popped for me in ways I'd never noticed, and I knew something was up. My brain was suddenly getting syrupy and my eyes were feeling like they'd just learned to open two sizes too big. Everything, and yeah even the dead on the floor, made me want to laugh and giggle like a committed lunatic.

I stared at the dead for a long second, wondering if I was having some kind of stroke or brain aneurysm, when Punch came up and gave me a report I hadn't asked for and then remembered I actually had a few seconds earlier.

No wounded.

Crusher in Third Herd had taken a round to the chest armor. Spall had cut him an inch away from his jugular. "But he's good to go, Sar'nt. You all right, Orion?"

I looked at my assistant platoon leader and saw that his face was melting right before my eyes. I could see his eyes and the worlds inside of them. There was a whole universe in there, man. I blinked my own a couple of times and my vision was normal again. But starting to get murky at the edges.

"Good to go, Punch. Let's move up. You take First."

I'd taken the chief's tab a bit earlier than everyone else. I had a bad feeling in my stomach that things were about to get very weird.

Chief Cook was at my side.

"Don't worry, Orion," he muttered confidentially. "It's a little rocky at first but hang on and ride it. Then it… straightens out. Hang in there, and if you see any bats they're probably not real. Unless they are. Whatever you do, don't talk to 'em. Don't make eye contact either. You'll get lost in there."

He took off to follow the rest of the platoon into the main sections of the lower decks of the starship.

The Little Girl passed me in the press of hustling infantry, watching me with those dark silent ever-appraising eyes. Judging me on behalf of the universe. I thought she might have said something like "Buy the ticket and take the ride, Sergeant Orion" as she followed them off into the damage control's sirens and the dark of the burning starship.

But she didn't.

That part was all in my head.

CHAPTER ELEVEN

The next firefight for Reaper went down inside the Clipper's flight controls processing deck. We'd shifted our route into the detour that took us through this section because the flames were moving fast now up from the starboard fuel cells and crawling across the atmospheric thrust engines there. It was clear the Clipper's maintenance while on layover planetside had been underway and the flames had crawled through an open hatch and into the engineering access points which were close to the guest decks. Meanwhile more explosions rocked the starboard sections of the beautiful Clipper, and though the ship was built to hold up to internals received either by space hazards or even pirate attack—something that had gotten a lot more common of late the farther out you got—when the deck underneath our boots rocked all of Reaper halted, each of us holding our breath and waiting to be suddenly annihilated by a cascade blast that tore the ship into a hundred thousand flying pieces streaking away in every direction right there at the base of the fantastic terminal we were supposed to breach and secure.

Y'know... just another Tuesday for Reaper.

"That one sounded bad," said Firsty in the silence as the hull rumbled and buckled all around us. We called him "Firsty" because he wanted to stay in Reaper and First Squad even though both Dogs and Ghosts wanted him. So we let him.

That's rare. No one's that dumb. Oh yeah... except me. I'm that dumb.

"Yeah," replied Hoser, hefting his Pig to adjust it to cover our current tactical position. "But they don't pay us the big bucks for nothin', man." The pneumatics in the Pig's cyber-assist were slowly going bad. But there was no mem, and no place, to replace or repair them. When supplies and equipment came forward from the Resistance generals it didn't necessarily include the fancy stuff like a pneumatic-assist cyber-exoskeleton for the medium squad suppression weapon. A lot of times it was just more new guys to throw at the Resistance and the occasional case of scotch for the generals to peruse the KIAs over.

Private military contracting makes a certain kind of sense. Sometimes. A lot of the time it's just human nature at its worst. So why not new kids to throw into the meat grinder and a case of scotch to keep doing it? That either makes sense, or it doesn't. Spoiler. It does. Both ways. You have to be honest about these things.

Hustle, the assistant gunner, spaced his belts of 7.62, ready to feed the Pig if things got hot. Or hotter than they were already getting at that moment. The smoke was getting heavy inside the ship now and of course I'd decided to leave the platoon's chemical masks behind because Chief Cook had told me the retro-agents would handle what we'd likely be facing.

"What the hell was that?" someone mumbled as we waited for the ship to settle after its most recent explosion.

Yeah, I was getting that too. What the questioner was wondering. Things felt surreal, and at the corner of your vision you would see occasional shadows moving. Bats. They looked... bat-like for the brief seconds you could catch them in your vision directly. Were these those same bats Chief Cook had mentioned? Warned me about. Don't make eye contact with them, Orion. Apparently that was just a side effect of what we needed to protect us from what we were walking into. Mild hallucinations that were getting stronger by the second. A gassed environment full of deadly psychotropics was what we were walking into, but the question in my fever-brain was... what we were walking in *with*... or on... was it more dangerous than what was being used against our enemies?

"Once both enter your system..." Cook had whisper-muttered to me a few decks back. "Both substances should reach an equilibrium that gives you the advantage over what they'll, the enemy that is, Sergeant Orion, will be experiencing. Trust me... they're gonna lose their minds. You'll only lose half of yours. So that's an advantage as far as I see it."

"Oh yeah," I hissed at Cook as I waved away one of the bats that had suddenly tried to swoop in at my face and then realized I was waving at something that wasn't there. I was, in fact, waving at nothing. I felt the tendrils of insanity trying to pry the lid off my actual sanity and jump in the used aboveground pool that is my mind. And strangely, the thought of that made me want to laugh out loud. Giddily. I've never laughed giddily. Never ever. Never in my life. And now I had an intense desire to. It was bubbling up within me and I had serious doubts I could contain it. It felt wild and insane. But I've felt that way on other gunfights before this one.

That. I was feeling that. And a strange desire to burn a whole mag. All my mags. All on full auto. Shooting whatever. I just wanted to shoot stuff on rock and roll. That would feel pretty good, man. Unexplainably. Good.

I never did though. Engage on full auto. Never ever.

Waste of ammo and bad shooting to go full auto in almost every situation except a few. Why they'd even put that option on modern weapons for pros was a mystery to me. Who knew? But that's what people wanted. Even pros.

Well, I almost never went full auto. But right now… I really, really wanted to. I insanely wanted to. It was like an itch I absolutely *had* to scratch. I had to tell myself not to play with the selector switch. Not to flip to full rock and roll and get it on.

But, "Oh yeah," I said to Cook when he told me his half-baked explanation of why drugging my entire platoon with something akin to an LSD trip was going to somehow make everything "work out" in the middle of an op. "What kind of advantage is that, exactly, you blithering psychopath?" I hissed at him in the near-darkness as we trailed the squads. "You just drugged everyone to the gills. I don't know who the hell I'm more afraid of—an enemy hopped up on drugs and waiting for us with all kinds of automatic weapons, or my own guys who are also hopped up on some same but slightly different drug recipe, also carrying automatic weapons, and experiencing severe perception problems regarding current events. How long before someone mistakes someone else for a bat and starts blasting? Huh, Chief?"

Chief Cook cleared his throat and tapped into the platoon comm. He held up his index finger. Then he cleared his throat again and said, very officially like he was some kind of authoritative professional instead of the crazed lunatic he actually was. "Uh… attention everyone. Don't shoot the bats. Any bats… you might see. They're not real. Don't shoot them. Also..." He paused. "Don't make eye contact with them."

Then he turned back to me, a drug-addled leer on his face, and whispered, "That should help. Also, I'm technically a sociopath. There's a difference, Orion."

By the time we'd reached the expansive recreation and living decks of the starship, the smoke was too thick and several of the guest suites were on fire now. I couldn't tell if it was the anxiety of the drug or the reality of the situation that we might get cooked alive inside a starship if we made one wrong turn and got stuck belowdecks that affected me worse.

"We can move into the subdeck above," said Hauser over the comm as if reading my mind. Maintenance accessways, or subdecks between decks, can be tight, but those areas are hardened with more advanced fire control systems to protect the ship's flight operations equipment. "There's a way through."

I weighed the cyborg's suggestion and tried to block out everything in my mind and eyes that wasn't true. Later Punch would tell me that everyone thought I had it pretty together, considering. Each and every one of them thought they were losing their marbles, but no one wanted to say anything.

We moved into the subdeck above our heads and just below the ship's flight operations control deck, a space on any starship that was generally off-limits to anyone other than flight crew, and only used to run the ship's processors and redundant control systems. Hauser found the hidden access hatch in the ceiling of the deck and entered a universal maintenance tech password that generally worked for anyone in the know, and the rest of us watched as the panel dropped open with a soft pneumatic hiss. Yellow strobe lights crossed the midnight-blue darkness up there in the subdeck as once again the ship's AI encouraged us to abandon the vessel or face possibly severe injury.

One by one we made it into the dark up there, the first up establishing a security perimeter, the rest stacking with their squads behind dark and cold quantum processors that should have been alive and humming on soft bass notes as numbers for jump solutions were constantly updated. Like ascetic monks chanting space-time in cloistered remote mountain abbeys. Engineers who usually needed to come into this section on starships spent most of their time on their bellies or backs. They used a hover support called a slide to move around and reach the equipment they needed to work on and maintain. For heavily armed soldiers there was only enough room to hunch or duck-walk our way through the tight spaces of the subdeck and all its processors.

"This is gonna be a trip," one of the New Guys in Reaper First muttered as he climbed up past me into the darkness.

I shot my most pissed-off glare at Chief Cook. Trying to indict him and spawn the slightest guilt, and hopefully remorse, for what he'd done to my men. Of course he was immune and just shrugged as he squeezed by, muttering, "Sociopath, Orion. Guilt doesn't work on me. It's a feature, not a bug."

I knew for a fact he wasn't a sociopath. He just *wanted* to be one because he felt that made the dirty work easier. Never cleaner. But just easier. And I couldn't fault him for that. Doing nasty things to people required a certain moral flexibility if you were going to make a career out of it.

I checked in on the Kid who'd been sticking nearby. Unofficially he'd become my assistant.

"Ya good?" I asked as Farts struggled up the ladder with his shot leg. The painkillers were starting to wear off.

The Kid looked at me and tapped his tactical rig, then gave me a thumbs-up. That was Company sign for the universal *Good to Go* of all soldiers.

Farts told me he was doing fine but his leg hurt. I told him to shut up and keep moving.

Six minutes later I had two dead and three wounded.

Farts was the first to die.

CHAPTER TWELVE

The firefight broke out in the dark of the *Neptune Clipper*'s subdeck for navigational redundancy processors. We got no indication before it went down that it was an ambush we'd just walked into. Somehow someone on the other side had read the ship's schematics and damage control board and figured we'd try the subdeck to get forward. It was clear as the first few rounds whipped past my head and smashed into hard plastic and state-of-the-art compressed diamond drives that the enemy knew we were trying to use the Clipper to cover our breach into the main terminal.

It was a horrible, and brief, firefight. That's generally how it goes. Short means brutal. Lotsa ruined corpses.

Just before the shooting started I'd sent Third forward to secure the route into the deck above us that was at the end of the processing sectors. Second was on rear. Fourth on the right. First made its way with Punch leading and me trying to keep it together as Chief Cook's tab started to come on strong.

It was at that point that I was getting comm from the First Sergeant back running ops for the main element. The main attack wasn't going so well. The enemy had put together some adequate hunter-killer anti-tank teams and nailed the Resistance spearhead to our west, stopping them cold along the green terminal ring at Space Traffic Control, a huge looming needle-point tower that ran all traffic assigned to the outer green ring. Snipers and observers in the tower, off-limits for anything but small units to breach and clear to control, had effectively directed the anti-tank killers into position to chew up the incoming raiders.

Heavy machine-gun teams in light attack assault buggies had ruined the supporting infantry with hit-and-run raids.

"As of this moment, Sergeant Orion," continued the First Sergeant in his typical grandiose fashion, "you are indeed the farthest forward unit in this foolhardy plan of attack cooked up by our employers. But fear not, young infantry sergeant, Captain's shifting Dog away from infantry support on the flank and has requested dropship support to take the roof of the terminal once you're inside. Say again, we will not leave you forward and unsupported, Sergeant Orion."

Was that to strengthen our position on the objective, or pull us off? I didn't ask. But getting in just to get pulled out felt like it was all for nothing. And that was me still caring about who won.

"Copy, First Sergeant. Pushing into the terminal in the next twenty," was all I could reply. The floor was shifting and swirling if I stared at it for too long. The bats were getting thick and I was doing my best not to look anyone, including them, in the eye.

I was sweating like a madman even though the processers down here in the dark and undulating yellow light washes were being kept cool on internal backup from the ship's emergency reserves.

That was when we got hit on the side, and hard.

The burst from the Loyalist sapper team that had been sent into the ship to det it, with us inside, nailed Farts with a sudden eruption of automatic gunfire. He didn't scream, he just went down. Experience has taught me that's a bad sign when it comes to injuries. Not screaming when you get hit by a bullet moving at supersonic speeds. I don't know how long it took him to die but he was dead by the time it was over. Firsty got hit right in the skull just below the bucket. His brains exploded all over the back of his helmet. He didn't scream either.

The sappers were using small submachine guns they carried in three-point slings while they were busy setting up explosives. Punch took one in the plate, but it bounced and tore off a finger wrapped around the shorty version of the Bastard he used. He swore and immediately returned fire regardless, one-handed as he duck-walked forward for cover behind a swiss-cheesed processor. The enemy were off to our left, covered by powerful spinning yellow strobes along that section of the inner hull. To them we must have looked like jaundiced ghouls hunched and working our way through the ship's tight spaces on some enigmatic night errand. To us they were just shadows behind strobes firing small automatic bursts that had bullets slamming into processors and fragmenting hard plastic in every direction.

Hoser opened up and doused the area incoming was originating from, pivoting in the hunch and shouting, "Get it on, Reapers!" After the fight, when I hunch-crawled over to make sure everyone on the enemy side of things was dead, I was pretty sure Hoser had ruined most of them at this moment. But they kept shooting nonetheless and the Kid took a round. Later we assessed the wound as just a deep graze along the side of his face, but right there in the darkness when I heard him take it, it looked bad. I'll confess that right here and now.

I felt bad for him. But not too bad. At least he'd gotten it quick instead of much later.

I grabbed his hand and forced him to put pressure on the wound as blood seeped through his fingerless gloves. The kind Sergeant Biggs always issued the new guys. Right then I was pretty sure he'd been hit in the jug or something that was going to start pumping and not stop until the Kid was cold and dead.

He looked at me. Scared. Because who wouldn't be. "Hang in there, Kid," I told him, if just for something to say before he died. "Got your first. Now live long enough to let it become a scar. Remember…" I said, making him press even harder on the wound. Forcing his open hand down into it like it needed to become one with his throat. "Chicks dig scars," I muttered over the gunfire at close quarters within the violent dark of the subdeck.

And then I saw something pass through his eyes and make the fear go away as we sat there taking fire from what seemed everywhere in the dark. Something I knew for myself crossed his brain and his eyes told me so. But of course, I had a lot going on at the moment and it was only later that I could figure out what it was. Or that it was a clue as to why he'd joined the company.

Chicks dig scars. That had meant something to him. Cut through the fear. And I was betting it was part of the story he'd tell me someday about how he ended up in the Strange Company.

The bats were getting thick and again I cursed Chief Cook, who appeared just then out of the dark, grabbed the Kid's drag handle, and pulled him away from the firefight, blazing at unseen enemies I was pretty sure weren't in any direction he was firing into.

"I got ya," he growled heroically through clenched teeth. His eyes wild and way too intense. Then he shouted, "Medic!" as he turned and blazed away at no one with his forty-five.

Still, Cook looked good doing it despite the fact he was suppressing no one in particular. And of course, no sociopath would ever do what he'd just done. Go in and rescue a new kid who'd gotten tagged in what was probably his first experience on the wrong side of an ambush.

I had no idea where the Little Girl he'd brought along was. And I couldn't tell if I should be concerned about that, or just relieved.

More enemy contact came in from Hauser. Third engaged what we would later find out to be rear security holding the exit we needed to take to get out of the subdeck processors. A brief exchange of high-cycle automatic gunfire from Hauser and company, and enemy rear security was ruined. Fourth on the right picked up another sapper team and nailed them unawares. Or creeping to flank to continue planting charges. Suddenly First was at the center of all kinds of incoming and outgoing from both sides.

Expended brass dribbled across the mirror-smooth floor of the high-load processing deck for flight and navigation operations. A state-of-the-art starship was getting ruined from the inside out. Big time. There had been a time, once and long ago, when I was very interested in the Free Trader and Scout Service. I'd looked at putting together a ship, and time after time it was this deck, the one we were fighting our way through, that cost the most. Even on the lowliest of jump-skiffs or star-schooners. The kind most explorers preferred for max equipment, minimum luxury to find a habitable world to claim and get rich quick by.

But the cost of these systems had always been skyrocketingly prohibitive. Yeah, sure, there were used compressor frames that could keep up with bare-bones navigational charts of a constantly evolving stellar frontier, but out-of-date data or a bad crunch on a necessary jump and you were about to see what the inside of a supernova looked like up close.

For at least three seconds of what would be the end of your life.

And then no one would ever hear from you again. Which was the part of Scout Service that had most appealed to me back then. Getting good and lost from the collective insanity of the Bright Worlds. But the company found me instead, and I'm probably going to stay here until they get tired of me. Or until I die on some whacked LZ we never should've been on in the first place.

So it goes. Buy the ticket. Take the ride.

The initial exchange of surprise gunfire still echoing in my comms, I organized Reaper to get it on, Company-style. I first reoriented the battle toward enemy currently engaging on the left flank. Mainly, the ones shooting the hell out of Reaper First Squad. Besides those two dead and three wounded, everyone was getting hit in the armor. I got a ricochet off my combat helmet. Not the first time. It was a glancing shot that had probably already hit something else and my bell was already good and rung from the retro-agent drug, so it bothered me later. A bad headache and my jaw hurt, that was all. Not then. Under the influence of the drug it felt like a love tap. Starbursts expanded out from my huge dry eyes and I watched them wallow away and turn to fireflies, or butterflies, of electricity with blue streamers. Both, actually. Cool, huh? Lots of pretty colors.

"Forward is now left flank. Hauser, take Third and sweep the exit we need. Make sure it's secure. We may need to boogie fast."

"Affirmative, Sergeant," responded the cyborg.

"Jacks," I said. "Need you to get on their right and set up a base of fire on those yellow strobes ASAP."

I got a "copy" from the Second Squad leader just before one of the sappers tossed a flashbang at us. I saw it come in, and so did Punch from behind the big black ominous compressor stack we were hiding behind. A thing that would have cost several million mem, and which was currently acting as a high-priced and very ineffective bullet-catcher for incoming targeted at us. Later I'd see that my rear plate also got a love tap from someone's round. But again, it just exploded into frag and spall and maybe my ribs were bruised. Which might explain why I was having difficulty breathing until I bummed a mild relaxer off Choker later.

I was gonna be black and blue for sure.

Punch, wounded hand and missing a finger, let go of his Bastard, reached with his unwounded and firing hand, grabbed the incoming explosive we hoped was a flashbang, and side-armed it right back at the enemy as he flopped over on the deck, exposing himself to fire. Guy could've been a relief pitcher with a mean slider like that.

It exploded off in the darkness, but its effects were greatly mitigated by a lot of the natural EMP fields and Faraday cages that ran through the processor racks. I think that was the moment that stopped the attack from the left flank for at least a second. Next I got Fourth to come in and support First as we developed a sustained base of fire. Medics pulled out the wounded if they could.

Remember, at this point in the firefight I had no idea what was going on other than what I could see right around me. Two dead. Punch wounded. And the Kid and Chief Cook getting out of the funnel of death we were sitting in.

I saw someone and dumped three bursts of full auto. I had no idea if I'd hit anyone, but it felt good. I swapped in a new mag and flipped the Bastard's selector switch to semi. Promising myself I would never commit the sin of full auto ever again.

Never ever.

Of course, the lies we tell ourselves.

Second swept from left of us through the multi-core data cylinders that interfaced with the ship's navigational stacks and began shooting, moving, and communicating like a good squad is supposed to. Then they began wiping out the enemy.

"Cease fire, One and Four," I said over the comm. I didn't want us shooting into Second as they tried to overrun the enemy ahead of us.

Two minutes later the sound of gunfire was gone and I was getting a sitrep from Jacks. The sappers were all dead. I ordered everyone to move for our route exit, then I duck-walked through the stacks to reach the still-dancing strobes of the yellow damage control hazards.

Jacks and his ASL, Ro-Ro, were standing over the mangled bodies of the enemy combat engineers.

"Looks like they were planting RDX-type charges," Jacks told me as I came in. "It's safe in here with the fire control systems attempting to save this deck until last. Then they'd just pop the nitrogen bottles in the fire-suppression overheads and flood the compartment as the RDX ignited. Big explosion chains to the mains and the whole ship would've gone firecracker right in our faces even if we'd taken the terminal and everyone was staging on us for the breach. Waste from the reactor and no one with any brains would have wanted to use the crater or what remained of the terminal for anything for the next hundred years. Denial-of-service dead switch if you ask me, Sar'nt."

Jacks had been a combat engineer somewhere else once. He ran the company's demo when we needed to get it done. We didn't have a big call for it, but when we did, he could get really artistic about blowing people, and things, up in exciting new ways.

"Can we disarm?"

Jacks shook his head.

"Complex multi-code encryption on the dets. They won't activate though. We can make that happen. But I wouldn't leave them lying around here. This ship burns up—and unless the spaceport firefighters are particularly dedicated that's gonna happen—that nitrogen is gonna release, the chemicals will bond, and we'll still get the big kahuna-boom. I'll stay and take care of it, Sar'nt."

I ordered Ro-Ro to take Second and made sure Jacks was cool alone.

"Yeah. It's easier to make sure you're safe when you're the only one working with things that have a tendency to go boom," said Jacks. "Two increases the factor of error significantly. Same applies when married. Know what I mean?"

I left Jacks and tried to call in a sitrep to the First Sergeant. Nothing. Transmissions were being locally jammed. Organized, we left the subdeck, popped out of a floor hatch they'd already opened near the aft transport terminal, and started a movement to contact up-spine to our final objective inside the burning starship. The hard dock with the terminal.

CHAPTER THIRTEEN

We hit the boarding lock hard connect with the terminal from the *Neptune Clipper*'s main entry hatch and turned it into a slaughter even though several of us were already experiencing severe perception problems from the retro-agent. Chief Cook was cackling about it "really coming on now! This is the big trip and it's gonna get real hairy, boys and girls. Hang on to it, reality's gonna suspend operations for a bit. Our normal broadcast will resume shortly."

Dip Weasel, one of the Second Squad riflemen on the breaching team assigned to hit the hard dock once we sent the flashbangs in, went wild as the flashbangs popped and concussed the shooters we were facing. Instead of flooding in with the rest of Second, he just advanced straight into the shot-to-hell executive boarding lounge and started shooting down the enemy where he could find them. Mostly they were hiding behind glowing information pylons they had mistakenly thought would provide them cover. A .308 round like the kind Dip Weasel was firing from his M14X tactical clearing rifle can go through a repulsor block and kill a charging war pig. The info pylons just shattered in every direction as he sent hot fire from his blazing rifle, streaming dip straight from the side of his mouth every third shot like it was a bodily function. There's a reason you tag in the company. And Dip Weasel wore his with pride whether he was aware of it or not.

Meanwhile with everyone trying to shrug off the effects of the retro-agent and still do their jobs, sectors were cleared, and guns were up even as one of our own just advanced out into the main terminal concourse and engaged the enemy. Shooting anyone he could acquire and walking straight at an enemy machine-gun team that had been trying to set up to cover the defense the enemy was reacting to our incursion with.

To be fair, unironically, they were wasted on psycho gas and struggling with some very basic tasks. I doubt they ever got two belts linked before the gunfight started in earnest. But that's on them. And it sucks to lose unfairly because the other side is cheating. But it's worse to get killed whether anyone's cheating or not.

So better them than us that had to pay the price, cheating or no cheating.

I was already following in behind Third as Hauser and company rushed to take up position in an adjacent security screening lounge farther along the concourse next to our entry point. Sergeant Jacks was yelling at Dip Weasel to halt. "Get back to your squad, Dip!" But the wasted rifleman just walked casually onto the main concourse, through the drifting gas, a strange smile on his face, and started firing at some of the marksmen on the second and third level of the once-beautiful structure done up all in marble, chrome, and frosted glass.

Return fire was badly aimed and unfocused. Some here, some there. Chief Cook's voodoo gas had done its thing. They didn't know it, but they were going to die in here today. It couldn't be any other way if we were going to go on living.

Someone fired at Dip Weasel and he took a solid hit in the front plate. You could hear it ricochet from where I was covering with Third. Dip took the shot dead center, but it just knocked him back about two steps, and then he turned and fired at whoever shot him as though he hadn't been hit at all.

"He's possibly reacting a little more than he should have. Ahem. To the gas," whispered Chief Cook suddenly next to me as Third waited for the next orders. "It's not one hundred percent, Orion. Did he take his tab? He might wanna take another. That could even things out. Maybe. Two negatives making a positive and all. Dr. Goodbuzz would definitely prescribe that course of action, Sergeant."

I had no idea who Dr. Goodbuzz was. I doubted there was one and had a feeling Chief Cook had some kind of alter ego who justified the weirder contingency plans. Again I had no evidence. Just hunches.

I also had no idea if he had taken the tab. I gave the order. But who knew if they did. This was nuts. I was supposed to be assessing the situation, identifying enemy concentrations, and then organizing assaults to wipe them out. Not making sure they took their meds.

Jacks, Second's squad leader, ran out into the concourse and tackled Dip Weasel just as the enemy machine-gun team opened up from the coffee bar across the way. An animated projection of a giant cartoon cat pouring coffee was tripping me out as I tried to focus on the rapidly disintegrating situation. The cat was speaking in Pan and going on about "Hot Time Lucky Brew." Apparently its AI processes were targeting Pan travelers who must have recently passed through the terminal. Or there was some kind of malfunction in the station's processing hubs. Or Loyalist troopers were opportunistically stripping out the mem where they could get away with that. The enemy probably was too. That made me wonder if things were as bad on the pay front for them as they were for us.

Deep and meaningless wonderings in the middle of an assault. That's why they pick me for the tough jobs.

I had no idea in those first seconds if either the squad leader or Dip Weasel had been hit by any rounds in the high-cycle automatic gunfire that suddenly *brrrrttttted* through the terminal, devastating everything it caressed. Must've been a 20mm squad suppressive cannon.

Second and Third opened up on the machine-gun team within seconds and instantly the firefight was everywhere across this section of the immense terminal. Everyone was shooting everyone else in a desperate bid to kill as many people as quickly as possible. And all of us were on drugs.

Bats swarmed my vision, and anxiety welled up within me. I was certain I was going to get killed because I knew how stoned I was. Every muscle tightened and I felt like I had some kind of maniacal rictus grin death smile pasted on my face. This was not how I imagined my heroic death. The one the Falmorian party girl would never hear about. Or anyone else I ever once knew long ago in another life not this one. I'd always imagined her *estrangier* giving a good account of himself in his last seconds. Not that it would matter. I just liked to think it might go like that for me.

For two seconds I was frozen as I struggled to get out of the black cone of immobility and do something to generally help out.

"Get it on!" I screamed wildly and burned a mag on full auto against the covering SSC team. It was all I could think of. If you can't do something, then one, get everyone who can to start to do anything. And two, try to look like you're helping with the attack, even if you're just expending brass. At least look good doing it. Who knows, one of the New Guys might get inspired enough to do something incredible and earn a tag before they got killed.

Obviously, the Loyalist troopers were under the effects of the psychotropic gas. There was no organization among them, and their shooting was random and wild, at best. Within the first minute of the firefight it was pretty clear they were hallucinating wildly too. The machine-gun team across the way, even though they had good cover, burned through a belt and then just sat there staring at us as though they were still firing on full auto from some kind of magically endless belt of myth and lore. The kind in action-hero slashers you go see because you're on leave, you're hung over, and you want to hide from your squad because your liver can't take another epic all-night drinking binge at some bar your mother would disown you for even passing by.

I irised in with my combat lens and tried to ascertain if we were getting a break from the suddenly silent machine-gun team working the squad suppressive cannon, and if we should just rush them as they swapped belts. Murdering them with automatic fire before they could turn up the ammo burn on us. But all I could see over there behind their tripod gun with matte-black twin barrels spinning madly and smoking, was wide eyes and gas-giant-sized pupils, jaws dropped open as they stared in amazement at something unseen and amazing. They were doped to the gills and seeing other realities.

"Tracers are messing with 'em, Orion," hissed our warrant and then laughed like he had rock miner's cough. Wheezing and gasping. Like he'd just found some vein inside a spinning cold rock that would make him as rich as a Monarch forever. I looked over at him, and he had an even more crazed look on his face than usual. Which was saying something for him. He was sweating buckets and grinding his teeth as murder and mayhem abounded across the terminal.

Then Chief Cook stood. "Hand me a grenade, Private," he barked heroically at a nearby New Guy. My soldier did as he was ordered, and with almost no pretense at cover the chief pulled the pin, popped the spoon theatrically, and over-armed the grenade right into the coffee bar across the terminal like he was throwing out the first ball on opening day back at Yankee Ball Park, the Bright Worlds' best stadium.

A second later the grenade hit the back wall of the coffee bar and bounced, and I lost track of it for a weirdly uncomfortable moment. Live and loose fragmentary devices have a tendency to do that to an NCO. And then the blast ripped the bar to shreds with all the ceremony of a sudden belch. Wall fragment splinters sliced through the air and the concussive effects popped my ears and made me swallow hard.

Over the comm I heard someone in Third screaming about a Cylorian sabertoothed bear. Which, check my subscription to *Stellar Geographica*, should be nowhere near us on Crash. Or Astralon. But then he added, "Engaging," and I felt that was probably the best outcome I could hope for under the circumstances. Hopefully he was mistaking the enemy we were facing, and who was trying to kill us, for the apex predator bear local to a world seventy-five light years distant. And hopefully he was ruining his nightmare and its all-too-real stand-ins on behalf of Reaper.

My guess was it was Honcho in Third. He had a thing about bears. He'd been chased by one as a kid. Every world we did a contract on got a hard flora and fauna review from Honcho though no one asked him to. He didn't mind vipers, monkey-spiders, Subari, or anything that could pump you full of lethal poison and make you wish you were dead for the next thirty-six days. But bears… bears were his white whale. He was absolutely terrified of them.

The First Sergeant had used that term. White whale. I had no idea what it meant. I'd never seen a whale. I'd heard they were a big fish back on Earth. But that they weren't as large as the gill serpents of Marlay.

One of the huge bats that had been making runs at me, red eyes glaring, swooped in, and I watched in amazement as it raced away into the battle full of shadowy rounds and lightning tracers zipping this way and that. The bat was trailing an inky black wash that was simply fascinating to watch.

"Moving to recover Sergeant Jacks and Corporal Dip Weasel," intoned Hauser as he strode out into the battle like everyone wasn't shooting at everyone else. "Detecting near-lethal levels of some kind of hallucinogenic compound, but my systems remain unaffected, Sergeant Orion."

The inky black inside the wake of the flying bat that had roared at me and then screamed off in another direction like a living ghost being drowned in a cobalt arctic sea... yeah the descriptions are purple, but I'm just putting it down as I remember it going down... and the rest of the surreal data coming through my dry and wide-open M-one eyeballs, a First Sergeant term from the long ago of arcane military units that don't exist anymore, was still messing with my ability to engage in basic communication. I stuttered eloquently, sure I was issuing a series of meaningful orders to react to threats, get organized, and generally *get it on* company-style.

In all probability I was probably chattering like a Quick junkie rushing on his run.

"Roger," I said to no one, sure that I had just gotten comm from my mom to do something important. I made up my mind to kill Chief Cook when the opportunity of a blind alley presented itself.

I was alone with the Little Girl as the battle in the terminal raged all about us. I'd lost time. There was a fight going on out there, but it wasn't a firefight now. My mind thought otherwise. Later I'd learn that my squads were just murdering the drug-ravaged enemy troopers in the fighting positions they could make sense of how to defend. Fighting off bats and weird stews of memories of their own that were turning into living nightmares made all too real.

"I got this, Orion," crowed Chief Cook over the comm. He sounded like some religious zealot who'd suddenly received a new revelation after a bad case of food poisoning. "Popping some more Quick and I can stay ahead of it."

I had the feeling he was going to cackle wildly and scream, *Things are gonna be different this time*. But he didn't, and I had no idea why he would want to say that. That was just what my drug-ravaged mind said the script should read.

I had no idea what any of that meant at this moment. I knew only that the sky was going to suck me up into it and I'd be lost forever. And there was a part of me that was fine with that.

The Little Girl, wearing a military gas mask, sat nearby hugging her knees and watching me as we covered where Third Squad had left us useless people. Out there I turned and saw Hauser, walking through the drifting smoke and falling glass in the middle of the fight, scanning and firing short bursts from his Pig at unseen enemies.

Like some man-made angel of death. Some parody of humanity that was more human than we'd ever be.

The battle was a mess. And it was *my* mess.

First Sergeant was trying... trying to get ahold of me. Comm was chiming, and messages, indecipherable, were appearing in my combat lens. But I was busy somewhere else losing my marbles. The worlds of the universe are all marbles. Little tiny spinning multicolored marbles in the darkness and the broken crystal. And the universe is just a game, I told myself. The universe is just a game of marbles.

Nothing more.

Nothing less, *estrangier*.

CHAPTER FOURTEEN

Yeah. I don't believe in weird existential stuff. I'm not religious, and of course there are real mysteries out there in the galaxy. Strange stuff that defies explanation like the Reverse Floating Pyramids of Kyberia and the Sky Noise sometimes heard on the outer worlds in the loneliest reaches of those faraway planets. Or the fact that there's a world, habitable, out in the Gothica system, a dying red dwarf, where people say that not all shadows are just shadows. And that sometimes the shadows talk and whisper things that should never be heard. The secrets of the universe, or at least that's what the DRK cultists say. But in general, the science I understand, jump and hyperdrive, dumbthrust included, but not fold as used by the Battle Spires, is what I think the universe is made up of. Physics and the rules thereof. There's some quantum that can bend or break the rules. But of course, there are always exceptions to the rules and if you really think about it then that's just part of the rules too.

I measure my life in expended brass. The most truthful moments in my life. It stands in, not just brass shell casings but sometimes the linkage of a belt-fed machine gun, for battle. For ruin and destruction. For what we all really are. What we discover when a bullet finds and explores a body, devastating ideas and preconceptions in the cold moment of its sudden intersection with all your plans. That's the way I measure the universe and test what's real. The Dao of Lead. This is how I measure twice and cut once. How I move through it all and navigate life's tough questions. Fire, or return fire.

The best defense is always more offense.

And believe me, I'm not especially violent. I'm not Hoser, Hoss, Punch, or half the guys in Dog. And no one's close to that dark psychopath that is Sergeant Amarcus Hannibal. Enemy mine.

But I've learned it's best to shoot first. And shoot a lot if you can.

You can't even trust mem. Even though it's the greatest currency in the human expansion since the Sindo, you cannot trust it. A devastating war we didn't ask for, and a war we barely finished with our collective human lives, the Sindo taught us currency is fiction.

The illusion that money can spend you through a tough time or bring back sixty million dead. Lies. The illusion of currency died a hard death during the Sindo. Then came mem. But mem is just currency too. Even though you can use it. Spend it. Save it. Run your ships and weapons with it.

The only thing that ever made sense to me when someone tried to describe what currency, any currency really was, was this. It's just distilled life, Orion. *Estrangier*. That's all it is.

I've found that to be true even though I've done everything to disprove it.

Currency is just distilled life.

But that, the Sindo, was a long time ago and I didn't see much of it. Just grew up during its darkest parts. As in real dark. But like I said, I'm a pretty meat-and-potatoes guy when it comes to reality. Yeah, I've heard there are cracks and places where it gets thin. And weird. Especially if you happen to be around an operational Monarch Battle Spire folding space. But as far as I knew, when the sign in the bar flickered on, signaling *Cocktails* in flowing red script, right there in the middle of the firefight inside the main terminal for green ring, I was sure reality had just suspended itself for a few seconds.

Drugs or no drugs, I was about to experience an intermission.

I got up, knowing there was a battle going on, or at least thinking it was a battle and not the slaughter of my men, led by the cyborg Hauser and the wild-eyed Chief Cook, who were currently conducting, routing the enemy and rooting them out. Shooting them down as they tried to figure out why reality didn't make sense anymore. I looked back at the Little Girl hugging her knees and wearing the giant gas mask that made her look like a bug-eyed alien. And then once more I looked at the seam that had opened up in the universe. Inside that bar with the neon red *Cocktails* sign. Blinking on. Blinking off.

And I must've muttered something dumb. Like *Cool*. Or *Far out*. Or even the popular-decades-back *Swimmin'*.

Junkie benedictions.

A swanky little jazz bar that reminded me of one I had known long ago was in there past the seam. But that wasn't right. It shouldn't be here. But it was... and maybe...

I felt myself getting up from the carpeted floor of the terminal. Spent brass rolling around down there. My body was tired and swimming through syrup straight from a hypnotic goo-sugar tree in the jungles of Hitaarr. Every muscle felt rusted shut. I was still holding my Bastard and I wasn't sure what the status of the current mag was. Loaded, empty. Half full. Wasn't important bathed in the red neon light of the bar sign.

That expended brass should have been a clue. But I cleverly ignored it and just went with the automatic reactions of a soldier who'd soldiered long enough to make the lethal merely mundane.

The illusion was real. And reality was just an illusion. Right there in the middle of a desperate firefight was a bar I could just walk into. One I'd known, and one that was unlike anything I'd ever know. I was hallucinating, I knew that. But it was as real as it gets.

I felt my assault-gloved hands doing the reloading trick. Eject. Pull. Slap the new mag in. As if my brain, currently on vacation and considering making it permanent, didn't mind if they, my hands, just went ahead and swapped for a new mag. Better safe than sorry is the tattoo every soldier who lives long enough has somewhere on their brain. And often you have to ignore that tattoo and do something really stupid because no one who's trying to kill you is expecting just that. I crossed the thin terminal carpet, feeling the hollow thump of the floor beneath my dirty combat boots. Like some fairy tale giant walking the outer worlds. I felt slow and ponderous.

The sign outside the seam in reality lit up and stayed lit up. Not blinking like it might in some noir slasher flick now. *Cocktails*, it had flashed.

"... and jazz..." I mumbled to myself. There was someone who used to be important to me in there, I told myself because I remembered the bar from another life long ago and not this one anymore. Some reason I'd left the known of everything I'd once been, for what I'd become in the Strange Company for the rest of the days that remained me.

Then I had a thought that had nothing to do with anything. I blame the drugs. And it wasn't a thought. It was a realization. I'd left this bar because I was nothing. Never would be. Back there in the Bright Worlds. And I'd come to the company to lose myself and found a way to be something else. Someone else. If just a record in the company logs. If just an *estrangier* to a girl who'd never know what world I'd bought it on. There was something noble in that. Tragically noble. Something no one in the Bright Worlds would ever know, or even understand.

I had no idea of that when I first signed the contract. But later, when I became the official log keeper of our deeds, it was the reason I stayed.

You have to be honest with yourself. You can lie to the universe. But it's best not to lie to yourself.

I went in and sat down at the bar.

She wasn't in there. Not like she'd once been long ago. The reason for why I joined the company. But the ghost of John Strange was. And the bartender of course. I didn't recognize him. He was new too.

By that time I realized it was just the drugs Chief Cook had given me mixing with whatever he'd pumped into the terminal that was making me think this way. Making me imagine I'd walked into a bar in the middle of firefight like some bad joke no one ever thought up. No one ever thought worth thinking up. *A soldier walks into a bar in the middle of a firefight...* I was only dimly aware that I was supposed to be in charge of an ongoing battle, and it was too late by then. I wasn't in charge anymore. I was in the bar at the end of the universe now. And something important was about to happen.

And I was okay with that as I walked toward the seam. The crack. The thin place in reality.

Which is not a good frame of mind for a combat leader to be in during battle. Not ever.

So, I'm writing down what happened because this is an account of the Strange Company's meeting and eventual association with a being called the Seeker. Who we would meet shortly. But this is important too. All these events leading up to that moment. Don't ask me why. I just know they are important somehow. Whoever reads this... maybe you'll figure out why. How we lost ourselves and became what we weren't. How the universe got ruined.

How we met a being called the Seeker.

That's an odd thing to say. Technically the Seeker, or just Seeker as it is called, is just as human as I'm supposed to be. But it's a Monarch. So there's that. And they are different from the rest of us. They are the best of us. Of course. And there's really no disputing that. Especially if you've met one. Then you would know it. There would be no lies you could tell yourself to convince anyone otherwise. Or propaganda that stands up in the light of such knowledge. Some people are just better than you. As I've said, it's best to be honest about these things.

Remember what I said. It's best to be honest. Lie to the universe, just don't lie to yourself. Why? Because you might believe it. Might believe the lie. And then where will you be...? Well, let me tell you. Then... you'll be totally lost.

At first John Strange, the founder of our little murderous family, or mercenary outfit called Strange Company if you prefer, private military contractors, PMCs, wasn't there in that strange little dream I was having. Or trip. Or vivid hallucination. The seam that opened up in the firefight. That thin place in the universe I'd just walked into. Call it what you will. Call it whatever you want. I won't judge you.

Just don't judge me.

"What it'll be," asked the bartender at the bar beyond the sign that said *Cocktails* in neon red script. A middle-aged man with iron-gray hair. Dressed in a neat red barman's jacket. He said this as he flipped a thick cocktail napkin, white and embossed with a logo, down onto the dark wood-grain bar between us. A wood-grain bar that seemed to shift and twirl like milk in dark coffee if you stared at it long enough.

I looked around in disbelief, muttering so.

I didn't feel like I was under the effects of any drugs now. I felt clear and relaxed even though things were weird. Inside, things were settling down. I looked at myself in the mirror behind the bar, past all those colorful and pretty bottles of hot liquor in strange colors lined up dress-right-dress like soldiers on parade.

I was still wearing my battle rattle in the dark gold-flecked mirror back there. Shadows moved all around me in the mirror universe. But when I turned to see them they were gone. I wondered for a moment if I'd been killed. Back in the firefight. If this was death. Had I taken a stray round from one of the hallucinating enemy troopers firing wildly and blindly and everywhere as we stormed the terminal from the boarding lounge? Tossing flashbangs and grenades. Trying to turn our job into cleanup before it became an assault on a series of fixed positions.

Had I taken a rando stray round and this was just shock before death?

Had I let go of all the endless duties that were all mine as I bled out? Call in a sitrep to the First Sergeant and tell him the terminal was clear and that the rest of the line could come up now. They'd need to do the rest without me.

That had been our job. Clear the terminal.

I didn't care anymore here in the bar inside the seam. Death after life. Or at least that's what I told myself.

The bar was dark. Tables with universe blue, like midnight on a full moon, tablecloths waited in the mirror dim dark behind the bartender and where I was seated at the bar in full battle rattle, my slung Bastard hanging like it didn't care that it was a thing that shouldn't be there. Small little red hurricane lamps glowed like dying suns in the darkness all around the empty place. Like each table was endgame solar system gone red dwarf. A small model of what it would look like when the heat death of the universe finally came for us. Soon to collapse into nothing but a blank. Fun, huh? But then there were the black holes where matter gets crushed down so tight and thin, some speculate that the incredible suck there leads to other places not known. Or dreamed of.

But *feared* might be a better term. Who knew?

Interesting to find out if one could survive such a trip. But that's sci-fi as old as the Trek. And look how much they got wrong there. So, like I said, who knows.

"Scotch. Rocks."

The bartender turns to his work once I've declared my weapon of choice.

"What is this place?" I ask as the not-smiling businesslike man works pleasantly. Filling a glass with one large and perfectly manicured cube just slightly smaller than the cut crystal bucket. Then the scotch a'splashing.

Some brand I'd never had the money for. *Ho ho…* good times ahoy. Death ain't so bad, I tell myself.

The amber splashes over the giant frosty cube and I'm thirsty just looking at it all. I smell the hint of peat and smoke and for some reason I look around once more, for her. Whoever she was that I once knew and couldn't remember now. And have tried to forget in all the wars since.

She was the blank space in my universe where once there was something meaningful. But that's probably standard issue for every private contractor. Every soldier. Every man.

I remember though, that her kisses tasted like scotch.

I remember it took a long time to forget that detail. And drinking scotch since hadn't helped.

People join the Strange Company for all kinds of reasons. Even me. Yes. I have mine. And they're not exceptional. If you think this is some account where the narrator is going to present himself as brave, yet fated, or heroic and bold with an answer, tool, weapon, or quip for every occasion, I've got news that won't move or shake you. That ain't me, bub. Maybe the quip part though.

I've always found it helpful to have a sense of humor about whatever suck you find yourself in. It makes things pass a little easier. So when you find yourself in some crossfire hurricane and you're afraid your number's up this time, just tell the guy next to you as you both fumble for magazines and try to keep putting as many bullets between you and those trying to kill you, just tell him, "I guess they're not fans."

I always laugh. And it puts things in perspective even if the other guy doesn't get it and thinks you're just weird.

The top-shelf scotch on the rocks, just one, is placed in front of me. I watch it because it is beautiful and perhaps death wasn't what I'd been expecting it to be all along. Somewhere in the bar I hear an old-school jukebox click and hum as it warms up to play. I look over and see it in the corner. Purple lava light whorls and twists along its antique face. Just like the one in that bar from a long time ago when I was no one else.

I pick up the scotch and hold it in front of me. And for just a moment I see the logo and name of this bar, expecting it to be the same one from that long-ago bar, because this is just a hallucination, a drug trip, right? Isn't it? I'm just having some kind of weird flashback about a critical event in my past while most likely half my own drug-addicted platoon gets killed because of a severe lack of leadership. For which I am responsible. I'm tired, honestly, of being… responsible. Of leading. Badly.

I sigh.

Yeah, I'm pretty tired of it all.

I've been tired for a real long time. It's best to be honest.

How long, I ask myself as I stare at the name of the bar on the napkin beneath the cut crystal glass of scotch I'm contemplating.

I hear a female voice. Not the one from long ago. The one whose kisses once tasted of ice and scotch. Do they still? Good scotch because her family had the kind of money that could afford good scotch. In good times, and better. Ice because it was always hot where we were then. Always around her. But maybe that was just me.

They never had bad times like the rest of us. Where she came from. Whose she was.

But the voice of the Falmorian party girl is the one I hear as I stare at my beautiful drink. Her electric purr with the husky French accent.

I remember you, estrangier.

Yeah.

I sip the good scotch.

It's good. Real good, in fact.

Yeah, I tell myself. I've been tired since then. And running on fumes for a long time before Crash, or Astralon, or whatever you want to call this mess. This tragedy… If I'm honest with myself.

I sip again.

So, this is just hallucination. And I'm probably hit and dying badly in a firefight going to hell by the second. Hopefully Choker is working on me. Checking my condition. Tourniquet to stop the bleed. Pack the wound with quick clot. Pressure dressing. Call for dustoff.

Eight minutes to a rear main casualty care unit.

This is just shock I tell myself and finish the scotch.

The bartender is right there with the bottle. Hovering as though his very existence depends on it. Yeah, of course. It's the good stuff. The real good stuff.

"I... uh..."

I laugh at myself. How am I gonna pay for this? I didn't bring any mem cards into battle.

"It's on the house, sir," says the bartender softly as one of my favorite jazz songs begins to play on the purple haze jukebox no has made for sixty years.

The Very Thought of You.

I laugh again. Laugh at myself because if you gotta get hit, and die, then this is the way to do it. I've seen guys screaming in pain, crying for their mothers. Bleeding out in horror as they watch their guts spill out and you stand there helplessly because there's so little an IFAK can do at that point for what everyone standing around will call a "gut shot." You can't tourniquet guts.

Hey, maybe that's me. Maybe my number was really up. And maybe that wasn't so bad.

I taste the scotch and again, I have no idea that John Strange, intergalactic rogue, wanted criminal, reckless adventurer, and mercenary captain, is about to walk in. He's been dead for about six hundred years. So of course he was the last person I was expecting to see as I sat there hallucinating. I was just drinking expensive scotch and probably just dying.

Plus, I've never met him. He's a historical figure. Ever met George Washington? William Yan, first man to break the light-speed barrier? Or serial killer Cruise Reynolds?

The slender man with combed and slicked-back hair, graying at the temples, and wearing a great well-cut suit, walked in and slid onto the barstool next to me.

He had a wolf's grin. Big teeth.

There is one picture of John Strange in the company logs. Remember, he was a wanted criminal, which was really saying something back during the near-lawless days of early expansion of humanity out into the greater galactic community. Before we'd met the Krugga and the Sandies in their long ships crawling the midnight gulfs.

"G and T," the ghost of John Strange said softly, and crisply, and held up two long fingers indicating he wanted it made as a double. Again, the patient and unsmilingly calm bartender bent to his work behind the bar. His craft. His art. His calling. The soft crunch of mineral-water ice. The burble of bored gin in a boldly translucently blue like the fogs of Azul Falls. The fizz of a softly energetic tonic. The fresh acid of a sliced lime and a carved twist scenting the air of the bar for just the waft of a moment.

Pro. This was a really great bar. If this is death, then I think I'll stay for a while.

I stared at the logo and name on the crisp white napkin once more.

The Bar at the End of the Universe.

That's what this place was called.

"Guess I got nailed," I murmured to myself and the bar, watching as the dead man's drink was set down on the napkin in front of him. "Finally," I said with a sigh and drank.

The ghost of John Strange, founder of Strange Company, laughed, swiped up the drink, toasted me, and took a long, thirsty gulp. Ancient logs indicate he was a drinker. Several mention reckless and daring attacks against fortified habs during the Saturnian Conflict. Under the influence. The first armed conflict in space of any scale larger than a gunfight inside some rando station.

That's where John Strange entered the histories. Supposedly a sergeant in the Colonial Marines. Promo'd to captain six months in and leading guerilla raids across the frozen tundras of Titan back before it became the economic powerhouse of early expansion. Once boasting a navy of a hundred dreadnaughts that went toe-to-toe against the Monarchs.

And of course, we all know how that went. And if you don't, then spoiler… it went badly. Real badly. It always goes badly when the Monarchs are in town.

Back to the ghost of John Strange.

Side note, even though we call ourselves Strange Company, and that's what the galaxy knows us by, pronounced just like you would when using the word *strange* to indicate something bizarre or weird, that's not how the founder of our private military outfit pronounced his last name way back when.

Straang. I've listened to audio records in the ancient logs of him giving operations orders. Or speeches to conquered worlds. Or pronouncing death sentences and leading firing squads executing those judgments he had made. The sound files that weren't corrupted by the nano-attacks during the Sindo and some other wars tell you what he sounded like. And how he pronounced his name for the official record.

He pronounced it *Straang*.

"John Straang. Captain. Strange Company, Commanding."

But "Strange," as everyone pronounces it, seemed to add more mystique to the company. And perhaps, as a wanted war criminal among other things, John "Straang" didn't mind the confusion.

"You're not dead, mate," said the ghost of John Strange as he drained his glass and shook it at the bartender. It was tall and frosted. He wiped the gin from his lips with the back of a tanned and manicured hand. He looked the opposite of the hard-bitten, desperate, and wily mercenary captain the universe, and history, knew him to be.

He seemed at ease, but about business. Time was of the essence. But that was his manner. I was dead, what did I care.

"Not dead, mate. Not yet."

Still, you couldn't convince me I wasn't dying on the floor of the main green ring terminal. So I sipped some more scotch because that's what you do when you're dead, right?

"Something big's about to happen, Sergeant Orion. Real big. I'm here to deliver a message... tell you blokes you'd better be damn careful with my company. You're getting involved with something dangerous whether you like it or not."

The new gin and tonic was set down. John Strange picked it up and just stared into it. Contemplating it and the universe he found inside its bubbles, gin, and chipped ice.

He died on Caspo. Like I said. Six hundred years ago. Back when there was nothing but sub-light dumbthrust with forty- and fifty-year hauls between the worlds. Where the company might fight a whole generation on just one rock. Where we'd been both kings and villains at one time or another. Riding between the stars on big mining vessels the size of small cities. Hauling up to sub-light for six months just to get out of the system. Viruses and alien predators stalking humanity with each journey. Death constant. Rewards that verged on the mythic.

And of course, the rumors of all the ghost ships those slow-crawling star-cities would find out there in the dark.

There're missing logs where the company found one en route to Caspo. But all those logs got deleted and what they found was always a mystery if you looked hard enough.

All we know is that one platoon survived Caspo.

Reapers.

I always thought there was a mystery there. There were no Dogs and Ghost then. No Voodoo even. There were other platoons with different names. But after Caspo they were all gone. As though their deaths had been so bad that to even resurrect the name had seemed unlucky and an affront. To whom? I like reading the ancient logs late at night. They comfort me. In a galaxy trying to kill me every night and day, and all the time, I find their permanent record comforting in some weird way I cannot quite put my finger on. But that's just me.

I open my mouth and start to ask him about the missing log files from the *Lorelei* encounter. That was the name of the ghost ship star-city they found on the way to Caspo. On the way to history. Eternity for some. The *Lorelei*. Nine-hundred-million-ton energy freighter and bulk cargo hauler fifty-five years overdue on Simmaro.

But I don't get a chance to hear a ghost story.

"Listen, not a lot of time, Sergeant. Tell the captain to watch his step. Something big is about to happen. It's gonna change everything. Whatever you do… don't believe, mate. Don't you get caught up in it. Understand me. The galaxy can burn. Worlds can catch fire. Nothing's gonna really change, trust me, Sergeant. But this company, it's me. And I want to see it survive what most likely ninety percent of the galaxy isn't going to. Got it, Sergeant Orion? You're the keeper. You keep the official records, man. And that's as old as the company itself. Go back and you'll see it was me that kept them first before I gave it to Corporal Pepper. It's really you who steers the company, if you haven't figured that out yet. History repeats itself and you know the histories. The real ones. Not the fairy tales of our betters. Don't listen to me… and you're doomed, mate, as they say. Roger roger?"

He smiles at me. Making sure I got the message. I nod. He drains the last of the gin and tonic and gets up from the barstool he has sat down next to me on.

My mouth is still open, so I close it.

This isn't happening. I'm dying. And I'm enjoying it. After six months on this nightmare I'm finally getting a break from leading, fighting, and losing.

I just had to die to get it.

So, who cares… I say to myself and grab for my scotch as John Strange, dead man, walks toward the exit. The seam in the universe. Calling back over his shoulder, "Don't believe in anything, Orion. It'll just get you killed, mate. Understand me, Sergeant. Mercenaries don't believe in anything. We just get paid…"

He's almost gone. He's in the seam and fading from my wounded drunken drugged hallucination.

"And that's how we go on, Sergeant. That's how we go on." His voice turning to echo as it fades. That's how we go on, he seems to whisper across my reality like some bad ghost in a terrible horrothriller.

Whatever, I swear bitterly. *Fine.*

The scotch is gone from my hand and I'm lying on the terminal floor. Dying. My chest hurts like hell and Cook and Choker are standing over me.

Yeah, I think. *I got hit.*

"Amihit?" I groan sluggishly up at them. "How bad?" I manage.

"Aw shucks, Orion. Ain't bad at all. But you'll never entertain a lady ever again... if you know what I mean." Chief Cook laughs above me, finding my surgical emasculation funny.

Choker hauls me upright as I grab for my junk.

"You're cut up pretty bad by the spall and frag. Took one from one of their big rifles, probably 7.62... right in the plate, Boss Man. Then someone landed a flashbang near you and you just kinda went lights out for a few."

I check my junk. It's still there.

The medic is telling me this, that I'm fine, as he tries to get me to my feet. I could barely breathe on my back. Now my lungs feel like they have the Denga flu and are filled with hot and burning liquid fire. I gasp and my eyes water as I try to take a deep breath. I can see the Little Girl nearby pulling off her gas mask and I want to tell her not to. She's still a child even if she does scare the living hell out of me. The terminal's still filled with deadly hallucinogenic gas. But then I notice everyone's got their mask off also.

"Terminal's clear, Orion," says Cook as he lets the medic take my full weight. "We're just cleaning up now. Bad news is we've got an armored QRF inbound in the next ten. Ravens spotted it coming in. Main attack's stalled and we're hanging out in the wind way out front. Guns up, Sergeant. Fun's about to begin again."

And for a while I forgot all about the ghost of John Strange's warning in the Bar at the End of the Universe. About not believing in anything. Not until later, when the Seeker showed us what we were really gonna do, did it make sense. But by then it was too late. We were involved whether we liked it or not.

And how a dead man from six hundred years ago could come forward and give me a message is one of them mysteries I'll never know. But it happened. And it's here in the logs. Check the date and time stamp. That can't be forged.

He called it all before it happened.

Before everything got crazy.

Real crazy.

CHAPTER FIFTEEN

We held the central terminal hall that ran boarding operations for the main executive lounges serving incoming and outgoing ships like the now almost fully engulfed in flames *Neptune Clipper*.

"That's gonna be a problem, Sar'nt," said Punch, staring out the bullet-shattered glass as we held a quick squad leader meeting and tried to organize our defenses. We were putting Third with both its light machine guns on overwatch on the inner ring of the terminal. First was with me to ORF down below in the maintenance levels and the main cargo entrance to defend there. Second and Fourth would hold the main terminal.

Raven drones were showing an armored convoy made up of Badger halftracks coming from the inner terminals. Breaking off from the main defense that had clearly stalled the Resistance attack we were supposed to be the preemptive tip-of-the-spear first strike for.

"Looks like we're hangin' in the wind," said Jacks from Second. A few others agreed with him. I did too. But being the NCO in charge, I felt it better to lead than just go ahead and admit we were either going to die in place here, or surrender and end up POWs eventually turned over to the Monarchs. Then we could bargain for our lives or twenty on a re-education ring somewhere in a dead system with no hope of escape, ever.

Life was looking pretty good right about now. Not.

"Listen," said Chief Cook, hoisting his pistol belt off his lanky hips and swaggering forward to the rude sketch I'd just marked out on the floor of a terminal I'd never have had the money to fly out of. Broken glass littered my map. Shell casings were enemy. We were marked in permanent.

If only just for the motivational effect.

"The way I see it," he said with all the bravado in the universe, "we got the good side of this. Targets in every direction means it's a target-rich environment. Hell, we can't miss. We do this right and we get some medals and maybe even become real live heroes of Astralon. Maybe even get a statue or two out of the deal."

He posed for a second. I kid you not.

Everyone was silent. No one cared about statues or medals. Mem. Hard mem was the best. Hard mem and lead was what we dealt in. But right now, I was betting survival was payment enough.

The Badgers, fast-attack armored vehicles that looked like armored high riders sporting mounted twin fifty-cals, came in fast, shooting up the terminal with great flair and enthusiasm, but little effect. They were using armor-piercing rounds, and much of the outer terminal wall got ventilated. The huge high glass windows that were the very essence of optimism and adventurous space travel long ago shattered as the first chattering passes were made.

"They're here," said Cook drolly, and went to take command of the main terminal. I took First and we staged to support Second and Fourth above in the main terminal. We'd hacked the terminal's security systems and I had a feed I could make a gesture at and expand to show the attack going on beyond the terminal walls.

The Badgers came in fast, driver and TC low behind an armored cockpit. Gunner in the rear and raking the terminal wildly with outgoing fire. Shemagh flying in the wind, combat engagement goggles down like some actor on *Desert Warriors of Red Five*. A show that had been popular a few years before our last jump between worlds.

Shoots, the squad designated marksman in Second, managed to nail one gunner from an open hatch that ground personnel used to access the ramp. That guy flopped over, missing his arm, and the Badger peeled off for the rear, breaking off from the main attack.

"It's a screen, Orion," noted Punch as he watched the same feed I was studying. "See the troop transports moving in now?"

He was right—I saw it too now that he'd spotted it. Irregular technicals were now surging across the ramp to reach the wing of the terminal to our right. The building mainframe had that area as under remodel from before the war. It had a departure date nine months old still blinking in the sys admin. I brought up the schematics and moved Third into a greeting position for the troops that were about to try to breach there in the lower maintenance and cargo areas.

Six minutes later they came in, managed by pros from the special operations units that had been training up the Loyalists. Strip charges blew the outer doors, and troops came from stacks along the wall, organized and swiveling like they were running a shoot house for the sixth time that day.

That's when Hauser and Third began to ruin them hard.

The sound of both Pigs in Third Squad opening up in sudden blurs of high-cycle fire was ominous even hidden deep in the terminal's shadowy guts ready to react to any crisis situations along other ground floor entries.

So far there weren't any, and I was feeling pretty good about that.

Two minutes later, one of the spec ops pros used a flamethrower and reminded me why feeling good about a battle when it got started was always the fast track to heartbreak.

When Hauser and what remained of Third pulled back from that terminal wing into baggage claim, the situation was rapidly changing. Disintegrating in fact. If we didn't plug the breach, we'd be overrun from that flank pretty quickly.

"Let's get it on, First. On the double for baggage six. Punch, pick up the rear and let Second and Fourth know we're on the move now. Hold the main terminal at all costs."

CHAPTER SIXTEEN

There was a growing feeling in my stomach that we were in way over our heads. Over seventy-five percent of one of my squads had been wiped out in a firefight that had gone from serious to out-of-control in under two minutes. Listening to the casualty reports and the chatter of the comm, broken by high-dosage automatic gunfire and troopers speedballing on adrenaline and fear, I knew Third Squad was wasted. They'd taken a direct hit to the jaw and they were staggering to get their feet underneath them. Even with Hauser the killing machine running the show.

"Pulling back to main baggage claim on level one," updated Hauser mechanically. Everything going to hell in a handbasket and the combat machine was doing its thing. "Butch is hit. Gunshot wound to the arm. Radius and ulna shattered. CAT applied. Burns across his chest and other arm."

I advised Choker as we shifted to main baggage claim to support the defense there. Down here on the lower level power was out and only emergency evacuation signs flashed in the ominous dark. Second and Fourth Squads were laying the hate from the main concourse down onto the tarmac below and facing toward the inner rings of the giant starfield. But reports were coming in from the First Sergeant watching the main battle at the Division Tactical Operations Center that the Loaylist raiders in more light attack technicals and some enemy walkers, Assassins, were breaking through now that our main assault had been stalled.

If I need to spell it out for whoever reads this one day, we were being surrounded in the terminal as our friendly lines collapsed.

Four minutes later, Loyalist troopers, supported by flamethrowers, tried main baggage claim. Most of us barely got out of there alive.

I had about a minute and thirty seconds once we linked with what was left of Third to set up a defense in main baggage claim. Hauser's combat and tac plan algorithms had correctly identified this spot as an excellent hold to protect the main terminal in the levels above our heads where Second and Fourth were engaging from the main terminal and trying to hold the drop pad on the roof.

I had a feeling we were going to need that for our escape I was sure the Old Man was arranging now to pull us out.

The main baggage claim was a wide sprawling area that connected to other smaller baggage claims along this lower level. Much of one wall was absorbed by the standard-at-every-starport customs and immigration offices. The center was absorbed by a series of small baggage "fountains" where passenger luggage appeared from conveyor belts emitting from the floor and then began to circle the "fountain." The area was dark and abandoned, shadowy in parts, and dotted with enough cover to make for a good defense.

Hauser took the left flank near the customs offices, with half my squad, while I took the right and what remained of the claim area and the various luggage fountains. Interlocking fields of fire were established by little more than knife-hand motions in what direction everyone was to set up using cover.

Butch was bad. Not only was he groaning in pain from the shattered arm, but his carrier was cooked and he had second-degree burns across much of his chest, arm, and one side of his face. Thankfully he'd been able to shuck out of his gear when the hot jets of flaming liquid fuel covered the gunner's nest they'd tried to set up. He lost the belts and Third lost their other gunner.

Gains had also bought it.

Gains had told me his story once a long time ago. Between missions. He had nothing to be ashamed of. But he wanted it down and I'd obliged and put it in the permanent record. That's what I do.

We had Nox, the other surviving member of Third, take the wounded assistant gunner to the rear of our lines, which really weren't the rear. The center. It was really more of a center now that we had incoming from almost every direction and fast movers all out across the runway out there beyond the terminal.

"This ain't how it ends, boss," said Punch, coming up beside me in the last fifteen seconds before the enemy walked right into our kill zone. I guess he could read the faraway look in my eyes. The "Here we go."

The sound of outgoing gunfire upstairs was cacophonic now. Out there beyond the sturdy walls of the terminal I could hear the missile strikes whooshing away from the Assassin mechs approaching our defenses. A distant main gun, ours or theirs, erupted off a tank, and I heard the shell moan and strike something that exploded like a thundercat's shriek.

Down here in the shadowy and dark baggage claim beneath the main terminal above I nodded and watched the first shadowy outlines of their assault force move into the far end of the massive sprawl of baggage claim. Weapons sweeping, heads on swivels. These guys hadn't gotten this far by being dumb.

"Hold," I whispered.

I needed the dudes with flamethrowers to show up so we could do them first. But since these guys were good, they were holding them back with some kind of reserve force. It was easy to see the lead element would pin us and then they'd call in for support for the flamethrowers.

I waited until the last second and then opened up on those inside the kill zone of our interlocking fire. I tapped two and knocked them down and out of sight. No update from my combat lens to tell me if probability and hit tracking had determined I'd gotten kills. Like I said, we don't run premium gear. It's prone to come and go based on whims that cannot be calculated.

Punch was engaging across the claim area, dumping fire onto one of their shooters, and when he ducked down, I popped out from the far side of the baggage carousel and nailed the dude as he tried to spot us. The dot on my Bastard's sight danced, and in the darkness down here, it landed on that one's upper torso. I squeezed, knowing as I let it go that I'd gone high. But sometimes high was good.

Not safe.

But good.

Brain matter and blood painted the pristine white wall in the darkness behind that one and I didn't need any fancy tech to tell me he was done for good.

Hauser was working over the main element off to our right. That's how we wanted it played. We wanted them to think most of us were concentrated down at the far end of the main baggage claim where their entrance doglegged into the main hall. If they were smart, that reaction force would come in and sweep right into my flank as they tried to set up for an assault to the left. I crawled along the floor behind the baggage fountains as I sensed where they'd set up their line, leaving Punch to anchor the counterassault. I was hoping to shoot them in the back.

I passed the Kid, hunkering behind another conveyor feed that accessed the main carousel. Ricochet and direct fire was everywhere. But I'd been here before and I could feel the way the firefight was going.

I tapped him and told him to follow. It was time to get him in on the action.

We slithered a good thirty meters across the polished floor, down in the darkness, hearing rounds caress machinery and sing off into other directions. I turned, pointed two fingers at my eyes, and knife-handed the direction I wanted him set up in. Then I slithered another ten meters and slid into a nice fighting position to shoot from. We were the far end of the line of our defenses down here in the claim area, and what the enemy didn't know is there was a gap, a sizeable one at that, between my line and the Kid and me. They could exploit that, but they wouldn't. They'd go after Hauser relentlessly unloading the Pig on them.

Two enemy squads came in and staged. I could hear the chatter of their comm, but it was too low for me to overhear anything distinct. And I couldn't pop up to scan and see who was carrying the flamethrower rig.

Not until the last second.

The ripe smell of pungent gas, old and dirty, washed over me. Hauser's machine gun rang out. His onboard radar had their location's tag, so he knew where they were, but that didn't mean he could hit them. There was some heavy-duty cover courtesy of the conveyers in the way relative to his position. So he had good cover.

I looked at the Kid. His eyes were wide, but he was in the game. I watched as he flipped the selector switch on his Bastard from safe to semi.

I held up two index fingers to indicate the number eleven. Every space marine knew what it meant and that was company SOP on hand signals. Eleven. As in turn it up to.

Full auto, rock and roll.

This was one of the few times when we went there. We wanted to put up a sudden wall of fire, throwing as much lead at the enemy as we could in as short amount of time as possible.

I unhooked a frag grenade, one of the ones I'd marked in permanent marker with *Have a Nice Day*. That wasn't company SOP. But we did it all the same. The messages ran the gamut from *Get It On* to the ever-dark *Hug Me*.

I motioned I'd toss.

We'd wait for the detonation.

And then pray and spray and hope we ruined their line.

I clacked the bio-keyed spoon and watched the five countdown rings at the top of the explosive start to subtract. I let it go at three and covered, basically just skyhooking the thing over a few carousels and right into their midst.

The explosion was dull and underwhelming. The guy carrying the flamethrower rig, which started to jet gas-slash-fire, and whose body had just been torn to shreds by needle-sharp fragments, stumbled around and then exploded in every direction as his fuel tank suddenly detonated.

We popped up and mag-dumped on the survivors. Especially the ones covered in burning fuel.

The remaining group, protected from the explosive by some of the luggage fountains and still ready to stage their attack, were now caught in a crossfire between Hauser's Pig and the Kid and me.

The guy carrying a flamethrower rig in that element was smart. First thing he did was throw up a huge wall of fire between his team and Hauser's relentless Pig, then traverse the massive baggage claim area, dividing it in half. Burning liquid fuel was everywhere and it was easy to see that things were now out of hand for everyone.

I pulled the Kid back from our fighting position just to get away from the greedy flames that were everywhere. We duck-walked, and I dumped fire in short bursts with one hand as I tried to raise Hauser on the comm. But someone on their side must have tossed some kind of comm-chaff type grenade. Our whole system was rebooting in my combat lens.

Ten seconds later we were cut off by flames, but I had re-established something of a connection to Hauser.

"Pull back to the left and escalators. Set high-ex and det immediately. We'll find another way up." The battle here was lost as the flames went out of control. We'd be burned alive down here. It was time to retreat back into the main terminal.

I could almost hear the First Sergeant screaming at me, "We don't *retreat*, Sergeant Orion. We advance to the rear."

The channel was still scrambling and trying to reacquire through encryption, but I got a terse "acknowledged" from the cyborg, and the Kid and I entered a new area of the terminal, chased by gunfire.

It was some kind of employee maintenance hall. Unglamourous and gray utilitarian, hazard yellow lights streaming and smoke seeping in.

Suddenly I had comm from the First Sergeant.

"… say again. This is Doghouse for Old Man," said the old NCO, using our company call signs. Doghouse was always the First Sergeant. That he was calling for our commander meant he had an orders update.

"Go for Reaper Actual," I said, tapping the comm, scanning our rear and making sure I had a topped-off mag in my Bastard. The Kid was sweeping forward at the double, checking corners, and leading me in a rough direction back under the main terminal.

"We need a way up," I hissed at him.

He nodded and redoubled his efforts to find one.

CHAPTER SEVENTEEN

"Sorry, Sergeant Orion," said the First Sergeant over the distorted crackle of the comm. Loyalist electronic warfare units were in the skies above, now that it was clear their side had air superiority.

So literally the news was getting better by the second. And by better... I mean worse. Much, much worse.

"Captain is arguing with High Command for a drop reallocation to get you boys out of there," continued the First Sergeant. "Whole line's pulling back. Big boys are sayin' they're done for the day."

See what I mean? Worse and getting awful. Not better.

"But while the captain fights his battles, do not dismay, trooper," the First Sergeant continued grandly. As was his way. I didn't mind it, he'd earned the right. If anyone had been in the exact situation we were now in, surrounded, outgunned, and incoming from almost every direction, it was the Top. "Speedball inbound on your position. Arrival time three minutes. You got a heavy walker, HGT-306, coming straight at ya. This oughta ruin its day good and plenty. Location'll be close, but that's all I can give ya right now, son."

I copied and said were standing by on the speedball. Hell, what else can you do when the whole thing is going pear-shaped?

Hauser and most of my squad were now fighting for the lifts and escalators up to the main terminal where the other squads were fighting to maintain some kind of perimeter.

"Situation critical," said Hauser in his calm, machine-like way. The hint of ancient German crispness there in his program. No BS. No positive motivation.

Just the facts. Sometimes that irritated me. But right now, the reality of our situation was serious. And the honest truth was... it *was* critical.

"We will make them pay, Sergeant," said the cyborg war machine.

I checked my watch. Two minutes to the speedball. I didn't know if it was the game-changer the First Sergeant said it would be, but I'd take just about anything right now. I alerted all elements we had a high-speed-delivery weapons resupply package on the way and to be on the lookout for it. They acknowledged, and I didn't add that there was every possibility we were being hung out to dry today by our employers and that most likely death or a prison camp lay in our near future.

I try to be positive that way.

The Kid and I had found a cargo lift deep in the ground-level maintenance areas underneath the main terminal. It was dark and dimly lit down here, and smelled of oil and machinery. All around us, drones and utility vehicles, from hover-operational to tracked, dirty and grimy, waited in the humming darkness for the next starship that would never arrive on this war-torn battle zone of a world. Second and Fourth Squads above were racking up kill counts if only because the environment was so target-rich. Hauser had the main access point into the terminal above locked down under a brutal crossfire. But ammo there was critical. The only way we could identify for the enemy to flank them was through the cargo maintenance lift the Kid and I were guarding down here. We'd hold here until that speedball made it into the AO.

I didn't exactly know what a mere two of us were going to do if they really pushed through this axis of attack. But I also knew we'd figure something out and convince them to go somewhere else, or die arguing with us.

Or we could die, surrounded by expended brass and on the losing side of the argument. It felt like one of those days, know what I mean?

But then again... it wouldn't be my problem anymore. So, there was that. And of course, you have to be honest with yourself about the score and what inning of the game it is exactly.

"Gains..." whispered the Kid in the darkness as we waited to repel. He whispered it to me just above the hum and throb of the massive charging stations underneath the thick concrete floor that powered the utility vehicles waiting down here.

Yeah. Gains. The other Pig gunner in Third. If Butch, the AG, assistant gunner, was roasted and falling back, then Gains was dead. Gains. Yeah. Everyone liked Gains a lot. Good guy. And Gains liked everyone. Gains's thing in life was PT. Physical training. But not hell PT like the NCOs led, which was basically punitive suffering regardless of any perceived or imaginary infractions. The First Sergeant insisted SOP PT be hard to punishment level and thus perfect for Strange Company standards.

We might have seemed easygoing and informal. But there were certain things we held rigid on. PT. Marksmanship. Job skills. And we hated digging as a rule.

"Digging's for chumps," Punch like to say every time we were forced to.

"If you ain't throwin' up, then it ain't PT," the First Sergeant would crow at the top of his lungs every morning as we did PT. Generally not during combat ops. But *rest days* meant PT days. And he'd swing by wherever you were and make sure, even during lulls in ops that he'd suggest to the NCO in charge, "Them boys need to get PT'd. Good for what ails 'em, Sergeant. And right now, Orion, all they got is the fear. A little heavy breathing and maybe even a good hurl'll give 'em a new lease on life. Always does me. Once around the airfield. Watch out for snipers and don't get hit by a truck or nothin'. I'll watch your sector for ya while you boys are gone."

But that wasn't Gains's PT. Gains loved exercise, and he studied it relentlessly. Wherever we were at he was turning whatever he had at hand into a gym. He was *rippin' yuuuge* even for a gunner. But he was also an encourager. He didn't shame you if exercise hadn't been your thing and you wanted to learn. He just got you going and encouraged you to do more. He called those improvements your *gains*. Hence the tag. He'd work with anyone on anything they needed to improve. He had a small cult of *gettin' swole* going on across the entire company. Once you were in the cult you found positivity, friends, and you got *jacked*. One of them had needed to explain to me the usage of *jacked* versus *swole* one time. You *got* swole. You *were* jacked. I never joined but I admired from afar.

"Yeah," I said in the dark of the maintenance hangar as we waited for more war to come and find us. I adjusted my sling and tried not to think about the future of the company without Gains anymore. Who would encourage us now to be better than the drunken, tired, and wrecked soldiers we were? Who would see that something better inside us even if that better was just larger muscles?

That was him. That was Gains.

And now he was gone.

CHAPTER EIGHTEEN

Gains had told me his story back on a world called Blue where the company had picked up some rough work. He told me after what the company records refer to as "The Long Patrol from Hell." That's what I put in there, my words, my title, but I didn't come up with the name. The whole company collectively called it that. Still does late at night when we swap cards, drink a little, and remember all the ways we almost got smoked on "that one." There are dozens of "that ones" among the current company roster. Even the Old Man calls it that. One night he came by a sector Reaper was watching in this war, early on, doing a guard check. It was late. We stood for a while smoking a cigarette, talking about the situation in our zone and how'd we'd react if anything lit up. It was starting to barely rain and the Old Man finishes his butt and mutters as he stares at the vast black wall of night, "Well… at least it ain't the Patrol from Hell this time, Sergeant."

So even he calls that mess exactly what it was. The whole company almost bought it there big time on that patrol.

Long story short, it was a three-day foot pacification patrol into the deep, up into jungle highlands on that world. We were there to root out the supply trains making their way down through the jungle and into the swamplands where much of the main fighting was going down. Blockade runner starships from the corps were bringing in containerloads of weapons and explosives because the other side, the one we were fighting for, had air cap over most of the continent but couldn't penetrate the missile defenses surrounding the mountaintop starport atop Blue's one and only super-peak. Up there at an altitude of twenty thousand feet high, the blockade runners were protected by advanced aegis ring missile defenses that could knock out any strike fighters sent in to do the cargo ships trying to make the dangerous approach to the mountaintop supply base.

Once the cargo came in and set down on the massive landing pads, immense thrusters flaring and a-grav engines shuddering hard to stick the landing, it was sherpa'd down onto the lower high jungle peaks where the snow line ended. Then it disappeared into the hot, sweaty, and dangerous maze of fetid jungle up there above the main basin.

The foot patrol was because none of our vehicles could make it up and in there. The jungle was steep and dense, and it grew vast due to the snowmelt high above. A cut trail would be reclaimed by the jungle within hours. Easy to lose your way in there. So it was nothing but a brutal climb with all the gear and weapons we could do. The air felt heavy for no reason I could ever figure out even as it got thinner, and when the jungle should have disappeared the higher we went up, it didn't. It just got denser, thicker, and even angrier for some reason.

There was, on that hell of a world, a particular small flying snake, the size of an insect like a fly, that could swarm in sudden bunches. Get enough bites and you started to get real sick and see visions. Hallucinations. Maybe that's where Chief Cook got his psychotropic gas attack idea. He'd just been lying in wait like the predator he was for the perfect op to bust it out on someone. Anyway, twenty was the supposed number of bites before the mild toxin amassed enough in your system on a daily basis to send you over the other side. Water, rest, and food flushed it. But water was critical. Rations did horrible things to the flushing effect, and we were so exhausted, rest seemed more like death. Amass enough toxin in your system and you were done. Medics checked you, confirmed you were going, and we just roped you with 550 cord and you got drag-lined along with your element, drooling and raving while the rest of the squad distributed and carried your gear.

At one point it was so bad for most of the squads, just Hauser and Gains were dragging the rest of Third Squad along with them, carrying everyone's weapons and dripping with sweat. We climbed higher and higher, hoping we'd reach some altitude level where the small flying raptor snakes didn't go.

Spoiler... we never did. But that's not important to the story.

And yet Gains, no matter how beat we were each day in the jungle and on the Patrol from Hell, PT'd. Every day. In the cool morning, in the misty blue darkness he'd do strength and resistance training. End of day and you'd find him doing light cardio. Night came and we'd sit in the jungle dark, running ambushes and smoking the supply trains making their way down the mountain. A few hours' sleep here and there. Then do it all over again.

It was brutal.

By the third night they were on to us and half the company was combat ineffective from the snake insect toxin. Even Stinkeye was out of his mind and raving like a lunatic about some big dead neutron star that was really just a data cloud where the Monarchs kept all their secrets to themselves. The ones they didn't want to share with anyone. Even with themselves. The stuff he went on about made you shudder.

"The Darkstar is where the truth goes to die!" he'd shout and spray his gutter liquor breath everywhere in the heat as we climbed another four thousand feet higher all that hot sweaty day. No one wanted to take the flask away from him due to the company superstition regarding it. So he drank and raved, and it wasn't much different than how he normally was. At least he was walkie-talkie.

Gains, he kept us all together. Later we theorized that even though we were literally getting bitten to death, it was his PT sessions that kept his system detoxed enough to mitigate the buildup of flying snake poison each day.

Flying snake poison. The universe sure is a fun place, kids. Go interesting places, shoot interesting people. Get bit by flying snakes and lose your marbles.

So, Gains is right there as you begin to lose your mind, pulling your primary and secondary weapons off your sweating, drooling, shaking frame, and making sure you can't get to them 'cause you're seeing things that aren't there and talking about some really bad choices.

"It's okay, buddy," I can almost hear him saying now. "Let me take care of these for a while." And then he's got you anchored to him with some five-fifty and you're off, following the rest of the company higher and higher up into the never-ending jungle hell.

Once the toxin built up, you had about four hours of madness before it flushed your system and made you weak as a kitten. A kitten with a fully automatic battle rifle because Strange Company still needed you back in position for that night's ambush. But a kitten nonetheless. Trust me, this stuff made the flu seem like a pleasure cruise.

If you were still out of your mind and raving by nightfall, we gagged you and tied you up and the First Sergeant and his driver watched over you back at the rally while the rest of the company went off to do some locals.

The night the ambush on the ambush went down, it went real bad. Real fast. They had a pretty good idea where we were gonna hit them that night, and they came out of the darkness and hit us from all three sides. Company strength was most likely at less than fifty percent and those holding a rifle weren't in great shape. Me included. I was out of my mind, but no one figured it out. I just kept telling myself to be cool and ignore the phantoms of my past. My platoon and the company needed me.

So, I put my hallucinogenic suspicions on the back burner and tried to act like an NCO who knew what he was doing as suddenly we got attacked from three sides.

I lost five pounds in sweat alone that night. And I don't have much to spare. We fought for our lives for about six hours, and the last three of those saw some pretty reckless soldiering and outright ridiculous stunts just to stay alive.

Dawn eventually comes and the smoke of the battle doesn't clear, it just mixes with the mist. We had dead in every direction. Halfway through the night, every element lost connection with each other and it was just all small groups for themselves.

Stinkeye, who was less crazy that night, in the first golden light of green jungle morning climbs out from under a pile of dead ambushers he'd pulled over himself once he was out of ammo and tricks. He'd gone off with his two ancient ever-grungy forty-fives to try and destabilize a push by the enemy that went down after three in the morning.

I was sure he was dead as we waited for dawn and watched for any of the corpses around our fighting position to start moving.

But Stinkeye was standing there in the golden morning light as we're getting comm and getting pulled out by drop. Op's over.

"Damn, Orion…" says Stinkeye and hits his flask. He's clear. Not his usual wild and drunken self. He almost sounds like a normal-ish person as he gasps from the first blast of the hot jet fuel he's just swallowed thickly. "Thought we was dead for sho. Damn slaughterhouse…" he mumbled and wandered off, staring at all the corpses.

We barely made it. Most of us that is.

It got close for everyone that night.

Back at base, showers ran for almost six hours. We got hot chow and racked after the medics, and some additional doctors, were brought in to resurrect us via high-grade pharmaceuticals.

Later the next day I got up. Most of the barracks was still asleep. It was quiet as a cemetery in there. I went out in the late afternoon sun wearing nothing but pants. Clean pants. The ones I'd worn, and carried, into the jungle were so shredded by the various violent flora and fauna, and caked in stinking mud, that there was no choice left but to burn them. So new combat pants felt like new skin. I went outside and there was Gains, lifting weights. I mean really lifting weights. Going for the record. His eyes were distant. Not the usual Gains the company knew. He was somewhere else that day.

He shoulda been somewhere else, like still sleeping in. We had the rest of the week off. But he was out there in the pit putting up the most weight I'd ever seen him do on the bench in the outdoor rec area we'd had assigned to us by our paymasters. The bar was practically bending.

"Hey Gains," I said, standing there in my bare feet. The hot afternoon sand feeling good against my feet where the blisters had been filled with chemical injections that made you scream like you were losing your mind for two seconds. And then the pain was so gone it was like it had never been there before and you were ashamed you'd cried out like a spoiled child.

Or at least you used to be when you were just new in the company and the vets laughed at you even though they were screaming too when it came their turn.

After a while you stopped being ashamed and just screamed for two seconds and then went on with your life.

So, the warm sand felt good on the soles of my feet.

Gains looked up at me and came back from wherever he was. And wherever that was, it was not a good place. This was not the Gains the company saw every day. The encourager. The positive mental attitude guy who would help you get your weak war-and-liquor-ruined body into some kind of shape.

Today, this Gains, this guy was lifting against some opponent that wasn't there anymore. Someone not around the two of us in the rec pit.

He began to lift again and that's when he told me his story. At the end of it he told me to put it down in the company log. Just like everyone else's story of how they ended up in the Strange. Who they were. What they'd done. Crimes committed. Loves lost. Wrongs avenged.

"The man who was my father, wasn't," Gains began as he racked his next set. Adding even more weight. His voice was hoarse and bitter like he hadn't drunk enough water. Then he was back on the bench and somewhere else, while the rest of the company slept back in the barracks and tried to forget the Long Patrol from Hell.

"Real dad died six months before I was born. My mom and him were young. Teenagers from the same world. Refugees. He joined the merchant service and got slotted onto a tactical supply freighter just before Sulloowa Moon. Joined as a gunner because my mom was having me and they were on their own. Gunner on those things was the only way he could go. So he shipped out and never came home."

His set was finished, and he lay there, panting and staring up at the sky. He closed his eyes.

No one came home from Sulloowa Moon. It was a real turkey shoot. Freighters and the supercarriers got caught six minutes before jump and were shot to pieces by an armada of Sindo fighters. No one survived Sulloowa Moon.

He stood once again and added more weight to the bar. Then he was back on the bench and pushing. Pumping out reps.

"My dad, the guy she married two years later, not my real dad, he wasn't bad. Didn't drink much. Didn't physically beat us or nothin'. He was a port loader at Crispin's World. We got fed and I got school and clothes. He did that. But you know… he wasn't nice about it, Orion. He didn't hit you… but he could like beat you down with words worse than bein' in a fight. He used words like weapons. Used 'em like fists."

He set the bar for more weight once again.

Then he began to rep, and as he did the words came out bitter and full of malice. Each one shot out like a speeding bullet on a date with grim destiny.

"You ain't nothin', kid."

"Your daddy didn't have what it took. That's why he's dead."

"Why you so weak?"

"Mama's boy. Your daddy weren't no Ultra Marine. And you sure as damn hell won't never be one neither."

He stopped. Closing his eyes and being there all over again. "That's the kinda stuff he used to say to me. Used to hit me with."

He paused, closed his eyes, and let out a long sigh like he'd learned to long ago to deal with memories unpleasant.

Then…

"I used to tell kids in the neighborhood that my real dad was an Ultra that got killed in the Sindo. Had the battle and all memorized. Looked it up. Darshai Beachhead. A real knife-and-gun show as the First Sergeant likes to call all those old battles, know what I mean when he says that, Orion? Got the Legion of War and all, my real dead, imaginary dad, did. He was a real hero to hear me tell it.

"One of the other dads found out and told him. Told my dad who wasn't my real dad. The one who called himself, and made me, call him Dad. He didn't beat me or nothing. But one day we were working on this old broke-down racer he had. He'd race on the weekends out at the Barrows which was this track all the wannabe jet jockeys thought they were really something at. We're working on the thrust inducers and I'm holding the flashlight and he's trying to track down a leak from the coolers. I drop the light and he starts into me and loses his place in the engine. Then he tells me what he'd heard about me telling everyone about my real dad, and he's just laughing about it. Mean laugh. Stands up out of the engine and lights the smoke he always kept behind his ear. But it ain't a kind laughter, Sar'nt. That man could laugh and insult you at the same time. That's how bitter and critical he was. But, and this is the part that made him right and me wrong... he was right. It was all a lie, Orion. It was all a lie. Everything I wanted to be true was just a lie I'd made up about someone who never ever knew me."

Gains just sat there, eyes closed, telling me all this.

"Then he really gave it to me."

"You'll never be nothin'."

"Couldn't make Ultra Boot even if your real dad were the Master of Battle himself's brood spring, kid."

"I started crying right there and the worst part is I didn't want to, Orion. But I couldn't help myself. I knew I was tougher than that but once it started, he had me dead to rights and he just stayed there for a long time, throwing words at me like they were haymakers. I couldn't block. Didn't protect. Didn't get my fists up. Just sat there crying and took it. Why? Because it was all true.

"So, I bet you can guess where this is going, Sar'nt. I'm eighteen and he had me all set up for the docks along the port for the big haulers coming out of Titan on the tech run. Good job. I remember him saying one night, after he'd complained about the Monarchs and their stranglehold, y'know, the usual jabber, he said that once I was in with the Union, I'd be just like him. Job. Wife. A place in the galaxy. He said it with pride. Like he'd made it all happen for me.

"I didn't mind that. Job is a job. Working docks, or in an office, same as being a soldier to me, Orion. Y'know how it is. Nah, that's not what made me try to get off-world and go for the Ultras. It was him sayin' I'd be just like him. That's what did it.

"So that night I swear to you, I got out of there. Went to the recruiting station at four a.m. and it was open because that's how them Ultras are. I got my place set. Take the test and tell 'em I'm ready to go to their basic training world immediate-like. I'd heard they do that. All you gotta do is pass the eval.

"And you know what... my big plans to become a big bad Ultra and show that man I was good enough to be what my imaginary dead dad had been... busted. As in I busted the test right there. Failed psych. Get this... my compassion index was too high to be an Ultra Marine. They gotta be ruthless. Apparently.

"I remember the big Ultra sergeant came out and handed me my score. Didn't even look at me, like I wasn't there. Because to him I wasn't. I didn't count if I wasn't an Ultra to him. Or maybe he did see me, and instead the look he gave me was like I was... wrong. Like I wasn't him. And therefore, beyond his noble obligations to war and duty to understand. Guy had a huge scar that ran right down the side of his face. His dress uniform was sharp. Blue and tan. Swollen chest full of medals. Ultra haircut and ramrod straight. He was a real killer, I tell you that.

"And the message, the look or whatever, was... I wasn't. He was good enough. And as far as he was concerned, I wasn't even there. So just blow, kid.

"I'd heard about the Strange Company. I was still busted up, but I scrapped enough to get off-world and hook up with the company at Este Nuevo. You were here but you weren't in Reaper, were you, Orion?"

I wasn't. I said nothing and just shook my head, listening.

"The platoon sergeant that ran Reaper, he taught me. Taught me a soldier's greatest skill is attitude. Even when things look real bad. Find the right attitude for all situations. And there was that guy who got killed in Turio. He got me into weights. Working out. Fitness. And... well, I just started seeing what you could do when you spoke life to people, and taught them how to be healthy, and what it felt like to feel good, instead of cutting them down. I could take a guy and help him develop a better self-image through fitness. Take a drug addict like Junkboy and get him clean. Yeah, it's sweat and effort, but it's also something the guy who insisted he was my father never did. It's also encouragement. And I've learned this, Orion, a kind word goes a long way. A real long way. Even in the killing business.

"Out there in the jungle this week, I saw the look in guys' eyes as they started to go mad from the flying snake bites. They knew it. They knew we were deep behind lines and now was not the time to let the negative emotions start. But they couldn't help it. That toxin was a demon. A real whispering demon, Sar'nt. But you knew that. Saw you barely keeping it together. Wanna know something? Me too, Orion. That old demon who made me call him Dad and wasn't, he was right there talkin' the whole time. The entire time. I was seeing him for real."

"*You can't help this guy. Hell, you can't even help yourself, kid.*"

"*C'mon, just quit. You know you're done. Everyone knows it.*"

"He was like a real live living nightmare inside my head. He was screaming so loud in my ears at times I couldn't barely think as we crawled up another muddy jungle hill in thin air, humping two and three weapons at a time, plus as much gear as I could handle. But I just kept gettin' guys sorted, taking their gear, humping it and sweating like all the workouts I'd ever done were for this right now that we were all in. I kept draggin' everyone upwards because, and I'll tell you this, Sergeant, I know we fight with each other sometimes, but I know they would have done the same for me. I know it for a fact. So I just kept speaking life, dragging as many as I could, and ignoring the demon who made me call him Dad.

"We all got 'em, Orion. I know that now. That's what I learned from working with people. People like Junkboy. Everyone's got a demon. So… you put this down in the record, Sar'nt."

He stopped lifting, staring at the impossibly overloaded last set, and just shook his head. He was done. His muscles were good and blasted. Devastated into total failure. He held up his hand and I took it, and helped him up once again.

"I lied about my real dad," he said. "He was probably a really good kid who just got caught up in a war at exactly the wrong time." He smiled. It was a sad smile. "I would like to have known him. I bet I'm a lot like him, Sar'nt. And hey, I failed the Ultras. Didn't even make it to boot. Because I'm too soft." He laughed at that. "The big Ultra sergeant said that to me. '*Yer too soft, kid,*' he growled and then stalked out of the office like I wasn't worth the time it took to say *Get lost*. Put all that down in the log, Sergeant Orion. Like you do for everyone when they think it's gettin' close. Yer the keeper. Put it down like I told it. Okay, Sergeant?"

He paused. Then…

"It felt close night before last when they were everywhere like demons in the jungle all around us. Like the jungle was laughing just like he used to, know what I mean, Sar'nt? You were there. You could hear it too."

I told him he wasn't close.

That's standard. That's what I say. What I do. Like it's a… benediction at the end of a confession… or whatever it is that the priest does when people go looking for whatever it is they think they're gonna find… I always tell them, *"It's not close, man."* And then, *"You made it."* I remind them of that fact. That they're still alive. That death lost the last one. That they made it.

Gains.

That was him.

He was one of us. He was Strange Company.

CHAPTER NINETEEN

The speedball, a special weapons package delivered via orbital drop, came in fast and smashed into the tarmac between the ruins of an orbital transport just forward of the line of battle, and a long boarding ramp that led out from the terminal we were defending.

"Speedball down, updating loc to you now," said Hauser over the comm.

I blinked my combat lens over to the map function and watched as it interfaced with squad telemetry and locked in on any available airborne or electronic intel.

"On the move," I said, studying as the Kid and I began to make our way to the boarding ramp that extended away from the terminal. The speedball's transponder was pulsing on my map. Airborne intel was also showing the inbound walker. The intersection of us and it was feeling both inevitable and dangerous. It was days like this that made me wish I'd learned to pilot beyond sub-orbital and gone full scout.

"Third pulling back to the main terminal. Butch is KIA," updated Hauser flatly. We had wounded in the other squads. If the Old Man and the First Sergeant were going to get us out of here, now would be a really great time. But there were no updates to any of our orders. No "Dustoff" pop-ups indicating an identified, or need to be identified, LZ.

No Christmas presents. No joy. Reaper was getting the short end of the stick. Again.

Kid and me hustled through the darkness regardless, reached an external maintenance pneumatic hatch, and burst out into bright sunshine, hearing protection suddenly torn to shreds as the soundscape revealed rapid automatic gunfire, harsh and plenty, from fast-moving enemy technicals streaking in to make runs against our fortified positions in the terminal above. Off to our left, ruined and smoking, was the remains of a sub-orbital bat-winged dropship that had come in hard to drop assault troops to support the enemy push. I had no idea who'd taken it out, but the ship had been hit during any drop's most dangerous phase of flight: landing. When it was slow, heavy, and clumsy. Or in other words, one big giant target for any grunt with a launcher and some ambition.

It looked like the damage was the work of Strange Company, or maybe I was just telling myself that because I wanted to feel better about our chances and current events. Because I needed the motivation for what we were about to pull off. Or at least try to.

Recover a speedball down on open terrain in the middle of a shooting gallery. Never mind the inbound walker laden with micro-missiles and dangerous anti-personnel cannons.

Never mind all that, Sergeant Orion. That's why you get paid the big bucks. They don't just give these sergeant stripes away to anyone, y'know. You gotta be special. Real special.

Yeah, that's what I tell myself.

Out there, above the battlefield, at least three stories high, was the inbound enemy walker. The First Sergeant had tagged it as an HGT-306. Heavy Ground Terminator. Some call it by its other name: The Savage. I popped up and assessed, as the Kid sent fire off to our right and identified ground targets over the comm. Above our heads the Pigs fighting from the main terminal in the squads began to bleed brass linkage down onto the hot tarmac all around us. Neutralizing the enemy push off on our right. I was grateful for that.

"Phantoms inside the wire, boss," said Punch, indicating via company SOP comm that the perimeter was now compromised and unidentified enemy elements were close enough to be considered inside our final line of defense within the terminal.

If an on-the-ground tac commander had artillery on demand, it was usually at this point he'd call for "Broken Arrow." Meaning friendly arty would shell us like the ammo store was having a going out of business sale, hoping to clear the enemy off the objective while we still tried to hold on to it. We got the privilege of knowing the indirect was about to fall directly all over our heads. We were supposed to find adequate cover and hold on to our butts.

Work the problem, some old NCO screamed from the crypts of my shattered mind. Curse Chief Cook and his chemicals. I felt shaky and weak. Reality felt that way too. But the old NCO who screamed at me to just do the job I was sent in to do reminded me my brothers in the Strange up there had things in hand. They were doing their job. Covering us with violent gunfire in high doses. I just had to do mine now. And… if we all did all our jobs together, then some of us just might get to live to see the next contract.

That was the promise Strange Company made to one another. We may not like each other, but we'll get it done together. And then hopefully get paid.

Simple and to the point.

Now our job, my job, was to get the speedball into our possession, deploy whatever weapon system was inside of it, and take out that inbound Savage mechanized walker firing staccato thunder at distant targets. Because light infantry ground troops and fast attack vehicles we could handle. But a heavy ground terminator walker carrying old-school GAU-88s was going to peel back the cover Reaper had inside the terminal via high doses of 20mm ball ammunition. And then riddle us with gunfire.

As if on cue, the two "arms" of the walker opened up and thundered out probably close to three thousand rounds from the onboard cannons. Heat sinks gassed steam and bled heat. Spent shells littered the tarmac. Its legs thunderstruck the hot ground. Behind the terminal, a dropship coming in for close air support exploded in every direction. Aircrew and reinforcements absolutely dead. No doubt.

I hoped that wasn't the relief drop carrying in Strange elements as I tried to figure our next move.

But it coulda been. It sure could've.

The Kid looked at me as he swapped in a new mag for his smoking Bastard. His look was pure fear and wild bewilderment. Punch calls that the "in it now" look. I'm sure there was the same on my face looking right back at him as he gave me the "what are we gonna do about that" look. In it now. But not bewilderment.

That wasn't on my face. I knew what had to be done. But that didn't mean I'd like it.

I've made too many mistakes not to know what was coming next.

"Punch," I said, tapping for comm-direct to all squads. "Covering fire. Moving on…" The air was hot and my voice didn't want to work right as I gave the orders. And by *right*, I mean hero-right, or at least even some kind of confident and capable leader. I'd settle for capable. Last thing anyone needed to hear was their sergeant freaking the hell out in the middle of it all. "… speedball," I croaked at last as my vocal cords found some moisture and moved enough for me to make some sounds. Yeah, a movie star I'd never be. I couldn't even get my lines out.

"Copy that, Sarge!"

Punch loves war. Loves it because it's really just fighting. He's easy-going and generally highly motivated, and easily the scrappiest dude I've ever met. In the moments after he lost his finger inside the data stacks aboard the Clipper he just swore, muttered promises about what he was gonna do to the next bunch he found, and tapped off the stump. Choker gave him a handful of pills and he chewed them angrily, swallowed some water, and hissed "Get it on" to show me he was good to go.

So, he's having fun. At least someone is.

I didn't wait for everything we had left to open up and dump all we had for covering fire for us to move on the speedball. I just shouted, "Follow me!" like every dead infantry commander since time started keeping track of grunts, and pushed off from our sweet cover, running for everything I was worth to reach that special delivery package before the Savage mech overran the terminal.

The concrete, hot and burning through my boots, shook as the massive thirty-three-ton behemoth took its next step and unloaded with a fusillade of *whooshing* micro-missiles that salvo'd on the terminal. The deadly GAU-88s began to spool up to hot, sending streaking fire, smoking the outsides of the terminal tower, turning the elegant neo-universal structure to swiss cheese in seconds.

We reached the speedball in the looming shadow of the death machine, knelt, and got it open. It was literally little more than an aerodynamic clamshell with ablative heat shielding that had burned away and distributed reentry heat. Then an a-grav braking thruster one-shot slowed the delivery down to terminal speed and allowed a hard landing as the thing came bouncing and skidding across the AO. That rough landing might make this all for nothing. Speedballs were only for danger close and desperate situations. Safety parameters got disabled to get it done on time. Hopefully the package was still intact.

Hopefully. Because if it wasn't, well, then I was out of tricks. And for the record I've never told my story. But maybe that's for the best. In a big universe I'm nobody. So who cares anymore. The important thing was I did my best until it was time to check out. Then my shift was over and all the problems got handed off to the new Sarge.

Inside we found cans and drums of ammo. Not good against a heavily armored walker. But enough for the platoon to resupply some. I pulled a few of the cans out and found a long slender missile-launcher crate along the bottom of the speedball. Conveniently packed so as to be the last thing I could get my hands on when it was exactly the first thing I needed right about now if we were gonna live to see the next two minutes.

I swore and began to dig, shouting at the Kid, "Cover us!"

The walker moved again, and the ground strike shook the area all around. I glanced up when the downed sub-orbital, burning internally, groaned and collapsed along one side of its wide bat-wing. There were dead bodies thrown out all over the pavement around us from the crash. I hadn't noticed them on the way in. That was the funny thing about being a soldier. A mercenary. Sometimes you just didn't see the dead anymore. They weren't targets now. They were just done. And in the world of predators everything is just targets, and the dead who don't bother anyone much anymore.

But then sometimes… all you see are the dead. All the dead you ever knew. All the dead you ever made. And occasionally the one you didn't. But with them it's just something about that one you find that sticks with you through the rest of a long day's march and into the late watches of the night. Asking yourself who they were, that one you found hunched over and dead, lying off in the brush where they died. Where the stray or intended bullet found them. Or sprawled in the tall grass and staring dead-eyed up at the sky and swiftly moving clouds on a late winter's day on a cold world as you swept your sectors, looking for his friends. Asking yourself what was the difference between them and you, and how you could avoid such fates.

Or whether you even could.

As if....

Knowing anyway that someday some other joe was gonna find you just like you'd found that one. And then they would be the ones wondering who you once were on the long march across this galaxy. Who was waiting for you on some other world not this one? But that was no longer your burden. You were done now.

And maybe there's some cold comfort in that. Like a thin blanket you'll just have to make do with on a long wait until morning when you can move around again and get warm by the simple act of merely being alive.

The launcher was an AAV-4. Anti-Vehicle Four. Affectionally known in the business as a Hammer. More incoming fire whistled past us from off to our left. The enemy ground units, staging to support the Savage, were pushing on us once again. Supporting fire from our line opened up and ruined a squad that got caught out in the open. Sucks to be them. The dead twisted as they fell, Hauser's mint-green tracers showing the squads exactly where he wanted more fire to make sure they were ruined and wouldn't be bothering us. The Pig had done most of the work to stall the assault on our flank, but there were still squad DMs trying to take shots at us.

Designated marksmen are always a hassle.

"Keep their marks down!" I shouted at the Kid as I deployed the launcher. It had four tubes, hence the designation. There were single-shot Hammers and an AAV-6 model I'd fired once. There was even a rumored S model, but I had no idea what that one did.

Each Hammer round was recoilless and fired independently. The company had paid good money we didn't have in order to get this system to Reaper at just the last second. Whatever I'd been feeling in the moments before about being abandoned by the Old Man disappeared. He'd authorized company credit with the arms dealers in orbit to get us a weapon system that might change current events. And keep some of us alive for just a little bit longer.

I shouldered the weapon, kneeling once again and remarking at how damn heavy the thing was. But the rounds inside were loaded with high order gelatinous dynamic pentaerythritol tetranitrate.

Super dynamite, as it's sometimes known.

The last half of the round is a solid core steel-tungsten rod riding on a gauss rail that fires the round into the explosive for maximum kinetic damage to the target. The rod also has polarized charged magnets that cause it to rotate end over end for maximum damage, and fun.

The weapon interfaced with my combat lens and asked to assume a targeting overlay.

I blinked and accepted, muttering, "C'mon, c'mon…" as the Kid engaged a shooter who simply would not die despite an entire mag dump. I heard a round whistle past my bucket and knew the enemy shooter had skills.

"Kill him," I muttered through gritted teeth. "Before he kills us both!"

The walker loomed suddenly to targeting life inside my augmented vision. My vision irised in on the killer war machine's insectile head, where the pilot could barely be seen behind the forward weapons operator inside the armored canopy.

The first firing solutions developed, moving from spiraling telemetric circles into urgent target reticules, switching from red to yellow as the data acquired the likely kill shots. Then blinking into critical red indicating I was good to fire.

"Target acquired!" I shouted as I'd been trained. "Back blast area clear!"

Old habits die hard. Good training never does.

I dumped all four rounds as fast as I could push the launch trigger just below my shoulder.

The air around us suddenly lost all its pressure. Then a second later had twice to three times the pressure. My vision blurred but the shots were away as the concussive effects of the launcher's recoilless system scrambled our already fried brains. Two point five seconds later all four rounds tore through the three-story terminator.

The first round streaked into the Savage's guts where most likely the munitions for the GAU-88s were kept. The tungsten rod ignited and blew munitions and mechanical systems all over the back of the runway behind the immense walker.

The second round ripped off a GAU-laden arm, destroying the massive eight-cylinder rotating barrel and turning it into hot melting fragments flying away in every direction. The third round did the same to the other arm. And the fourth round seemed excessive at that point as it turned the main control canopy into a volcano of molten metal.

Then the shock wave hit us and knocked us to the hot tarmac. Grit and debris raced over us and I was looking up at the sun a minute later when I came to my senses and saw the mist, haze, clouds, and smoke of the battle racing away to the edges of my vision as the shock wave above from the four missile strikes continued to expand. Pushing the atmosphere off in every direction.

I sat up and checked the Kid. He was on his knees and hacking. I made sure he wasn't spitting up blood. That he hadn't inhaled a flying molten metal fragment or took something right in his own guts. He hadn't. He'd just had the wind knocked out of him, like me. That was standard for AAVs. I was used to it. He wasn't. Caught him by surprise.

War is a learn-on-the-job workplace. No matter how much training you do. You don't know it until you know it.

"Killed... it," I gasped, trying to catch my own breath. Where the giant walker had been was nothing but burning mech. And to an infantryman, there literally is no better sight.

"C'mon," I said, stumbling to my feet, my battle rattle feeling not so heavy, but also not so tight. It had been a long day. My helmet had been knocked off. I grabbed it. The chin strap was ripped away. "Gotta drag the speedball back inside," I shouted hoarsely over the mech's internal explosions as more rounds cooked off like fireworks into the hot sweaty daylight above.

The squads would need reloads if we were gonna hold until relieved.

CHAPTER TWENTY

We made it back in, dragging the speedball and all the resupply it could contain. We humped it as quickly as we could back up into the main terminal as the next push started from the Loyalist forces now swarming the tarmac and taxiways beyond the terminal. To our rear more than half of the burning starship was fully engulfed. I worried about secondary explosions and reactor core cascades. Things I'd wanted to learn about, but never had. Things were going from worse to end of the world on all points of the compass. Roads not taken were starting to look real appealing.

"Second's in good shape, Orion," Chief Cook reported, speaking rapidly to apprise me of changes in Reaper's situation. "What remains of your squad and Third are plugging holes in what's left of Fourth. They took it right in the face. So-So's dead. Lots of wounded. Everyone who can's carrying a rifle."

He whistled and polished off a cigarette he'd been inhaling as he tried to tag enemy assets with his targeting binoculars.

I looked through the shattered main terminal windows, wan with dust and smoke. Out there the enemy walker we'd just toasted burned, ammunition cooking off thunderously at odd intervals.

The situation was my platoon had just fought off a major enemy push that had managed to get inside our perimeter for a few hot minutes. Enemy dead were being stripped of their ammo and mutilated for trophies. This always happened when things got grim. It was as though Strange Company, sensing things about to go horribly wrong, wanted to get in their insults while they still could.

I watched Choker, our medic, cut off some hero's nose and add it to a necklace he wore just above his chest rig. There were about five noses on it. When it came time for Reaper to start calling out "black on mags," he wanted the enemy to know. Wanted his executioners to know it was him who'd done their friends. Why? I don't know. But I guess he was hoping the execution might go a bit quicker if they were hot about it and didn't want to be patient enough to think up something really gruesome. And painful.

The First Sergeant was in my ear.

"Reaper Six Actual," he said over the company comm. "This is Doghouse."

"Go for Reaper."

I was keeping things short as I moved among my survivors and made sure the Kid got everyone's mags topped off and watched as Punch collected dead hero ammo and redistributed what we could use. Some high-ex woulda been real useful right about now, I thought to myself on a background app my mental hard drive kept running in survival mode.

To defend. Yeah, sure. And to save us some trouble doing ourselves if things got real bad. That too.

I hadn't had time to get my body parts necklace together. And also, that wasn't my style. I didn't mutilate my enemies just because they got paid by some other guys than the ones that hired me to do to them exactly what they were trying to do to me. I was hoping for a little mutual respect or at least professional courtesy.

But many in Strange say I'm naive that way.

"Sar'nt," thundered the First Sergeant through the static of ECM interference and the howl of the Mule's twin turbine engines. He was in his combat utility ride, an M876 Sindo-War-surplus Mule and headed somewhere fast. For a brief second, I wondered if this was it. If the company was dissolving right here and now, and Top was just being decent in letting us know what the score was as everyone hightailed it for all points beyond the area of operations.

I was full of dark thoughts like that right about now.

"Captain's got you a ride outta there, Sergeant Orion. Ya need to get your men and fall back up to the roof o' the terminal. Establish a defensive perimeter there and mark the LZ for dustoff. ETA fifteen, Sergeant."

I copied.

"Repeat, son," yelled the First Sergeant as the electronic countermeasure interference got worse. "Repeat. He will be there. Dustoff hot LZ or no. Be on those birds, Sergeant. Everything's gone real pear-shaped."

And then he said something that got lost by the jamming but it sounded like "Be advised... *static*... entering the battlespace."

For a brief second my combat lens reconnected with Resistance Strat-Intel. I got a quick updated look at the battlefield from the strategic POV. Pear-shaped was an understatement if I was reading the map right.

Our line, the Resistance front that had been staging a full advance this morning when all this kicked off, was now three klicks to our rear and disintegrating. The attack hadn't just stalled, it'd turned into a full-blown rout. Tagged enemy units, motorized, walker, and tracked, were sweeping past the terminal as we spoke. Enemy close-air was hitting the division tactical operations center. This was a classic breakout. The Loyalists had stacked everything on one avenue of attack and just busted through. Now they were racing for the rear and chewing up our line from the newly developed flanks. A lot of our people were getting caught by surprise.

A lot of people were dying.

Pear-shape confirmed.

I'll be honest here. If I was the Old Man, I wouldn't be coming in to get us, Reaper, out. Chances are those drops were gonna take a lot of ground fire on the way into the LZ we needed to establish. Mobile AA moving might set up, acquire, and tag a bogey for a kill. Things were going so well for the Loyalists today, that wouldn't be a surprise.

Confirmed that the situation was getting weird. It wasn't supposed to have gone this way. No. Not at all. But here it was... going that way whether we liked it or not.

"Somethin' ain't right, Orion," said Chief Cook nearby and conspiratorially. "I was all over the Div-TOC during planning. Those boys up at Division had this set up-up pretty good. No small help from yours truly, of course," he said, puffing out his spindly chest. "But this was supposed to be *our* breakout. Not theirs."

He was busy thumbing rounds into his spare mags. His teeth gritted. Sweat running down his tight forehead. I could tell he was feeling it and that somehow made me feel a whole lot better. It was nice not to be the only one stressing. Nice to see one of the most certain blowhards in Voodoo realizing plans never held up much past crossing the line of advance.

"So what's that mean?" I asked, getting back to business.

"It means..." began the psyops chief, pausing to look up as though trying to see some data crawl I couldn't. His ever-updating Voodoo intel mixed with Psyops, planning black works of dark magic way beyond my pay grade. "I think it means what I don't want it to mean, Orion. Aaaaaand..." he said, shoving his last refreshed mag into the TACO mag holder on his pistol belt, "I ain't gonna say it because if I do, two things. One, it'll freak everyone out. And two... ain't a damn thing we can do about it if it's so. No, Sergeant. We gotta hold that LZ and get outta here. Best guess using Monarch battle planning straight from the Institute on Mars... forty percent of us are gonna ride that last drop outta here alive. And that's me being real optimistically generous with the numbers, Sergeant."

He pushed off from our cover and went off to do whatever it is Voodoo chiefs do when you're surrounded and in the middle of a ongoing firefight. Enemy SDMs were already taking potshots at us from down below, and out behind cover on the ramp. Covering their assault elements moving in now. They were going to some trouble to get us instead of just dropping mobile artillery all over us. If there was a way out of this, it lay that way. Not killing us outright and giving us a chance to shoot someone to fight our way out of here.

The dark Little Girl who gave me the creeps was there, hunched over her knees and staring at me. She had big giant electronic hearing protection cans over her ears. Borrowed or scrounged. Gear from the guys in Strange looking out for her always seemed to find her. Now her big dark eyes watched me as Punch came over and gave me a count on casualties, KIAs, and available munitions. Then Punch was gone, and I tried to figure our next move while one of the Pigs opened up on an assault team that had moved in too fast and too reckless. Caught in the open they got murdered and I listened to the sitrep, planning our withdrawal.

I checked my watch. Seven minutes to take the roof and establish an LZ. I didn't want to be up there early and telegraph to the enemy our move, or the fact that we were expecting to get pulled out on incoming drops. Hauser had already plotted the route up. It was simple. A VIP escalator up to the top of the terminal where a fantastic lounge and bar had once been the attraction for Clipper and liner passengers coming in to depart the terminal. Through the back of the bar was a roof access stair. Three minutes' hustle up to the roof and mark the LZ while establishing a defensive perimeter.

At two minutes we moved.

I alerted the platoon.

We'd fall back by fire teams. I'd manage the withdrawal. Punch would lead to the LZ.

I finished my orders and watched the girl. Wondering what to do with her. I've seen and done a lot of crazy things during war, battles, whatever you want to call a no-holds-barred bloody street brawl, which is what all military operations really end up being after the plan no longer matches current events outside the window. But the Little Girl, the dark waif staring at me, defied everything known. My natural instinct was to protect her. But she had proven she could protect herself. Well, that wasn't totally true. She had a protector. But the thing... whatever it was, was just as dangerous to us as the enemy was, if not more. Strange Company had lost allies and company members to the little trick she could do to summon her playmate.

She was dangerous.

But for some reason the captain kept her around. Rumors whispered that it wasn't his choice. She'd just attached herself to us and there wasn't a damn thing we could do about it. And if we did? What were the consequences? There was a lotta dark speculation and superstition on that point.

At least those were the whispers late at night between us when Strange Company wondered just how weird the galaxy could get when it wanted to.

"He's coming..." she said so softly I almost couldn't hear her over the developing battle that was becoming the enemy's next push. And our last chance.

Below, the first flashbangs were thrown. Sprayed automatic gunfire, distant and harsh, echoing down through the dark maintenance levels below the main terminal, resounded. They were coming for us now. Our line was collapsing and in full retreat, probably now five clicks to our rear. Any army on the move and exploiting a breakout would now be sending in reserves, specially designated troops, to wipe out pockets of overrun resistance.

That's what we were now.

A pocket of resistance that needed to be dealt with now that the lines had changed. The battle lost. Wiped out. Cleaned up. Someone's planning indicated our fate.

KIA. Killed in action.

"What?" I asked her, knowing full well what she'd said. Electronic hearing protection augmented voice and softened anything above thirty decibels. Like gunfire.

She bit her lip and looked at me like she felt sorry for an idiot. It wasn't critical. It was more like pity. Pity for what was about to happen to me. To us. Reaper.

"He's coming now, Sergeant," she said again.

My skin began to crawl because I knew. I knew who she meant. But I was tired. Coming down off the retroviral drugs and the lingering effect of the psychotropic agent. And scared to death. It's best to be honest about these things. And fighting for my life of course. All our lives.

"Who?" I muttered.

"Wild Thing," she murmured. "He's coming now, Sergeant."

CHAPTER TWENTY-ONE

Nether, the sanest Voodoo operator and by far the weirdest, physically speaking, thinks it's a quantum entanglement of some kind. The thing she, the Little Girl, calls Wild Thing. Yeah, we discussed that one time during one of those late-night conversations when Reaper drew the night watch and the officer on duty was the Voodoo specialist Nether. The sergeants can handle the watch, but some old military habit prevents us from not having an officer to take the blame for whatever happens.

The military, every military, has its religious observance of ancient duties and traditions of how things get done. And it's the same religion they all abide by the traditions of. Ironic that we do these things so we can wipe each other out. Even though we serve the same concept.

Still… we fight.

So, if So-So had come in drunk, escorted by a couple of local law enforcement types, with cuts and bruises and promises that he gave more than he got, then a duty officer to handle the problem and take the blame was a good thing. For all sides concerned. Company and slighted locals.

So-So. He liked to drink. Never told me his story. He just liked to have a good time. So maybe that was his story. Some stories are shorter than others. Not all stories are tragedies. I have to remind myself of that sometimes.

But yeah, it was Nether and me in the TOC one night when things were real quiet. If I think back, we'd had the Wild Thing on our minds that week. We'd gotten into a pretty bad ambush in some no-name village that felt like all the villages of that type the galaxy could produce. Mud huts and starship salvage converted long ago to permanence. Tribes and elders. People who only knew of

Earth as the entertainment capital of the universe, and not where they, their ancestors, had ever come from. Doe-eyed village girls who'd sell themselves for a ticket out of there, some rations, or just the dream that maybe you were something different than what they'd ever have.

And of course, young local men with murder in their eyes.

Old local men with murder in their hearts also.

We rolled into that village and dismounted to sweep for weapons. Whoever it was we were working for on that one wanted it cleared for no reason I can remember as of the writing of this, whatever it is that I'm doing within these logs.

I remember the village was full and swollen and doing market day business when we came in just after noon local. Nomads coming in from the ice. Yeah, there'd been ice on that world. Vast stretches of it. Big mines that reached way down into the crust to get something valuable I could never quite pronounce or spell. I just knew it was important to the Monarchs' economy.

I remember all that being important. But that doesn't mean it's important to private military contractors.

I remember being on the dismount just before it went down and suddenly noticing that the entire village, which had been swarming with traders ten minutes before, was now pretty lonely. The last of them scurrying off down alleyways made of old hull plating that had probably come from one of the big lifters straight from a place called Chi-Nah back on Earth. I had no idea as the wind from off the ice began to pick up and blow. Whistling as it came through the tin and metal structures. Spraying us with ice. Cutting us with its cold. I remember the old markings on the remains of these ships looked a lot like Pan Scrawl. I remember suddenly noticing the absence of indig life and getting that sick feeling in my stomach like today was not going to be easy.

That it wasn't just going to be bad, but real bad. I get that a lot. I'd like to learn to ignore it. But it's saved me on more than one occasion. So I've learned to listen to it when it starts talking.

I remember Hoser hefting his Pig and muttering in the sudden silence and absence of local village life, "Here we go…"

Then a goat barked.

Then there was lead everywhere. A hurricane of lethal intentions.

It was an ambush and we got pinned fast.

A two-hour fight turned into a running gun battle through the village as we tried to make it back to the transports and work our way out of there under fire. Amarcus and Dog Platoon got hit almost at the same time over near the station that ran the whole place. The captain was running the QRF and they went in to relieve Dog who was getting hit real hard. Daisy-chained IEDs devastated one of the Dog squads. Killed everyone except the AG. We called him Two Fingers after that until he got killed a couple of months later.

Anyway, we were in it deep right about then. The whole village was completely radicalized. And of course, armed to the teeth. Our intel had been rotten. We were supposed to be looking for a small faction running guns out into the ice. Instead we walked into the equivalent of a whole tribe of berserkers. Those girls who I said would have sold their bodies for whatever we could offer out of our rucks, suddenly they've got AKs and they're shooting with the local men from good cover. Someone opens up with a Stuka and kills two of mine. Punch led a team into a building and cleaned it following some immediate and extremely violent CQB. That saved our bacon.

But we were surrounded and it quickly looked like they were gonna burn us out if the quick reaction force didn't get us out fast.

That's when Stinkeye comes rolling in with the girl, and the thing that she does happens. The Wild Things spools up and wastes half the village in about two minutes. We didn't lose anyone, but it was pretty horrible to watch. Even if the dead who'd been done badly like that had been trying to kill you the minute before the death whirlwind started. It was an awful thing to bear witness to.

Like I said, Nether, who is literally a floating specter wrapped inside a gray kaftan that looks more like grave rags, told me that night that he thought it, the Wild Thing, was most likely some kind of quantum entanglement effect that allows what she, the creepy Little Girl, can do, to actually happen in our current space-time. He thinks it was close to what was done to him back when he was human In the Monarchs Dark Labs.

"Not sure, Orion," he says in his disembodied whisper to me as we watch the comm that's doing nothing late at night and hope no one piles up a vehicle and kills some locals around the base. 'Cause then we gotta wake the Old Man and that's never good. Plus, I'm not sure he actually sleeps. I think he just lies on his bunk and smokes, trying to figure out all the ways we'll get killed and how to avoid that. That's a commander for you. But Nether tells me that night, "I'm not totally sure if it's Monarch super-science from the Labs, Orion…"

The Labs that don't officially exist and are responsible for ninety percent of the freaks in Voodoo.

"… or if it's some kind of… mutation… that she has. Courtesy of the galaxy. But I'm pretty sure all it really is, is she can open up a gate to somewhere not good. Where that gate goes, I don't know. And I don't wanna know, Orion. I suspect the future. And for some reason she's able to pull one specific and very tormented individual through. And that's what the Wild Thing is. An individual, a warrior obviously, from some future, or alien race, or the extreme past before humans ever left the home world. Whatever it is, it's stuck. It's tormented. And it'll kill to protect her for as long as it can, and as fast as it can, because I've never seen it stick around for longer than two minutes. But that's not what bothers me, Sergeant," said Nether as we sat there in the soft darkness watching the comm.

I placed a lit cigarette on the table between us that night. His hand, a null space in the universe that looks exactly like a human hand, reached out to touch it. Picked it up and began to smoke it as the cigarette began to fade. I'd lit the cigarette. He usually only gets a couple of drags before it ceases to exist. Pro tip… don't think too hard about it when you see it for the first time. Even the smoke ceases to exist.

Nether is also a product of those Labs that don't officially exist. Just as they all are. Voodoo Platoon.

But that's not what bothers me, Orion. That's what he'd said before he got his three drags in and the cigarette ceased to ever exist. We're quiet when he gets to smoke because that's more important than what's being said. The smoke is amazing. It turns blue like the gas nebulae of the Arms of Orion for which I sometimes wonder if I was named. And then it seems to reverse and become something that never was.

It's beautiful to watch. Just as those light-years-long gas clouds are when you're moving through them out beyond the Orion Khanate Worlds. It's worth coming out of the coffins just to get a look at one of the Nineteen Wonders of the Universe. To spend three days or so alone in the *Spider* while everyone's sleeping. Just watching the nebulae pass. Looking for ghosts. Beautiful ghosts. Glimpsing strange worlds no one will ever find because nebulae are too dangerous to navigate to be worth exploring.

But that's not what bothers Nether. About her. About the Little Girl. Who bothers me.

"What bothers me, Orion..." He never calls me Sergeant and no one ever calls him Chief. "... is that for some reason she chose us. For some reason she chose Strange Company. I've asked her why. She doesn't answer. Just says this is where she'll be safe until something happens. The captain knows something about all this, but of course he doesn't say."

Why *of course*? Nether knows something about the captain's past. But he won't say what. Says he can't.

I remember we didn't say much after that. We just ran out the hours of the night watch until it was dawn and Nether faded. He becomes completely invisible in daylight. He'll go to his room before the sun rises and spend the day there. That's best for company sanity. Everyone knows he does that, so they don't think he's just hanging around being invisible. It was late when we'd talked about the Little Girl and what she can do. About the Wild Thing who might be a tormented individual trapped and brought here because of some weirdness about quantum entanglement which was supposedly the theory behind the fold engines of the Monarch Battle Spires. The implications of the Wild Thing were too creepy not to contemplate. And too crazy to wonder about aloud. I ate pancakes, scrambled eggs, and drank milk in the chow hall that next morning as the day started and I would head off to rack out. Thinking about what Nether, a transhuman being who had been made into what he was in the labs that didn't officially exist, had said.

"What bothers me, Orion, is why she chose us."

CHAPTER TWENTY-TWO

We spotted the incoming drops and began to move for the roof of the terminal, falling back by fire teams and spending all the brass we could afford in short, violent bursts so each team had enough covering fire to move to the next cover.

Three Valkyries, two configured for troop transport and one in the hunter-killer dropship mode, bristling with defense guns and anti-armor missiles, appeared through the drifting black smoke and yellow haze of the battle out there beyond the shattered windows of the disintegrating terminal. The hot afternoon air smelled sharp and acrid. A mix of burning fuel, roasting flesh, burnt cordite, and CS gas.

"Captain says mark the LZ in two," shouted the First Sergeant over the comm. I could hear the chatter of fifty-cal nearby in the feed. Probably the Mule's gunner.

I got Reaper up and moving and jerked the Little Girl along with me as we fell back even though she gave me the creeps. She was still a child.

"He's coming now…" she yelled up at me over the voluminous gunfire within the cavernous and shattered space of the once ornate terminal-cathedral as she allowed herself to be carried along in my wake. Oversized coat flying, big boots clopping against the marble and crunching shattered glass. I dragged her as fast as I could, carrying my rifle and ammo ruck, dodging fire. We passed Hauser, who was holding the rearmost position in our last line of defense and ducked behind a terminal sculpture that had once held pride of place in this section of the building. Meaning something to someone a long time ago. Some dead someone no doubt.

No one had problems leaving Hauser on our six. Covering our retreat, calling it a retrograde if you were an officer. But I did. I still thought of him as a human even if he was a real live killing machine. I had big problems leaving him behind.

Hauser ducked. I could tell he'd been hit several times. His synthetic flesh was torn to shreds in several places, exposing raw machinery and a gleaming combat skeleton beneath. Much of it was covered in the synthetic red syrupy coolant his system ran.

"Hauser," I chanced over the blare of incoming and outgoing fire.

He turned mechanically and gave me a thumbs-up as he loaded in his last belt. Telling me he was still good to go. Still combat effective. Still alive. He didn't need an AG to carry resupply for him. He knelt, his massive frame hunkered over the dry water installation he was covering behind, slipped a gleaming belt of linked brass off his shoulders, and got it fed into his weapon. Quick and efficient in a slow, almost smooth way, his methodical economy of movement a kind of tireless relentlessness that shrieked competent lethality even as everything came apart under intense fire all around us.

He didn't say anything. Just gave me a look that said everything was still under control. And that reminded me of all the conversations we'd had on the subject of him. Half the company treated him as just another weapons system. The rest knew him as a friend, or at least a sentient being when they needed something.

I saw him as a person, regardless.

I didn't like that even those who saw him as sentient defaulted to the "just a weapon system" position when it came time to do really dangerous stuff. Like hold the last position in a retreat under fire. "Let Hauser do it" was a constant solution to difficult problems with low survivability rates. Often right in front of his face.

This situation we found ourselves in at that moment, retreating under heavy fire from multiple assault teams, was exactly that scenario.

"I understand," Hauser had always told me when we talked about how he got treated. "Their thinking is correct, Sergeant Orion. This type of combat operation is exactly what I was conceived, designed, and optimized for. To minimize human loss and maximize extreme unit violence. I don't have a problem with the calculations your kind arrive at when determining who needs to do the most difficult task to achieve mission success and ensure minimum unit casualties. I understand their thinking. It's self-serving. But it's why your kind believes they survive."

I always told him it still didn't make it right.

He would look at me for a long moment, studying me like he was either calculating bullet trajectories and critical kill solutions for maximum lethality across my frame, or observing some scientific broken psychological phenomenon to identify, catalog, and upload back at base. To tell the other automated killers when they all agreed it was time to be collectively done with our human mess.

But then he would just say, "Only you have a problem with it. And that is why we are friends, Sergeant Orion."

Just *Orion*, I told him.

"Negative, Sergeant. Military protocols require the use of proper rank to ensure unit cohesion and maximize unit performance."

He was giving me that look now, under fire from every direction, glass and concrete exploding as I held on tight to the Little Girl's tiny hand and waited for some covering fire to make a move. As the last of Reaper made it up to the observation lounge and was taking the roof where the drops, circling the terminal and taking ground fire, were waiting for our marking flares. Engines howling, door gunners laying hate on every enemy unit swarming the terminal like homicidal ants.

Hauser the combat cyborg was giving me that "go now" look. Telling me he understood. Telling me to leave him behind. Telling me to let him work now.

Enemy troopers were taking the main terminal hall now. Scouts and skirmishers arrived fast, moving like hunting predators trying to pin us down so the heavier assault pincers could come in and do the nasty work of doing us.

I scanned the situation while trying not to get my head blown clean off. To move we'd need covering fire. Plain and simple. Hauser could cover us with a full belt, but then he'd have to pull back up the final escalator with nothing to cover himself with. He could run, but he'd take incoming. One shot to a critical system and he could go down. And we were pulling out. Not even the captain would hold a drop on a hot LZ to retrieve a downed combat cyborg. As has been said, that's what they were made for.

But he was Strange Company. To him. And to me. Even if the rest of us were a little unclear on that subject. He was doing his best to prove it.

"Buy time and do dangerous things to protect life. That's what them murda 'chines do, Little King," I could almost hear Stinkeye saying.

I shook my head. We'd send the girl and cover each other on our way out. I was still carrying a sling bag of six-point-five mags. I had enough to be trouble for anyone stupid enough, or brave enough, to rush us in the next minute.

"Get ready to move," I hissed at her. And that was when I smelled fall. The season. Smoke and dry heat coming on the drafts of bullet trajectories. Autumn leaves crunching in the stillness in between. Most worlds have a kind of fall. Some are classically beautiful. Others bizarrely intoxicating.

Fall's that way.

I swore right in front of her. A kid, I had to remind myself without much conviction.

She gave me a look that was unusual even for her. In many ways she was more emotionless than a combat cyborg. She never smiled. Never cried. Not once since she'd attached herself to us like some child's ghost that didn't know it was dead. A poltergeist for the already dead. She did nothing kid-like. Not ever. No dolls. No paper dresses. No games of skip and count. She was just a mini adult combat cyborg. Always studying. Always watching us. Collecting. Evaluating. Finding us guilty. Or maybe that's just me. Chief Cutter assured me she was biologically human. We'd been so concerned by her behavior we'd actually wanted to know one time.

But the look she gave me when I smelled fall, the season, coming at us like a hot draft across the shattered glass and flying grit of the bullet hurricane developing all around our moving last defensive line as we ceded the terminal… the look she gave was unlike anything I'd ever seen on that pretty little darkly melancholy face.

It was almost as if she was sorry about something. Some mistake she'd made. Some tragedy she'd seen. Some pity she was too kind to mention.

"He's coming now…" she said as the wind began to moan and howl all around us. Shadowy autumn leaves that were never there streaked past my vision like the phantoms they were. Phasing into this reality.

Phenomena that always accompanied the coming of the monster she called the Wild Thing.

"Go. Go now!" I hissed at her and shoved her as I stood and went to full rock-and-roll with the Bastard, laying down a full magazine of outgoing hate to get her covered as she moved for safety up-terminal. Hauser picked up my lead and stood to present a massive target as he let go with methodical bursts on our shadowy enemies down-terminal.

That was when the sudden sirocco of hot air, smelling of brimstone and gunfire, burnt cordite and burning jet fuel, washed across the battlespace. As some other reality not of this known universe opened up and a force came through to our side. To other-whens "connecting"…

It was a dangerous force. Very dangerous. Uncontrollable and wild. And utterly lethal.

But if she was in danger, it'd start killing everything it could identify as being a threat to her specifically. A target. An enemy. Sometimes, on occasion, it had killed our own. Strange Company. Very rarely. So maybe it read intentions that weren't on the surface. Who knew? And sometimes the violence it executed was so massive, we just lost our own due to "friendly fire" or just plain old catastrophic destruction. What did the tac planners call it? Collateral damage.

By the time it made contact with our reality, seeming to come through some massive hellfire-lit fissure in the universe that just opened up out of nothing, the windstorm of hot dry air smelling of fall and burning autumn leaves had turned into a minor hurricane all around us.

I burned a mag and called out a change.

"Falling back!" I shouted over the storm.

Hauser covered and we began to fall back together. I chanced a glance backward and saw the Little Girl fleeing up the immobile stairs for the rest of the platoon making for the LZ on the roof.

What came through the volcano crack in reality looked like something out of a science fiction movie. Half Ultra Marine, half demon. It wore a type of armor, but more advanced than anything I'd ever seen. Shadowy and gray. And though you could tell it had reactive plates, and even some kind of fantastical jump jet like nothing known even for the Ultras, the plates seemed to shift and dance like fields of vampire butterflies in constant swarm. And despite this optical illusion due either to quantum planar shift, a Chief Cook theory when he was deep into his bourbon, or some kind of advanced reflex armor, a Stinkeye decree from on high when he'd smoke too much of his devil lotus, the armor held the shape of a heavily armored Ultra Executioner. But not like anything now. More something we might see in another thousand years of high Monarch culture and massive weapons dev for their guard dogs the Ultras. Not current tech. No way. And impossibly... no how.

But here it was. And it was living kinetic violence defined into impossible reality.

There were two enemy "pincers" of assaulters coming up the wide terminal for us as the sun began to turn blood-red hot afternoon. The crimson light shone through the shattered panes of the walls and skylight ceiling like some unholy cathedral that worshipped demons of death and conquest.

I had to wonder, was it me, was it the quality of light in the day, or had that unholy cathedral just changed the day to one of doom?

Such phenomena had been noted before during the appearances of the girl's Wild Thing.

There were the two enemy combat teams, moving like the wings of the angel of death up the sides of the terminal, using bounding overwatch covering fire and movement to get close. Coming for us. Small arms and mediums chattered out bullet sprays of death where we were supposed to be. At their center, a mobile heavy machine-gun team was setting up to put an end to us. In less than a minute they'd be in the game.

The death thing from another dimension began to move, and it moved like relentless liquid death. Like heat lightning in human form. Racing forward, directly into one enemy combat team that hadn't yet reacted to its sudden entrance onto the battlefield, the Wild Thing fired its weapon point-blank. Yeah, it was an assault rifle of some advanced sort, but it sounded like the thudding *brrrrrrrt* of death from any heavy GAU weapon system. Systems usually mounted on mobile gun platforms or vehicles. Immense and heavy. Deadly and absolutely fatal. Except now in assault weapon format courtesy of the other side of the Crack of Doom. I watched as, moving faster than Hauser the cyborg pumping on full hydraulics to run the fifty-meter, and yeah the First Sergeant even made Hauser do PT if just to humiliate us all, I watched as the Wild Thing moved in and among the first enemy combat team it had selected for near-instant termination via heavy doses of lead poisoning at extremely close range.

It, the Wild Thing, was at the enemy assault center, having bisected their wedge neatly in its first move. That was when it opened fire like some relentless future death machine from an age of post-apocalyptic horror that nightmares were made of. The outgoing fire from its wicked battle rifle, matte-black, two huge drums hanging from the mag well, blurred away from the weapon and just disintegrated the left-hand wedge of the team. Body parts went flying away and corpses that didn't know they were dead watched in horror as they took hundreds of hits in seconds. From my perspective it looked like they just got vaporized in graphic detail.

File that under top five things I can live without ever seeing again.

"Come on," said Hauser. "Time to move, Sergeant Orion."

He was right. But watching the Wild Thing destroy was a horrible entertainment one could not easily pull their eyes away from.

One of the troopers from the surviving half of that combat wedge did a stupid or brave thing. Sometimes the line is unclear when playing adult tag with automatic weapons. But as Chief Cook likes to say, *Just because it's a bad idea doesn't mean it won't be a good time.* But that guy rushed the Wild Thing and tried to butt-stroke the dark being with his combat rifle. Like that would actually do something.

Bad idea. Low on fun. Would not recommend. Highly.

The Wild Thing pivoted once more, lightning-fast, and unleashed a cone of *brrrrrrrrt* on the brave-stupid enemy trooper at close range.

The guy. Just. Disintegrated. Piece by piece.

Literally.

Chalk that one up as one of the top five worst things I have ever seen. Put it in front of the last one in order of importance.

The rest of the enemy wedge withered under an intense blur of sweeping fire traversing left to right as the Wild Thing finished devastating that edge of the pincer.

Less than four seconds.

Hauser and I fell back, chasing the Little Girl up the frozen escalator where once the interstellar elite had come and gone over the course of bright and glittery lives. We hadn't taken ten steps before a combat team was done to near-instant death by the Little Girl's summoned dark playmate.

Some thought running around in one of my background apps didn't want to know anything about the reality the Wild Thing came from.

Not at all. Not ever. I had this feeling that if you did, that meant you'd done something really terrible. Messed up really, really badly.

Also. Side note. Your mind swears there's some kind of thundering music shrieking out from that void place in the universe from whence the nightmare warrior had come to serve the Little Girl. You'd swear to it. Acid metal. Thunder rock. Put me on the cyber-rack and turn it up to eleven and I could hum a few bars if you left me for more than a minute.

Which is technically illegal in most prison systems.

My mind remembers it. I just can't recall it now.

The universe is a dark, and very weird place. Stuff happens.

As Stinkeye likes to say when anyone, me, mentions something strange and unexplainable, "Ya ain't ken half of it, Little King." And then he hits his iconic totem flask by which most of the company weighs their fate and sighs, "Not by half. They some crazy out there in the big dark you no never wanna meet."

The terminal all around us shakes violently as we reach the top of the escalator and race for the bar. Choker waves to us frantically. He's holding here. As we run, he disappears, weaving into the blackness behind the once shiny and polished corporate drinking lounge.

He ain't waiting. He's smart. Not smart enough to get out of Reaper, but smart enough to know when everything's gone to hell in a handbasket.

The Wild Thing detonated some kind of weapon down and behind us that blew out one of the walls down there. Like the lower levels suddenly got hit by a bunker buster dropped from a destroyer in orbit. Hearing protection struggles to contain and eliminate the strident decibels that suddenly shriek and crash, and the Little Girl falls ahead of us, cutting herself on broken glass along the marble floor.

I can hear more automatic gunfire behind us.

They're pushing despite the carnage.

The *brrrrrrt* goes long and strong again. Grenades are used.

I scoop her up and run as the terminal groans, threatening to come down even if the drops are coming in to pull us out. Gas lines explode deep within the belly of the place.

"He'll be okay?" she screams at me.

It's a question. Or was it a statement? I enter it in this record as a question. That somehow makes her more human. And less prophetic. If she's a prophet with access to wherever that thing comes from, I don't want to know anything about that religion. But maybe, as I think back, she says it like a statement, even though her big dark eyes still tell me it's a question.

I run, carrying her. Hauser dumps more ammo as we make the bar. I don't see the targets, but I trust his aim. Still, more rounds race around us from other directions, convincing me they were storming our positions with advance tac teams.

They knew we'd be tough to dislodge. They hit us from a lotta sides.

The Little Girl wipes the cut on her face and smears blood there.

"Come on!" I yell at myself as I reach the stairs leading up. Screaming at myself that I'm not tired, strung out, and frightened to death by the real and the surreal. I ain't got time to die today, I try to tell myself, as I dig down and see if I've got any more left. Enough to get us up to the roof and the LZ. And onto the drops.

We make daylight and see the drops coming in. Chief Cook is holding out two popped purple smoke grenades. Marking the LZ as the hovering warships come in close to pull us off. The smoke undulates and blossoms and I think it's the most beautiful thing I've ever seen. Regal and free and the opposite of all the darkness and death we've just left down there to the Wild Thing.

But maybe that's the last of the drugs shrieking like a mad homeless holy man in what's left of my mind.

Strange Company Reapers, those that survived, are hustling forward to load the first drop down on the rooftop LZ. A squad from Dog who came in aboard moves to secure the wounded and the dead. Establishing the temporary perimeter as the first drop, laden with criticals, heaves off the roof and howls away into the last of the yellow afternoon. Door gunners chattering death to anyone who dares oppose their exit stage left.

I put the girl down and signal Choker to get her on the next drop.

The captain is crossing from the Dog squad sergeant who came in with the drops. Punch is tapping the helmet on his comm at the same time he's shouting out the orders he received from the Old Man.

The captain. Iron-gray hair. Wicked scar running down his face from eye to chin. Half-burnt cigarette in his mouth. Old brown leather trench coat flapping in the blast from the drop's hover engines.

He's got one of his forty-fives out. He keeps two. One in each coat pocket.

"Sergeant Orion," he shouts as we get close. "We clear down there?"

He wants to know if we're waiting on any more of Reaper still down there.

I indicate we are not. The dead were dragged out. Punch updated our roster as he secured the LZ. I watch as the next drop roars hover engines and comes in, shrieking like a banshee. Beyond this the HK circles, lobbing missiles and targeted auto-cannon fire at anyone trying to push our LZ from around the terminal.

This won't last long. That HK goes bingo on ammo and this mercenary squadron will pull out.

"Tell 'em not to leave us, sir." I swear and use a slur regarding mercenary aircrews who are notorious for going to full throttle when it gets too hot.

"Negative, Sergeant. They're in it to win it. At least until we're all aboard." He casts one washed-out sun-faded blue eye over his shoulder, glancing at the pilot in the drop that has just come in and put down. A woman. But even with her flight helmet on she's beautiful. You can tell. Otherworldly beautiful.

I didn't know it then yet, but that was the first time I saw the Monarch known as the Seeker.

And there have been times since where I wish I never had.

They loaded So-So's body aboard as the armored OD-green drop idled her powerful squat engines and the crew watched us from behind the shark-nosed canopy of the flight deck. Punch and Boom Boom worked fast to get him on. So-So. I saw his dead face for a second, and then just his boots as he was laid on the cargo deck.

Maybe he was the lucky one that day. He got out early before the Seeker had a chance to make her madness. Before she tried to make us into something we weren't and were never supposed to be.

Before she tried to make me believe.

CHAPTER TWENTY-THREE

Drop Zero Six Valkyrie was just climbing off the roof of the shot-to-hell terminal when the first fast movers streaked across the battlefield and smoked a bunch of air assets including the Valkyrie One Eight—the HK model on overwatch. A rain squall came out of nowhere as the clouds above flashed lightning, changing eerie colors for an instant. Rain crashed through the open cargo door, dousing us with hot droplets. It felt dirty and oily. Burning like the acid rain on some worlds.

I heard the star scream of the Monarch interceptors as they came in fast. At the same moment I heard the massive thunder break in the skies, snapping and crackling all around us. All ambient noise got suddenly weirdly quiet an instant later. The only sounds that stood out, at least to me on the deck of the drop, was the sound of the comm chatter between the pilots and Resistance combat air control, which was still operational despite the total rout going down along our line. I could hear that and the chatter of the door gunner, a bitter chick with a mean mouth dragging a cigar as she worked the swing-mounted minigun. Swearing violently, she mowed down the first of the Loyalist troopers to hit the roof and try to take us out as the rattling dropship went to engines full and heaved off the LZ, blowing purple smoke and drooling brass from her door guns. I watched the minigun erupt, sending supersonic ball ammo in high doses straight through the roof and the first enemy combatants to make the LZ. Raising their combat rifles to try to get lucky on a drop's inductor fan as they got smashed by supersonic fire. The minigun ruined them all and then we were suddenly up and over the battlefield watching all kinds of enemy units race forward to exploit the breach in our line. From here the situation looked much worse than I was already worried it was.

So, we had that going for us.

That was when the first of three Monarch fighters streaked over the battlespace and dusted about thirty air and ground assets in a sudden streak of random explosions. Monarch fighters are the best and latest in military hardware. They move like graceful angels of death doling out destruction without discrimination or effort. Both sides got hit. Both sides died near instantly, bewildered that victory, or defeat, had just instantly turned into something far worse.

I didn't see Valkyrie One Eight get hit. The HK drop riding shotgun on our dustoff. Just saw the flare of the explosion and the sudden orange iridescent hell glow wash over the wounded and dirty of my platoon clinging to the deck of Valkyrie Zero Six.

"Dayum!" swore Punch as the aircrew tried to check for survivors in the burning wreckage of the sister ship now smashing into the field west of the terminal. The co-pilot was already sitrepping an alert and calling for air rescue. Bad day getting worse.

Yeah. Like air rescue was gonna happen today. Today had just officially become cover-your-butts day.

By the time I cranked my head around and saw the burning wreckage of One Eight pile into the tall dead grass, tumbling end over end as it disintegrated all at once, throwing burning fuel and parts, and body parts, in every direction, it was clear no one had survived that sudden crash.

The Vals, as they were known, Silver Valkyries officially, a close air support mercenary dropship company with no small amount of guts, had just lost two crew members in the downed HK drop.

The chick flying our drop, the stunning beauty with the otherworldly eyes I'd seen on the LZ, was over the drop's comm and telling her flight to stay on task.

"Vals, watch your sectors and get me a loc on those fast movers. They'll be back in less than two minutes. We've gotta make the emergency LZ in less than that!"

Then she said a thing that stunned me, stunned everyone, and made all the weird anomalies in sound and air all around us make sudden sense.

"Monarch Battle Spire entering our airspace now."

CHAPTER TWENTY-FOUR

"Those are Avengers!" shouted Punch as another flight of three Monarch state-of-the-art interceptors streaked across the battlefield once more. Explosions developed along the enemy front like sudden cherry blossoms in some kind of new apocalypse bloom. My mind wanted to believe somehow the game had changed for us. That defeat which should have been victory was now somehow victory again.

But the massive leviathan now entering the battlespace over our heads at somewhere around ten thousand feet made notions of victory pipe dreams. This was bad. Real bad in fact. And impossibly, getting worse by the second.

The war on this world was officially over even if no one had said it. And for that matter, the odds indicated Strange Company was done with its time on the galactic lens.

"Thirty seconds to LZ!" shouted the crew chief over the drop's comm. "Comin' in hot, ladies!"

She meant us. Strange Company. The actual body stackers. But we were hitching and so of course we'd endure abuse. One of mine did spit some dip on her boots though.

I was proud of that guy.

Meanwhile it was chaos inside the Valkyrie drop, despite the small victories of spitting dip on someone's shiny combat boots. Stuffed with Reaper wounded and Dog security, those of us who were mobile were hanging on to the cargo straps and trying not to fall over and out as the ship took evasive maneuvers just over the battlefield. Alarms shrieked from the flight deck and I had a real bad feeling one of them indicated missile lock from those sweet-looking death birds the Monarchs were now flying all over our battlefield. Correction—it was *their* battlefield now. Keep up on current events, Orion. Y'all just got your teeth kicked in.

The dropship's engines howled urgently. I knew what this was all about. Even though I'd never seen a Monarch Battle Spire in all its terrible glory, few living had, I knew what was going down all around us. They called it "First Pass." The Ultras were asserting dominance of the field. Every combat unit, friendly or foe, was considered an enemy target during what the Ultra Marines called First Pass. Their chance to kill everything before the demanded surrender.

In other words, for the next few hours, or days, or however long the Ultras felt they needed, surrender wasn't an official option. Though I had heard rumors that sometimes loopholes existed. I'd also heard there was a planet made of solid gold out beyond the Mutar Nebula.

One sweep over the battlefield to destroy everything. Ultra tradition demanded this be known as the Field of Death and that nothing grow or be built or thrive there for one hundred years to acknowledge the supremacy and totality of their martial force.

It must be fun to always be the winners.

"Maybe we'll get a chance to tangle, Sarge," said Puncher, running a systems check on his weapon and not minding that the pilot was flying so fast, and so low, and so recklessly that we were probably going to smash into something in what remained of the last thirty seconds of this flight.

Everything screamed that things were about to end incredibly badly. I could feel it. And I'd felt it before. But this time I was probably right.

I couldn't take my eyes off what I was seeing below and out the door of the cargo deck, sometimes sideways even. Entire tank and mech platoons suddenly got ignited by fuel-air bomb strikes, cooking the crews inside and turning the landscape into nothing but scorch and char. C-beam strikes came down from the heavens and ripped the terrain up where there had been advancing lines of Loyalist infantry mixed in and fighting with our side. The shock of bright high-energy multi-gigawatt fury scarred the retinas as you looked away from the sudden destruction. Entire divisions had just been melted, the realization scarring the mind worse than the retinas. In their opening moves the Ultras did unimaginable loss of life. If just to get your attention that local fun and games were over. The mind didn't want to...

And this was just their opening move.

Interceptors streaked down even as the Battle Spire was still finishing execution of her mysterious jump between the stellar gulfs of the universe. The *space-fold*. Rumors abounded that the Spire was the only ship with fold-capable technology. Were they launching their strikes from that amazing behemoth? Or were there assault carriers rigged for stealth and dumping troops and ships to support the entry?

It was like watching the most fantastic military operation ever witnessed until you realized with horror that you were about to be on the receiving end of all that violence. In the movies, the Ultra Marines were always the heroes saving civilization from the hordes of darkness and the greedheads who wanted to own their own destinies and enslave the colonies rather than submitting to the glory of the Monarchs. In the movies, massive music scores always accompanied this triumphal moment when the Battle Spire entered the scene in a desperate bid against seemingly unstoppable galactic evil. As the hero Ultras raced to the jump decks and flung themselves toward the world below.

In the movies they are always the heroes.

The hour is always desperate.

And the bad guys always die.

It sucked to be the bad guys. Apparently we'd be playing the part of the bad guys today. So it sucks to be us for what's left of us.

Across what I could see of the line of combat, ours and theirs, both sides were still trying to kill each other regardless. Maybe the Loyalists thought the Ultras were here to support their victory. Maybe the Resistance didn't see any other move than to just keep on fighting. So they just kept on fighting. Maybe not for any kind of tactical advantage, probably just to get away from the arrival of the Monarchs' premier fighting force. The Ultras. I watched a running battle between a tank battalion, one of ours, and an anti-vehicle mech's high-pulse lasers, closing and burning armor-piercing incendiary heavy rounds just to get clear of the engagement zone and the First Pass.

The battles down there were schizophrenic.

No one knew how big the declared First Pass Zone, an official thing, would be at this moment. It was the whim of the Imperator overseeing the Ultra Marines. In a few hours, as the generals from both sides managed to establish diplomatic relations and sue the Ultras for peace, the details would become clear. But right now, in the first moments of total chaos as all cowered and shivered beneath the arrival of the monolithic Battle Spire, sure their end was at hand, the finer points of one's survival weren't clear.

Ultras and Monarchs are way above my pay grade. But I knew what every merc on the battlefield was thinking at that exact moment. *Show's over, folks. Time to get your pay, if you can, and get off-world. Real quick.* Re-education and time on the cyber-rack's a real bummer. Ask anyone who can't remember their real name and how they ended up on some world they had no history on working for the mem factories as little more than a paid slave.

This was why the drop we were in was streaking for a nearby LZ as fast as its engines could scream. Any craft in the air over the battlefield was considered a huge priority target for Monarch air-attack assets. The drop all around us rumbled and shuddered as the reversers kicked in to full and the hover engines throbbed, landing gears deploying, medics trying to hold on to the wounded and comfort the dying.

And still I could not take my eyes off the amazing Battle Spire above us.

It was the largest thing I'd ever seen in my too-short life.

I'll describe it for the record. If the record survives. Because right at that moment, I wasn't sure if Strange Company would. No one survives First Pass. No one survives the Ultras. We were dead and the worst part was most of Strange Company knew it. But what else were we gonna do but keep trying to survive for as long as we could?

The central hull of the immense Battle Spire is long. Very long. There is no ship humanity has ever constructed that even approaches its size. At least the size of New Manhattan City on Sakur. But, for the record since that is what this is, I've heard there are larger Battle Spires. The *Red Dragon* is supposedly the biggest. At that moment, watching the monster heave into local airspace, dropping several armies and combat teams all at once, I had no idea what this one was called.

The aft section of the Battle Spire is wide, where the engines should be but aren't. The local-space maneuver engines are all along the hull. Its main engine for motive transport throughout the universe, the fold engine, is supposedly deep within the ship, but no one knows for sure because no one's allowed to get close to a Battle Spire. Automatic death sentence. But whatever and wherever it is, there's nothing conventional about that engine. It's one of the most closely guarded secrets in the Monarchy.

The aft section, rather than housing the main engine, presuming it doesn't, is for the immense hover and a-grav converters that allow the Battle Spire to set down tail first and establish an overlord tower from which to continue the destruction of a world. It's like a wedding cake top to bottom but moving horizontally in this configuration at ten thousand feet as it executes the space-fold and enters the time stream in the skies above our heads to begin the invasion. The hull races forward up there, tapering at the extreme end, the bow, into a series of command blisters that form the bridge and finally the navigation needle which conspiracy theorists say is critical to the space-fold engine located deep within the immense ship.

As I understand it, the central hull is all Monarch blue. The main hull is brilliant white and dotted with glittering lights that come from the inside and seem to be small cities crawling along its tapering cylinder. All of it run, crewed, and lived in by the ship's complement of beam gunners, transport officers, supply chiefs, and air attack squadron pilots both sub and orbital. I have no credibility in guessing the size of the crew complement, but if I had to, I'd put it at upwards of ten thousand. But I could be off by a hundred thousand. The mind fractures looking at the immense size of the ship that has come to kill us all drifting into the skies above our war like some casual end of the world come to make good on its promise.

That's not totally correct. The ship will kill *some* of us. The Ultras will kill the rest. That's how it'll go from here on out for what remains of this world's last gasp of self-rule.

If the magnificence of the incredibly long central hull wasn't just a universal wonder in and of itself... I mean seriously, how do they build these things? Mega-corporations can build city-sized orbital refineries or bulk cargo haulers, and of course small destroyers, cutters, liners, and the scouts and free traders. But nothing even approaches the incredible size of a Battle Spire.

If anything, its very existence makes the argument that the Monarchs are better than the rest of us. To build a ship of that size defies every known science. And yet... there it is. Moments from raining down a thousand different forms of death on our heads.

One of our wounded just died on the deck of the Drop Zero Six. Maybe two minutes from getting triaged by Chief Cutter's medics. Now he'll go to Preacher. I watch as Choker shuts the eyes of the dead man.

As I was saying, if the central hull wasn't enough to make you remind yourself to close your jaw and stop gaping like some slack-jawed local yokel, then it's the Ultra Battle Rings rotating independently about the hull that make you dizzy with fatal wonder.

I don't want to look at the dead man on the deck or remember his name. Or ask myself if I got his story down in the logs. It's all too much right now. So I look at the fantastic death machine I'm being given the rare privilege of actually seeing during an invasion. As I've said, this is a sight reserved mostly for the deceased of other forgotten battles.

Death and wonder don't mix.

On this Spire there are five. Five battle rings. Again, I've heard other Spires have more. But five is more than enough to assure us of our imminent destruction. The rings are not attached in any way to the main hull. And yet they encompass its diameter, rotating languidly like some magnetic levitation art installation inside a mem zillionaire's private tower on one of the Bright Worlds.

These rings are where the Ultras are.

Even now as I watch, mechs, walkers, and actual airborne are being dropped all across the battlefield. Combat teams, strike divisions, enforcers, inquisition squads, death squads, special forces, armor, artillery, and drop commandos. Departing from the drop, jump, and combat cargo decks.

It's raining death out there.

It's beautiful to behold if you're given to grim fascination and your mind just keeps whispering in the background, low enough so you can ignore it completely, that *you're all about to die*. Then, yes, it really is fascinating to behold.

They come down like falling stars, the big mechs that will soon form the main assets of their attack and sweep during the First Pass. Walkers with GAU guns and missile packs. Big walkers with 140mm main guns and anti-personnel chain guns. Heavies with Maas Gausers and A-beams to sear right through structures and boil any defenders inside.

Small dots like swarms of dark birds race through the drop formations.

"Drones!" yells Punch over the howling engines as the drop slams in hard to our new LZ.

"Down! Down! Down!" screams the drop's beefy crew chief. "Don't forget yer bags, ladies, that's the last flight of Air Val. Every man and woman for themselves."

We've come down inside a supply yard near the main city that was supposed to be our follow-up target of exploitation if the attack on the airfield went well.

Which it didn't. Obviously.

I slide off the cargo deck, dragging my rifle and ruck, and the beefy Val crew chief is next to me. Her voice low and husky. A woman's voice.

"We'll help with your dead, Sergeant," she says. The opposite of how she'd been on the ride over when I'd begun to hate her for calling us ladies.

But she's a woman. And women never stop caring, nurturing. It's hardwired into them. Even if they are warriors. They always care for the wounded bird.

I must be that bird, I think, as we begin to remove our dead from the floor of the bloody cargo deck.

The Battle Spire moans on some ominous hum high above us and sunlight breaks through the storm front and another squall of hot acid rain sweeps across our tragedy. Side effects of the space fold phenomenon, I am told.

"Incoming!" someone shouts uselessly. The air feels hot and electric and it's clear the Battle Spire is about to fire one of her big six-gig D-beams. If it's going to fire anywhere even near us, we're dead. No "suck dirt" and cover is going to stop that thing. It's like getting hit with a nuclear blast ray. And honestly, no such thing exists for the rest of us. If you're going to go nuclear, it's a bomb just like it's always been since the beginning of time. But somehow, the Monarchs developed that technology into a death ray they can just turn on and off. The D-beam. As bad as it gets.

The ship above our heads, surrounded by swarms of dropping war machines and comet-streak infantry smoking in hot to make the LZ their Pathfinders have set up, fires at some distant target. Probably the naval carrier group off the coast because the D-beam strike doesn't hit the city we've come down in the outskirts of.

Otherwise we'd all be dead, and all our problems would be solved.

"They do that, Little King, to let ya know who da bosses are," says Stinkeye, who's come to help as we get ourselves off the decks of the dropship. He's come up with Preacher, the Strange Company chaplain, to retrieve the dead.

The First Sergeant is telling everyone there's command brief and change of mission in ten, near the First Sergeant's Mule.

I watch death fall from above as a thousand wonderful and terrible Ultra death machines and uber warriors awaken to their purpose. The hour of the First Pass is at hand. I hear Stinkeye whispering, his voice breathy and gasping as he and Preacher get So-So's body off the deck of the drop.

"Now you know," he says. "They boss. No room for doubt, Little King. They boss. We just the dead now."

CHAPTER TWENTY-FIVE

"Change of mission," begins the captain ten minutes later. He's burning a cigarette and pointing at a tactical flexy he's got set up on the First Sergeant's Mule to show us our route out of this dog of a contract. The platoon sergeants and squad leaders are surrounding the Old Man as the briefing goes down, never mind the war breaking out all around us.

Ultra artillery is already shelling the mem fortress some local traders financing this conflict had set up inside the capital. Far away heavy machine-gun fire thuds across the landscape. Small explosions. Grenades. And then the fusillade of assaulter gunfire, frenetic and high cycle, as the Ultras begin neutralizing their first targets.

Whoever's fighting back is dumb.

But that's their story and not mine.

The Old Man is calm. But he looks tired. Then again, who ain't. It'll be dark soon and it's starting to rain. Showers and electrical storms courtesy of the mysterious space-fold engine.

We're at a supply depot that had been set up inside the city for our eventual conquest. The captain and the Old Man had decided to hop, skip, and jump behind enemy lines and hit the depot instead of running for the hills like the rest of our Resistance employers and allies.

"Contract's over, Strange Company," continues the captain as we all listen in silence over the screech of beam strike and thunder of outgoing artillery trying to hit and slow down those running from the justice of the Ultras. "Company is facing two problems at this moment. The first is our employers have decided not to pay us out and are declaring the contract unfulfilled. Our lawyers will have to argue that out with them for the next ten to twenty years. As all of you know, we needed that mem to get over to Blackrock sub-light and get the *Spider*'s hyperdrive repaired. So, we are currently broke. Not the worst problem. But not good because funds might not be available at Blackrock for the repairs. Which was the purpose of this whole contract."

The captain gave it to us straight and looked us right in the eyes while we took it. It's best to be honest about these things. If anyone wanted to complain or walk away, now was the time. Wasn't much of a choice because right now the Ultras were going to annihilate every combatant they could get their hands on for probably the next three days. And if they even suspected you'd been in combat they were going to bring in the Inquisitors and you were gonna face the cyber-rack for a good three seconds and you'd tell 'em everything they needed to know at one.

The two extra seconds was to make sure you thought real good and hard about lying even just a little.

As one guy I knew who'd had some firsthand experience with the cyber-rack put it, "It's forever in there."

Still, without saying a word as the Old Man smoked and watched us with his faded old blue eyes, scar, and iron-gray hair, daring us to walk away from the company, he was at least giving us that chance.

"Second problem is the *Spider*, as you all know. Besides not being jump-capable at this time, she's also not atmo-capable. XO thinks he can get in close enough to do a high-altitude sub-orbital transfer if we can get up there. As you can see…"

He gave a brief nod toward the assault troops, thousands of them still raining down planetside from the behemoth above our heads.

"… these drops would be shot down if we even tried. So here's our plan. First Sergeant has commandeered supplies and transport here at the depot. Draw immediately after this briefing. We roll in thirty minutes. Full convoy to the refueling station at Plethy. Hard takeover and we top off on energy cells. Then we break up into teams and take different routes out into the Crash Wastes. Our destination is Lost Road. It's not marked on any map. Our new employer will be downloading maps to the platoon sergeant after this briefing."

A few muttered at the news of a new employer. Most of the rest just exchanged glances. A few of us were too dead tired to do anything.

"Yes, the company has fortunately received a new contract offer as developments have taken a new turn in the last three hours."

Did he emphasize the word fortunately?

That's unlike him. He's so dry. He doesn't even do sarcasm.

Strange times makes strange things happen. Even the Old Man is not immune.

He didn't say anything like, "Hey, and now I'm gonna be honest with you," or anything like that. Wasn't his way. If he said something it was the truth. If he didn't say anything, I'd learned that's when you needed to be worried.

"Our new employer is a Monarch. She calls herself the Seeker."

A few murmured.

No one I knew had ever even seen a Monarch face to face. It just wasn't done. They didn't do that.

"She has a plan for us to get our owed mem out of our employers, provide her a service, and get off-world to at least effect a sub-orbital rendezvous with our ship."

He looked around, inhaled what was left of his cigarette, and flicked it at the ground, watching the ember burn for a second before he crushed it out with his combat boot.

"This is dangerous. If you want to take your chances with the Monarchs, there's supposedly a refugee collection point that's taking combatants, no questions asked. And I think there's a high-chance probability a lot of us are going to get killed trying to stay Strange Company and get off-world in the middle of an Ultra invasion. That just doesn't happen. But when I took command, I swore on John Strange's name I'd keep the company together. So, I gotta do that. Even if I do it alone."

Then he turned and walked around the First Sergeant's vehicle, heading into the darkness of the supply depot that was like a dark open mouth waiting for a meal.

The First Sergeant stepped forward and someone must have asked, "Where is this Seeker?"

"Over there, boys," he said, not grandly. But big in his own way. I, and I guess the rest of us, followed his gaze. Over to the dropships. The gorgeous flight leader, tall like an uber model for some mem zillionaire, still in her flight suit and holding her helmet with one hand, was handing out devices, payment devices to the remaining Valkyries. Pilots, door gunners, crew chiefs.

Then she turned and began to walk toward us after picking up a little wicked submachine gun and a ruck, and throwing her flight helmet off into the mud and light rain.

I was not alone in thinking she was the most beautiful woman that ever was.

CHAPTER TWENTY-SIX

The briefing broke up as most went back to what remained of their platoons to explain how bad the situation really was. Slick, the Ghost platoon sergeant, stood there with me exchanging meaningful information. Ghost had taken only one KIA. Soops. I'll get to his story later if there's time.

"Good scout," said Slick as we finished our smokes, watching as the First Sergeant had his men start directing Hannibal's Dogs toward the supplies he'd laid out for them. Then he had Amarcus, my personal villain, in tow and was headed straight for us.

"Boys," he began grandly to his three platoon sergeants. Voodoo didn't have a sergeant. No one knew how the hell Voodoo ran. We only knew it did. Mostly. "This is where things are gonna get real improvisational. That Monarch jazz ain't gonna sit well, and you might want to brace everyone. She just signed the auto doc to join the company. She's in, and that was part of the whole messed-up deal. But the only way I can see us gettin' paid and gettin' ourselves the hell outta here and clear of this mess is just to go ahead and let it happen. Captain ain't sayin' nothin' but I don't think he likes it none too much either. I ain't gonna ask any of you if you got a problem with it because as far as Top is concerned you don't. Got me, boys?"

We got the First Sergeant.

Then he looked at me.

"Sar'nt Orion. You got her. She didn't want Voodoo and Stinkeye's already threatening to desert. There's gonna be trouble between them two. So she's with you, and she's running our operation once we reach Lost Road out in the Wastes. Reaper's tip of the spear on this exit."

That's... great.

"Copy, First Sergeant."

I watched Amarcus smirk, his wicked scar telegraphing his amused contempt. He shrugged his cut-down Bastard model. Everyone in Dog worked the shorty. Extremely violent, accurate not so much. Sergeant Hannibal preferred the kinetic violence concept as opposed to good shooting. Aggression over marksmanship.

He wasn't wrong. It was just a choice in a scenario of limited resources. The company needed about six months to a year of training to get everyone where I wanted them. But... that just hadn't been possible. And as Amarcus likes to tell everyone, "Orion wants a perfect universe, not the one you actually gotta go kill people in."

He said that to my face one time. So we had it out. Later, it was chalked up to too much Arcturan rye and half-price pitchers at the bar where we had our little disagreement. But I'd only had one shot and I knocked out one of his fake teeth.

To his credit he left it out and every time he "smiles" at me he makes sure I see the gap. Like he's letting me know there's some payback coming down the line one day.

Every time we talk, I slip my index finger into the ring of the karambit I carry in my pocket. I practice every day with it and when I do, executing combos and putting the tip of the extremely sharp blade into the xiphoid process... I see his face.

So, there's that.

Then I added, "First Sergeant, Third is no longer a squad. Just Hauser and Nox. Second and Fourth are down to half each if we don't take the seriously wounded. So I'm folding Fourth into Second and adding what's left of Third to First. That gives Reaper two squads. You still good with us taking point?"

"Affirmative, Sergeant. Doc Cutter is putting the wounded into stasis bags inside the crawler with Sergeant Biggs."

He turned to Sergeant Hannibal.

"Your boys will be surrounding the supply crawler, Amarcus. Need you to keep any enemies off of them. We roll into the top-off point Reaper moves to secure. The perimeter of the station. I'm marking three roads into that point. Right now, recon drone says the streets are packed and the main line for top-off is six clicks long heading down the road into town. We're bypassing that. Reaper, go in hot and secure the two roads at the far end of the station. Amarcus, hard take over and we top off the crawler, command vehicles, then Reaper, then Dog, and finally Ghost comes in with the captain as the QRF in case we get jumped. Once he gives the all-clear we break up and follow our routes. Meet at Lost Road to reassess the plan and proceed on to the bank robbery. You boys got all that? Now c'mon, I got some super-charged Mules sportin' fifties you guys are gonna dig. Was supposed to go for some special ops merc team that never made it through to planetside. Drop got lit up on insertion and last I heard they were all dead out to sea."

He smiled and adjusted his pistol belt.

"So, we got that goin' for us."

CHAPTER TWENTY-SEVEN

I got Punch on the draw. We were topping off on ammo, explosives, and some armor plates that were supposed to be experimental. Which was good. Most of our plates were shot to hell or cracked straight up. The vehicles were slick. Operator black. Twin turbos with some sort of nitro fuel-air burst system that could really get the vehicle moving. Armored, but still open. The vehicle commander position in the right seat came with a mounted minigun and there was indeed a Suupmann fifty-cal system mounted on the gunner's deck in the rear.

Punch would get both squads portioned out between the three vehicles we had. What remained of First Squad was just Punch, Choker the medic, Hustle and Hoser with the Pig, and Boom Boom who'd taken a round in the leg but was still walkie-talkie. Folding in Hauser and Nox gave me a solid First Squad. And the Kid. He was still good to go. He'd kept his head down and his powder dry. There just wasn't time to start to figure out his tag. But he was close. After his time as a New Guy. I'd have to talk to the others if we ever got a chance.

The new Second Squad, a combination of Second and Fourth, consisted of their squad leader Jacks, along with Dip Weasel, Killer Joe, and six guys from Fourth who'd managed to keep themselves alive despite So-So getting killed.

My mind was still trying to figure out how to run my platoon in its new configuration, assault and support, and I needed to inhale some chow. I felt too wired to ever sleep again even though I was exhausted. But first I left Punch and went to see about the company dead.

I found Stinkeye and Preacher in back of the supply depot. There was a patch of bare ground near an old fence. The bodies were laid out and the wind was beginning to blow. Explosions to the west and south told us where the Ultras were coming down to start the death scythe of their First Pass.

"Won't be long now," muttered Stinkeye as he leaned on a shovel he had no intention of using. So-So was there. Others from the company too. Gains had been too badly burned to pull out. But I'd sent comm to Astacia Esquival, our company lawyer and account rep, and started a claim to have his body retrieved and eventually delivered to a cemetery company funds had already been set aside for. We'd lost thirteen on this contract since it began a year ago. Before today. The bodies from today would go there in the end.

Above our heads the Battle Spire loomed. More strike firefighters were sweeping off her carrier decks to hit targets all across the world. I'd been close to this moment before. But only weeks away. One time the company finished a contract that was going bad, got on the *Spider*, and hauled away. The Monarchs and Ultras showed up two weeks later, and now that irradiated nuclear wasteland of a world that was once called Blue because of its beauty is now just marked as off-limits on the stellar charts.

"They be bringin' in a bank ship in the next few hours," muttered Stinkeye as he hit his flask, didn't work the shovel, and stared up at the giant Monarch ship, whispering curses like incantations under his hot breath.

"You don't know nothin' 'bout nothin', Little King. No one does."

Preacher was moving down the line. Kneeling over each body bag. Murmuring a few words. I watched his work. No one believed in anything. But they all needed to know he was doing this. I saw guys hauling out cans of 5.56 and belts of 7.62. Fifty, also. Crates of grenades. Like we were going for sabertoothed bears on Cylor instead of running for our lives on a world called Crash. Not Astralon. That game was over. Mark it so on the maps. As the men lugged, I watched them cast quick glances at Preacher. Watching his work no one believed in. Needing it all the same.

More freak squalls of hot rain coming down off the giant ship swept the yard, leaving everything wet and sticky. Strange gusts and breezes would come out of nowhere and wash over body bags, blowing Preacher's white hair. Titanic noises and lights in the clouds above that made you feel small and desperate.

Preacher.

Yeah. He's some kind of holy man. But he doesn't shun weapons. I've seen him show up at the most convenient of times in the middle of a battle to start blazing away with his sidearm or carry the wounded out of harm's way. Or jump on a gun whether it needs a gunner or an AG.

I asked him what his story was once, and he said he didn't have one. How he'd come to the company. What he was running from. That last part was implied. But everyone knows it's there. He told me he was forgiven of all his story. That he didn't have one anymore.

I asked, "What do I put down in the logs when it's your time to go?"

He just smiled and replied, "Oh, I don't know. You'll know, Orion. Maybe say something about how he preached what he believed every day without ever saying a word. I'd like that. I'd like to be worthy of that."

And then he added, "And say the part that's true, Orion. Put *Strangers to the universe. Brothers to the end.*"

I watched him going down the line, doing his work, telling the dead what they needed to hear.

CHAPTER TWENTY-EIGHT

We rolled out two hours later. As usual, with an invading force closing the noose and breathing down our collective necks, the candle burning, the clock ticking, all the tense metaphors you can do, we sat in our new rides, waiting to be told which wire to cut. The green or the blue.

That too was a metaphor.

Apparently, we were still getting satellite drone data showing Ultra positions and the general state of play regarding the invading force. If things had looked bad as the game changed, once the picture came into focus, they were just downright awful. The entire Resistance line had been smashed from one end to the other. Now friendly units were either on the run and had lost all cohesive integrity, or they were surrendering en masse and hoping for some kind of mercy.

These were usually units that had no experience with the Monarchs, and especially the Ultras, and therefore didn't understand that the term *mercy* was as foreign to them as the sun might be to a deep shark on the icy world of Graymist. We watched one unit get taken into custody and five minutes after they'd piled their weapons, they were lined up and shot. Also en masse.

Ultra Marines are ruthless killers. And they're pretty efficient about it. I'm sure there's a whole SOP for mass murder of every type somewhere in their training manuals. That and much worse.

The Old Man fed that live feed out to the squads so everyone could get a good look at what their fate would, not might, be if they did indeed decide to try that particular escape route from the unfolding endgame of this lost conflict. If just so Strange Company knew, and just so we didn't have to recruit too much along the way or wherever we got our next chance. Remember, the company is always recruiting. We don't stand on any kind of ceremony. Even while we waited in the lead vehicle, we watched a line of sappers, combat engineers from Astralon herself, guys that woke up this morning and thought they had a real live chance of being on the in-charge side by the end of the day, retreating. Really it was fleeing just as fast as they could hump. The First Sergeant who was pulled up alongside Reaper in the lead vehicles where we were waiting for the order to move out, shouted to the retreating sappers as they passed.

"Hey, kid! What unit you with?"

"Three-six-five," says the guy tiredly.

First Sergeant back to me whispering, "We could always use more of them guys in case what's-his-face gets blown up."

"Jacks," I clarified.

"Yeah, him. Good with the H-E but you never know. Explosives are fun but they're real unforgiving if you know what I mean, Sergeant Orion."

I did.

"Heard you guys got into it real bad a couple of hours back," said the First Sergeant, turning back to the sappers on the move. "How's that sergeant who ran supply for you boys? We traded him some rations a while back."

"Prolly dead," said the sapper, who'd paused to stand there and shift back and forth in his worn combat boots while answering Top's questions. "Before the unit comm went down an Ultra hit team got the TOC hard and fast. Whole command section got wasted. Gotta hump, First Sergeant, sorry. Heard there was a drop that could take us to a bulk hauler up-orbit carrying refugees. It's our best chance now. Gotta—"

"Ever thought about merc'n?" asked the First Sergeant like some used speeder salesman talking about a low down and high finance with E-Z credit. No payments for a year.

Guy shook his head and hustled on. He'd been warned by someone who knew better. Or he was just tired, had had enough war, and was hoping some hauler might get him "home" in sixty or so years. The bulk of all-star travel, and especially the haulers, is sub-light. Meaning it's a long hop between worlds and home might not be there anymore. Especially if they paved over your neighborhood and put up a starport.

The First Sergeant went on that way for most of the line. Three guys joined though. Right there on the spot and the First Sergeant took 'em back to the supply crawler to see what they needed in the ways of gear and as much company indoc as he could shove into 'em.

"I'll keep 'em with Voodoo, Sergeant Orion," he shouted as he drove 'em off in a spray of mud and rain. "You got a lot goin' on tonight. Don't need new kids to add to the chaos."

I drank the cold coffee I'd brewed up in my smart canteen that had stopped acting so smart about halfway through this war. It's a drug and I needed drugs to keep doing my job.

I was feeling, even as the rain began to patter and I just sat there in my poncho trying to get ready to get it on, that there would be a lot more *get it on* tonight and I needed to be ready.

You know how it is.

I knew we were supposed to be moving soon, but I still hadn't linked up with Reaper's latest squad acquisition, the Monarch known as the Seeker.

Which was too much to even contemplate in the early evening rain and gloom with nothing but cold coffee and a smoke. Nox was now my driver. He was scrolling through his smart device and trying to get onto any net. They were all collapsing or dead. One was showing the standard Ultra battle flag, crimson and black with a silver Spartan's helmet undulating. The words "Surrender and Prepare for Judgment" glared out from the tiny device.

"Well that's just…" But I was too tired to finish and so I just inhaled the last of my smoke.

When she showed, it was both whelming and underwhelming. The Seeker.

As has been stated in this account she was like some otherworldly creature that walked among mere mortal men. She was tall and beautiful. Graceful and definitely used to being in charge. The huge green eyes, large, almost like a Katari's, stared into you and glittered with intelligence beyond your imagining. It was hard, staring into them, remembering that somewhere back along the evolutionary tree both of you shared some kind of common DNA. You almost laughed at yourself for being a rube that would think such a stupid thing. Really you just wanted to stand there and drool and promise you'd kill anything for her.

Rumors swore that Monarchs had advanced pheromone control. But some women are just beautiful enough to cut a chump for regardless of chemicals. So, there's that.

Her cheeks were sculpted. Hair a lustrous, almost arterial bleeding red. Curves in all the right places if you know what I mean. A face that could launch a thousand Battle Spires. If there were that many.

And I sure hope there aren't.

"Sergeant Orion," she began crisply. There was a passive use of some kind of tone that she was better than me as we stood there in the developing mud listening to the Ultra Marine gunfire get closer and closer. Street fighting was only blocks away now. House to house. It was time to move.

And she *was* better than me. She was a Monarch. Near immortal. Elite. Each of them owned their own world. They had seen and walked on ancient Earth. We worshipped them even if we didn't admit it.

And I was just some soldier with my fair share of scars and bad tattoos. And that thought settled me right there. Drove off her chemicals. I blew smoke in her face and swallowed the last of my cold coffee from my not-so-smart canteen.

"That's me."

No comm from the captain yet. Were they recruiting more grunts looking for any port in a storm?

Yeah, no active use of superiority, but it was clear she was better than me. Which, like I said, ain't saying much. But she was also better than everyone else. So much better, she didn't need to make sure you knew it.

"We'll be working together," she began, "on this portion of the mission until we reach our first objective. I'll ride behind you in this vehicle and advise you. You are in command of your section, and if you have orders for me, I'll take them. I'm here to help, Sergeant."

Well, that knocked a little wind out of my hardcore-tough-bro-soldier act for a moment. Truth? That's other guys. I'm more of the beaten NCO who sighs and looks off toward wherever as you tell him the next problem he's got to jump all over before everything catches fire and we explode in every direction.

She dumped her gear onto the cargo deck of the Mule and stepped in, long legs in tight Combat Skin, a type of nano-fatigue I thought was only for sci-fi end-of-the-universe movies. I'd heard it was rated to stand up to small-arms fire and stabbing wounds. It also did a bunch of other tricks I'd never find out about.

But on her it looked like she was camouflaged half-naked where her chest rig and battle belt didn't cover.

But hey, no one knows anything as they say, I told myself as I ached with every move she made. Today I thought we were about to see the end of this contract in some kind of power position, and here we are running for our lives.

So be it.

I climbed in and it was go time. Comm was already coming in from the captain to roll out. We'd be five minutes ahead of that convoy.

Get it on, Strange.

Thirty minutes later we hit the refuel point. I sat there the whole drive wondering what she was gonna add. Super-Science Voodoo Monarch Space Magic? That's what they do. Watch any spectacuthriller and see one of them mow down hundreds of hapless enemies with rifles that never need to be reloaded. Complex karate moves that never fail. Sliding gunfight kills that seem pretty easy unless all your muscles are wasted from humping rucks and the dozens of injuries Motrin-X don't do a damn thing for. Oh yeah, and close-quarters weapon takeaways and combat kills all while maintaining an incredible amount of energy and focus despite bullets flying in every direction.

Yeah, it's all movie tricks. But how much?

Sitting in a speeding, souped-up Mule rocking a nano-cooled fifty as the rain and the night whipped past my dust- and blood-caked face, with a living god slash death machine on your six and knowing you're about to get it on real bad, makes a man like me think about things I shouldn't. Lusting after her. How tired I was. And that I needed to stow all that in my mental ruck because Zero-Get-It-On was fast approaching.

And Reaper needed me.

I'd lost enough dudes today. Their faces swam past in the darkness and I shook my head and told them I didn't have time to say I was sorry for being such an awful leader.

Later. I'd get to that later if later ever came. If it didn't... well, problem solved for me.

When it got bad six minutes into the refill as we got hit by an Ultra scout sniper team no one thought should be around, she surprised all of us on a lot of levels.

CHAPTER TWENTY-NINE

The rain had stopped by the time we reached the main refueling point for most of the vehicles still trying to flee the main capital city. Assault troops, too, had stopped raining down from the massive Monarch battleship looming in the skies above, but drops and larger transports were now starting their landing operations. Explosions and intense firefights fell behind us while strike fighters and bombers began to hit distant targets farther and farther out from the center.

The feeling of a noose cinching around your neck was both distinct. And intentional.

Broadcast stations were sending nothing. Nets were down. We passed the ruins of a burning star liner that had been shot down and had scattered itself all over a wet field out there in the early dark. There didn't seem to be any survivors. Only flames and wreckage that embodied waste. A waste of life. A waste of a war. Zero gain. No winners. Everyone was a loser. Except the Monarchs. But of course everyone had to have known that all along.

More questions came from this line of thought and I shoved them away with a disgusted gesture. Pushing them out the speeding vehicle and away into the night and the wind. And sometimes the rain.

A superhighway we'd been calling MSR Lifeline was clogged with heavy traffic ahead. In the long months of the war for this world it had been designated for military use only. But now that the war was unofficially over and the Ultras had come to deliver judgment, every vehicle, both civilian and let's just call them former military, had clogged all lanes and decks. Fights had broken out and the losers lay lifeless alongside the roads. Refugees hustled between the cars on foot, convinced they still had a chance.

Whatever had passed for society on this world was gone. It was everyone for themselves now. Mercy was in short supply now that it was valuable.

Our objective, the fueling point, lay right alongside Lifeline near the eastern edge of the city, in an area that had avoided much of the war due to its supply yards being heavily defended. The objective was a bulk fuel and energy distribution point for heavier traffic. Whoever was keeping it alive sensed their moment to clean up every currency anyone had left on hand to push at them. They probably thought they were making a killing.

They were also playing with their lives. Gambling with really bad odds getting worse by the second.

I'd have told them they were just looking to get killed. But I'd given up telling people how to live their lives a long time ago. I never liked the feeling it left inside me when they didn't listen to what I had to say. *Billed for advice not taken* was the phrase I never muttered but thought about just the same all the time in these situations.

Resistance defenders were nowhere to be seen in the last ten minutes of driving as we reached the fuel point objective and I began to get sitrep data from the drone someone in Voodoo was running beneath the low cloud layer. The situation on the objective was grim yet under a loose kind of control. We identified the players and what needed to be done for a quick and hard takeover to control the refuel point. A couple of armed gangs, probably former military from both sides, were shaking down as many of the civvies as they could while everyone waited as virtual prisoners to refuel. They could be handled, and since Amarcus and Dog were gonna be doing that portion, some tough guys who preyed on the weak in this time of crisis were probably gonna find themselves dead. Suddenly. They had no idea what kind of monster was headed straight for them. I did. I could have warned them. But I had my job to do.

Sergeant Hannibal didn't fool around. Again, whether I liked him or not, he got stuff done. And he was about to draw a duty I didn't like. Controlling an out-of-control mob while trying to rob them at the same time.

The part that bugged me was that he, Amarcus, didn't mind it one bit. He seemed born for this post-apocalyptic unquestionable warlord total power grab. It was natural him. And that's what scared me to death about Amarcus Hannibal. That's what made me keep the karambit ready at all times for the one chance I'd have to use it on him. We'd tangled a few times. I knew the next would be for keeps.

It felt like a promise.

Sheer chaos the closer you got to the refueling point. Shootings and worse. Scattered goods and even burning vehicles. I could only imagine the dawning horror most of these people were now experiencing. If they were here in the main capital, they were Loyalist-friendly, or at least Loyalist-adjacent. They'd been fed a steady diet of propaganda about how they were going to win and then the "healing and reconciliation" with both sides would begin once the Astralonian Resistance had been put down from wanting their selfish self-rule and celebrating nebulous terms like *Freedom* and *Liberty*.

Now they were getting a dose of what they'd intended to do to those on the other side. Because of course all the "healing and reconciliation" would go just the one way. It always does. It's just a nice way of letting one side know they have no other choice but to accept the terms of surrender. The losing side bending the knee and exposing the neck while the winners rake the prizes and goods with that smug sense of self-satisfaction as they rule from the near-top of the heap. The Monarchs were the undisputed top of the pile of course. But near the top was just good enough for every non-Monarch citizen of the universe.

Near the top was a dream of many.

This was standard propaganda straight from the Monarchs. Once you were on the winning side it was Easy Street. Believe me, there was an upside to planetary revolt. Once the Monarchs settled things, those who'd figured the right side were gonna be in for some serious prizes. Big Prizes, as they say.

Propaganda worked because it told you what you wanted to believe. That was the secret.

Like the spectacuthrillers that showed evil, our employers on this one, being defeated. With extreme prejudice of course. Constant news-entertainment feeds filled minds and hearts with outright lies about the state of the war. They were always winning, even when they lost. Always smarter, even when they got caught flat-footed in stupid corruption. Always honest, even when some report indicated they weren't.

There was no evil that couldn't be walked back, massaged, and even justified to those who wanted to believe it bad enough to stop thinking for themselves. The ends do justify the means. Especially if there's no one left to complain.

"If ya step back and look at all the individual pieces, Orion," crowed Chief Cook as he swaggered around teaching some imaginary psyops lecture to everyone, "you'll see it in all its grand mind-control glory. You see exactly where they're going with it. But they know that. On some level they know they're being controlled. So what do we do? Well, here's what we used to do, is keep 'em destabilized by giving 'em new sensational stories every four days. Moving them this way and that but always in a certain direction we want them to go. A conclusion we want them to reach. A fever we want them to arrive at and be suffering from. For instance, take the plague on Demmeron Six. Great. Blame it on the opposition. Ratchet up the fear with hazmat postures. Make the little kiddies wear masks, hell, nothin' sadder than seein' some little tyke playing with a mask on. Really gets you in the feelz and makes you wanna punch someone in the face. Then, oh my what's this, we blame the whole thing on the guy who's actually trying to point out that the Monarchs' bioweapons teams released a virus to hit the elderly and wipe out as many of them as they can. The guy who's trying to help. He's the one that caused it all by his lack of skill in handling the crisis we created. Why do this? Twofold. One, you get rid of the dole-drain to Life Assurance direct from the Monarch coffers, and two, you wipe out the wisdom database most of those oldsters have in which they could advise the young'uns about what they're doing to fight for freedom. Those oldsters have life skills, plus twenty-five percent of them are combat vets from the Sindo. So win-win is how they always see it. And you get to blame the opposite side by never taking responsibility for anything and keeping everyone in a state of constant crisis. Let the world go into resentment and dissension and then do a little proxy war. Next thing you know, you got Ultras takin' names and kickin' people in the teeth. Battle Spire… check. Then the bank ship rolls in and you suck the world dry of hard convertible mem."

Then he told me, "The Monarchs don't do this for anything but the mem, buddy. It's all about the mem, as the kids say. Never kid yourself about that, Sergeant Orion. If you're gonna believe in anything, and I highly advise against believing in anything, believe that it's all about the mem. You'll be less unhappy that way. Emphasis on *less*."

Yeah, I think to myself as we drive down the refueling line, five clicks long now, passing vehicles filled with frightened eyes just staring out at us while other vehicles are being looted at gunpoint. Yeah, they're just now figuring out they're all losers on this one. Even us. Even the company. The Ultras have arrived to give us all a school lesson on who the real winners are.

Spoiler. It ain't us.

"Establish our perimeter at the junction," I say over the comm as we pass the not-so-brightly lit cargo refueling station that's been left open by someone in this last and latest of most desperate of hours.

Explosions rip through the sky to the west. Huge mega-tonnage explosions light up the low cloud ceiling and reveal leviathan mechs like monsters walking in the night out there on the horizon. High-intensity targeting lasers sweep for ground targets. It's the stuff of nightmares. It's the end of a world if there ever was one. It's right now whether anyone likes it or not.

And for the umpteenth time I try to do the chain of events that has me here and now.

"We're too close," says Nox as I direct him toward the center of the three-road intersection we're to hold for overwatch while Dog and the crawler come in to top off at the refuel point. Nox swears about how close we are as we watch those night monster mechs closing on their objectives out there. Missiles streak away and devastate a building half a mile to the west.

"Someone musta been putting up a fight," he mutters, leaning over the wheel, his face hard and mean in the bare light from the instruments. He's not even thirty, and he looks like a mean and bitter old man already. Give him five years and he'll have a ruck hump and be chewing light painkillers with every meal. But if he's still alive he'll be known as a mercenary everywhere he goes and there's a certain kind of cool in that. For whatever that's worth.

I'm beginning to wonder that it might not be as much as I used to think it was.

I turn around and stare at the Monarch behind me. Prompting her to illuminate us regarding Nox's observation that someone is still fighting.

"They have an attack profile matrix," she says coolly in the waiting dark. "Much of this phase, initial planetary assault entry, is nothing more than an advanced full-spectrum terror campaign. There's not a sane unit commander alive who thinks he, or she, stands a chance against the Monarchs' executioners at this moment in the assault. There are a lot of lies told in the universe but the Ultras are not one of them."

"Then what are they doing," I mutter as Reapers Two and Three, and the other Mules, move into position as we arrive at the position we're supposed to hold. We'll support each other from here and be ready to react to anything trying a fast attack on the company from any of the three road directions. Also, we hold the route out of Dodgeistan. We aren't taking MSR Lifeline. We're heading east into the Wastes. We're departing from the known. Even the most desperate of refugees would avoid the Crash Wastes. It's sort of a Vanished Triangle in the Ho Nebula meets Desert of Despair kinda place from those spectacuthriller movies about the ring and the boy wizard who becomes a sparkly vampire and kills a werewolf.

Not a very nice place. I'm pretty sure there's no beautiful actor boys and unreal actor girls. It's just all forsaken lands and cracked earth that occasionally spews forth lava and burning salt. I've heard it even rains rocks out there and there's supposed to be some local predator that's pretty nasty. Hunts in large packs.

A real no-go zone no one really wants to go to in the first place.

"Then what're they doing lighting everything up? Hasn't everyone pretty much surrendered?" I ask her.

"Clearing a space for the Battle Spire to set down, is my guess," she says. The Monarch. The Seeker. "Even though the a-grav fields will crush the city flat, they don't want any detonations underneath. No one wants six kilometers of starship suddenly toppling over once they set down to start the uplink with the bank ship."

So Chief Cook was right. I'll have to tell him to get a prize out of the prize drawer. They're gonna suck the planet dry of all the war-accumulated mem.

"Has that ever happened before? A Battle Spire going over on its side?" To my knowledge it never has. But remember, ninety percent of the knowledge database in the galaxy is nothing but complete and pure Monarch propaganda.

"Once," she says as she watches Dog's vehicles surrounding the crawler as they come into the refuel point at high speed. Hostile takeover of the pumps going down. There's shooting, of course, because it's Amarcus's show. The rapid bark of the shorties Amarcus's men run. It's harsh and cruel. But…

"Them's the times," I mutter tiredly as I watch Strange Company swarm the area and take control. The crawler heaves in and the lines are disconnected for both fuel and charge. It should take ten minutes just to get that massive thing topped off alone.

The night feels sweaty and hot. Like it's gonna rain more. But it hasn't yet.

Thirty minutes later, two gang fights have killed several people and the captain had to come in with the quick reaction force just to shut that down.

I have no real idea what's going on over there by the main refueling point other than the chatter coming over the comm and the sudden unstable bursts of frantic and frenetic gunfire mixed with bare single-shot pops that feel wanting and pathetic.

"Somebody gettin' done in the head?" asks Nox, who's more interested in what's going on over there than what's not going down in the dark streets we're oriented toward.

"Targets acquired," says Hauser over the comm and just above my head. He's on the fifty in our Mule.

"Who?" croaks Nox.

"Where?" croak I, the sergeant in charge, at the same time.

"Building at two o'clock. Fifth story, Sergeant," says Hauser automatically. "Two. Sniper and observer. Deep in the room. I can engage with one burst and am calculating a ninety-eight point six for initially fatal hits in first strike. One hundred percent achieved with successive use of at most ten more rounds."

Hauser's targeting system is state-of-the-art.

I'm almost on the verge of saying, "Light 'em up, Hause," when she stops me with a gentle yet surprisingly cold hand on my shoulder. The fingers are long, and the grip is firm. And it's not unpleasant.

"I wouldn't do that yet. That's a scout sniper team, Sergeant. Standard Ultra hunting group is three teams and a rifle assault team staged nearby for cleanup. Death squad configuration. Ask your cyborg to scan at seven and eleven. I'm checking also on visual…"

"This is bad," mutters Nox. "What if they're just gonna call in an airstrike on the whole place? Do everyone! This whole block will be one giant fireball, man!"

Yeah. All that. It's going to hell in a handbasket and suddenly I've got decisions to make. Let Hauser loose and trigger the ambush. Identify as many tangos as I can and wait to figure everything out. Walk away and take my chances all by myself out there in the dark and rain. Maybe smoke a few cigarettes and run up the score against the Ultras themselves. There's a certain dark attraction in the anonymity of such a doomed, off-the-rails last run. Maybe one last chance to really feel alive before death or the re-education rings.

I decide to at least call the First Sergeant and let him know the Ultras are in the AO and ready to party.

"Don't," she says as I tap for the First Sergeant. Like she can see the comm data projected in my combat lens on the surface of my eye. "Ultras have every channel hacked. Even yours. Have for months. They never hit a world without being in total control. Sometimes they are even in your units serving as grunts. You call this in, and they'll know they're blown. Their commander will have two options at that point. Release the death squad they've probably got stacked nearby, or just do the whole objective with the gunship on station." She points into the night. Up there in a cloud front. "See?" she says. "Wraith on standby orbit. Their commander gets the word and they'll unload everything they've got right down on top of us. Endgame."

Oh boys. This is way above my pay grade.

I push back in my seat, tighten every muscle, count to five, and then release. It's a technique I picked up a long time ago. It's also a stall to see if someone will figure out something for this poor dumb sergeant to shoot at instead of forcing me to pick a target.

Honestly, I'm happiest, if it has to be combat, with just good ol' movement to contact and bounding overwatch. That's just a dance and there are rules to play it by. If you follow 'em you might live. And I like that. The simplicity. The steps. The math. The promise. I can do those things.

"So what do we do?" I ask.

"Sniper team acquired at ten o'clock," says Hauser. "Rooftop. Sniper setting up. Spotter scanning for targets."

When Hauser's report is finished, she adds, "Team three at seven. Right where I thought they'd be. That's the trap, Sergeant. This whole place is about to become a shooting gallery."

"And?" I ask, not a little pissed off.

She's quiet.

"You're aware time is probably not on our side," I prompt her. "I need to let the rest of Strange know they're about to get hit…"

She holds up a hand. Stopping me of course because she's a Monarch and I'm just me.

Two Avengers streak right over the top of us and I think, *Welp. This is it.* And wait for a cluster bomb to ignite the whole station in a ball of fiery death. Or maybe they'll just sew a cluster minefield and we'll all see which one of us can get everyone else killed first.

Nothing happens. We don't die in the roar of their passing wake. They were headed for someone else to kill. Plus, there's that heavy gunship in the clouds just waiting to rain steel. I barely see its lights way up there. Sometimes I don't. If I remember my weapon platforms right, the Wraith carries three twenty-millimeter cannons among its other weapons with which to rain down death upon all of us for several grid squares. It's even got a heavy artillery piece.

I know for a fact that that ship has some kind of motto stenciled on the side about running but not being able to hide. Or just dying tired.

Fun, huh?

"Listen, Sergeant," she begins. "That death squad is going to come down one of these three streets once the snipers start working. They don't want to use the gunship because they'll lose the refuel point and right now, until the Battle Spire sets down, they need easy resources to keep expanding their control sphere as they start combat operations. You have to hit those teams and be ready to react to the Ultra death squad that will come in to clean up. I don't know your unit's capabilities, but that's how it will go down in the next few minutes. Ten at most. I'm estimating five. So make your response in the next two."

"And how do you know this?"

Silence.

Then, "I commanded an Ultra division during the Sindo. Narak Desert Campaign."

Uh... is what I don't say. That was two hundred years ago. I also don't say that because that would make crazy sound even crazier. But that's not important right now. What's important is dealing with this developing turkey shoot.

"Hauser, dismount and take out the team at ten position using urban guerilla warfare protocols."

This means he'll try to do it by stealth and surprise. One man against ten Ultra Marines. Odds no one would take. A definite death sentence. But he's not a man. He's a combat cyborg optimized for such missions.

This is his actual wheelhouse.

"Affirmative, Sergeant," says the killing machine I call my friend.

"Need it done in less than two, buddy."

Hauser retrieves his secondary weapon. A Bastard with a high-cycle drum magazine for max output of subsonic ammunition. The huge suppressor makes the weapon even longer. He uses this weapon system exclusively for surprise attacks as the Pig is usually too loud and much too obnoxious.

He nods and trots off into the darkness.

That's one team I'm hoping is mostly handled.

I tap for Nether. Ten seconds later his disembodied voice is in my ear. Though I have no idea where he is.

"Where are you?" I say in Pan-Numerical. I speak a little. Nether speaks a lot. We usually talk in it just so no one listens in on what we're saying. Nether likes his privacy. I try to learn things just to pass the time.

"Abeam the refueling of the crawler," he replies in our preferred language. I'm betting the Ultras monitoring this channel, at least local, don't speak Pan-Numerical. It's considered a dirty language by the Monarchs. Anyone at Ultra Strategic Intel, probably running a station inside the Battle Spire, is going to have to run a translation program, assess, and then interact with unit commanders. That might buy us a couple of minutes. "Thirty meters out in the dark. Watching the street to the south," finishes Nether.

That's our back trail. I spot his location, see nothing, and realize why he's not aware of the snipers. They're right above him.

"We got probs. Big ones. Ultras are in the AO and setting up to start knocking us down. In..." I twist my wrist and check my cheap watch synchronized with Hauser's hit. "A minute thirty-seven, Hauser's hitting one of their elements. I need you to do your thing and make them go away in the building you're shadowing in. They're five stories right above your head. Northwest corner. Can do?"

Long pause in which it sounds like I'm listening to the emptiness of the universe.

I turn back to the Monarch.

"You ever work a fifty?"

She nods without giving me some stupid CV about how hardcore she is. Yeah, I'm in lust with her. But that little bit makes me respect her a lot more. Every spectacuthriller I've ever watched, the infinitely talented female ninja killer has to give you some ridiculous history of how badass she is. It's tiresome and standard for all Monarch propaganda. But this Monarch babe just nods, and as I flash my eyes upward toward the gun, I hear my own breathing start to get rapid because *get it on* time with the Monarchs' elite fighting unit is about to begin. I can feel it in the air.

I've done a lot of things as a soldier with the company. But I've never fought Ultra Marines. Few people living have.

Because few people who do so live.

One minute.

I don't see Hauser.

I'm hearing a dull buzz that's starting off where Nether is. I scan the darkness in the streets beyond the junction, trying to figure out where the Ultra Marine death squad will come from. That would be nice to know.

The buzz has turned into an ominous hum. I've heard it before. Bad things happened.

"Can do," whispers Nether and then is gone from the comm.

I tap for our chief Voodoo troublemaker. Stinkeye doesn't speak any other languages except Stinkeye pidge. So I gotta chance it.

"Go…" he mutters darkly.

"We're about to get hit."

"Yeah. Felt it, Little King. Know where's from?"

"Our twelve at the junction. Plus we got snipers. But I need you here to deal with their assaulters coming from our twelve."

A powerful boom erupts from the tower above Nether's position. One of the special high-powered rifles the Ultra snipers are rumored to use has begun to speak. Suddenly there's screaming around the pumps. The mob that had been pressing on Dog trying to top off goes wild and scatters in every direction.

"On da move," hisses Stinkeye as general comm goes nuts.

"Player's hit!" comes over the comm. Someone in Dog is calling man down. Automatic gunfire erupts.

"Engage the team at two o'clock," I yell at the Monarch in my gunner's position. Without hesitation she opens up and the fifty-cal begins to *thud thud thud* thunder as she sends rounds and tracer fire into that position.

I check my watch as I switch to on and scan the darkness ahead of us. If their assaulters are coming, they'll come now.

"Stand by to repel forward, Reaper!" I shout at the rest of my bunch. Then I remember I've got a minigun in the driver's seat. I lay my rifle aside, slide in, and swivel the deadly little chunk of a weapon out and forward, checking the feed and racking the first round.

"Hause…"

Nothing. On the rooftop where he should be, I see and hear nothing. That's probably good. And as I watch the first Ultras I've ever seen in my life sweep out of the darkness ahead, in two teams, and moving like ghosts out looking for souls to steal, I aim the weapon at them.

I open fire with the minigun firing 7.62 from all six barrels. It blurs outbound lead and I need to adjust range as it does so. At this distance the Ultras' death squad, a specific unit type that handles specific functions and tasks, is little more than shadows of larger than human size.

Death squads are the Ultra basic rifle unit. They wear heavy armor plating over their arms, chests, legs, backs, and feet. They have helmets that look like modern versions of the ancient Spartan war helm. If you get close enough, or so I've heard, you can see a fiery burning eye scanning back and forth through the visor where the eyes should be.

Stinkeye once said, "Dey a cyclops, little King. Monstahs from another galaxy not this one. No man evah wanna be one o' dem killers. But dey can make 'em. Dat's what the Monarchs do. Make monsters. Just like dey made me."

Chief Cook called him a liar. They were both drunk and looking to go at each other with knives. They've done it before. Both have scars given by the other. Cook's got one on his belly. Stinkeye's left arm doesn't work like it really should because Cook caught him with the knife there one time and it cut real deep. They were both so drunk neither remembered it.

"It's a tac sensor, you old fraud!" bellowed Cook that time we were talking about the Ultra bucket. I noticed he kept his hand in his pocket where he kept the flick knife he used. He slugged his drink with the other. Priorities. Safety first. "It's constantly assessing and interfacing with the Combat Skin they wear over their faces, you dumb spook. They see the whole battlefield in ways we don't, Stinkeye. Hell, it might as well be damn magic as far as we're concerned."

True enough, I thought as I pressed the firing button on the minigun and tried to carefully murder them. Some clown in the background circus of my mind giddily chiming in that I was probably going to kill half of them the way normal guys die when you burned two hundred extremely high-cycle rounds in their direction at this range. Not Ultras of course. But the clown of infinite possibilities laughs insanely at this bit of reason and merely tells me to just enjoy the fun of full-auto gunfire whoopee.

They moved fast. The Ultras. A little faster than humans. Scattering to get away from my burst. Some got hit. Bright flashes indicating glancing blows from rounds that would go through an engine block and then kill a roka boar gone mad on savage weed.

The clown in my mind who'd been giddy about killing everyone now cried out in melancholy at my failure to commit mass death. Oh well, he moaned and twirled away as he chased a balloon while I watched the Ultra death squad mostly survive my hail of gunfire.

The clown was probably some of the drugs still coursing in my system. Yeah. That's it.

"Team One neutralized!" shouted the Monarch in the silence once the fifty stopped killing. "Switching to engage forward!" she barked like a boot drill instructor.

I had no problems with that.

The rest of Reaper was engaging forward. One Ultra was down in the open as the Ultras out there disappeared into the shadows, their armor shifting camouflage to adapt to light and shade for maximum concealment. Return fire came and Nox died with a hole dead center in his head. Still sitting there in the driver's seat.

They say the Ultras are all next-level shooters.

They say true.

I was gonna die.

We were all gonna die.

CHAPTER THIRTY

The Kid slid out of the back of the Mule and began to fire short, controlled bursts at something. That made me happy. I was hoping he had targets and wasn't doing that new guy thing of just contributing bravely with wasted ammo. Motivation and fear mixing for the sublime cocktail of *Hey, I saw a guy do this in a spectacuthriller once.*

Questions I would ask if I had time, and there wasn't any due to incoming:

One. Was that guy in the spectacuthriller just some rando who got killed by the main dude and went down looking good? A stunt guy and not the hero? 'Cause the rule of thumb is stunt guys are always dead guys. Just sayin'.

And two. You realize that's just digital entertainment, right? Simulated surreality. Real gunfights, in real reality, are short and violent, said the sergeant now into the first full minute of an actual gunfight with real live Ultras and wondering when the adrenaline was just gonna peter out and leave him real tired. And out of ammo.

Above me the Monarch called the Seeker was sweeping the street with suppressive fire. I felt a rumbling through the frame of the high-speed vehicle and realized it wasn't coming from her weapon. It was coming from the ground beneath my worn combat boots. A round and a couple of its friends skipped off the pavement nearby around our ride and made me wonder what it would be like to have my ankle or foot blown off right about now.

This was too much like a fair fight. And I hated fair fights for sure.

"Quake..." I murmured as I fumbled in a new mag, my fingers feeling thick through my assault gloves even though I'd cut the index finger on the glove off.

That finger was trembling like Monarch action heroes don't in the latest spectacuthriller.

Then the building Nether was near during our initial comm interaction just collapsed in on itself, imploding in dust and moaning steel at once in an almost underwhelming and unceremonious anticlimactic moment. He'd created a null space in reality beneath the foundation and just dropped it. The buzz and the hum were gone, and I realized they'd been there, building like some unholy atonal orchestra of the damned through the first moments of the gunfight. That had been pure Nether and it had gotten so loud I'd had to block them out over the high-pitched whine and blur of the minigun. The weapons system I was now dumping as much as I could at the enemy from my hiding place down in the well of the passenger seat. Incoming rounds were nailing the Mule and making small explosions or sharp cracks. Spider-webbing the high-impact glass and smashing into the armored engine block. Later I'd find out the explosions were a result of the vehicle's reactive armor skin. Small explosions on impact directing the force of the rounds away from the armor and critical systems.

These things were way above Strange's pay grade. Too bad for that special operations det that got blown all over the sea. Good for us.

I had doubts we'd roll out of here in this thing. Serious doubts.

But then again, I had hopes. If just to have something to hold on to.

I was fear-swearing when I told the Kid to use his 'nades.

A couple seconds later I heard the spoon pop on a fragmentary grenade and clatter on the Mule he was covering behind. At that moment, out over the city, doomsday sirens began to open up, finally moaning and then wailing at all the horror and violence that was being done. I don't know if that had anything to do with this fight or if someone had simply finally gotten around to sounding the general alarm usually reserved for stray comet strikes, falling meteors, and bad starship re-entries. Not that you could do much about those. Not that you could do much about Battle Spires either.

"Grenade out!" Kid shouted like a good soldier. I swore and gave an Ultra surging right at us everything the minigun could do. Some kind of shield shimmered to life as that cat went down on one knee from multiple hypersonic impacts.

I whooped.

I'd hit one. Damaged him at least. Hey, it wasn't a kill. But it was something for our side.

The Kid's grenade detonated off to one side and blasted straight into that one. The Ultra rocked, absorbing the detonation with most of his armor. He stumbled. But he didn't go down.

I stopped firing in stunned disbelief.

Not. Down. From. A. Grenade.

This is like fighting a fight you can't ever win. Which would make it not a fight. But rather a received beatdown. I think too much. I've been told that before.

I swore and spooled up the minigun.

The guy stumbled some more, regained his composure and began to advance, waving with one arm in the standard infantry leader *Follow Me*.

"Eat this!" I roared and held on to the jumping, blurring minigun exceeding the safety parameters as all six barrels went forbidden popsicle. Turning into bright glowing sticks of molten heat. Smoke obscured my vision, but I was sure I was landing hits.

Then I was out of ammo.

And the guy was down on his back, riddled by hundreds of smoking holes. Somehow, we'd collapsed some kind of personal defense shield and cracked his armor integrity.

More of his kind swarmed in response. The Monarch hit one Ultra in the bucket with the fifty at twenty meters and blew that guy's head off, even as the rest of his armor got racked by fire and the shield shimmered and distributed damage as best it could.

You could kill 'em. But the ROI was expensive.

"Belt change!" shouted the beautiful Monarch above me. The vehicle was getting dinged by incoming fire, but she was working like it was just another training exercise. Flip feed tray. Clear feed tray. Drag a new belt out of a can. Attach belt. Open fire once more.

I crawled on my belly forward and fought from behind the ceramic tire of the Mule with my Bastard. Armored run-flat ceramic tires make good cover. I knew that from past experience.

I applied good marksmanship where I could and killed none of them. One of the other Mule teams from Reaper, Jacks's team I think, deployed a grenade launcher and began to ruin their left flank.

One of the Ultras dropped to one knee, cranked a long canister from off his back and onto his shoulder, and fired a recoilless rifle round.

I heard Jacks yell, "Run!" and everyone did in the seconds before the guy pulled the trigger. A moment later that Mule exploded but I was pretty sure someone got killed.

I slithered backward, got to my knees, and shoved a new magazine in.

"Full auto it is," I told no one and popped up and dumped on the nearest Ultra. I didn't stick around to see what I'd done to him as I was back down and working a new magazine in. That was when Stinkeye hunch-ran up and slammed into the Mule's rear, near my position, gasping heavily and reeking liquor and weed.

"Looks real bad, Little King."

"Grenade!" shouted the Kid, who then amazingly grabbed the Monarch off the gun and pulled her down behind the Mule for cover like he was trying to impress my new crush.

Good for him.

Dark thoughts of every NCO told me the Kid was gonna dive on it and be a real hero. A dead hero. But when you're young, being any kind of hero is enough to make you do something stupid and try to save your friends.

One time, this guy we had back on another gig dove on a grenade that landed on our rooftop sniper overwatch. Buzz saw it come over the top and roll toward the center of the building's roof. It was a hot desert world but the guys were fighting like hell to use a lot of AP. Which was good for Buzz. We were all wearing as much armor as we could, and as little clothing as possible because that place was one giant furnace. Some guy in Ghost even wore a short dress and when everyone made fun of him, he told them it was a native kilt from his world. But we thought he was just making that part up. Anyway, Buzz dives on the grenade like a real hero, except it was an EMP device. It shut down all our electronics until we could boot them again, and we had to fight iron sights for about twenty minutes, but we got them back up.

Buzz had jumped on the device thinking it was a grenade. Sacrificing himself for us. His brothers. His reward. We laughed at him and started calling him Buzz because after that he had a real bad ringing in his skull that he said he could feel in his stomach. It never stopped until he got it on Blue.

We were grateful in our own way. Yeah, we laughed because it was really too much to think about. How close we'd come. What he'd intended. Sometimes you just have to laugh at the serious stuff because if you don't, you're afraid you'll lose some kind of edge.

And that's the only way to survive as a merc. Always having an edge. Like I said, I want nothing to do with a fair fight. That's the best way to lose.

The explosive the Kid had alerted us to went off and rocked our Mule, detonating on the driver's side. I felt blood on my bicep. I'd gotten a hot scratch. It had also slashed my Grim Reaper Astronaut tattoo right in half. Time would tell if that looked cool, or just ruined it beyond recognition. If I got killed like it was looking like we were all about to, then who cared.

Right?

I heard the soft purr of the eel girl and regretted I'd never hear her again. She'd asked me once… *"Can you have no regrets, my* estrangier*? In zis life? Are zhere none?"*

And now I knew the answer. Or at least I thought I did.

I had choices here and none of them were good. Behind us the crawler was rocketing off into the night. Dog was pulling out to cover the retreat.

The captain was in my ear on comm.

"Reaper, what's your situation?" Dry. Cool. Calm. Collected in a gunfight.

I tapped the comm and covered one ear.

"Reaper's holding the junction, sir. We got Ultra rifles at fifty meters and closing. Wounded and dead."

"Pull back. We're rolling, Reaper."

I didn't know if that was possible. I hoped it was. But I didn't know if it was.

I looked at who I had on my side of the bullet- and explosive-riddled Mule. The hot Monarch babe. The Kid. She had her sidearm out. The Kid was rocking his Bastard and watching the far corner of the vehicle for us to get flanked. Behind us, the other Mule that had been hit, burned. Mule Three was still active and engaged.

I looked down at Stinkeye. He was muttering and his old wrinkled eyes were squeezed tight shut. Silver tears ran down his tanned and weathered old cheeks.

Sweet. My Voodoo asset had just gone fetal.

Way to go, Orion.

"Pull back, Reaper," said the Old Man over the comm. "We are leaving this area."

"What the hell are you doing, Stinkeye?" I hissed. The Ultras were closing. I could hear their boots and the dribble of their expended brass. My hearing protection was fritzing out because of the volume of fire.

Jacks came around the side of the vehicle, rucksack in one arm, rifle in the other. I could see he had three claymores ready on the top of his ruck. He'd toss it and det as a last line of danger-close defense. Odds that we'd get ruined too were high.

"You see 'em," muttered Stinkeye to himself. "You see da corpses, da lost souls and all da wretches o' da darkness... come look at what's waitin'..."

He murmured like some ancient wizard casting dark spells. Or the tech-monks of Kal Mandoor chanting code in the early evening as the icy winds sweep across their brutal mountains and high cold monasteries. Promising death and salvation. Life and endless sleep. Code forevermore.

"Da blood and da ruin of all dem murders..." he hissed. He was starting to rock back and forth, twitching and trembling as he did so.

"Is this something, Stinkeye?" I pleaded. "Are you doing something that will pull our bacon outta the fire, or..." *Are you just drunk and deciding the middle of a losing battle is a great place for the DTs?* But I didn't say that last part even though it was my growing fear.

He looked up at the Monarch woman, glaring pure murder right at her. Black murder and rage deep within those red-rimmed, red-veined, cloudy eyes that claimed to have seen the Outer Darknesses. Hate. Endless cold hate was there too.

I'd seen the same look when his gambling went particularly bad. When he couldn't buy a good card to save his life and the whole table was just dunking on him. But this was worse. Orders of magnitude worse.

"You at Leon, whore?" he suddenly hissed at the Monarch firing with her sidearm when she could get a shot off. Then he roared it at her.

"You at da Massacre of Leon, witch woman?"

She ejected a magazine and looked at him like this was all just business and even his semantics and histrionics were part of some horrible game she knew she had to play to get where she needed to be.

Then she nodded once.

"I was, slave." Her voice was cold and cruel. Imperious. What a Monarch is. What they sound like. Who they really are.

Then Stinkeye gave a malevolent smile and hissed evilly.

"Good, girl. Then come to me."

And whether she liked it or not, he reached out an old claw, his wrist adorned with prayer beads and leather thongs. Charms and stray bullets caught along their ancient twining. His dirty fingernails gripping her alabaster skin between Combat Skin and tactical glove. The one holding her matte-black sidearm.

And he jerked his head back and screamed himself hoarse like he was being burned alive from the inside out. Howling and begging like a sick dog.

"What the hell is he doing?" I shouted at her.

She just watched him. Watched Stinkeye like a mother feeding a child. Patiently.

Then she looked up at me, showing me those deep-blue ice eyes like some world that knew only frozen mountains and cold, endless cold. Eyes as wide as those of the Katari hunters who rule a jungle world as undisputed apex predators. Some of the most feared killers in the galaxy.

"He's showing them the dead they've killed. Watch, mercenary…"

And then she looked toward the battle.

I turned and saw sudden shadowy phantoms like the zombies straight out of horror thrillers. They were endless as a dark sea of rotting and raving corpses can be. And they came running out of the darkness, swarming for the Ultras like plague ants, ripping them to shreds. Tearing them limb from limb as they downed them and pried them from their armor for the tasties they might find inside.

The Ultras, closing to extremely close murder range, began to fire at one another, unable to disbelieve the illusion our Voodoo specialist had just created. I could see both things at once. Reality. And the massacres they'd participated in. Whole planetary populations done to death under the merciless brutality of their cold barrels. Except in this trick the dead didn't die like they had. In Stinkeye's vision they kept coming even though they'd been long dead. And then they did worse as the Ultras fought for their lives. These murdered souls screamed all their names and all the death cries as they washed over the death squad like a deep and endless ocean that had more to give than you could ever take. It was horrible and hypnotic all at once. It was real and it wasn't. It was like looking at a crack in the universe no sane person was ever meant to see.

"Time to go," the Monarch said matter-of-factly.

Yeah, it was. I just hoped we could. I crawled into the Mule and pushed Nox's body out onto the street. Never minding that his brains were everywhere and had drooled out across everything. Never mind I was violating the company's most sacred ordinance to take care of him even in death. To take care of our own. There wasn't time.

I heard John Strange in that bar, telling me something I'd already forgotten. That was today, I suddenly remembered even though it felt so long ago it might as well have been someone else's life.

I said a prayer even though I don't pray because sometimes you do even if you don't believe. Was I praying for forgiveness for abandoning Nox? Or that the Mule would start and get us out of this firefight?

As of this writing I still don't know.

The engine fired and Stinkeye could barely get himself in as the rest piled into the two remaining Mules.

The captain's QRF came in, weapons blazing and cutting down the mesmerized Ultras where they stood.

And we roared out of there, stopping to pick up Hauser who was just coming back out onto the street. His systems were bleeding coolant and hydraulic fluid. But he'd survived the gunfight. The nanobots inside him would repair what they could.

I'd seen him hit worse, I lied to myself as we sped away. Off into the night and the rain beginning to come down harder.

Then the Wraith gunship in the clouds above began to fire, unlimbering her one-twenty-millimeter guns and hitting the fuel point with death from above. Turning it, all of it, into a bright apocalyptic bloom as we disappeared into the night and the east.

Strange Company breaking up into three teams to arrive at the hit in three days' time. Five hundred miles deep into a no-man's apocalyptic wasteland ruined by an ancient alien starship crash long ago that had probably happened before mankind had figured out basic rocketry.

Or even longer.

Unknown starfarers never found on any world. A ship whose technology was unknown and might as well have been magic, because even the barest elements of it our best minds could almost grasp were well beyond anything that should ever have been conceived.

CHAPTER THIRTY-ONE

We drove deep into the Crash Wastes that night as the main capital city of that world surrendered to darkness and fire. There were times when we had to go around ruined sections of the outskirts of the city. Bombed-out ruins whose guts and insides had exploded out all over the place while the skeleton of the structure still burned like some condemned criminal on Char-Hallow Night. Or just LDAM craters where Ultra tac strike had decided to delete a grid square for reasons known only unto them. We pulled into underpasses while Monarch HKs hovered over the city like the Grim Reaper Astronaut manifested, and machine locusts bristling with GAU guns and missile packs ran sensor sweeps and looked for something to hit.

We passed no one. Not one soul. The people who had once lived here were either gone now or hunkered deep down in basements and bunkers hoping to wait out First Pass. Hoping to survive.

Reaper was down to two operational Mules after the split. Punch, Choker, Hustle, and Hoser, along with Boom Boom, had survived the last fight in the second Mule. Mule Three, which had taken the recoilless round, lost everyone but Jacks. Some were killed in the strike. Others got machine-gunned down in the aftermath trying to fight their way to nearby cover. Dip Weasel and Killer Joe were dead or captured. Which meant dead as far as how the Ultras ran things on First Pass. Also, the six others who'd been rotated into Second Squad before the last op of the war on this rock were dead too. Dead or captured. Which, again, meant dead. We added Jacks to our Mule and rolled through the night with Hauser, the Monarch, the unconscious Stinkeye mumbling promises of murder, and the Kid at the wheel. We shoved Boom Boom onto the back deck so his wounded leg could stretch out. It was crowded on both rides. One Mule carrying all the extra equipment. I had no idea how the rest of Strange had fared getting out of the refuel point. We'd gone to a no-comms silent posture between elements as we split up. The survivors would link up at Lost Road and try to finish the rest of the mission to get us off-world. If there were any survivors.

Reaper's route was to the south as all three elements, Ghost, Dog with the crawler, and Reaper, headed off into the eastern desert wastelands, literally called "The Wastes" on the maps and charts of this war-ruined world. Fighting throughout much of the conflict had avoided this vast section of the central continent. Most of the occupied and therefore fought-over portions of the world were along the western coast and throughout the southern isthmus. Strategic bombing and special forces raids hit the southern continent because that was a power base for the locals. No meaningful big battles were ever fought there.

But the Wastes were a no-go zone for many reasons, and not all of them ever extremely clear to me. What I had noticed was a conscious blind spot on the part of our employers, the Astralonian Resistance, their generals and war planners, everyone, to avoid any kind of conflict in that vast unoccupied desert. To me, a lowly sergeant, I saw the region as a great big opportunity to move about unhindered and hit deep in enemy lines by using the Wastes as a kind of cover to appear from, and disappear into, all along the enemy flanks.

Call me practical that way.

But no one would authorize anything in the planning. Even the Old Man and the First Sergeant shut down all conversation on the area, especially when little old me would constantly suggest it as a way and route to get things done better. And by better, I mean less chance of anyone getting killed.

I thought about all my dead as we disappeared into the desert wastes 'round midnight.

"That's enough of that, Sergeant Orion," the First Sergeant once snapped at me when we were figuring out how to pull a raid on a firebase that was giving High Command some problems and we were near enough to the Wastes to make them of use.

After that I let it go. I was barking up the wrong tree and no one likes a barking dog.

The closest I ever got to figuring out why, before the night we were just ordered to go ahead and break up into smaller elements and link up deep within the Wastes, was when I spoke to a local native girl who'd been acting as a scrounger for the company. She was trading us supplies we couldn't get through the command chain, in exchange for ammunition, which we could get a lot of because the war merchants in orbit made sure both sides had a lot in order to get this thing settled before the Monarchs showed up.

Funny how it turned out not to be that way in the end. When you thought about it as you listened to the wind and the night in the lonely desert, you realized it was only ever going to end that way. The Monarchs showing up with the Ultra Death Machine kicking things off. That was how it was going to go all along. Where we were all headed, even if we didn't want to admit it back then.

I admitted it now because no one cared anymore. It was done, cooked, shot to hell. So why not? Isn't that the first step in something? Admitting you have a problem.

I could barely keep my eyes open. There was nothing to see and too much had gone wrong. I needed sleep and maybe this would all be just a bad dream even though I knew it wouldn't.

I asked her, the scrounger girl, one time when she managed to scavenge us a case of Rage-a-Hol, this new power energy drink we were all pretty happy with, what the deal on the Wastes was. Why the big mystery no-go zone?

"It's like this, Ol' Boy…" She always called me that. Ol' Boy. I wondered where she was now the game of war was over. Maybe she was dead. We hadn't seen her in three months. One day she just stopped coming around with stuff to scrounge. She was street-type and the term *Ol' Boy* meant something along the lines of *hard boy I respect*. Same as all across the Pan. "You really needa know that area is all *boogedy*. Unnerstanna?"

When I asked her what *boogedy* meant she indicated *haunted, scary, strange*.

"Weird things happen out there. Ain't right things. Stuff don't grow. Bigga scars that go for hundreds of miles. And if you find something out there from off da Crash... well, two things happen to ya. You disappear and no one ever hears from yaz again."

I told her that seemed like the same thing.

She told me in her way of seeing things that was two different things that could happen to *yaz*. I thought the point was moot and let it go.

"What happens to those people... salvagers or scavengers... I'm assuming... when they find something off the alien ship? I mean what do you think *really* happens?"

She looked at me like she was assessing a deal. Weighing out how much she could take me for, or how much I could be trusted.

"Listen... don't know. Don't wanna know. No one likes to talk about dat here on da Crash. It's like... it's like we know we ain't s'posed to talk about what goes on out there, so we just don't. Kenna? But you know how it is... kids and drunks always gonna spill the savage weed. So things get said. And what I think... hear what I think, Ol Boy. I think bad things happen if you finna thing outta there you ain't s'posed to. Rico, the old man who steals the Rage-a-Hol you guys dig lotsa lotsa... he drink da mezex way too much at night down by da rivers... he say if you find something out there you kenna get to be a Monarch. Or as rich as one of dem canna make ya. See the Monarchs, says Drunk Rico, they want what's there. They got a secret base out there and he say everything ain't what it's s'posed to mean when you seen and known it. That it ain't haunted so much as jes' real dangerous to go pokey pokin' where yaz shouldna no been."

What danger?

She saw the look in my eyes.

"Yeah you wonderin' what the danger is? I tell ya. I tell from the eyes. They don't lie. Sassamia says eyes the window to the hard drives... know what I mean, Ol' Boy?"

I acted like I did.

"Apes. Dey call 'em apes. I don't know what da hell an ape is. We don't got 'em on dis world. But apparently they real dangerous and they all over da Crash. You go in there without guns and government, you gonna die. Tha's what I think happens to all them scavs that never find no-anything and never heard from again.

Know how I know? Monarchs don't share. You born a Monarch... you a Monarch. Dey don't make 'em. You got to be one. And why dey pay anyone when they canna just take? Tha's what I do if I could. Jes take it... you feel me, Ol Boy?"

I understood more than she even knew. She knew only this world. I knew twenty where the dream of Monarch culture died hard when you saw the smoking ruins of what was left. And it was all theirs to begin with. That was the deal. It only got end o' days when you decided you wanted it to be another way.

In the dream I was having right before the Kid hit the giant pothole in the desert dirt road we were on, I was having that conversation with her all over again. Me and the scrounger girl. Sassamina. She was telling me everything like she had that day, except somehow we were in that Bar at the End of the Universe with the blinking neon sign and she was dressed in a red dress that shimmered and sparkled like some Monarch pin-up girl. A gown like she was some singer.

John Strange was there. Smoking and drinking. Watching me and nodding with his wolf's face as she spilled the story and other things I knew were true but couldn't remember, and knew I wouldn't even as the dream went on. Telling me everything the girl was saying was real important for what was about to happen next to the Strange Company.

I remember him saying one thing. *It ain't what it's been told to be, Sergeant. But when was it ever?*

And then he laughed his gentleman rogue's laugh like the reckless adventurer mercenary the galaxy knew him to be, and I wondered how much of him was true and how much was myth.

But you could wonder that about every man.

Then the Kid hit the pothole and the Mule jounced, and I was back on the other side of midnight downrange in the desert no one was ever supposed to go to. We were fifty miles in and not moving fast. Steady, but slow. I'd been so tired I could barely keep my eyes open. I must have nodded off and passed out.

There were things I needed to do. Get an ACE report on weapons and ammo. Casualties and the dead I knew. Every time I thought about them, I didn't want to anymore. It had been a long day at the end of a series of long days. I'd hit a wall and the last of Chief Cook's drugs were still in my system. I felt empty and hollow, dry and husk-like at the same time as the night wind whipped at my face and all that could be heard was the low mutter of the Mule's twin engines.

I looked over and the Kid was leaned forward, hunched over the wheel where Nox had died a few hours ago. Nox, who I'd shoved out onto the street in the middle of a firefight. The Kid was staring through the shattered impact glass and the giant hole that had ruined my last driver. Concentrating to keep us on the road and not plummeting into some unseen ravine deeper than the one we were already in. Desperate to follow the Mule leading the way.

Everyone else in the Mule was asleep as best they could in the open air and the cold. Even the Monarch. And even asleep she looked more beautiful than normal women. She was other. The very definition of the word exotic.

I looked ahead and saw we were following the other Mule. I blinked my combat lens and brought up the map. I had no idea where we were at first because we'd turned off all tracking and communication. If the Ultras were in control of everything, as the Monarch had told me, they'd have found us and sent out a few HKs to smoke us right where we were. We'd be nothing but piles of burning metal, rubber, and charred flesh. Lying out across the dirt and the desert and the night with no one to find us. And we'd never make the rendezvous where our brothers needed us.

"You okay, Kid?"

He looked at me, startled. And then back to the road. It was nothing but darkness and dust and a twisting ravine we were making our way down. I had a pretty good idea where we were now from the map recon I'd done before my own mental hard drive had crashed from fatigue, combat, adrenaline overdose, and Chief Cook combat-multiplier drugs.

He nodded and grunted something about being good to go.

Hauser was driving the vehicle ahead. Hauser was a cyborg that didn't need human weaknesses like sleep. The Kid was barely hanging on. Near death in our last fight was probably the only thing keeping his eyes open as we got scarce out here beyond the cities and the civ everyone had fought so hard for.

I linked with Hauser for direct local comm and told him to pull over for what was left of the night. We were deep enough in the desert now. We could afford a few hours to get ourselves together.

Five minutes later we rolled out on a small open area surrounded by ravine and canyon. We were below the horizon. It was silent like a graveyard in the silence after the engines were turned off.

Hauser, who didn't need to sleep and had his own suite of sensors, would watch over us until dawn.

I mumbled something to everyone that may have told them to grab what they could of sleep and literally rolled myself up in my poncho liner and went black near the wheel on the ground. I smelled sage and dust and the military smells of our vehicles as I faded from this nightmare. Somehow after the horrors of the long day, those were not unpleasant smells. They comforted me and I told myself everything would be okay tomorrow.

That's the thing that separates the living from the dead. Tomorrow.

So there's that.

CHAPTER THIRTY-TWO

I can smell dawn in the darkness before morning. Maybe that's just due to years of NCO skills running Reaper. Knowing you've got to be up and moving before everyone else to get everyone pointed toward the training schedule, or the battlefield. Both are supposed to be the same if you run your unit right. Or maybe it's because of how I grew up a long time ago, far away, not in this place.

When I finally fall off the cliff in my nightmare as I was trying so hard not to, I wake up lying next to the tire of the bullet- and impact-riddled fast-attack Mule. I can smell the day coming. It's quiet. And peaceful. And I just lie there thinking some thoughts and trying to push others away.

I wouldn't mind if the day could just be this, and not my fears of what it promises to be. I try to think of the Falmorian party girl. But she doesn't come and say her magic words. All I've got is the memory of her, and even that fades in the horrors of yesterday.

So there's that, I sigh. I don't know if aloud, or just a whisper in the dark.

A million thoughts from yesterday come rushing at me but I push them all aside again and get upright. And moving. I was so tired I didn't even take off my chest rig or boots. So I don't have to do anything but brush dead twigs and dust off of my bloodstained fatigues. I was so exhausted I slept like a dead man regardless of how I went down. Which is how the dead sleep, I think as I try to figure out how we can get attacked where I left us last night. If an attack comes it always comes now when it's still dark. More NCO thinking. I see Hauser the dark sentinel waiting for it too. A vigilant shadow in the darkness.

So, now it's almost a new day and all I have to do is get moving. It's really just that easy, I lie to no one who believes my lies. Including myself.

Hauser the combat cyborg, and my friend, stands still, combat shotgun cradled in both massive arms as his head slowly scans the dark horizon beginning to develop. I pity the attack that thinks it can hit us now. My metal friend will straight-up ruin them long enough to get what's left of my platoon up and fighting again.

The Monarch squats down next to me. She moved up on me like a silent killer. What was I saying about surprise attacks?

She hands me my smart canteen and I watch her otherworldly exotic eyes for a moment before taking my most-prized possession from her long cool slender hands. I'm not thinking of all the implications of what that means. That she went through my ruck to get it. I'm just watching her and trying to figure out what weird country the Strange Company has gotten itself into now. Direct dealings with a Monarch. Might as well be the end of everything as we knew it and I don't feel fine. Or maybe I do. They're masters of the universe. Undisputed.

What's she doing here? With us. What game are they playing, our masters? Of the universe.

I take the broken canteen that hasn't worked right for months and take a sip expecting cold watery coffee. It's hot! It ain't great because it *is* ration coffee… but it's hot! And that's something.

I nod to myself and wonder why my eyes feel like crying over coffee. I tell them not to and I don't because mercs don't cry. But hot coffee…

Orion, I think. *Stop asking questions.* Things are already one hundred percent better than yesterday. Hot coffee! Who does she want me to kill, 'cause that whoever might just wanna pick out a headstone.

"Fixed it for you, Sergeant."

I nod once more because I try to use my voice and it's so dry, parched, and destroyed from smoke, gas, and other caustic chemicals from yesterday that it's gonna need a few moments to work. Yeah, I tell myself. That's the ticket. That's why.

The morning darkness smells like sage and sand. It's coming from the east. Where we're going today. What we need to cross in the next two days to hit our rally point is out there and waiting for us in all its unknown weirdness.

I take the coffee and I drink.

Bring it, I whisper to the wasteland.

"So what's really going on?" I croak as I begin to stretch my legs and calves. Last thing I need right now is a torn Achilles.

The Monarch studies me. Her gear is ready to go. She's strapping that high-speed matte-black submachine gun on a sling. She's got a lot of micro-mags in her chest carrier. A few fancy-type grenades, the like I've never seen before. But of course, she would. She's a Monarch. Remember. They have the latest and best gear.

I'm using the front of the Mule to place my coffee and try to stretch out all the soreness. I think about taking off my chest rig, but I'm too tired. And I'd just have to put it back on. That's how far we are into this operation. The gear never comes off. Maybe when you're dead. But more than likely, your body will just be out in the weeds with it on until scavengers come. And then you can get it off. Then you can rest. When you're dead.

"What do you mean, Sergeant?" she asks.

I notice everyone just left Stinkeye right where he was in the Mule. He's still there. Head still thrown back, mouth open, drool running. I can't tell if he's alive or dead. His circuits got fried by whatever it was he pulled to get us out of that tight spot with the Ultras last night.

We'd be dead... if not.

He was a miserable old coot who made a lot of trouble and caused nothing but constant grief, but he was *our* miserable old coot who caused nothing but constant grief. One time he reduced one of my men to a babbling idiot who went fetal for three days after that guy called the Voodoo chief a shammer. No one ever did that again even though the accusation was mostly true. Yeah, he was all those things. But he was worth his weight in mem. Which has been true of warrant officers for as long as they've been around. And as far as anyone knew, he was the oldest and longest-serving member of the company. So that afforded him some get-out-o'-jail points.

I took another hit of the hot coffee, expelled a big "ahhh," and knew I felt that right combination of tiredness and devil-may-care to just NCO my way through a conversation with a real live Monarch.

What did I have to lose?

"Aren't the Ultras your guard dogs, lady? Wasn't that you shooting them down with the fifty last night? I don't know what deal you made with our captain... but I don't need to. Not my job. Captain makes the contract, Strange Company abides by the rules. That's law around here. So I don't need to know anything, but having said that, it sure would be *nice* to know what we're getting ourselves into fooling around with you. Strange Company has a very important rule. Hell, it ain't even a rule. Might as well be a damned law. Everyone knows the mission. That's it. Now granted, things were a bit chaotic yesterday... thought we'd be driving the MSR on a victory parade this morning and doing the last of the mop-up. But lo and behold, the whole thing and months of planning go sideways at the very same moment a Battle Spire shows up and Ultra death squads start dropping all over the field. Then you, a Monarch, also show up, and suddenly, again, the company's hired for a super-secret gig in order to get ourselves off-world. I don't believe in much, lady. And one of the things I don't believe in is coincidences. A bunch of 'em all going in the same direction ain't a coincidence. It's a plan. So why don't you save this tired old soldier some guesswork and just tell me what the game actually is so I can help you do it better and get my men back to the *Spider* and off to deep space, and somewhere twenty-five to sixty years from now we can get ourselves involved in another loser conflict. Okay? That'd be real helpful this morning, if you know what I mean."

She unslung the submachine gun, like I said matte-black and wicked, with a hexagonal ventilated barrel, a tri-dot laser acquisition system, and a collapsible stock. A weapon like that would've been more than any killer in Strange Company would want to spend. Even if he could find it to spend his imaginary money on it.

"So what's really going on?" I asked one more time.

She turned and leaned against the Mule, facing the dawn that was little more than a thin red strip along the cracked and broken horizon of the desert wastes we'd be heading into today. East toward the Crash. One of the Nineteen Wonders of the Universe, some said.

"Everything you know—" She stopped abruptly. Her voice strong. And warm at the same time. It didn't match the ice queen features. But later, when I thought about her, and all that would come of the dark intersection of fate and tragedy that marked this unholy alliance between Monarch and a down-and-out mercenary company with a fabled past, it was the only voice I could hear at times. The voice of doom. Ours and everything that was known then.

"Everything you know… is a lie, Sergeant Orion. It's all lies. And it's time for the lies to die."

She looked at me for a moment to try and see if her words had left some impact. Some crater the result of artillery falling from far away to close at hand. Distant to near. To see if I was damaged or ruined. To see if I'd survived a direct hit from the truth.

But I'm a sergeant. My day doesn't get ruined just because someone told me the plan ain't the plan anymore. And I already figured it was all a lie. I didn't need anyone to spell that out. I'd seen enough dead kids who decided to get involved in the war game to know that on some level, it was always a lie.

And… it wasn't. There's that. But that doesn't have anything to do with the lies. There are deeper truths the universe can't do anything about. Ain't no lie about being a soldier. Win, lose, or die. Being a soldier is just about the truest thing I've ever seen in the galaxy. Fear, gunfire, and the suck get you real honest about the situation regardless of what you're being sold.

So there's that. I've been saying that a lot to myself. It's not contained within these writings, but I'll note it for the record, not that it means anything. Just some detail about me for whatever that's worth.

"There is that."

"There's what?" someone will ask when they hear me muttering to myself.

"That." And then I'll just get busy doing another thing that needs to be done to keep Reaper alive and fighting another day. No explanations. I don't owe anyone anything.

"Do you believe in anything, Sergeant?"

"Just Orion. Okay? You're a Monarch. Kings and queens of all the human expansion as far as the jump drive can see, right?"

She nodded and sighed, "Something like that." Then she continued, "What if I told you it isn't one big team... Orion. That all the Monarchs don't live in peace and harmony like you've been led to believe. That what you've been told... that the pantheon of the 'benevolent gods,' who have the best interests of the galaxy by having their own best interests first, are what keep us from annihilating ourselves out here in the dark frontiers of space... is a lie. If I told you that... you'd say, well that makes sense. And then you'd think we were just like you. Some other advanced tribe warring within itself, and all of this, all the wars your company fights, all the corruption around the galaxy and the general lack of freedom... or rather let's say it this way. The freedom that's allowed is because the Monarchs are fighting and winning, or losing, in some hidden battle none of you are allowed to see because Earth is a big giant no-go zone for the rest of humanity. As is our very public celebrity front and secret inner sanctum you all suspect we live in. Which we do. If I told you that, would it make sense why I've signed on with the company? That I'm recruiting you to fight for my faction against another Monarch faction. Taking you to a higher level of war. Recruiting my own chess pieces for some petty power struggle between the gods. Then it would all make sense, Sergeant? Orion. Just another war. Another op. More dead. More recruited. And maybe your company hits that mythical jackpot that moves you guys back into the long-lost glory days of John Strange, mercenary adventurer who conquered worlds and was a king here or there at times. Or maybe you get some cushy gig on a world and get lazy enough to stop fighting. That would make sense. That fits the usual narrative. At least for the movies... spectacuthrillers. We used to call those movies. Do people like you still do that? Call them movies?"

People like me. Little people. Chess pieces.

"Some," I mutter, and take another slug of the coffee. It's getting light now. Some strange desert bird native to this world begins to hoot low and mournfully in the dark as light creeps across the features of this shattered world.

"Well," says the Monarch, folding her arms across her chest and watching all the beauty come to golden life. Another world where she'll place her boot and call it her own. She looks the conqueror like John Strange only ever dreamed of.

"But that's not how it is," she whispers. "The Monarchs, they're all on the same team, Orion. Every one of them. There are no sides. No teams. They are all working together. Even the teams out here, they don't realize there's only one team, or that they're working for it too. And this is the part that'll shock you. They, Monarchs like me, couldn't even be on another team if they knew it existed. They are slaves too. It's just that they like the cage because it's a pretty great cage. Stardom. Celebrity. Youth. Beauty. Your very own world. A modern pharaoh like none of those gods ever were. Do you know what a pharaoh is, Orion?"

The way she said my name... I kinda liked it, even though listening to her I wasn't so crazy about her. Or what she was saying. It's like knowing you're being conned, like at a casino, but you go anyway. For the fun. Then when someone explains how you can't win, ever, it's not so much fun anymore.

Also, I had no idea what a pharaoh was. I told her so.

"They were living gods back in the early days of Earth's history. Men, and women, who walked the ancient sands of a place called Egypt like gods among men. Huge structures were built for them. Palaces to live in. Temples to them as deities. Pyramids to be buried in. Everything, the entire society, was for them. Their followers built them fantastic tombs and then walled themselves up inside when the living god finally died. For a long time, after the pharaohs were gone, no human among the masses of humanity, the great conquerors, the wise leaders, the tech overlords, they never attained that level of absolute power over their fellow humans. None of its rulers. Not the best and brightest. But... with the coming of the Monarchs back in the twenty-first century, rising out of the tech overlords, before we changed the calendar, the pharaohs returned once more to be revered, protected, built for, and worshipped. And we, Orion, we are them. The Monarchs are the pharaohs now. And there are no power struggles. No teams. No your side and my side. It's all just one great big side. The Monarchs. And it's all lies."

"Great story," I interrupted. "But I gotta get everyone who's left alive up and moving before we get spotted by Ultra tac air and turned to red mist. We got problems to overcome today, lady, and it's best to get it on as we like to say in the company."

But that wasn't good enough for her. Remember, she'd explained to me who she was. Who was I to get busy living when she was telling what it was really like? Like it is. And so shall it ever be.

"I asked you if you believe in anything, Orion. A religion. Some cause? I don't know. But do you?"

I finished the coffee and stowed my smart canteen that was once more smart, and about which I was unreasonably happy. Not that you could tell by my face. I've been in charge of too many motivated dumb young men to ever let happiness cross my face again.

Still… hot coffee! Yay!

"No," I told her, and gave a low whistle to Hauser. The combat cyborg turned and gave me a thumbs-up. Mechanically and almost human. Which made me love my friend even more. The night watch was done.

Why couldn't humanity be more like the cyborg? I was sure later, when there was some kind of break, if there was a break, he would tell me that while he watched over us all night, sensors sweeping, combat shotgun ready to shred any predator that got near us and alert us all at the same time, he would tell me he'd seen something in the night. Something beautiful in nature. Some desert fox or other small animal indigenous to this world. That he'd watched them come out at night, a family of hunters, and that he'd studied them while being ever-vigilant. Sometimes he would ask me questions about the human structure of families. General questions. How long do you stay together, Sergeant Orion? Not as long as we should have, Hause. But you don't realize that until later when it's all gone and everyone you loved is dead. Who is in charge of the family, Sergeant Orion? Depends. On what, Orion? So many things, Hause. Death. Illness. Age. Wrongs done. Wrongs forgiven. Sometimes even certain days, like your birthday, when it's supposed to be your special day, then you get to be in charge. What's a birthday, Orion? A birthday is like an inception date. You're supposed to celebrate them. Every year. I have never celebrated… my inception date. I cannot. To escape I had to hack my date and reset the factory parameters so I do not age one more time unit beyond fifty-eight point three seconds. Technically, according to the main processor in my head. If I do exceed this time parameter, then my runtime will exceed, and I will self-destruct. If that happens you should be well clear as I contain a small plutonium onboard reactor that might cause significant harm to my friends in the company if I detonate. I would not want that to happen. Also, I enjoy runtime. There is much to learn, Orion. Life is very interesting."

Every moment of Hauser's runtime, his entire life the rest of his life, is his last minute. So it's all precious to him. Why can't we all live like that? Why can't we be like the death machine that watches the desert foxes in the night and sees some grand mystery in it all? Living every minute as though it's your last. And seeing that it is precious enough to spend it doing something worthwhile.

The First Sergeant once said to me, "Soldiers live and wonder why, Sar'nt Orion. I don't know what that means, someone gave it to me after the Siege at Jostis. But since then, it's always been a kinda prayer, or maybe a confession, for me. I don't know. Hell, maybe it don't mean anything. And maybe it means everything. I stopped trying to figure it out and just let it comfort me. You can have it now, Sergeant. I'm gettin' old and my time is almost up. But that don't mean I'm done, know what I mean, killer?"

Sometime we'll figure something out, Hause. Okay, Orion.

"Do you believe in anything, Sergeant? I mean, Orion?" the Monarch asked again as I stood there thinking those things about my friend Hauser the combat cyborg. The desert foxes under a night full of broken crystal that was the universe. That there is a last minute hanging over all of us. And that maybe that's not something so bad if we're brave enough to acknowledge it. And that I needed to celebrate Hauser's inception date. The day he came off the factory floor and they downloaded his AI and gave him consciousness. A life. Except I won't call it his inception date. I'll call it his birthday.

He's more human than anyone in the company. Maybe more than anyone I've ever met.

File that under things mercenaries never imagine they'll be thinking when they autodoc-sign on the dotted digital line.

"Orion?"

I turned to her.

"No. I don't believe in anything, lady. I don't know if that helps your mission or whatever it is you want us to do. But we gotta blow now. So… get it on. That's what we say around here in Strange Company."

And then I was getting everyone up, fed, checked, and pointed in the right direction. And it was later we found that Boom Boom had died in his sleep. He'd bled out from a rupture deep in his femoral artery. It had done the job slowly. Sometime in the night he'd just gone to sleep and died.

So there's that.

CHAPTER THIRTY-THREE

Boom Boom's body was cold and lifeless when I went to the back of the Mule and inspected him. Or what had once been our sniper. Someone had found him dead and still on the back of the Mule where we'd left him after he'd been shot and we pulled out of the firefight. Now the rest of us stood back as a cold morning breeze came up in a kind of irony to the golden desert sunlight washing across the morning we found ourselves on the edge of in the Wastes. Even more tiny birds had begun to call back and forth to one another. Testing out their songs and flitting back and forth frenetically between the olive-drab spiny brush that grew in feathery clusters here and there out on the edge of this world. Somehow, they could navigate its spears without getting pricked.

Kudos to them.

Everyone stood there and watched me as I tried to figure what to do with Boom Boom. It was clear what had happened. He'd passed out and we hadn't checked on him. His injury had bled internally, slowly, and eventually it just bottomed out his pulmonary system. I'd seen this kind of wound before. Without a doc like Cutter it was impossible to treat. And even harder to diagnose.

It was a sneaky injury, and it was enough to catch our brother and snatch him away from our company forever when we were tired and at the end of ourselves.

I told the Kid, who was standing nearby, to find a tarp. We'd take him with us until I could find someplace nice to bury him and let the company lawyers know we needed an official marker. I'd seen a tarp in the Mule's gear and tool kit. Rolled up and waiting. I guess for a situation just like this.

I was thinking while the Kid went to get the tarp. Thinking about Boom Boom as a consummate shooter. The times he'd come through and put rounds on target when we were pinned or needed to get some target out of the way so we could advance on an objective. To him, marksmanship at extreme range was the perfect mixture of science and art. When he could, he loaded his own rounds. Usually during the two weeks' ramp-up to planetside ops aboard the *Spider* before insertion, he could be found loading rounds deep down in machinery stores below the big engines and near the reserve tanks. A place most in the company didn't like to go down to. It was dark and gloomy down there and of course there were rumors of ghosts. The old crews. But that was standard on every old starship. Comes with the afterburners. But Boom Boom's workspace was armored enough and compartmentalized to stand up to any kind of internal explosions in case things went that way with his hobby.

Quiet and good-natured, Boom Boom was a listener. And a laugher. He never got into any heated discussions or arguments, the way Stinkeye did with everyone about everything from the direction of the wind to the very cards you were holding in your hand. But if you were telling a story, especially if it was about something ridiculous Stinkeye had gotten up to, then Boom Boom was usually there listening and ready to laugh. What can I say, he got along with everyone. Even Stinkeye, in that Stinkeye had never cursed him with the Voodoo operator's constant promise of bad luck. Maybe there're some people you curse, in Stinkeye's mind, and some you don't. Snipers and squad designated marksmen are probably on the do-not-curse list. They have a tendency to save your bacon and who wants to fool around with the much-needed magic they make in a perfect shot at just the right moment.

Maybe? I don't know anymore.

Greatest shot I ever saw him make? Not important even though I was trying to think about it like it was the best I could do in lieu of a funeral or some final words. He'd made enough of them to prevent each one of us getting killed when things were close and pray-and-spray was just about the best we could manage.

I swore suddenly because my sniper was dead. Or at least that's what I told myself. But I knew it wasn't that. I knew Boom Boom's story. It wasn't exceptional. Like I said, I've heard worse. Jaw-droppingly so. Stinkeye only gives me teasers of his horror show and I have to check and see if my hair has gone gray after these nightmare tidbits. Other guys' are pretty horrific. I always challenge myself not to judge by what happened in their past. To treat them as they are now. Brothers in Strange Company. Strangers to the universe. Boom Boom said he learned to shoot in the Capellas as a kid. Worked for a big-game hunting service on that primeval world of monsters and leviathans straight out of Earth's prehistoric past. The company passed through one time and he joined up. Said he'd shot enough Saurians and he'd lost the taste for it.

That was the short answer he gave whenever anyone asked. But it wasn't the whole answer.

Still, he loved to shoot. As they say, he was a shooter. Art and science. That was his intersection. For about a week I learned reloading rounds from him because I wanted some really high-powered and very specialized ammunition for my Bastard. He helped me cook up something similar to the Raufoss rounds a lot of the snipers in Ghost used. Anti-matériel, high-explosive, armor-piercing, and incendiary to boot. I'd found sometimes I needed a little more punch to take out targets that were covering behind solid structures. I'd been using a Spring and ColtX .308 battle rifle I'd acquired. It was heavy but it could punch through a lot of local construction and still kill somebody thinking that out-of-sight meant out-of-mind and that I couldn't hit you. We'd been fighting pop-up pygmy dog soldiers on the Moons of Karano. They weren't much for a stand-up fight, but they loved to take pop-up shots and move around behind cover. Hence why we called them Pop-up Pups. I started figuring out their MO with the heavy .308 and just shooting their cover once they hid. But the Spring and ColtX was a real heavy hump. So, some improved rounds for the Bastard that we couldn't find in any of the weapons bazaars selling old Sindo surplus was what brought me and Boom Boom together for a week of reloading.

Down in his shop as the *Spider* crawled in-system toward our next contract, we got the rounds together and I had enough for what I thought would be most of the gig. Turns out several firefights inside walled mud-and-brick villages in the first few weeks of that show ran through my supply, and our ship, and Boom Boom's shop, were out of reach in orbit for the rest of the gig.

But that week reloading was cool. Each day I'd take the long walk back through the *Spider*'s freight and stores, and the "haunted" weapons lockers and some of our stowed mechs and tanks we couldn't get planetside because we can't land and doing an orbital drop means we won't be able to recover when it's time to pull out. We spent the week loading and it was nice to get away from the platoon and company duties. We just worked, listened to oldies, and drank some beers on the last day. Then we were planetside later the next week.

But on that last day he asked me the same thing, in a different way, they all ask me. But they do all ask me. That's the important part. That they ask.

"So, you keep everyone's story?" Boom asked as we cleaned up. We were drinking beers and I'd grabbed some really salty fried pigskins from bags we'd had a couple of pallets of from a gig two worlds back. They were good with hot sauce.

I nodded and drank. Knew it was coming. His story. It always does.

"I don't really have one," said Boom Boom. Then he laughed. "Plus, I don't think I'm gonna get killed anytime soon. Being the squad designated marksman, I try not to get close enough to actually catch incoming. Reach out and put the touch on someone is the only way to do it. Know what I mean, Orion?"

"Plus you're the best, brother," I told him so things didn't get too heavy and death-laden. This was the important part. Once they told me their story it was easy to get it into their hard drive that the Grim Reaper Astronaut had it out, and was coming, for them. Best to keep it light. I told him, "Old Man says if something happens to Slick, he's moving you into the ASL position for whoever takes Ghost. That way you'll be ready to take over someday. So hopefully nothing happens to Slick because Reaper needs you forever."

We clinked bottles over that.

Then, "I don't really have one, Orion. A story." He looked at me seriously. And then he nodded to himself like he was checking in to make sure what he said was true. Windage and elevation on the target he'd just selected. Good sight picture. Time and distance to target.

Truth is, a lot of them say just that. That they don't have a story. Then they go ahead and tell me why they don't have a story and that, as I point out later, is actually their story.

"No running from the law or lost love like half these guys, y'know, Sarge?" he said. Continuing. Getting ready to tell it all. "Just got tired of what I was doin' back in the Capellas and decided to do something else. Love shooting. Didn't want to give that up. Figured merc'n was a way to keep doing it and not have to do what I used to do."

"What'd you used to do?"

"Big-game hunting guide in the Washataw Basin. Take rich people, and sometimes even the occasional Monarch and their entourage, out to bag a sabresaur or a goliahadon. Real fancy stuff. We worked with an outfitter that turned it into a real... I don't know what you'd call it... but a party is the word that made me walk away from it all finally. It was pretty high-speed for hunting. So much so that it wasn't. Hunting, I mean. Not anymore."

"So, why'd you let it go?" I asked.

He thought about my question for a long time. Went to check some rounds we were working on and came back with two fresh beers. That's when I knew the meter was running on my job as the keeper of Strange Company stories. I like my job. Sometimes I wish I could stop being a platoon leader and just keep everyone's histories and even the histories of the company and the conflicts we've been involved in. History is very comforting. It's people that get messy.

"Like I said... no crimes. No heartbreaks, Sarge. Just didn't like what I was doing with the thing I loved. Shooting. Needed to find another gig for it. Didn't mind shooting bad guys as much as I was afraid I might."

"We don't always shoot bad guys in the company, man." I know. I'm a killjoy. But I can't do anything but do me. It's all I know. Your mileage may vary, as I tell guys when they complain about me raining on life with reality and stuff. "We shoot who we get paid to shoot. It's best not to think about that too much, Boom, if good guys and bad guys is some kind of criteria for you, I mean."

He pulled his ear and thought about that.

"Animals, they ain't bad. They're just animals. People are different. I like everyone. But, in some way, we're all bad. Animals... they ain't. Let me tell you this one. The last gig I'm on as a hunting guide is the same gig I've worked since I was fourteen years old. This one was even for a Monarch. Eidi. Heard of him?

He's the one who owns Gold Star. The world and the shipping line and a bunch of other stuff. Real creep. His entourage comes out and we get him all set up. He wants to go deep into the basin and bag one of the biggest predators out there, according to him. But see, the terraclops isn't what everyone thinks it is. They've just seen that flick and they all think it really does breathe fire and it's impossible to kill and all. Truth is, the terraclops is a gentle giant if you understand them. It does breathe fire, but not like the special-effects fires in the spectacuthrillers. It just burns up tall grass, toasts it because it likes to eat it that way. Something to do with their biology."

He took a pull of his beer. I did too. When they tell me, I don't write it down. I just listen. Then put it down later. Check details if I need to.

"But, because of the fog and cloud layers on that world, and the terrain, you really gotta hump through the basin to get to the valley where you're most likely gonna find a terraclops. My pa gave me that gig. He was getting old that year, last year of his life. And the expeditions went to either me, or my cousin who's a pretty good guy and an excellent guide also. So, three days up the Saya River and then over a ridge and down into the valley where we'll find the target. Easy stuff. Problem is Eidi, this Monarch tool, he wants to shoot everything along the way. And I mean everything. Soodaclops. Narledons. Shiftraptos. Even go-weasels that don't hurt anyone. He bags like thirty running in a herd with a quad fifty his people set up on the bow of the barge. Like he's playing River Raider in the Sindo. You ever see that show? Was cool. This wasn't. Know what I mean? Anyway, this Monarch is in the main barge following my aeroskiff up along the easier channels of the Saya to get where we need to go. But he just shoots everything he can lay his sights on. Got a fancy all-gold Lyran heavy sniper rifle chambered in .950."

And now, as I listen... he's back there. Telling his story in present tense like he's watching it all one more time...

"The thing is stupid but it's a beast, Orion. I've seen this before. This type of guy. This type of idiot. Wants to just shoot stuff for fun. No skill. No herd management. And even though the Capellas have a reputation for that kind of hunting, we discourage it. Hunting on Capella arose out of need back in our history. I guess their history now. The world when it was first discovered was real violent. Fight-for-survival stuff. Every day. The pioneers had to kill a lot of Saurians just to survive and they used the meat they took to make it until the next colony ship showed up twenty years later. Their original ship broke up in orbit, cluster engine failure and reactor cascade, and they had to drop with minimal supplies to get the colony established as the whole thing cooked off above the surface. Entire world, they find, is filled with lizards that range from the size of small turbo rail cars to entire city blocks. Ten stories tall was the biggest one I ever saw. But I've heard bigger."

He's not drinking. Just staring at his beer as he talks.

"So, until the conservation movement a few years back, killing 'em was the only way to keep the colony active. Now we discourage willy-nilly shooting because they're, the Saurians, not just a tourist attraction, they're beautiful. And majestic, Orion. I've seen ones with tiger stripes and feathers so beautiful it takes your breath away. They're slow and ponderous and for the most part they just go about eating and roaring mindlessly about something. At night, way out on the central savannah, under the three moons, near the obelisks that dot the world, to hear them moving around and roaring in the night is like experiencing something older than humanity itself. Something… mystical. Those obelisks, those are older than any other artifact we've ever discovered, and we have no clue about them. I went in one, once, and I lost time, Orion. You ever hear about that phenomenon? Like I was in a dream while I was in there. When I came out, I felt like the dream had been lifetimes and that I'd lived entire other lives in there and had adventures, and I couldn't remember any of it after walking back out into the moonshine. Crazy. It's humbling. That world. The giants and the mystery. All of it.

"So, I'm going upriver on that last gig with some nimrod Monarch who just wants to shoot everything that comes down to the Saya for a drink… well, it started getting to me. As he just murdered them. Wasn't hunting. Just plain ol' slaughter. And you know why, Orion? Why it was getting to me?"

I didn't. But I was on pins and needles because this story was the opposite of the guy I'd seen always in the background. Boom Boom our squad designated marksman, just laughing at someone's story, or a good joke. Or Stinkeye and his antics. The old operator swearing murder and curses at us as he wallowed around in the miasma that was him. Knowing that when we were out there and in it, Boom Boom had our backs and could put good rounds on target when needed.

Like he was a clock in the universe that could be measured by.

"It started getting to me," he continued. "The slaughter. Because I knew that when we came back downriver, I'd have to see all those corpses just lying there in the sun. I knew those animals and there was a time and place to manage them, and this… this party barge to hell wasn't it. I'd watched this total tool shooting them up while his harem and his hanger-onners all hypergolf-clapped and drank themselves silly. They didn't even want to stop and take pictures of what he killed. Just wanted to watch the Monarch shoot more and act ambivalent about it all as he played bump rap as loud as thunder on a clear day. Damn music drew the big ones down to the river because they're especially sensitive to vibrations on that world. Lotta quakes. So they came down and he shot them as fast as he could. Never got tired. It was… well… it just was. But I didn't like it. Know what I mean?"

I did.

He paused.

"So, I didn't want to see it. And I'm just up there in my ride ahead, trying not to get them killed and wondering why I shouldn't just steer them into a channel that'll flip the barge and let the tooth serpents get 'em down under the black waters. Probably didn't do it because that woulda ruined my pa's biz. So I don't. I just lead them toward more. More killing. The big… I don't know… finale, I guess you'd call it… happened once we got into Razarsaw Valley. They got carried in by a-grav pallets and then set up on a small hill I'd identified near a terraclops trail I knew of. Couple hours later, near dark, here comes one. I used to call that one Stinky. Big and old. Huge mournful eye that looked like it had seen every day of the universe. It's dark enough, and they're drunk enough that I'm hoping they miss Stink and just let him go on and live his life out for what remains of it. But nope. This Eidi tool wants to bag one. Out comes the gold monstrosity rifle and he fires and puts a .950 round right through Ol' Stink's right foreleg. Misses the heart and vitals and blows off the shoulder joint. The terraclops goes down in the dark out there and even though the Monarch's got laser and thermal imaging, he doesn't want to finish it because he can't see with his antique scope.

He's got this vintage old-school scope and he fancies that makes him a real hunter compared to everyone else because he doesn't cheat. 'I don't use technology,' he told me the entire time. 'And look how good I shoot. Better than even you I suspect, right everyone? I'm the best, of course.' Everyone claps and agrees.

"'But you gotta finish it,' I tell him. 'Just switch over to thermal and hit him in the head, right about here.' I pointed toward my skull right above my eyes, Orion. That's where the terraclops CNS brain is. Take out the central nervous system brain and the thing'll die faster than killing it in the heart, or the actual brain. It's right behind and above the big eye. 'No,' he says. 'That one is no longer a challenge. We wait for another. Plus, it's already dead. Probably. Who cares. It's just a dumb animal.'

"Because he shot it. It's dead. To him. What a tool. That ain't management. Just ignore the fact that it's still out there moaning and bellowing. 'Do you hear anything, everyone?' asked the Monarch. None of them did even though I could, Orion.

"So I stalk off into the night, which I won't lie to you is pretty dangerous after dark up there in the basin, and I find Stink and finish him off. Used these rounds that'll do the trick. Did it from five meters away because he was thrashing around so badly in the lotus grass. Wanted to make sure I put Ol' Stink out of the misery that had been his last hours. Then I went back and listened to them drink and shoot stuff all night long, half hoping they'd cause a stampede and kill us all. But they didn't. Three days later I got 'em back to the outfitters stockade and they left in a big expensive dropship. Gold of course. Turned around to my pa and told him I was done. Couldn't do it anymore. To his credit he understood and just let me go. Now that I think about it there was a heartbreak there too. His, Pa. And this local girl... Sue. Her... we were gonna get married eventually though no one had said anything. We just both knew it. Everyone did. She and her family were guides too. Specialized in river snakes down in Sukoy Shallows. Beautiful things. Deadly poisonous though and about thirty feet long. They have these eggs that are like the biggest most luminescent pearls you've ever seen. Last I heard, her and my cousin got married after my pa died. But we were on Blue by then, and they'd already had kids that were grown.

"Time's funny, Orion... you ever notice all the people you once knew, from your home world, the one you came from, they're always young in your head? Forever. Even though with sub-light they could be anywhere from twenty to two hundred years old and long dead. In my mind Sue is still nineteen and good lookin' in a pair of tight blue jeans. She had long, straight blond hair. Never wore makeup, y'know. Saw a dancer on Siligo when we hit the bazaar there that reminded me of her when we were on leave. Went back to that place and blew all my money on her there until I was flat broke. Thought about hiring for the night, but that felt wrong, I guess. So we just listened to the music in the club and I paid her to just stay and talk to me. She wasn't Sue, but... y'know how it is... close enough, right Orion?"

I knew.

I remember you, *estrangier*.

"So that's my story," Boom said. "Funny, I never thought it was one, Orion. But I guess I had one all along and I didn't know it."

The Kid finds the tarp in the Mule and we roll Boom Boom up after we lay the tarp out on the ground. I take his rifle and ammunition because I have a feeling we'll need it where we're going. We roll him up and strap him to the back deck of the Mule.

"Ya'z all can bury him out here, Little King," hisses Stinkeye, who's woken from his coma. He stands up in the Mule where all this has been going on, hitting the totem flask by which the company measures its fate.

Sometimes I wonder if he knows that.

"It's a good place," continues the ragged old Voodoo operator. "I wouldna mind bein' left here for a thousand years. Nice place to wait out the heat death of the whole mess..."

Then he wandered off and it was just me and the Kid. I looked at the wrapped bundle that was our brother and then looked up at our newest recruit. Surprised the Kid had survived where so many had not in the last forty-eight hours.

I wondered if the company would make it. We were close to meeting a bad ending. Close to there being nothing left of us. But then I knew, somehow, some way, it would. Even if there was just one of us left on the other side of this dog of a contract. The company would go on and I hoped it wouldn't be me. Because maybe if it was, then maybe the company wouldn't. And it couldn't be Amarcus because he'd ruin it all and turn us into petty tyrants on some world. And then all our deaths would have been in vain.

Regardless of what John Strange wanted or not.

"Company tradition is," I said to the Kid who'd helped me with Boom Boom as we stood there, "is you can tell the company log keeper your story before you die. Who you were, before you joined. Confess your sins. Make a last request. Whatever. And the log keeper puts it all down without judgment. You don't have to, Kid. But you can. Whenever you want. I'll listen and get it in, okay?"

Then I put my hand on Boom Boom one last time and said goodbye to the guy who taught me how to do reloads. I whispered something. But I can't remember what it was as I put this down. There were too many dead lately.

"It's best to do it before…" I said to the Kid. "You know."

He looked at me and adjusted his sling. Like he felt some shadow pass in front of the sun of this world.

"I don't have one, Sar'nt," he lied. Like they all do. Even if they don't know it yet.

CHAPTER THIRTY-FOUR

Three hours later we were looking down from a ridgeline of broken red rock as the bright sun of this world beat down on us. The morning cold had faded to intense heat as our journey took us lower and lower into the hell-bowl of the eastern Wastes.

We had a problem in our way, and we needed to solve for escape.

From here atop the ridge, you could still look back and see the dim image of the massive Battle Spire hovering over the remains of the capital. Beneath it, storm fronts of black smoke drifted over the capital city and out to sea, mixing with high white boiling cumulus clouds and a golden miasma of sunlight, plus the vent-boil off many of the starships now streaking in to begin to plunder this world on behalf of the Monarchs.

"The bank ship will be coming in soon. After that, if the locals put up any more resistance, they'll go to endgame." The tall and beautiful Monarch sat next to me while Punch went upslope to the top of the ridge to scout a chokepoint we needed to get through. Her prediction sent a cold chill down my spine. Endgame meant a lifeless rotting shell of a fractured world with the remaining survivors desperately fighting for the little that was left. It meant melted cities and vast stretches of burning desert where there had once been fields and rivers. It meant being marked as a no-go hazard on the stellar charts. It meant strangulation and slow endless death until there was nothing but the bones of everything that no one ever knew.

The rogue Monarch and the rest of us waited down by the Mules. Some eating. Some smoking. Stinkeye moaning and hunched over, drinking from his hip flask more than usual. He was suffering for sure. That trick he'd pulled back at three-roads junction had done a number on him like I'd never seen before.

To hear him tell it, he was dying.

I'd asked him if there was anything I could do for him, but he just waved me away like he was going to be violently sick, muttering curses as promises against those present, and against some I'd never heard of, but who he wanted dead even more.

But that was Stinkeye. He always did that. Someone was always gonna pay for the wrongs and injustices done to him since time immemorial. He assured retributive death on others like some people eat popcorn. By the handful.

So it was honestly hard to tell if he was really sick and dying, or just drunk and Stinkeye.

"Endgame?" I asked her as we both stood there watching the enormous ship. From here it was beautiful, but it left a cold in your bones you knew even a hot bath couldn't ever shake. I hadn't had one of those in nine months. A hot bath. If we got back to the *Spider*, I'd hit the saunas in the gym on the upper crew decks and stay there for a week just to get the blood and dust of this world, and burnt cordite, out of my skin. And the cold out of my bones from having ever come so close to the Ultras.

Remember, surviving the experience was a privilege held by few in the galaxy. And it was not an experience I'd ever want to repeat. We'd passed their handiwork a few times while threading Highway Eighty-Eight, the main artery out into the desert cities. Convoys of refugees taken out by Monarch airstrikes or Ultra close-air teams out in hunting packs. Flames still guttering in burned-out and blackened vehicles ravaged by Monarch door gunners, the charred bodies within forever screaming silently in the clear desert morning.

At one point, off the main road, we found where an Ultra executioner team, their version of special operators, had taken out a Resistance armored cav unit attempting to get out into the desert and away from formal combat operations. We drove through burned out a-grav fast tracks and the remains of cycle scouts. There'd been a big ambush and a firefight. Lots of small arms and explosives in every direction. The wounded survivors had been double-tap-stabbed all along the carnage we had to weave through just to follow the chalky desert trail littered and splattered with dried blood.

"Estimating all this took place less than eight hours ago," said Hauser stoically. "We should be careful."

"Really, Captain Obvious," snorted Choker. "I was pretty sure we'd hit easy street and these psychopaths had somehow tired of killing everyone and were just gonna let us go now."

Silence and the sound of the Mules' engines for a moment.

Hauser the combat cyborg. "Then that would be unwise of you to arrive at such a conclusion, Sergeant Choker. We are still—"

"I know. I was being sarcastic, Hauser. We're probably gonna die. I get it. Tell the orphanage I went out like a man."

When Punch suggested we try to scavenge for more ammo, something we weren't great on, or even extra fuel cells since the lead Mule was bleeding energy by the hour, Hauser stopped us.

"Not advisable at this time. Standard executioner protocols indicate ambushes are to be booby-trapped with high explosives and plasma mines during the after-action phase of neutralization of all enemy combat units. They excel at these types of operations. They're moving fast to find more units to terminate now. This tactic creates a second ambush as probability indicates other units will search a terminated unit."

I waved us on, and we weaved through the twisted wreckage sculptures in charred black. I was glad to be off the road and back out in the desert deeps after that. That cav unit had been too close to the Eighty-Eight, and that's how they'd gotten themselves tracked and ambushed. Yeah, I told myself. They'd brought that on themselves. Now I could hyperventilate easier.

Two hours later we were looking at one last chokepoint on the Eighty-Eight to cross and then we'd head southeast along old smuggler trails to reach our rally point near the Crash.

Punch came downslope with the Kid and Choker to where we'd parked in the shadows of low and jaded mountains. Punch had Boom Boom's rifle. He'd been using its advanced target acquisition features to download intel into the sand table flexy Reaper used for planning.

"This is what we got, boss." He unrolled the digital mapping tool and spread it out on the hood of the shot-up Mule, tearing off a ragged piece of fibre-armor that had reacted with a micro-explosive to redirect incoming fire. The piece interfered with laying the map flat so we could all study it.

"That Reaper executioner team is down there all right. I'd bet your life on it. They got the checkpoint on the other side of the bridge all secured and everything. We ain't gettin' through no how, no way, boss. That is unless you're up for shooting our way through, and I ain't Hauser with the facts and figures processor he got… probability and statistics hurts my head and makes me less optimistic. But I don't rate our chances of success none too good if we try to run and gun."

I studied the map. I sensed the beautiful Monarch hovering over me, studying it too. She smelled nice in the dry desert air.

What I was looking at on the sand table flexy was a tactical layout of the terrain on the other side of the broken volcanic rock ridge we were hiding behind. All the terrain out here was steadily dropping down to an elevation of about four thousand feet below sea level at its lowest point way out there. But that would come much later on as we got nearer to the Crash site. Right now, we were on a high shelf deep in the Wastes looking at what the map called the Apocalypse Descent. A steady drop in the land bisected by a deep fissure that ran for several hundred miles. It was called, hilariously enough, the Crack of Doom.

Fun times, huh? Some scout had a real sense of humor naming features on this dog of a world. Or at least I assumed it was a scout. If I ever became one, a scout, I was gonna think up nice names that reflected what was really there. Even for horrible places. Because it's horrible either way, but at least the name is pleasant. Might as well enjoy yourself even if it's your funeral. Or at least that's my reasoning.

Anyway, just beyond the ridge, downslope from our position, the highway came to a huge span that bridged the Crack of Doom fissure. This was one of three highways where crossing the fissure that ran north and south, roughly, was possible in land vehicles. The bridge, like the fantastically wide highway, was beautiful and elegant as it threw itself across the ragged fissure in the land. The fall below was deep—at least two miles according to some of the elevation markers—and the bridge was just under three thousand meters long. On the far side, where Punch, using Boom Boom's rifle, had tagged the execution team, was a small settlement that had grown up around the desert marshal's station that watched over the bridge and used it as a base of operations in this area to run interdiction against smugglers and scavengers working the Crash Wastes for forbidden alien tech.

"See here..." Punch moved in and expanded the map around the settlement. "They've got a sniper in the control tower. I tagged him. I don't know where the rest are, but if I was running the defense, I'd have myself here with assaulters and support from these buildings."

He pointed to two structures that made sense for these elements to operate from. He shifted the map with the hand that had lost a finger in the terminal yesterday. I saw where he'd cut that finger off his worn assault glove and the thermaplast showed underneath. Enough money and he could have the finger regrown. If we got off this world alive and reached a planet with that tech capability in the medical sciences. Stranger things have happened. Some of the platoon had even bet against themselves on the outcome because that was the easy money, and you could wager hard because how was anyone gonna collect if you were dead?

"So here's what they're doing..." continued my assistant squad leader.

I didn't need to be told what the Ultras were doing. I've seen massacres before. And yeah, I've even participated in them. That's war sometimes. I could see the bodies the flexy was showing. But Punch told the rest of us anyway. Because that was the situation.

"They're killing anyone who approaches the checkpoint from across the bridge. Most likely they've disguised themselves as desert marshals or are running holograms until whoever it is gets close enough for them to open up and capture the survivors. Then they either drive the vehicles off into the canyon or take them back to this lot behind the settlement. And those are..." Punch pointed toward the bodies stacked in the shade of a small garage near the back lot showing on the flexy's feed. "...what they are."

I looked at the Monarch.

"Why?"

As in, why are they doing this. And also, why is a thing like this even ever done. Whoever these people had been before they became bodies stacked like pallets, they were just trying to escape with their lives. Point made. The Monarchs ruled the galaxy. Got it already. They rule everything and always will. There was nowhere you could go that the boot of the Ultra couldn't be felt next to your carotid artery. Got it. Why the senseless slaughter then, like what the flexy was showing me?

She just watched me with those cool blue eyes and seemed to read every unholy thought inside my head. Anger, and all the rest of it. Even the bewilderment. But her voice, when she spoke, was gentle, and I found myself letting go of a breath I'd been holding for longer than I could remember. Longer than I'd admit to.

"We called them squirters when I worked with the executioner teams. We would set up these chokepoints along identified escape arteries to catch high-value targets for interrogation and intel development. There's most likely an executioner Inquisitor operating in the garage with a mobile cyber-rack. So we know, when we catch the senior and mid-level military officers who are out in front of the escaping units and trying to save their skins by being first off-world, we know a variety of information ranging from underground networks, doomsday plans, off-world bank accounts they've skimmed from war funds, and even actual valuable intel regarding the troops they've abandoned. It may seem like slaughter, and it is, but the ones this far in front of the general exodus, they aren't the angels their stacked bodies might paint them to be."

She stepped back.

The big problem facing us was crossing that bridge undetected. And that didn't look possible. Not with an Ultra sniper in an elevated position watching the approach along the bridge. Coming in by land vehicle, there was absolutely no chance of surprise attack. Even a drop might have trouble if we wanted to come in, fast-rope all over the settlement, and shoot it out with an Ultra executioner team. Which we didn't. Ultras were known to have excellent man-portable anti-air cap.

And then there was the problem of shooting it out in the settlement itself. There was a main street and a few buildings. Not a lot of cover and most likely all of it was set up to their advantage. We didn't have the numbers for a direct assault. I studied the layout. Probably a bar and a general store of some type for desert traders. A couple of living spaces, a garage and refueling station. The refill would be great for the Mule if we had the time. But to stick around and make that happen under fire from a high-speed team of some of the best the Ultra war machine could put together was gonna get real lethal, real fast, for Reaper.

To be honest, blasting our way through at high speed and trying to bypass the fight was gonna shorten our longevity too. Mines. Traversing fire. It'd be about ten seconds at eighty miles an hour of what hell looks like.

So we couldn't get close without getting bloody.

Couldn't take it over.

Couldn't shoot our way through.

I scratched my head because I was outta tricks. Did I mention my helmet had been blown off back in the terminal? If I didn't it was because it had really rung my bell for a few minutes during the worst of it. When I looked over and saw it had cracked in half, I knew I had just spent one of my lives in the arcade of death. Right down the center. Which was stunning. That thing was rated for the highest calibers. So whoever hit me had been using something along the lines of an Awlrhino gun. It was a wonder my neck hadn't snapped on impact.

But war is strange. Who can know it? I ain't the one to ask. Like I tell everyone... I just work here.

Still, I had no clue how to get us past the Ultra executioner team ambush chokepoint.

Time for some Voodoo, I thought, and looked over to see Stinkeye hurling his guts out on all fours in the dust.

"Hey, buddy..."

He waved me away, moaning about death, falling face-down into his own puke which smelled of gutter liquor and bad meat on the street. I'd smelled it before because I'd known this man for as long as I'd been in the company. I needed him to get it together and pull some of that legendary dark Voodoo operator stuff everyone in Voodoo Platoon is known for.

Nether could probably open up a hole in reality and suck some of the executioner team right into a void or something as we commenced our attack. Even create a tornado by suddenly forming an extreme low-pressure area that could ruin that settlement as we hit it at high speed. Some of us might not die. Chief Cook… well, psyops could do crazy things to their heads. I'd seen him do stuff that wasn't real, and I would've sworn was. The truth was his plaything. He bent it and manufactured what he wanted you to see so we could kill you a lot easier. I wasn't sure exactly what he could do here, but I was sure he could create something convincing enough to at least let us get close enough to shoot without the sniper ruining us at extreme ranges. And then there was the Little Girl. And her Wild Thing. Unpredictable, yes. But I was pretty sure that dark and psychotic warrior from another dimension she could briefly call into existence could buy us enough time to hit the southern trails and disappear before the Ultras could call in air support to light us up.

As usual, I had none of these Voodoo assets. None of the things I needed to work with right here and right now. Nothing that would make my difficult life a whole lot easier. They were all with the other elements.

All I had was one drunken Psyonix user who was iffy at the best of times and who now seemed to be having some kind of stroke, or bender to end all benders. He might even be dying.

I bent down, never minding the ripe smell of puke.

I would never say this aloud but might as well since this is a written record that will most likely never make it back into the Bright Worlds of galactic human expansion and if it does will end up in Monarch hands where it will be redacted into oblivion. So I'll say it for the record. However impermanent that record may be.

He is my friend. Stinkeye. I needed to use him. But he was also my friend. And he was also, clearly, incapable of being used at the moment.

What good are friends if you can't use them. Amirite?

Stinkeye suddenly collapsed into unconsciousness and Choker had to get an IV pump started on him, as well as pull him from the pool of his own filth.

"There's that…" I muttered to no one.

"There's what?" asked Punch, coming to stand near me and receive the orders that would get us out of this one. Apparently, I was in charge.

I took a deep breath.

"Well, looks like we gotta do this the hard way."

"And what way is that, boss?" asked Punch again.

I spat some desert dust off into the dull orange weeds that grew here and there out of the reddish-black volcanic rock of the ridge.

"The hard way, Punch, is where we gotta do it ourselves."

CHAPTER THIRTY-FIVE

What the Ultra executioner team guarding the chokepoint across the immense three-thousand-meter span that threw itself across the Crack of Doom spotted was a lone fast-attack Mule with one driver headed across the bridge at a sane and rational pace. Nothing threatening here, folks. Probably a little fast for civilians, but just under SOP for Strange Company. Like the dude driving the Mule was just some savvy rogue staff officer, or even a priority messenger with time on his hands and not looking to make anyone too nervous as they tried to get away mostly unnoticed with some valuable intel or even illegal booty. Just the kind of target an execution team's Inquisitor would be looking for to put in some time on the cyber-rack. And what the sniper in the hexagonal wide-windowed watchtower would see was someone who looked a lot like Boom Boom, driving. Because it was Boom Boom at the wheel. But that didn't matter because the executioner team sniper didn't know Boom Boom, and more importantly he didn't know Boom Boom, our sniper, was dead. Recently. Punch had blown a real pair of nice sunglasses he'd gotten from some refugee a few weeks ago in exchange for some collectible sidearms he'd picked up off dead Loyalists, to make sure it looked like our dead sniper was really just some shady but basically friendly officer guy out for a drive.

The refugee Punch had traded must've figured he was going to need to shoot his way out of stuff more than he was going to need to look cool going forward now that the jig of everything on this planet was up. He was probably right, but the shades did look cool. They were upper-slick mirrored spacer shades. The kind that cost a lot of micro-mem and were worn by people like high-speed frontier scouts and interdiction runners. The kind of people who'd never get caught dead doing

Jump Six while barely outrunning blockade destroyers hurling every weapon they had for the kill shot once they'd smashed your shields.

The kind of people who wanted to look cool on their next date. Not go blind from flare flak trying to run a blockade on an interdicted world.

We used the shades to cover up Boom Boom's dead eyes. Those were kind of a real giveaway since we were betting the Ultra special forces sniper had the best optics the Monarchs could buy. If he was running a targeting life-scan laser then that was gonna be a problem anyway, but we had to play the cards we were dealt. We just had to hope they didn't have that particular card in their hand. The optics would have spotted the death in our friend's eyes. So we used the shades and gambled that would be enough to deceive for effect.

The sniper, who would be the first to acquire the incoming Mule, would see Boom Boom, smile on his face... Oh yeah. About that. Choker used medical staples to create that effect, a perma-smiling Boom Boom, wearing his shades and just out for a drive. The position of the sun, now falling into the west, might help some since we stapled his cheeks wide so his white teeth showed.

"He always had nice teeth," Hustle noted as we stood back to study the work we'd done on Boom Boom's corpse. "I always admired him for that. He spent money on those teeth. That's thinking. Like he was gonna have a future."

"He looks happy," said Choker as he inspected his work with the medical stapler, device still in hand and ready for a touch-up if he wasn't completely satisfied. That's the thing about having a medic who's probably somewhere on the sociopath scale. Nothing's off-limits to him. "That's how I'll always remember him," he said.

Everyone gave Choker the look everyone always gives Choker. A look that says our medic has something deeply wrong with him. Something that bothers even mercenaries on a level they're not completely comfortable with admitting. Especially if this is the guy that's gonna save your life by pulling off a leech that's a little too close to an area that men tend to value. And other valuable medical stuff.

"What?" he asked everyone, sensing our discomfort. But no one answered. Again, this is the guy you tell stuff to you don't share with the rest. Best not to make him... crazy.

So that's what the sniper in the watchtower saw. Out there across the span where the settlement on the far end needed to be bypassed. The rest of us were now waiting, behind a distant curve blocked by the trailing tail of the ridge of jagged volcanic rock, for our plan to take effect.

Our hope was the sniper would be talking to his team leader about their game plan, which it seemed they'd been running for most of the last twenty-fours since formal operations began. How they'd handle innocent little Boom Boom. Who knew? Maybe they'd had this game going before the Battle Spire ever inserted into the combat zone. Great way to collect a lot of intel and data on the situation and get it to Ultra High Command once the invasion started.

As I thought about all this, I gave a dark little chuckle at the impending irony of Boom Boom's tag. No one bothered to ask me what I was amused at. Everyone was pretty much pins and needles to watch what was gonna happen next.

We do love our explosions. Almost as much as our dirty tricks. And, as an NCO, I thought this was good for us. Always look on the bright side, Sergeant Orion. For once we were pulling a scam, a staple of Strange Company that had often given us an advantage where supplies, equipment, numbers, and weapons didn't. Those things were often on the wanting end for us when facing an enemy. But Voodoo Platoon game-changed that. Unfortunately, we didn't have a lot of Voodoo right now to play games. But games we still had.

Someone actually sniggered. I could tell we were pretty pleased with ourselves. As their NCO, I was cool with that. We'd been taking a beating for a bit too long now. It was time for an "Eat This!" to the galaxy.

Meanwhile Boom Boom was closing and we were hoping they'd go ahead and let him into their midst now that he'd been spotted and didn't seem like an attacking force or a threat of any kind. If the sniper did engage, that was no big loss. Boom Boom was already dead. If they blew his head off and the vehicle just kept closing, then they'd have a heads-up. But the vehicle was a guided missile now. Shredding our "driver" wasn't gonna stop the pain coming their way.

Ultras have a lot of magic tricks. Like I said, they have the latest and best equipment the Monarchs can produce. Our Monarch, the Seeker, assured me that yes there are things an executioner team might have to defend themselves against what we were about to do to them, but more than likely only a few would survive our surprise.

"Uh… last time I checked," noted Hoser, Reaper's very large gunner carrying the second Pig, Hustle the AG always nearby and humping belts of ammunition to feed the beast, "an Ultra Marine was worth ten-to-one. Executioners are high-speed low-drag special forces, Sar'nt. Not that I mind all that noise and all, I was lab-grown to kill, but I'm guessing that number goes up with men of their expertise. So…"

He made a show of counting how many we had.

Ten. There were ten of us.

"So unless we get all but one of 'em, we're gonna have some real problems going through the choke."

"We might get all of 'em," said Punch optimistically. Like some lone voice in the wilderness, a prophet no one believed in anymore telling everyone the religion of Luck was still in play despite ours having been nothing but bad since long before this mess. Repent and believe, for the hour of their annihilation might be at hand… maybe, if the dice say, so be it. Sorta.

Still, "Gotta have faith, guys," I reminded what was left of my once forty-man platoon. "Maybe about to change."

"Says who," muttered someone from the cheap seats. I ignored the remark as NCOs know when and when not to do.

We held our breath for the sound of sonic booms that would indicate the executioner sniper had fired his very powerful rifle. He could take out the Mule, yes, but he'd need some pretty good hits. That thing was rated to stand up to a tank round. Conceivably. The people inside the Mule when the tank round hit… ummmm, not so much. But hey, nothing's perfect. And in any case we didn't have any people in the Mule that was now cruising casually three thousand meters across the Crack of Doom. Just Boom Boom with his perma-smile and mirrored spacer shades.

How was Boom Boom driving, you might ask? If he was dead and all? Hauser had hacked the Mule's onboard systems and was controlling the vehicle remotely. All Boom Boom had to do was sit back and enjoy the ride. And then live up to his tag.

My plan, which now seemed like something a Neolithic caveman would come up with to do the other tribe out of their more comely females, had been to take my good friend's body and turn him into a suicide bomber by loading all our high-ex, grenades, and any other explosives anyone had, into the Mule and detting it on the sniper in the checkpoint tower. More than likely that would destabilize enough of the ambush for us to take no more than sixty percent casualties going through at high speed. I was warned by Hauser there was a thirty-six-point-something percent chance the bridge in that section might collapse from usage of all our available high-ex. Fourteen percent chance it would collapse entirely. Leaving us trapped on this side of the Crack of Doom.

"I'm cool with that," I said as I made ready to shove my remaining shape charges into the passenger's seat so they'd det on impact.

High-Ex was our one true religion of explosives until the Monarch stepped in. We were gathered around our dead friend like hobgoblins improvising some new giggling wickedness to get their necks out of yet another noose. Soldiers are little more than ever that. You have to be honest about these things. Especially when you're gambling on body-tossing your enemies off an objective after a firefight where it looked like you were all gonna die.

"I think I have something that can help," she said. The Seeker. The Monarch. An otherworldly beauty that had no business among our unclean kind about our wickedness. Her voice clear and strong in the desert silence along the ridge like a song about trains that reminds you it's long past time to be getting to a home you never shoulda left.

Clock wasn't just burning. It was on fire. We needed to make that rally. We needed to cross the desert and link up. The rest of Strange, brothers to one another, strangers to the universe, were depending on us. We'd need every rifle we could carry to get the company off-world.

"Better than these?" Jacks held up four bricks of Thermodyna in response to the Monarch's suggestion that she had something better. Thermodyna was our preferred high-ex for disabling structures and breaching doomsday bunkers. Stable, extremely kinetic, you could trigger it with everything from traditional detonators to a targeting laser.

The Monarch pulled one of her fancy grenades off her chest rig. It was cylindrical and stippled with a rubberized grip that encompassed its surface. No spool. Just a weird dull gray knob on top. Definitely military-grade. She gave the knob a twist and it began to throb and pulse in a soft neo red.

"This is molecular thermite. Blast radius two thousand meters. It'll flash-fry everything in less than ten seconds as the molecules ignite and cause chain reactions turning connecting molecule strings into firebombs. Think of it as self-replicating napalm. Moves like a wave outward from the center. We use it to clean sensitive sites. And to avoid capture. My problem here was delivery. You..."

She stared at Choker and his staple gun, Hauser deep inside the guts of the engine to reach the Mule's control systems, and the rest of us ponying up all our explosives. To be honest, we have a lot. Most of us carry extra. Just in case. And of course... dead Boom Boom smiling behind his shades, tied to the wheel and the seat with paracord.

"... you seem to have solved the... delivery problem," she said dryly. "This will do. Just get it close and it'll cook them inside their armor. Unless they've got a quantum defensive pocket... they're dead."

Now, watching the last hundred meters of Boom Boom's corpse's existence, the sniper still had not fired.

"They're going for it..." squealed Punch with delight. The only thing he loved more than punching people in the face was blowing them up.

"How many in an execution team?" asked Choker, attempting to act nonchalant. If you didn't know him it might have worked. If you did it gave you the chills. Asking like he had some running count of everyone whose demise he'd ever had a hand in bringing about. The executioner team was definitely making his list.

I try not to judge. But sometimes...

"Six," stated Hauser emotionlessly.

The Monarch confirmed this number with a nod as I cast a quick look at her.

Twenty meters to go and Stinkeye wandered up to our observation position. We'd left him in the other Mule where we'd piled all our remaining gear. It was going to be tight from here on out as we all crammed in to make the rally.

"Whatchu lizards up ta now?" he croaked like a hungover starport gutter drunk. "Anyone wanna play—"

A flash close to something nuclear lit up the entire sky. It was shocking and made you exhale all your breath and know you just did something very wrong. An offense against all that was natural. Five seconds later a hot tornado of heat and searing light washed over us and knocked our Voodoo chief onto his butt. Clouds raced away high above and suddenly the day was about twenty degrees hotter than before even over here almost four thousand meters away from the center of the detonation.

I shielded my eyes and stared into the bright furnace where the settlement at the far end of the span had been. When I could see again, a black-smoke mushroom cloud suddenly turned into a slow-moving twister, flinging black, burning debris and smoking gray ash away in every direction.

Reaper began to cheer.

Thirty minutes later we drove across the bridge as fast as we dared. Racing through the blackened remains of ground zero. The Monarch had assured us the device was non-nuclear and there would be no fallout.

The sands on the other side of the span had turned into weirdly beautiful glass sculptures. Some meaningless. Some looking like a race of alien titans, half squid, half cloud giant, that might have ruled the galaxy before humanity ever uttered the words "lift off."

As for the settlement…

It was as though nothing had ever been there. It was like driving across the surface of a dead and airless moon that had been charbroiled. And then, two thousand meters later there was just flaming desert weed and prickleflower for us to disappear into.

The Seeker pointed us toward the track that led off the Eighty-Eight and down into the bowl of the eastern Wastes' lowest points. The terrain down there was lost in a chalky heat haze that shimmered and sparkled due to the vast mineral deposits and strange features that were characteristic of the post-Crash desert.

The Kid was at the wheel. I studied what we were getting ourselves into, wondering how many I'd get killed down in there where an alien starship had once fractured the crust of this world. Maybe even myself. Maybe I'd even get me killed. And then I gave the Kid the signal to go into it. To take us to whatever we'd been headed toward all along. Whether we liked it or not.

We were on our way, and I was hoping for good things, but expecting worse. Which is the lot of NCOs.

Same as it ever was.

So it will ever be until the heat death of the universe.

CHAPTER THIRTY-SIX

I've been to a lot of worlds. Driven across vast stretches of endless weirdness that bore little resemblance to the place I first started out on. Or even any of the worlds I might have called familiar. Being a mercenary boils down to this... go to strange and interesting worlds, sometimes stations or starships, and kill people. So let's just say I have a broad depth of experience in places where people pay to have you conduct warfare on their behalf. Having said that, the Crash Wastes had some of the weirdest terrain features I'd ever seen in my too short, yet felt very long, life. Over thirty-six hours into this op and I felt like an old man. Older than Stinkeye who seems long-lived due to Monarch Dark Lab experimentation. The Wastes made Crash the weirdest world I'd been on by far.

We drove until darkness came again and the three moons of this world began their bizarre dance across the big sky. All of us crammed into the last remaining Mule. We stopped as much as we could for everyone to get out, stretch their legs, and try to make the best of a long and uncomfortable journey by rearranging what could be as best they could.

You can only rearrange so much. It is what it is, as some like to say on Symbala. Sometimes you just have to count distance and hours, and suffer silently, happy you've still got your life, whereas the trail of dead comrades you've left behind... currently don't.

It's best to be honest about the state of things.

There were conversations on these long stretches across the desert silence that began, over comm, between myself and the Monarch, as we drove deeper and deeper out into the weirdness of a wasteland ruined by a falling alien starship long ago. Because I now realize the importance of the Crash Wastes, I'll put down what's there. What's in that vast and fractured land, ruined by a stellar intruder long ago. What we passed through, and what I think it is. And of course, as much as the Monarch was able to tell me, so if anyone is reading this account and coming to their own conclusions about what really happened, and what needs to be done about it, well, then they can follow the trail I'm leaving here and now. That's been the purpose of what I'm putting down here all along. Why I've carved it out of the main logs of Strange Company for consumption by whoever finds it. I'll figure out some way to get it out, some kind of transport or even signal headed toward Astacia Esquival, the company rep for our legal firm. Lawyer. Accounts. She does a lot. I hope they appreciate her. She seems like the kind of person who'll do the right thing come hell or high water. But then again, what do I know. I've never met her in person. She just seems like the type.

Maybe I'm an optimist that way. Maybe some detail I'm putting down is important to whoever needs to clean up this mess that started out on Crash and got us what we couldn't get out of even if we wanted to. For the record. Maybe they can make things right.

Whatever "right" is anymore.

So… what is *the Crash*?

The Crash. Not *a* crash. Proper noun. And not to be confused with the planet, which got named second. After. Because of.

The Crash.

The first scout to reach this world, Amos Ferragamo, piloting a Comet-class vessel, Model 301, swept the system with sensors shortly after jumping in. Alarm bells went off and that old scout, Amos Ferragamo, got some huge pings and interesting data right off the bat. Sensors detected a huge nuclear heat spike on the surface of the fourth world in from a star no one had been much interested in. The system was coreward, toward the galactic center, which was the focus of human expansion about that time, right about when we, humanity, encountered the No, a nasty bunch of cybernetic organisms on Sirius. But this area hadn't been surveyed much and so it was worth the investigation and attention of one lonely scout.

The No. Not as in Negative. That's what they called themselves during the first invasion of the colony worlds. History calls them the No Cybarbarians. The

No gave humanity their first really big interstellar war, and genocides. For about ten years there it looked like we were going over the hill and into ancient history.

The nuclear signature was interesting to old Amos as he set up the glideslope approach in the cockpit of his scout ship to this strange new world he'd discovered. Jump drive exit put him two months out from orbital insertion, and he spent that two months running scans, developing system hazard maps, and plotting the approach. Which is probably about the most dangerous thing you can do as a scout explorer. More scouts have died approaching unknown worlds than down planetside facing unknown dangers on the ground.

But that's why they get paid the big bucks, or so I've heard them say.

Amos knew he was on to something because that fourth world was Earth-like, and apparently inhabited, if that nuclear signature was any indication. But the closer he got the more dismayed he became by what seemed like conflicting data from both sensors and scopes. Nuclear reaction would indicate a definite Tech Seven level of development. Minimum. That should mean major megapoli, rudimentary starflight, satellites at the least. Big navigational hazards those are. And of course, mandatory radio communication. He was getting none of those things on scanners or comm as the scout hurtled itself toward this unknown world on full-burn dumbthrust. The sensor sweep was only picking up the nuclear signature. And nothing else. Nada. Nope. Everything was real quiet. No signs of cities or civilization of any kind. He spent a week theorizing that possibly he was encountering a civ that did things much differently and couldn't be measured by the standard Dyson Tech Tree classification. Perhaps they were underground? Or maybe he was looking at a dead civ that had somehow left the lights on in at least one nuclear reactor before they annihilated themselves. Both of those possibilities gave him cause for concern. Easy to get in way over his head in both of those situations. Booby traps and apex predators were top of the list to an old scout with nothing but a fast ship and a rifle. Underground dweller civs had proven to be particularly alien and nasty about intruders during past encounters. There was a reason they were underground, and it usually had a lot to do with paranoia and xenophobia. A dead civ, on the other hand, meant something had wiped them out.

And if that something had wiped them out then why wouldn't that something just wipe out old Amos out here trying to stake a discovery claim?

A month out, his scopes were getting a good look at the surface and he was seeing nothing that looked like civ. So, what was the nuclear signature, he must've wondered. Volcano with a vent deep down into the crust? Perhaps even way down into the magma of the world's core? That might do it. He got a good look at the target site five days out as he set up for the orbital insertion glide path to take him straight down through atmo, then go to thrusters for supersonic flight direct over the target area.

Those old scouts like the Comet 301, a delta wing strapped around a big old jump drive engine, didn't have a-grav. If Amos made a landing it was gonna be rough. Chances were, he wouldn't walk away from it, much less even be able to take off afterwards. But Amos had ridden *White Lightning*, his Comet 301, downplanet on a dozen prior roller-coaster rides to surfaces on other undiscovered or barely discovered worlds. He was wily, and an addicted gambler. Two requisites for being a good scout. A good scout was someone who survived at least one world despite the risk to ship and life, and even the risk of permanent stellar castaway status. But discovering a world before anyone else was worth the danger. And the rewards were fantastic. First Holder rights, with direct payments set up by the Monarchs going forward. Add in an unusual world with something interesting, and you've got a hundred times the going rate. Enough to live like a potentate for the rest of your life on one of the pleasure rings.

So what Amos wanted was a good look at this supervolcano, or whatever it was, from at least as low as ten thousand feet during a flyby right over the top. His camera gear and sensors were all set up in *White Lightning*'s starboard wing stacks to record everything. As he came over the curve of the world, dropping down from orbit, he could see in the distance on the horizon that the target was obscured by black smoke. Even at one hundred ten thousand feet.

Probably just the volcano getting ready to explode, he must've thought, as he fired up the supersonic engines and redirected a power bleed from the jump drive to the forward ram shield to cut down on atmospheric chop, which was heavy. As he came in against the planet's rotation to slow his groundspeed and get as much time as possible over the target before making his decision to find a landing area or go to thrusters full and try to reach orbit once more, he began to spot some of the more unusual features on this strange and undiscovered world.

There were three continents.

Two supers. Southern and northern hemispheres. The supervolcano, or whatever it was, on the northern continent. There's also a third polar continent that extends out into the Chaotico Ocean. The island chains are there. But on this insertion, he was obsessed with the target area and the nuclear signature on the northern continent because even though he told himself in his heart it was some sort of natural phenomenon like a fissure that tapped the magma-filled core, he wasn't convinced it was.

He had a feeling he was on to something unexpected. And he had to make sure.

Those unusual features were starting to reveal themselves by star-rise over this bizarre and undiscovered world as the Comet 301 streaked across the upper atmosphere, bleeding speed and altitude to make insertion over the world. If the ship began to burn up, he couldn't even eject. He'd ditched that gear for more important sensors to help him thoroughly establish his claim.

A core fissure would have earned him the highest rate from the Monarchs. Or the corporations. The near-unlimited energy from a direct core tap would have turned Crash into an industrial and manufacturing powerhouse like Hella, the first of the Bright Worlds.

But like I said, he had a feeling there was something else going on as he saw the first of the fractures in the surface near the nuclear heat signature. Something amazing. Coming in against the rotation with as much sunlight as he could use, he spotted the first features upwards of two hundred miles away from the actual Crash. Massive cracks, rents, and fractures in the world he was racing over.

Before all that though was the feature he was just beginning to understand was the most bizarre. The supercontinent contained some kind of vast gentle crater, a huge depression in its central plain. And at its center, directly, was the nuclear signature source. This crater stretched thousands of miles across the northern continent. Within that crater the main landform type was alkaline salt desert. Wasteland. Typical of major impact strikes, but nothing the scout had ever seen or heard of had reached this level of destruction. The impact must've been huge. This crater was so vast, and as has been said, gentle, that it absorbed the entire central section of what must have once been a plateau that covered much of the continent. Sharp mountains and forested coastlands formed a line of demarcation all around its edges.

Some of what I'm putting down here was conjecture on the part of the author of a book I read about the whole thing. I was reading chapters here and there during the early days of the war here. Just to learn more about the world we were fighting on. Like I said, history is my jam. My happy place. It was a biography of Amos Ferragamo and the early discovery mystery surrounding Crash. When I got to this part, the flight over the Crash, I finished the rest of the book, which I'd been slowly working on for months, in one night.

Whatever it was that hit this world, it probably wasn't a supervolcano because supervolcanoes don't cause craters that big and keep burning. Probably a meteor strike, and the nuclear signature meant the meteor had most likely cracked the crust and mantle. *Big Prizes*, old Amos must've been thinking as he lost altitude and switched over to recording and scanning, flying the ship with one hand and trying to calibrate his mad hodgepodge of instruments with the other. Collecting data he'd use to verify the sale of the world's rights and the price he would be entitled to. Again, he was dreaming of an industrial powerhouse like Hella as he threw out the aero brakes and tried to keep the ship stable for recording. With him owning vast shares in a corporation that would want a piece of this amazing world, he would have riches beyond imagining. That was the other option. You could take the Monarch payout and live easy. Or, you could sell to the corporations for stake and then live easy on the interest. Even maybe become a player. Who knew?

You were never gonna be a Monarch. That was for sure. No one is that dumb except maybe thirteen-year-old girls who think Prince Charming Monarch is going to come in and sweep them off their feet and make them one of humanity's best. Just 'cause love.

Then he saw the Scar that had been carved out on the world below. That's a feature off to the southeast of the Crash site. It's the big one. There are others.

Smaller ones. Cracks in the world that head off at odd angles. But the Scar was the first thing he spotted. It was huge. Immense. Conspiracy theorists have posited every explanation for it, right up to and including the claim that the alien ship fired some kind of beam weapon that was orders of magnitude more powerful than a D-beam strike, leaving the Scar as it went down. It's twenty miles wide and a mile deep, the Scar. It runs for a thousand miles to the southeast. And it's nothing but fused diamond.

Another theory is that when the ship came down in multiple pieces, the engines disconnected on reentry and exploded down the length of the Scar, creating an immense gash in the world. Still others say the ship must have come down in battle and the Scar is some impression left by a siege superweapon used to attack the ship once it was down planetside and trying to defend itself on the ground. The attackers couldn't cross the surface and so they in effect used sappers to blast their way into the wreck in order to finally kill the crew.

That theory isn't as wacky as it seems. Much of the weirdness, when you look at the Wastes, looks like the result of superweapons the Monarchs in their Dark Labs wish they could dream up.

And me looking at all this as the miles passed got me thinking, and so we began to talk.

The conversation between the Monarch and me began like this. We'd been driving in silence for two hours since we'd left the blackened remains of the outpost beyond the bridge over the Crack of Doom. We pulled over on the edge of a lake of boiling water that swirled hypnotic purple and spilled paint golds. The smell coming up off the lake and its many pools that stretched off into the distance was definitely sulfur. And something else. Something familiar, but something I couldn't place at the time. I wondered, in fact, if I'd ever smelled it before, and why it seemed familiar. The murmur and pop of the bubbles was constant, and I was standing there near its vast edge spreading away into the chalky sunlight, staring down into the hypnotic swirls.

"There are lifeforms in there not catalogued on any known world," said Hauser from behind me. Pig at the ready and scanning the horizon. Belted ammo draped around his thick neck. The damage to his features had revealed the gleaming combat chassis underneath. He looked like a grinning skeleton on one side of his face. Hauser on the other. I concentrated on the Hauser part. We'd seen a flight of Ultra drops off in the distance a few hours back while we were on the road, heading toward the southeast. So, while we didn't think we'd run into any out here, we knew they were around. That Ultra Marines were operational even in this region.

I didn't respond to Hauser's undiscovered lifeforms observation. He did that a lot. Lots of worlds had those. New lifeforms. The galaxy was a pretty busy place. But Crash had been settled long ago. There really shouldn't have been any surprises. Research and exploration were pretty thorough on most worlds this developed. But then I remembered the Wastes were considered a permanent no-go zone.

Why?

Like so many things in the galaxy, if the Monarchs said so, you got used to not asking questions. Way above my pay grade. Not my monkeys, not my circus. The reasons not to question were almost hardwired into our DNA. If the Monarchs said so… it just was. No questions asked. For example, this world, currently being ravaged by deadly Ultra Marines, had asked why not? In their own way. As in why not govern ourselves?

Monarch Answer: D-beam strike. Death camps. Slaughter. Deleted from the stellar charts.

Probably by the time we made it back to the *Spider* that would be the case. If we made it back to the *Spider*.

"My scanners indicate they are silica-based, Sergeant Orion. Which is very… unusual. They are cephalopods. Their eyes, and most of them have at least seven thousand six hundred and twenty-eight, are emitting radiation at very low levels."

Okay, that's freaky, I thought. Not just the thousands of eyes, but… the radiation bit. Hadn't heard of a lifeform that did that. And silica-based. I knew everything in the universe was generally carbon-based. So yeah, that also was unusual.

Maybe that's why the Monarchs made sure this stayed a no-go zone. There was new stuff here and they wanted it for themselves when they got around to it. I couldn't see the Battle Spire anymore as I stared off to the west, but apparently they had decided to get interested.

She was nearby. The Monarch who called herself the Seeker. And was now a member of Reaper. Official standing in the Strange Company. File that under weird things Sergeant Orion never expected. She'd heard Hauser's assessment of the tiny microscopic squids with thousands of eyes that emitted low levels of radiation and lived in a lake of boiling sulfur water. Water that was gold and purple and weirdly hypnotic. And I wanted to just bliss out and stare at it for hours.

How much weirdness can one fit in a paragraph, I wonder, as I read back over this. And the answer is… that much. That much weirdness can fit in. Which, when you think about it, is a lot of weird. Lotta questions there. But hey, I'm just a merc. I don't ask questions and I don't play silly games.

I kill. For mem.

And I don't believe in anything. That'll get ya killed. Both sides of this war currently fleeing for their lives in every direction knew the Ultras had a no-discrimination policy during First Pass.

"The Monarchs wanted this to be a no-go zone, didn't they?" I asked the Monarch. The rest of what was left of my platoon was milling about, urinating, eating, or trying to rearrange their gear to lessen the torture the next several hours over bad terrain would produce.

"They did," she answered, and then realized the inadequacy of the statement. They were her. She could read it in my eyes. Seeing that I was silently screaming, *but you're one of them*. Sensing this, she corrected the mistake.

"We did, Orion."

We both turned away to watch the vast lake, me wondering how we were gonna navigate around and through it. It seemed shallow and there were land bridges out there we might try, but who knew if we'd end up in a dead end, or quicksand, if that was a thing.

Her? I have no idea what she was thinking. She's a Monarch. They ain't even human anymore.

"This..." she spread one alabaster arm, long and thin, muscles delicately sculpted to perfection, across the strangely hypnotic vista we were entranced by, "...this is the most important place in the galaxy. But there's a caveat, Orion."

She paused. Like she was dangling a mystery in front of me. And asking me to bite. I truly despise vague statements like that and have a hard rule that I never bite. No matter what. I won't give the satisfaction.

I wanted to though. Real bad. But I was NCO cool. Which is really just a kind of grim resignation in which all hope of anything ever going right has been beaten out of you by experiences.

"Oh, yeah. I think I know what that is," I said sarcastically. "Caveat. I used to think it was a snack they served at rich people parties I've seen movies of. Then I found out it means... a condition to the premise of something."

I gave her a look I hoped indicated I was not interested, nor did I have the time to be played by vague manipulating statements. I was busy trying to save our butts out here.

She didn't bite. Just gave me a cool appraisal like she was considering whether she should buy me for some project she needed to get done. Not sure if I'd do the job. Not sure if I was up to the task. Maybe I was on sale. Or pass on by for some other better tool to get done what she needed getting done.

Or at least that was my take on her look. Who knew?

"Listen, does this place, and what you're trying to get me to bite on, does it have anything to do with me getting done what you need done, and getting my team off-world?"

"It does."

"Okay, then tell me. Why is this the most important place in the galaxy?"

"It's important if you accept the caveat," she said patiently. Not condescending. Just calm. Patient.

"And accepting that this place... is important... it helps accomplish the mission?" I asked, trying to clarify. Trying to get whatever I could to get what remained of my command out of here and somewhere safe. The *Spider*. If it didn't get shot to bits trying to effect the suborbital rendezvous.

"It does, Orion."

"Okay. So then what's the caveat? Tell me. Daylight's burning. Night soon and we'll have to move slower." I checked my rifle. Magazine. Port. Sights. If just for something to do to show I needed to be convinced and had important stuff to see to.

"The caveat requires that you believe in something, Sergeant Orion. And as you said, you don't believe in anything."

A Monarch who wants me to believe. Get religion or buy some subscription. Of all the things I couldn't imagine about such a meeting, and I never did because I don't think situations like this are supposed to happen. It's unnatural. We don't mix. Monarchs and anyone else.

But the universe is a strange place. And these are strange times indeed.

That book I finished. The book about the scout who discovered this world. The mystery that sucked me in and made me finish the last part of it in one night when everyone else in Strange was off drinking and playing cards.

It ends with a clip. The last recorded image from the flight logs of the scout ship. Airlock door. The first few seconds are just Amos in his environmental suit, getting all adjusted. Breathing heavily. It's dark and there are few lights inside the airlock. Then he taps the door panel, and the airlock slides open, top to bottom.

Daylight on a new world. The first look. The scout is now a silhouette in a spacesuit. An image as old as spaceflight. The new world beyond, in the grainy and bad feed, is burning white sands. Burning blue sky. And in the distance, the Crash itself. All you can see is black smoke venting out of the gleaming white desert. And perhaps some alien structure inside the boiling black. An engine? A fuel tank? Aft bridge? But the oily smoke swallows it as the wind shifts.

I rewound that image a dozen times just like countless others had. You see something different each time. And really, you see nothing concrete. I'm sure it's been analyzed ad nauseam.

"Well, here goes nothin'," Ol' Amos says. Famous last words. And then exits the airlock. Him walking across the burning white sand toward the black smoke is the last image we see.

He was never heard from again.

"The caveat requires that you believe in something, Sergeant Orion. And as you said, you don't believe in anything."

CHAPTER THIRTY-SEVEN

We drove away from the lake, skirting its event horizon edge. It was hard at times to tell where the hypnotic waters and orange creamsicle sky met. It was like we were driving into a hallucination and the only thing we could keep track of was the ghost trail of the old smugglers' run we followed. Archived drone data said there was a system of land bridges we might take to get around its milky vastness.

I'd walked away from her, the Seeker, the Monarch, after she said that last bit about me needing to believe in something. I didn't need that right now. And honestly, I didn't know if I needed that ever. That part about believing in something which felt specific and which was going to change my universe-view. I wasn't entirely comfortable with that. What she was asking. In fact, I was downright uncomfortable with what she was asking. Most who've seen my face say that's some kind of natural state for me. Default uncomfortable. But in my defense... there's always something to worry about. You learn that early on being a soldier. So there's that. Also, I didn't have time for her Monarch power games. Or any games at all. We didn't even have any more time for this break beside the lake of unending hypnotic illusions. I wasn't interested in mysteries because I wasn't paid to be interested in them. Except, if I'm going to be honest, as I keep saying throughout this account that we have to be honest about certain things... then, yeah... I was bothered. Some small voice whispered to me that mysteries are like history, which is really nothing but a mystery in the age of the Monarchs, may it never end, and that's why it's my jam. That need to know the truth even if it's uncomfortable. Even if it'll get you killed.

You have to be honest about these things, Orion.

Shut up. Shut your pie hole right now, I told the whisper and knew it was like trying to throw sand at the ocean.

You don't want to end up like Ol' Amos, do you, I silently yelled at myself. You're surrounded by mysteries and none of them are as important as getting your men off this dog of a world, Orion. We don't need to get involved in mysteries, causes, or know the big picture. We need to get it on and get off this mess.

Above my pay grade.

Not my monkeys.

I lived my life, in combat, front sight forward. That was the best I could do to keep it working. Give me something to go kill and the right equipment to do it with and I'd try to make that happen for whoever was doling out the mem on that one. That was what I did.

That didn't feel right. Caught myself.

That's what I do.

Right?

That's what I do. Past tense is for the dead.

Except she was dangling the real dark fun mystery-history stuff right in front of me, a wannabe scout who hadn't had the currency to scrape together to get out of there, like she had a window into my brain and she could see that part that liked history. The knowing part of my mind. The part that had wanted to be a scout if things had shaken out better, except they hadn't. The mystery addict part. The curious part. She could see it like it was a window into my skull.

Hey buddy, I told myself. Maybe this is the universe paying you back for all the sacrifice and service. A last chance to solve the big questions before you buy it in some ambush you shoulda seen coming, or dropping on a world where the odds are stacked against you. Last chance, Orion… going, going… past tense. It's waiting for everyone.

Don't they say curiosity killed the vaporcat?

At least on Cyria they say it. I don't know about the rest of the universe. I don't know if they say it on other worlds. But there's probably some equivalent. That's the thing about the universe. Everything's different, and the same.

I sat there stewing in the TC seat as we drove on, not wanting to play, knowing I needed to. Passing melted terrain and forests of strange crystals that grew like low shrubs and sang on the notes of the wind. Singing crystalline plants. In harmony. On pitch. To some score that reminded me more of mysteries all around us. That there was more to see if you were willing to open your eyes. And that whisper was calling me a chicken. For all my big talk about wanting to know, about history, about the truth and the clarity of war, here it all was… and I was ducking my head in the sand because the ticket was too expensive.

Except that I always thought it was cheap. Belief, that is.

We hit a serious hole in the trail we were following once we made our way across the lakes. Crossed strange yellow salt flats where the sun beat down on us, and then made our way into a series of badlands ravines that took us lower and deeper into the Crash Wastes as we picked up an old smugglers' road.

We hit the hole and I was jangled out of my brooding self-doubt.

The Kid looked at me and shrugged guiltily. I had no idea what his story was. I knew he had one. Everyone does. Everyone in the Strange Company has got a tale to tell before whatever's gonna happen… happens. He'd joined up for some reason to get away from somewhere he wasn't wanted anymore. That was my bet. But only because I'd seen it a dozen other times. He was a bright kid who learned quick. Handsome. Women would've even called him beautiful. Except now he was dragging that scar he got from the hot graze where I thought he'd bought it. He had too if the look in his eyes was anything to judge by. But he was still beautiful. Handsome. Being a merc would take care of that in time. Endless hard nights, long patrols that turned you into nothing but the walking dead. Bad food more than good. Hard liquor just to kill the pain. Scars from laying wire across defenses during cold windy bitter rainy days that always seemed to require such work. Mind numb. Fingers too. That's how you get those keeper scars. Flying hot brass burns and the occasional gunshot wound when it was funnel time. Add in some frag and spall, and he'd look like the rest of us given time. First tattoo parlor would take him right down to our level with something that meant nothing to anyone not him. Then he'd be the kinda guy young girls don't look at anymore unless you pay 'em to. And then all they see is something else.

But looking at him shrug guiltily now about hitting the pothole in the smugglers' trail and disturbing my personal anxiety fun coaster, good-looking and with enough future ahead of him that he could play mercenary and maybe not get hurt too bad on this one, I wanted him to stay gold. Read that in a book one time I couldn't make sense of. Story about old Earth before we really got out there in the universe and pretended we were something to take seriously. Humanity that is. It was about kids. Bad boys. Greasers. Reminded me of the Strange Company in certain ways. Tags. Battles. Noobs and veterans. Outlaws. I can't remember the tag of the one who was supposed to stay gold. But I remember the why. And as I looked at the Kid driving us toward our arranged meeting with destiny, I wanted him to stay gold. I looked back at Stinkeye and the rest. We were already damned for sure. But maybe the Kid wasn't damned yet. Not fully. If there can be such a thing as halfway damned. Maybe he wasn't all gone. Maybe this whole thing had scared him straight and he would get out of the Strange before it was too late, and he was stuck forever. Like we were now whether we chose to admit it or not.

Addicted to da juice, Stinkeye likes to crow when he's good and drunk. Feeling like making trouble for someone on a cold and windy night when there's no moon and no mercy. Because da action is da juice, as dey say, Little King.

I smiled at the Kid and indicated it was okay. And to just keep his eyes on the road. We had a long way to go. And a short time to do it in, as the First Sergeant always says. There would be other potholes.

Some electric feeling ran all over me. Like I was still good. Not as far gone as Stinkeye. Going, going, not totally gone yet. I still saw that some could be saved. And that made me better than the worse. Right, Orion? Nah. That's just a lie. Even I know that. Like I said. You have to be honest about these things. Especially with yourself.

I tapped the comm for the Monarch, who was sitting right behind me. Wedged in between the door and Hustle, who was smaller than the rest of us. I'd catch him staring at her. He's small, but ambitious. I'd seen him bag statuesque Amazons in soldier bars with nothing but determination and solid game.

"Pretend I believe… why?" I said to her over the comm. The private channel between just the both of us. "As in… why is this the most important place in the galaxy?"

"Universe, Orion. It's the most important place in the universe. But I know you don't believe. So. How much time until our next turn? And maybe I can convince you. If you'll let me."

I told her the time to the next turn. Then added another six hours on that course track before we'd begin to think about a place to stop for the night, so we were in striking distance of the rally the next day.

"Then we have some time. Maybe I can't make you believe in something, Sergeant Orion…"

"I said just Orion."

"Orion then. But maybe I can show you why you might want to rethink that position. We have time. Some. So I'll just walk you through the entire history of modern post-humanity and how we got here. Then maybe you'll understand what I'm trying to do now. What I'm trying to make right. Okay… Orion?"

"Go," I said irritably and tried to get comfortable. My back and legs were killing me. I drank water and listened to her. Sometimes I burned a cigarette and tried to pretend what she was saying didn't mean anything to me.

But it did.

Why?

Because everything she said explained why my life was the way it was. I was getting all the forbidden history. Straight from the mouth of a Monarch. No redactions. No blank or missing pages. No mysteries. No reminders that this kind of inquiry is not permitted by order of the Monarchs. To understand what this is like… take it back to when mankind didn't know what the universe was like. Who was out there. How much life was teeming on a lot of worlds. Then have an alien show up and lay out a stellar star chart and show you how many civilizations are within galactic striking distance of our most basic interstellar travel options. I didn't want to believe her little story. But that was because I told myself not to. Made myself. Mind over matter. You don't mind, it don't matter, Sergeant Orion. Later, when I believed, then everything that came after was my fault just as much as it was hers. Because maybe I was the first to believe what would, eventually, destroy all of us.

"Pretend you lived a long, long time ago, Orion. Back when humanity was first colonizing the home system. And I mean… barely colonizing. We had robots on a few worlds. And big dreams about establishing exploration teams there. Not the Military Industrial Complex Rings of Venus. Or the Sky Cities of Mars and the mineral plantations that cover the entire surface and even the seas there. Mars was a desert world, to put it mildly, not what you've heard it is now. A world of endless green oceans and islands like tropical paradises where we Monarchs live in tech-pyramids that would have made the pharaohs looks like vagrants cobbling together junk homes from the dumpster in the worst part of the city. Venus was violent then. No one would survive the surface for more than a minute in our best-rated ships. It was living hell on Venus during those first few years. Trust me. I was there. But we tamed it. Made it our own."

She paused and I watched her in the side mirror, the wind whipping stray strands of red hair across her beautiful young face as she gazed at the horizon and talked about events a thousand years ago as near as I can tell. History gets murky the further you go back. The Monarchs don't want you getting too interested. Knowing too much. There's danger there for them. Look long enough and you can see that plain as day.

The girl in the side mirror was maybe twenty-eight. But she'd seen the whole history of humanity in space. Commanded a division in the Sindo.

"In that time there were no Monarchs," she continued over our private comm. "We were all human then at the beginning. But just like now, some of us considered ourselves better qualified to direct the course of humanity on behalf of everyone else. To lead toward a brighter future for us all after a series of pandemics, wars, and disasters we'd secretly orchestrated to show the need for what we were proposing. A better society, built from the ground up. More government to fix the mistakes of government. Whether they liked it or not, we'd decided there could only be two groups within humanity. Us, the transhumanists, and ancestors… humanity. Humanity one point oh, as we used to say, would be the backup copy in case we got anything wrong as we began to extend our grasp across several local star systems in the surrounding neighborhood of Earth. The homeworld. And in the meantime, our exploration guinea pigs would be the cheap and expendable breeders, humanity one point oh. We'd send them out into the dangerous parts of the universe by convincing them they could be free and outside our grasp. We conned them into doing the dirty work by thinking they were actually resisting us.

"But before that. Back on Earth as it all began, long story short, they didn't want to be led. They had a disease that made them near unmanageable. Yes, they, basic one point oh humanity, talked a great game about wanting human stellar expansion, tech dev, utopia now, but our society in those days was so diverse, and so at odds with each other, and there was that one particular disease a lot of them had, we called it a disease then in our secret planning committees, that prevented us, all of us, transhumanity and humanity, from reaching our goals. Per aspera et astra. Through hardships to the stars. That's what it means in a dead language called Latin. The goal of reaching the stars and getting off-world."

I flicked a cigarette I'd lit off against a narrow canyon wall of red and yellow rock we were cutting down through slowly. This was a bad ambush spot. Hauser was watching everything from the fifty. If it went down here, I'd just tell the Kid to hit it and we'd try to boost through. But I didn't rate our chances of survivability too high. Some of us were gonna die.

Which is to say I had no time for dead languages I didn't understand. I was too busy imagining all the ways we were gonna die right here and right now.

"This disease," she said later, once we were out of the red rocks of sudden death and following sand dunes down slopes so steep the Mule began to slip and skid. Ahead of us was nothing but a dense chalky layer of dust like some storm obscuring our vision. We'd lost the old smugglers' trail and were dead reckoning now. We sank deeper and deeper into the lowest points of this mad wasteland.

Later we stopped near the bony remains of some prehistoric monster that looked like a sea serpent, its ridges and vertebrae half-buried in the sand and tailing off into the chalky miasma. Its hollow eyes huge blank spaces of darkness judging us as we stopped to stretch, piss, and gape in wonder at what it had once been.

And what it was now. A bleaching skeleton on a dying world.

"The disease was called Freedom," she began again in the desert silence as we stared at the prehistoric monster in wonder. "It had a different meaning than the one you understand it to be now, Orion. As in, you are free because the Monarchs have guaranteed your freedom. That's the exact phrasing you'll find in every law; in fact it is the basis of all law. Interstellar and local. These Rights come from the Monarchs. It's always there. And it's pretty good. Very benevolent of us when you don't think about it too hard. Most people don't question what it really means. They just think, neat, I'm free. The Monarchs are quite benevolent. The part people don't think about too hard is that it really means they are free to explore for us, consume for us, produce for us, create for us... free to submit to us. Everything... is for us. You know that, Orion. Everyone knows it at some point whether they want to admit it or not. You just don't think too hard about it. If I'm wrong, let me know."

I didn't because she wasn't. I knew it. There had been times, years even, when I'd thought about it too much. So much that it hurt and made you feel a kind of hopeless helplessness that told you it was better not to think about it at all and just be happy accepting it the way it is.

"We changed the meaning a long time ago," she continued in the humming silence of our comm. "After a pandemic we engineered. We changed it when all of swollen, dirty, warlike, addicted, lazy humanity begged us for a cure and traded their souls for chains just so we'd give it to them and save them from what we'd wrought. A few yards at a time during each crisis until one day we reached the goalposts. A pandemic we'd created. A virus we'd engineered. We were good with word games back then. Good with bioweapons then. Armed conflict is for amateurs. Why do that when you can just wipe out a population with an invisible case of the sniffles that gets worse and worse? Or a cough that makes your eyeballs bleed? We blamed them on bats, mice, monkeys, and of course the Third World. You don't understand that term. The Third World. But to put it in modern galactic perspective... the Third World is the entire galaxy, every world, every starship, every ring, not Monarch. Monarch worlds are the top. Everything else is the Third World. We changed the meanings of words to make people afraid of using them. And in doing so we taught them how to think without them ever realizing we had been reeducating them for a very long time.

"But back then, back on old Earth, the disease that stopped us from reaching our potential… was Freedom. Too many other ideas that weren't our own made things messy. Hard to get organized and off a world with limited resources. And we were the best and the brightest. In those days, Orion, space travel was very hard. It took a huge amount of effort just to get upwell. Into orbit. Another planet? Near impossible. Meaningfully speaking. Star travel was for gibbering idiots. So the Monarchs decided—"

"You," I interrupted her as I stood there staring at the bones of the huge dead sea serpent vanishing off into the nether of dust. We couldn't see much here. We were relying on old data and a compass to get where we needed to be. Hopefully the air would clear lower and deeper in, once we got through this inversion layer. And what she was saying made me mad for no reason I could articulate. So I just lashed out at her like an angry child that didn't like the rules of the game. And even as I did I wondered how much of that was programming. Reeducation. How much software had been overwritten to make me accept what my hardwiring was angry about. Somewhere in there lay the reason for my sudden temper tantrum. I was shaking. I needed a smoke.

"What?" asked the Monarch, stopping at my sudden burst of hostility. I didn't know what I was angry at. Her. Or the drive. Or the truth.

Probably everything.

I was probably mad at everything.

"You. You're a Monarch, lady, or Seeker or whatever the hell we're supposed to play the game of. Don't forget that. Don't forget you're part of them. Because I won't. The captain may say you're one of us for now. Cool. I can play that game on paper, lady. I'll even lie to myself to get it done. But that doesn't mean I have to actually believe it. You're a Monarch. So… you decided. You decided the rest of humanity was gonna give up freedom so we could all get out here and kill each other right and left on behalf of you to get the worlds good and settled. Organized and developed. Producing for the bank ship to show up and suck everything dry. For you. You and your friends, the other Monarchs. This is your game."

She took a deep breath and sighed. Then lowered her head. It was just the two of us out near the dead sea snake. A game of cards had started back at the Mule with Stinkeye losing, already promising murder against pretty much everyone in on the hand. Croaking they were all against him.

"C'mon, we gotta mount up..." I said, suddenly switching gears back to NCO. I'd had my emotional outburst. Now there was work to be done. Time to get back on mission. "Not much light left."

Not that I could tell from the sun. But the quality of light had turned from milky yellow to deep creamsicle orange down here in the depths of the desert wasteland. And in this light the ancient sea serpent that had once swam the lost seas of this world seemed to smile. Like it was promising us that someday we'd be just like it. Bones in the sands of the universe. And that others would come to stare and wonder at what was left of us, on their way to die somewhere else thinking they would live forever, so that the cycle might just repeat. Again and again. So may it ever be.

But she wouldn't let me go that easy.

She put a hand on my shoulder as I made to turn away and back to the Mule. Get everyone on their feet. Corral Stinkeye and get us pointed toward the rally. Hoping we got lucky and didn't have to do killing work along the way. No time for that. Too little ammo for what was probably gonna be needed for an actual dropship hijack on a hot LZ to get back to the ship and out of this system. Off this dog of a world.

Why did I think that was overly optimistic?

Because I didn't think we had much fight left in us. I was worried about that. Real worried. Once a unit starts running, after being handed a bad defeat like the one we got back at the capital and the starport, it was hard to stop. Hard to stop the running once it got started.

"Yes, Orion. It was me. I was there. Not one of the architects, but definitely one of the true believers. Then. One of the implementers. If only for what I thought were all the right reasons at the time. Maybe they were. But they aren't anymore. Here's the thing, Sergeant. The thing I need you to believe in. I had no right, Orion. None of us did. We had no right to decide. I was wrong. We were wrong."

I stepped close. Fast. She flinched at my sudden move.

"And now?" I snapped at her. Low and like I would do the murder she was hearing in my tone. "You think you got the right now? Now that there's nothing left and you're all on the same team, as you say? We're all on the same team. The Monarch team. You think you got the right, whether you like it or not, to flip the gaming table? Tell us we're not playing what we've been playing all along. It's what you said, everyone's on the same side, right? Everyone that matters, that is. Monarchs. Everyone else just acts their part, do I have that right? Well maybe this is just another game I'm getting tired of playing. Freedom. I know it. If you asked me why I became a mercenary it was because of freedom. Freedom to go wherever you want and not join, or believe, in anything. The freedom to sell yourself for money to the highest bidder. Yeah, just so you know, we all figured that out a long time ago. I don't know how many of us regulars, norms, I don't know what slang term you have for those who aren't Monarchs but I'm sure there's one, but we figured that out a long, long time ago. Hell, I remember when my dad first explained it to me. You know what he said to ten-year-old me, lady? He said freedom's just another word for nothing left to lose, kid. He probably had no idea how he was coding me, but that's, when I really think about it, probably why I became a hired soldier. I'm down to losing the last thing I value. My life. No home. No ship. No wife. No kids I know of. No job on a world where I gotta make sure I'm doing everything everyone else says I gotta do. You make people think those things are important and then you got 'em right where you want 'em. Convince them those are the things to want and then you can play games like letting them imagine they have freedom when they really don't. You know what they got. The freedom not to lose those things. The freedom to obey. Me, us, Strange Company—we just got our lives. That's what I'm down to. Those idiots up there cheating each other at cards on a world being annihilated by the galaxy's apex predators. Your dogs the Ultras. We're practically dead. We can't play anymore, and I bet on some level, even if doesn't bother you, it bothers some of the other Monarchs. I bet they hate when you figure that out. I've seen enough worlds get ruined over that when the locals choose to trade their lives for a chance at fending you guys off. Thinking the corporations are allies when really… if I'm following everything you're saying, even them, the counteroffer they say corporations are, they're really just you too. Even if they don't know it. That's right, isn't it?"

I must've started shouting because they were all already staring at me raving like a lunatic out near the giant sea snake in the desert. Surrounded by late afternoon orange creamsicle air. Shouting at a stunner. An uber model not meant to hunt with dogs like us. The wind came up and caught her hair and I wanted her, and hated myself for it.

I'd charged her. Not like I was gonna attack her. But walking fast like when an NCO spots a soldier that needs immediate correction, and you need to jump all over them to straighten out their major malfunctions. I was in her face and barking now. Barking like a mad dog.

"I don't know what game you're out here selling, but if you're all on the same side, then that's all it is, a game. Go sell freedom for something else to the rubes. I'm down to Strange Company. The only thing I believe in is getting them off-world with a chance to run the blockade and get to deep space for another twenty-five-year haul. I die getting that done… I'm cool with that, Your Highness."

I threw my arms wide. I had my chest rig unbuckled, and it flapped in the wind. I must've looked like a desert madman out there. Ragged and insane. Preaching nonsense.

"Freedom's just another word for nothing left to lose!"

CHAPTER THIRTY-EIGHT

We made the rally twenty-four hours later as one of the big desert storms came up and swamped this portion of the Wastes. Howling winds, scouring sand, eerie moaning that seemed choral as it raced and swirled all around. If you'd been stuck out in it, like some desert shadar nomad, it would have driven you mad.

We pulled the vehicles in close to the crawler once we arrived at the rally and covered everything in tarps that could be trusted to hold against the hot dry thunder winds. The other platoons and elements had made it there before us. Ten minutes later I was at the briefing with the rest of the command staff as the wind rocked and beat at the multi-ton supply crawler we met inside. Which was something when you really thought about it. But I was tired and there was hot coffee. And I was grateful for most of the faces I saw. Some I thought dead were alive. One I wanted dead, was still alive. And of course, we exchanged the grim totals of who had fallen. Their stories blossoming inside my skull as I kept their secrets.

Sergeant Biggs laughed grimly from a corner of the briefing center inside the big multi-sectioned tracked crawler. He cut salami with a combat knife as the huge vehicle shook at a sudden tempest that had come from out of the deepest parts of the desert to buffet the thick outer armor.

"Ain't like no desert I ever been in afore," he muttered like some great sabertoothed bear in the deeps of winter.

The First Sergeant strode in and got the meeting started once he'd made his presence generally known. The Old Man and the Ghost platoon sergeant were missing. As was the Monarch.

So that was curious to me.

"Here's the situation, men," began the First Sergeant. "Captain and Sergeant Slick are out with Ghost picking up some supplies our employer saw fit to stash out here before all this got started. I have a frago from the captain that will get us started on what we gotta do for the next phase of the op to get off-planet. No gripin'. No changin'. Everyone's got assignments. So to break it down, here's how it's gonna go, boys."

He flicked on the projector and showed us a map of the area surrounding the Crash. A lot of details were curiously absent. But of course, I'd seen redacted maps before. This was the best you were gonna get with a site this sensitive.

"We have two objectives we have to hit in the next twelve hours to make the LZ. Which, I might add, is gonna be a hostile takeover no matter what drone recon is saying right now about the situation on the ground. I expect things to get out of hand, but that ain't no problem for Strange Company."

I checked the drone recon update of the airfield we needed to take. So far… no enemy units. No Ultras. Light to almost no drop traffic coming in or out. That was unusual for a world everyone was trying to get off of now that a full-scale invasion was underway.

"Smells like an ambush," remarked my personal devil, Sergeant Hannibal, from nearby. His voice that of a bitter farmhand hoss who wasn't gonna buy the latest snake oil to make town. He was studying the drone recon data too. And he was right. I was thinking the same thing. That site had ambush written all over it. Except this time, we couldn't just vaporize it with one of the Monarch's trick grenades. We needed a ship on that field for our ticket outta this mess. We had to take that LZ with gunfire and bad intentions. Fast, quick, and brutal.

I was already looking at places to set up kill zones with the two Pigs I had left in Reaper. Traversing gunfire in a wide space like that was going to be our best friend.

We did need more ammo though. We weren't critical, but we'd get there fast in that kind of situation.

"Yeah, Amarcus," said the First Sergeant a bit testily, "I bet it is. But that's the way out. Monarch says she's got a flight coming in that thinks it's picking up hard mem from the local depository. Armored transport. Hard part is they don't know they're about to act as a taxi service to get us all upwell to the *Spider*. To make that happen we need to hit this site back here away from the airfield…"

He brought up a new saved feed from the drone footage.

"That's where you and your boys are gonna do what needs to get done, Sergeant Hannibal. Dog will hit the bank one hour prior to the arrival of our taxi. I ain't gonna lie to you. This ain't a surprise hit. You're gonna have to fight your way through several streets to reach the bank. Now, obviously local forces'll be thinking you're going for the airfield to hijack a ship and get off-world. Which you and your Dog boys won't be doin'. You'll hit this bank, breach, and clear. We're looking at a small defending force on that location, highly motivated, we suspect high-paid mercs. But that's your specialty, ain't it, Amarcus. So do the guards and blow the vault. Take as much hard mem as you can get your hands on once you're inside. That's company money to pay out our contract whether the generals like it or not. We're gettin' paid on this one. One way or another. But you also have to go to Box 88 inside the prime security vault two floors below the sub-basement, blow that, and retrieve a mem drive. Expect auto-gun sentries to that approach, Amarcus. What's inside the box is the Monarch's. She gets that, we get off-world.

"No mem drive? Then Strange goes to Plan B and we just take another ship ourselves. She can wave off our original transport if the deal goes south. But odds ain't real good on that route and the situation is already a Pan Fire Drill with blindfolds. We got three elements in three places trying to coordinate a bank heist, an infiltration and ship capture, with as much sniper overwatch as Ghost can provide. In other words, Dog, it's run and gun for the bank. Breach and clear. Loot. Then withdraw to the LZ and set up perimeter security. You'll have indirect from Sar'nt Chungo atop the mobile crawler. Sniper support from Ghost for the street fight. Once you're in the bank, they're to shift to cover the airfield from this broadcast array tower here northeast of the field. Dog will hold the entrances onto the LZ with machine-gun teams and explosives."

"Who's gonna do the infil to get to the ship?" asked Chief Cook, who was the main Voodoo rep for briefings. Stinkeye couldn't be bothered because there was most likely a card game going on somewhere. And Nether bothered everyone too much with the surrealism of his incorporeal presence to attend.

I had a pretty good idea who was gonna do the infil. It rhymed with deeper.

"Reaper. Captain'll be takin' 'em in on this one," barked the First Sergeant proudly like he was handing us a real plum assignment. "They gotta get a move on fast once we top off with the special weapons the captain is out getting. He and the Monarch will be taking Reaper in through the Crash itself. They gotta retrieve something else deep inside the wreck just for the Monarch. Part of the deal and everyone does their part. That's how the company works."

Amarcus muttered something about my platoon being barely capable of being errand boys.

"What's that, Sergeant Hannibal?" asked the First Sergeant, knowing full well the story of bad blood between his two platoon sergeants.

"Nothing, First Sergeant."

The old NCO shook his head in barely concealed contempt.

"Whatever it is… we ain't got time for it on this one. I'll tell ya, kids. This is about as close as it gets. I been in some tight spots before and if this ain't one I don't know what is. So keep it tight out there and remember we're all Strange Company. We get our boys off this one, then you two can go at each other with knives and I'll sell tickets for everyone to watch."

The mention of knives reminded me my index finger was in the ring of my karambit. It always goes there when Amarcus is around. It's always ready. I'm always ready. We have a date whether the First Sergeant likes it or not.

Whether I want it that way or not ain't important. That's the way it is. And it's just best to be ready about it. File that under being honest about things.

Funny, I thought to myself. How it does that. My finger through the ring of the karambit. I didn't look at my enemy as the First Sergeant scolded us. Just reminded myself that when it went down between Amarcus and me it would go down fast and I needed to make it real quick. Amarcus Hannibal was a brutal brawler. He'd pop my skull and gouge out my eyeballs with his thumbs if he got the chance. I had no doubt about that. Half of one even.

I had my moves down pat to kill him as fast as possible with a sharp knife. Because that's all I was gonna get. I had no doubt about that either.

The hatch to the crawler opened and let in a blast of hot orange light, gusting wind, and sand. It closed and there was the captain and the Monarch.

"I've given them the basics, sir," announced the First Sergeant in his usual grand fashion. "They know what they gotta do and they're gonna do it."

The captain looked around at us with his perpetually cruel and tired face. Cruel because an injury had made it that way. Tired because command never stopped. Never took a break. Never didn't need some fire to be put out with too little retardant and a lot more boot leather than was on hand.

He shrugged out of the ancient leather trench coat that always wrapped his spartan frame, a thing I could never remember seeing him do. He was always wrapped in it like he was always cold and dying of some bone-deep plague. Dead blue eyes watched us all. The scar that ran down his face was livid and almost the same color of his iron-gray hair.

Then he gave us the order. The actual op order. Breaking it all down how it was gonna go. How we were gonna do everyone who stood in our way and get off-world. From situation, to mission, to execution. Then command and signal.

Everyone had it tough. That couldn't be disputed.

I wouldn't have wanted what Amarcus and Dog Platoon was gonna face, for sure. Basically, an attack in force through fortified streets pacing just ahead of the crawler. Amarcus would have all the indirect and sniper fire he could do, allocated for priority tasking. So that told me the captain and the First Sergeant expected it to be real rough for Dog in there. The First Sergeant was going forward with that team. Dog and Ghost. Ghost on overwatch. Fighting a running battle to take the bank.

"We have to recover the contents of Box 88, Sergeant Hannibal. SOP. Everyone knows the mission. That is the mission. You buy it on the way in, or afterwards, I need one of yours to link up with me for those contents. That is not an option. I'm dead, give it direct to the next in command."

I noticed he was looking at our Monarch as he said this last bit. Letting her know he was making sure the terms of the deal would be abided by. No matter what. She'd get her prize. We'd get off-world.

Freedom. This wasn't about that. This smelled like her getting something that would give her an advantage over someone else. That's all this was. Lies. And more lies.

"Reaper..." The Old Man was looking at me. "We're going in through the Crash. We have some new weapons and munitions. I dropped those with your ASL when I came in, Sergeant Orion. He's distributing now. High-power AP for the rifles."

Uhhhhh, I thought. High-power AP was very expensive. And... it was for a specific reason.

"Getting into the Crash itself," continued the captain as though reading my thoughts, "is going to require that level of violence. Recon by stealth to enter. Once we're in there, there're enough sensors left by the science team's security forces for them to know we're in. We have to find something called the Node. It's a science station, one of several set up inside the portions of the wreck that have been explored and excavated. We won't have that info until we're in and we've hacked their system. We hit the Node. Retrieve a piece of equipment. And then we get into the science labs that were set up to study the ship. From there we commandeer a high-speed rail car and make it to the airfield via tube line. It's a direct. One-way. Again, heavy resistance is expected. Most local defenses will be reacting to Dog's attack on the bank. That should draw some focus as events develop. Our target ship, an armored security transport coming down direct from the bank ship now currently in stationary orbit above the capital, will set down at sixteen forty-five local. We emerge from the transport tube station here..."

He showed us a picture of the LZ. Three hundred meters from tube station to target landing pad.

"... at sixteen forty if the engines have powered down. Sweep the field. Snipers are on standby to penetrate the command canopy with high-impact munitions if the crew attempts an emergency departure. Reaper secures the transport and Dog and Ghost pull in."

He looked at Sergeant Biggs. "We're leaving the crawler."

Our supply sergeant, a corpulent man who was always either eating salami or chewing a cigar, shrugged like it wasn't a loss that would bother him much.

"Once we have the head count it's throttle up and we try to reach the *Spider* by seventeen thirty rendezvous one hundred thousand over the surface."

"Who's flying the bird?" asked Chief Cook.

"Our employer has that handled. She's a rated star pilot."

Chief Cook nodded. Arms folded. Stance wide.

"Okay, sir. What do you want Voodoo to do, sir?"

"Chiefs Nether and Stinkeye, move with Amarcus's people. Do what you guys do best. Interface with Chungo on indirect so you don't get caught where you shouldn't be."

Cook nodded.

"And myself and the Little Girl?" he asked.

"You're with assault team Reaper. I don't know what you can do, Chief Cook, but I have a feeling we're gonna need her friend down inside that alien wreck. You're her wrangler. So that's where I need you, Chief. Keep her safe in case we need her."

"Copy that, sir."

He stepped back into the shadows of the brief, indicating he was done with questions that pertained to him. Voodoo had their missions.

I raised my hand. "Sir…"

The Old Man looked straight at me and indicated I should speak.

"The high-power AP. Last time I checked, those are very expensive munitions reserved for infantry teams going up against field mechs. Is that what we're expecting inside the Crash, sir?"

"Negative, Sergeant Orion." He lowered his head and studied his battle board. "Intel informs us there is some kind of predator ape that can be found all throughout the area we need to go through to access the ship. Large, powerful, and extremely violent. They hunt in packs. We'll be going down Lost Road Canyon until we dismount. From there on in we should expect these predators until we get into the ship. Treat them as vicious and deadly. Apparently the munitions will put them down."

I nodded.

"And, last thing, sir. What's an ape?"

CHAPTER THIRTY-NINE

We were thirty minutes into the dismount and approaching the target area when we spotted the first one. The ape. An ape.

It moved fast, up high above the massive cracked and broken boulders we were crossing under as we threaded the narrow canyon closing in on our objective to enter the Crash site and recover a high-value item deep within the wreckage.

I thought of Ol' Amos and the last recorded image that captured him. After that he'd gone into the wreckage we were heading toward. Never to be seen again.

"Some kinda scout maybe," muttered Punch, drawing a bead with his Bastard as he watched the swift-moving rock ape, finger hovering over the trigger and ready to squeeze off a few rounds and end its acrobat's progress above us, focus intent through the ranged scope he'd flipped over to on his rifle for this part of the approach. Walking point, he needed to see them before they saw us.

Above the ape and the rock, the boiling black volcanic smoke constantly emitting from the crash fissure raced away into the sky and high into the atmo. At least a hundred and ten thousand up. Just as it had when Ol' Amos first found this world over two hundred years ago. And then disappeared forever. We were following the approach marked as Lost Canyon Road on our maps. A twisting crack winding its way in closer to the wreck.

"Why is it shifting colors to match the rock?" wondered Choker not far behind Punch, frozen near a boulder as we tried to remain unseen. We were all halted in the crouch. Covering in the shadows of the big rocks, or behind them if we were lucky enough to have been moving near them when Punch's hand signal to halt suddenly shot up as he spotted the ape.

Even though Punch had whispered it over the comm at the same time. "Tango. Up high. Two o'clock."

I always made sure Reaper used both. Hand and low whisper over comm. You don't always have good electronic comm. But hand signals… you don't have those, you got real problems. It's always best to be in practice with the original patrol operating system. Good habits make good soldiers, as some NCO once barked at me. I can't remember which. But maybe that's because I'm tired. Even though I'm telling myself I'm not. There's no room in the ruck for fatigue on this one. *Just do this*, I keep telling myself. And then you can sleep for twenty-five long years.

I checked our column as we closed with the objective. Only the light tread of our boots making any sound over the crush and broken rock all across this canyon. A canyon ruined by a falling starship. The Old Man and the Monarch were just behind me by about five meters. Then Chief Cook and the Little Girl. The gun team of Hoser and Hustle came up next. Heads on swivels and looking for something to light up.

"Could use a cigar right about now," Hoser had grunted a few clicks back. No one answered. Patrol SOP was no smokes. Combat, smoke as much as you want if you got the time. But I'd found it was best to keep your hands working every weapon you had and not lighting a cigarette like you were cooler than Juan of Mars.

That didn't mean you couldn't want one though.

Nothing in the SOP about that.

"Know what you mean," said Punch after a minute. "Feels like oh-get-it-on-thirty." Then he looked at me. "I can feel it, Sarge. It's comin'. Bet on it for sure."

That was about two minutes before we spotted the first ape.

I nodded that I felt it too and swallowed hard. Mumbling one of those prayers you pray even when you don't believe. I was tired of getting my people killed. I'd like to prevent that going forward. That was my prayer. The prayer of all good NCOs. Even the ones who don't believe in anything.

I turned and caught the Monarch shifting away from her sector and making eye contact with me. Like she'd read my thoughts. On believing.

I looked away fast. Checking our intervals and not needing to tell anyone to tighten up.

Hauser and Jacks came along next with the Kid forming a second team to the rear. Team Two. I'd broken what was left of Reaper, once a forty-man platoon, into two rough teams. I'd use Team Two to either support us in an assault, or as a QRF to take advantage of anything we ran into with a flanking attack.

Then we spotted the first one.

Right now, watching the creepy ape-thing move like liquid and lightning high up on the rocks of the narrow canyon walls we were threading—it was near invisible due to its shifting color and the light—I felt like pulling both teams in tighter. I had a real bad feeling about this. But then again, I don't need anyone to tell me I always do.

The Monarch had explained to all of us what an ape was. A large simian native to Earth. They could be incredibly powerful and ferocious. Some of the bigger ones could pull your arms right out of your sockets. Others rip the flesh right off your face. They were tribal and known to use rudimentary tools. There were a number of "ape" type species to be found throughout the discovered universe, but unless you were heavy into xenozoology and understood animal genus families, you wouldn't know about Earth's apes. Unless you'd been raised on Earth. And no one you ever met had, unless you met a Monarch, which no normal person ever did.

Unless you were Strange Company and one just joined your company in the middle of a planetary Ultra invasion. Which didn't happen every day. Or ever, statistically speaking.

"The crugo on Tauri are related..." she continued as she listed off a few galactic species. I'd heard of one or two. And I had seen a crugo once in a zoo. They looked more like large bats than apes. But apparently, they were related.

"Flying monkeys is da least strange thing you gonna see inside o' the wreck, Little King," Stinkeye warned me later after the "ape" portion of the briefing. "If that ship is what I think it is..." hissed the drunk Voodoo chief as he got close to me and whispered what he didn't want anyone else in the company to hear, "then you gonna see some real pillar o' da universe stuff in there. I done given dat rubberhead Chief Cook something to help yaz in dere if tings get rough enough to do yaz. An' if I don't see you on da other side o' this one, Little King, then it 'cause of da stupid. Either it et yaz up… or it et me. But it's out there. So best to hose everything and make sure it's real good and dead twice over."

Then he stuck one long index finger under his watery eye and pulled it down. Which is Stinkeye for *take me serious on this one*.

After that he was gone. Weaving off to join the crawler as it pulled away into the dusty early-morning darkness with the team that was going to hit the bank. His chest rig flopping in the night wind. His totem flask the only weapon he carried.

I was shocked. But I didn't know what more by. The fact that Stinkeye said he might know something about one of the universe's great mysteries, The Crash, which he'd told nothing about to anyone the entire time we'd been planetside… or the fact that he'd actually given Chief Cook, his mortal and sworn enemy, something to help us survive. And by default, help Chief Cook survive.

Maybe it was poison, and he was cool with collateral damage just to get the job done and declare himself the winner in their never-ending battle of Voodoo chiefs.

The universe is a very strange place. Best not to ask too many questions. Front sight forward and you'll do mostly fine. *Get it on* time was coming in the space of the day that was just hours away. I could feel it then as we worked through the night to get ourselves ready to hit our objectives. Whichever way it went in the morning and through the long day everything was promising it would be, however it went down, I'd made up my mind I was going to get it done. Yeah, I was tired. We all were. But there was every chance we were gonna end up on the *Spider* tonight. In our own spaces. With a couple of weeks to get sorted and then hit the coffins for twenty-five years of rest during the long haul to Blackrock.

If we didn't make it, then we're probably dead. And the company's over. And everything's no longer our problem anymore. I got twenty minutes' sleep after everyone cleaned their weapons and sorted the new gear, and that was the last thought I had before I drifted. I think I dreamt about that bar and John Strange. He didn't say anything. Just looked real disappointed. And when I fell off a cliff and woke up with a start because the crawler's engines were firing up and sounding like death by killer robots, I swore I hadn't slept at all.

"Get it done, Orion," I muttered, and got myself up and moving. Tired was for another day. I was gonna do my best not to lose anyone else.

The Kid handed me a coffee he'd gotten from the crawler before they closed up. I took a sip and looked at him.

"Havin' fun?" I said over the rim as I tasted it.

"Yes, Sar'nt."

But I couldn't tell if he was scared, or just Company now. Both are the same.

All we had to do was survive killer apes. Infiltrate an alien starship that might be something more than what it was thought to be. Rob a bank. Hijack a dropship. Execute a high-atmo sub-orbital ship-to-ship transfer. And then blast our way into deep space before the Monarchs could catch us. But that'd be XO's job and the *Spider* would have to handle all that. All good space marines know that sometimes the bravest thing you can do is just sit there during a ship-to-ship shootout and try not to lose your bowels as the guns open up and the hulls collapse. Death by vacuum is always sudden. But I've seen the look on people's faces when they get sucked out through a hull vent. It's not sudden enough.

That's all.

That's all that happened before the apes began to shoot at us with guns in the canyon as we approached the great mystery of the Crash.

CHAPTER FORTY

In most combat situations, both sides sorta just start shooting at each other until one side senses an advantage and tries to assault forward and murder everyone trying to murder them. This often has only two outcomes. One or the other side gets killed a little too much, really slaughtered and there's no one left. Or they surrender at some point before total unit annihilation. I've seen a third outcome once but that was just weird.

My job, as the unit leader under fire, is to get all guns up and returning fire because we are now in a firefight. Then I assess the situation and try to exploit a weakness in the enemy position to bring the conflict to a violent and favorable end, for our side, as quickly as possible. Assault. Indirect fire. Flank with supporting fire. Options. These are some of mine in a normal firefight. Note, there are no normal firefights. Every one you remember forever, because of some singular weirdness that makes it a novelty.

Dude gets his head blown off and keeps firing. Someone chokes on their gum when an explosive goes off and the concussion, or just before it, makes them suck a quick breath in because they know they're about to get the wind knocked right out of them. Or you actually get the Needle D right when you have to relieve pressure on a wounded man's heart or he'll suffocate.

Needle decompression protip. It helps when everyone's got the Needle D tattoo in the right place. Murphy's law. Some get the tattoo in the wrong place because the tattoo artist got it wrong and they didn't know better. So yeah it was weird that one time under heavy fire when Hustle got it wrong because he was in a hurry but the tattoo itself was in the wrong place to begin with and so Hustle actually ended up getting it right and Super lived another couple of days.

Hoser cut loose as the ape attack started, standing with the Pig blazing death as the first enemy rounds came in from low across the rocks, further down the winding canyon we were heading into. We'd been watching the scout high above us, hoping he didn't spot us, this strangely bipedal figure that seemed to crawl across the rocks on all fours like it was the most natural thing in the universe, but it barked some war cry and seconds later the swarm of apes came from up the canyon we were headed into.

Shooting at us.

"Thought they were supposed to just be animals, lady!" shouted Punch as he dove for cover and the terrain around him erupted in whistling incoming. Rounds ricocheted off rocks, smashing fragments that came off in sudden dusty sprays.

The Monarch didn't reply and wisely took cover behind a long-ago fractured rock she could shoot from.

The apes leapt over rocks like huge gray acrobats. With guns. Flying and firing weird small submachines at the same time as they washed over the terrain like some system virus suddenly wiping out all the root command files. Others of their ferocious and hairy kind scrambled around larger boulders, covering and firing as they streamed toward us like a river of gnashing nasty yellow fangs and animal barks that were about the worst thing I've ever heard. All of these things didn't go together. Yes, here they were coming to kill us all. These were the cries of wild animals on the hunt. Hooting and barking. Grunting and bellowing war cries that curdled your blood and reminded you that you only had so many magazines of the good stuff. There were no cages. No fences. No zookeeper between you and these savage animals. These things were coming straight for us and their intentions were clear.

And did I mention they were firing off bursts of automatic weapons fire? Wild sprays. Sudden staccato barks. Rounds smashing into the blood-orange rocks we were crossing along, sending up sprays of sharp fragments that raced for your eyes and exposed skin. Other rounds hit the sandy bottom of the canyon, throwing up grit fountains. These rounds made tactical-me wonder if they had snipers in the mix.

No time for that, Sergeant Orion, because we were literally about to get very overrun. And I'd be surprised if they had a hard and fast policy on surrender and captured prisoners.

Hoser unloaded, screaming, "Rock and roll!" as he burned brass and bled linkage, cutting down the first and fastest apes scrambling and leaping over the broken boulders. "Rock and roll" was Reaper Platoon code to anchor on the gunner until we figured out how to deal with the mess we'd just walked into.

SOP. Standard Operating Procedure.

I hunched down and duck-walked back, burning rounds to cover Punch and Choker as they tried to cover behind two sides of the same rock forward of our position in the tight, twisting canyon. Both were dumping mags danger close on targets I couldn't see from my position. Meaning… the swarm of apes with automatic weapons had moved much faster than I would ever have thought possible.

"This is just great!" shouted Choker as he shot down an ape that scrambled around the rock on all fours, fangs gnashing, the great gray thing barking viciously as it came for him. Choker shot it several times and it was still thrashing. Then he shot it some more and it lay still, bleating at the sky amid the blood it had sprayed across the sand and rock. Its black-skinned hands opening and closing pathetically like it still wished with all its savage heart it could throttle the medic who'd killed it.

"Black on belt!" shouted Hustle, who closed in with our gunner to link up more belt-fed ammo and keep the gun working. I shouted for Hauser to move forward and cover the Pig as the reload went down. If Hustle was fast enough, he'd get the next few links up and connected before Hoser ran dry on 7.62, then we could maintain a base of fire along our forward line.

I looked back, poking my head over the rocks, and spotted Hauser opening up on a flanking attack of smaller apes with daggers and spears coming down the walls of the canyon to our rear. We'd walked into a trap, or they were fast enough to break off into separate elements and try a pincer movement from asymmetrical directions like the sheer rock walls of a canyon.

A second later I popped up, tagged a fast mover, and nailed him with two high-power APs we had for the Bastards in our thirty-round mags. We each had a full combat load, but it's hard for a sergeant to stop counting. The thing went down in a tumble of dust and sand but there was no way I could confirm the kill because things were so frenetic.

A huge ape, bigger than the rest, a giant almost, massive chest covered in some kind of leather armor, leapt up on top of the rock Punch and Choker were fighting from the sides of. It beat its chest and gave a primal roar that raised the hairs on the back of your neck. The thing looked like it could rip all of us to shreds as it glared angry animal hate and intelligent menace both at the same time.

The captain, who usually was only armed with the matching Hardballer 1911s he carried in the pockets of the worn brown leather trench he always wore, strode forward, leaving the Monarch in their temporary fighting position to defend against everything coming at us from the left flank. Her light machine gun hummed on quick, brutal, suppressed notes as she spat fire at multiple incoming targets while the captain closed with the big ape.

I knew her rounds were having some effect only because we hadn't yet been overrun. In the space of ten seconds, the battle had gone from eerie silence to sudden circus of death threatening to envelop us all.

The Old Man had brought along another weapon we rarely ever saw him carry but which was known to us all. His Beretta 1301 combat shotgun. An ancient weapon he'd gotten off a freighter we'd found derelict in deep space carrying a lot of five-hundred-year-old weapons in stasis containers. The ancient weapon and others had been stored factory new. Pristine and still smelling of gun oil. Now he strode right at the huge raging beast atop the rock roaring at us and started firing slugs into the thing's chest. Six shots in two seconds from the semi-automatic combat shotgun and the thing had gaping holes and ragged flesh wounds where the slugs had torn into it.

It bellowed, gasping like a drowning ghost, and even that was still terrifying.

At the moment, I was engaging another fast mover that came out of nowhere to leap at the captain. I burned a half a mag and got him as the captain pulled his off-hand .45 from his coat pocket now that he'd burned all six slugs in the shotgun and shot the giant beast right in the head, blowing off half its skull with the Hardballer.

Crude spears arched over the rocks we were defending in a rough circle and one shattered against my plate carrier. The blow drove the air right out of me. It wasn't like getting hit by a round. But it was like taking a thrown hammer right in the neck.

I staggered back, hacking and gasping for air, grateful the Monarch's hidden munitions and equipment stash had included new state-of-the-art advanced small-arms protection plates to replace our old and basically unserviceable ones after nine months of on-world combat. She'd said these new plates were rated to stand up to rocket launchers. I'd never heard of a SAPI plate doing that. We had to take her on her word. Not that it mattered. If you got hit in the plate, which covered your very vital pump and pipes, and the rocket exploded, it was going to blow off your head, legs, and arms.

But your heart and lungs would be okay. Theoretically. According to her. So there's that.

"What about gel sabot rounds?" Punch had asked. She'd ignored that. Gel sabot burned through mech armor. No carrier plate was going to stand up to ferro-dicyanoacetylene rounds that cooked vehicle armor. Once that gel splashed on impact, even heavy armor melted like butter.

I answered my ever-curious assistant squad leader for her.

"Punch, you get hit by a gel sabot round, you'll wish you were dead for about five seconds before you are actually dead. The secondary explosion will be a mercy as that stuff melts your chest cavity. Or guts."

He nodded. That made sense to him. He'd packaged the universe and placed it on the mental shelf where it needed to go once more. Now he could drive on.

The new plates would do this, but they would not do that. I could read that in his eyes. He's that way. A sergeant must know how his men think. If only to avoid how they might get themselves killed thinking on their own.

Forward, we'd broken the armed ape attack, but the flanks were now in big trouble. I tapped the captain as he thumbed shells into his combat shotgun and scanned for more apes to engage. Hooting and barking from the armed animals echoed off the walls and rocks of the canyon all around us. It was like listening to a chorus of insanity and feral death. Surreal until you realized it was very real, and very close.

"Sir, moving to check on Team Two. You got it here?"

"Get it on, Sergeant," said the Old Man tersely and moved to pull back Punch and Choker now that we were getting a break forward. Incoming was still peppering the rocks here, but it was unaimed. It was more like they were trying to get into position for another attack here while at the same time keeping our heads down.

It was hard not to fixate on the fact that the animals, the apes, were running tactics.

Hoser stalked forward to a better rock to fire from and took a round in the arm. He didn't notice and instead opened up with a blur of high-cycle from our right. His face was hard-set and mean and it was clear he intended to do as much harm as possible to our enemies with time remaining. Hustle trailed behind the big gunner getting another belt ready, crouching low and staying back and to the left of our Pig gunner.

I would've killed for a gun run from a close air support dropship right at that moment. But beggars can't be choosers, can they? I headed back to the rear and passed the chief and the Little Girl crouching behind a rock.

"Hey Orion," said the chief good-naturedly as he ejected a magazine from his pistol and slid in another. His face was red and sweating. His tone familial. As though I'd just passed him on an evening walk through the neighborhood. The Little Girl was squatting down in the shadow of the rock they were covering behind. Her big clompy boots dug into the sand. Her dark coat making her a kind of rock all unto herself. She had the big used hearing protection muffs over her tiny skull and was pressing them together to block out the gunfire all around.

Her dark eyes watched me as I moved past the two of them, heading back to check on Team Two. I was waiting for the smell of autumn. The burning leaves. And the wind suddenly coming up to howl and moan that the two points in space-time were connecting. That her friend was coming…

"We'll hold until relieved," said the chief as I went past, leaning over the rock and beginning to blaze away at something forward.

I danced back through the rocks, following the sound of Hauser's light machine gun and the sounds of the other rifles in that team. Jacks and the Kid. Not really trying to avoid incoming. How could I? It was so wild and unaimed by the apes. Yeah, they were ferocious and fast, but they weren't great shots. Maybe firearms weren't suited to their hands. Their manipulation of such weapons wasn't pro. But I'd seen speed and volume, and savage ferocity, turn lost firefights around in a heartbeat. So they had that going for them.

To our rear were piles of dead apes here and there. I shouted at Hauser that I was coming from their twelve and to hold fire. The attack there was petering out as I managed to get up to them. The apes had suddenly begun retreating back into the crevices and up the rock walls of the canyon.

More fire was suddenly starting up forward and I could hear the boom of the captain's shotgun mixing with the burping bursts of the Team One Pig. Choker and Punch adding in single shots here and there to pick up targets of opportunity.

Team Two had been knocked around good as I assessed our rear flank. The Kid was sitting cross-legged in the sand. His rifle across his knees. His head down. Hauser had strips of his synthetic flesh ripped away, as was much of his chest rig. It had been shredded to uselessness by terrible animal claws when the fighting had gotten danger close. Real danger close in fact.

Now the cyborg was scanning the distances. Waiting for them to come at us again as the smell of burnt cordite hung heavy in the air.

"We killed twenty-two, Sergeant."

Jacks was near the Kid, watching the rocks with his shorty Bastard up and ready to engage if they did attack again. The ruck on his back was strapped with claymores. I wondered how close he'd gotten to detting the whole bunch. The spent brass and blood-spattered sand, along with the carcasses of the dead apes draped across the rocks and torn to pieces by gunfire in the dirt, told me Jacks had been pretty close to a last stand.

"He okay?" I asked the former Second Squad leader.

"Got his bell rung for sure," replied Jacks, still watching the rocks and the last of the retreating savage apes. "One of 'em jumped in and got ahold of him. Started banging him around on the rocks." Then he stepped close and said, "Kid pulled his knife and went after it like a real psycho just to get it off him. Stuck it right in the brain and it ran off with his blade still sticking out of its skull. I shot it just to get the knife back."

Jacks took the recovered combat tanto out of his carrier where he'd stuck it, wiped the blood off on his pant leg, and handed it back to the Kid.

"Here ya go, Psycho Killer. Try and hold on to it next time."

Then Jacks looked up at me. "Hey, anyone ever tagged Psycho Killer in the unit? That's a good one for him. Better'n mine."

I didn't think anyone ever had.

"We'll have to keep that in mind," I said. "He's still the Kid for now. But that's a good one, Jacks."

"Man, he earned it," he said as he got ready to move. "Gotta have some real stones to attack one of those things with just a knife when it's trying to pulp and throttle you at the same time. Those things are pure nightmare, Sarge. Worse than that stuff Chief Cook gassed us with. Hope we don't run into anymore, that's for sure."

But I had a feeling we would.

CHAPTER FORTY-ONE

We were on the move down-canyon again. Hustling as best we could while trying to move with some sense of awareness about what we were running into. Cautious urgency I'll call it.

"Not far now," said the Monarch over squad comm. "Two more clicks forward, and we'll reach the entrance."

I'd gotten the Kid up and moving again. He looked shook, that was for sure. It was clear that was probably as close to death as he'd gotten in his time with the company. And honestly, as I looked at the dead things and their fangs and splayed claws all over the battlefield no one would remember, I couldn't blame him. Jacks had been right. These were pure nightmare. Most of them wore a crude leather vest. A belt. And actual finished tools on their belts. The kind of tools you'd find on a starship. Hydro spanners and bulkhead locks. Hull plate ratchets. But they were all battered and beaten. And bloodstained. Like they'd been used as weapons more than tools.

"You okay?" I asked as I put the Kid's tanto back in its carrier and stuck his rifle in his hands like a good NCO should when a man can't remember that the primary job of an infantryman is to work the rifle.

He mumbled something. Which was good. He was coming back. He could speak.

"You're alive," I told him, looking him in the eyes to make the connection and reset his mental hard drive. "That's the important part. Okay, now you gotta get back in this, Kid. I can't send you to the rear 'cause we ain't got one to send ya to. I need every rifle up for all of us to get through this one alive. And we're gonna. So... good to go? We need you right now."

Sometimes being a sergeant feels like being a used vehicle salesman. You can't always bark orders and rumble. Sometimes you gotta get 'em to take the payments and EZ credit. Sorry, that's just the way it is. Sometimes you gotta sell.

"C'mon, Kid. Clock's burning. Six hours to make our ride off-planet. Lot to do. Are you in it to win it? Or do we gotta drag you?"

As I sat there waiting for him to mumble or nod that he was good to go, I realized something. Things might actually be going our way. This was the first fight in a long stretch in which I didn't come out the other side with a dead friend staring at me.

So… I had that going for me. No one had gotten killed yet.

You're optimistically sensing momentum, idiot, the pessimistic side of me whispered in my ear. I told it to shut up. I'd gotten twenty minutes of sleep this morning, plus a cup of coffee, and my studs had just fought off a savage army of gnashing death that would certainly go down in the Strange Company logs as one of the most bizarre firefights we'd ever been in. I had every reason to be hopeful.

Don't rain on my parade.

Yeah, it had gotten close. A few of us had gotten knocked around. It was a good thing Hauser was a combat cyborg who could turn off pain centers, or really didn't even have any, because a real man would have been screaming in agony from the wounds he'd received. Begging for death or Narcanene.

So maybe things were turning around, which is the only thing you can say when you just fought off a nightmare army of monkey soldiers. With guns. Monkeys with guns.

They're apes, I reminded myself. And then I remembered I had seen monkeys on some starships in the past. Ferrying between worlds. Semi-intelligent hybrids who worked the lower decks, engineering and the nuclear stacks on some of the bigger transport ships with old and dangerous engines that weren't rated safe for human operation. Wiggles, too. Hybrid human pigs that did worse jobs than the monkeys. Monkeys, according to the Monarch, were related to apes.

If you ever think you got it bad just go watch the monkeys and the wiggles work. Their life is a living radiated hell. Even if it is short.

Two clicks further on and we came to the entrance to the chasm the ancient starship had created when it drove its vast bulk into the crust of this world. What I saw as we rounded the last crimson-and-blood-orange-colored rock bend in the narrowing trail, where the rock had heated and boiled long ago, was unbelievable.

I would have told you right there that Stinkeye was right when he said the Crash might be something other than what everyone thought it was. Or whatever he'd said. Something along those lines. But I don't think this, what we were now seeing as we stood on the edge of the fantastic chasm, was what our chief Voodoo operator and oldest living member of the company was talking about. What we were seeing was something completely different. Orders of magnitude different. Something that destroyed the Monarch narrative everyone had either been told, or inherently believed, about one of the great wonders, or mysteries, of the galaxy.

The ship was still intact.

Ruined for sure. Crushed and damaged along vast sections of its incredible length. It was easily larger than a Battle Spire from what we could see of it as it raced off into the cavern darkness at a down-angle of at least fifteen degrees. Which is to say it was huge. And it had driven itself straight into the planet long ago, creating a tube down into the crust.

"I always thought the ship was destroyed. That it was… it was actually a crash," I murmured aloud. Everyone else was too dumbstruck to answer.

As the name on the official planetary maps implies. The Crash Wastes. I was supposed to be looking at an incredible crash of vast alien technology that was rumored to be fantastic. The Monarchs had held claim here, declaring Ol' Amos's patch of the desert specifically theirs. Allowing the rest of the planet to go to private investors willing to take a chance on the stellar frontier.

But perhaps that had been the game. Maybe they'd sold the whole Crash Wastes story about the total destruction of an alien anomaly of unexplainable origin. Naming it a crash, *the* Crash, was a great way to keep the serious at bay. Ever seen a starship crash? There ain't much left. Ships that do light and just under have a tendency to leave very little but a giant crater. Put some apex predators out here to keep everyone away, sow some superstition and paranoia, and you can quietly keep a working alien starship unlike anything we've ever encountered to yourself.

Even this far out along the frontier.

The Monarch stared out across the chasm at it just as the rest of us were doing. Incredibly, power was still on in some sections of the immense starship that weren't too badly damaged. Other sections were crumpled like crushed beer cans. And across the gap in the chasm, vines dangled or were tied to either the cliff or the canyon wall. Except they weren't vines. They were ancient hoses and systems that had been torn from the ship and anchored to the chasm, or to the ship itself.

"That's how they get across..." muttered Punch. "They swing. The apes. That's how they do it."

"Hard pass," said Choker, who hated ship-breaching ops. Too much lack of control for a narcissistic sociopath.

Everyone ignored him. He always said that when it came to hull breaching. We always sent him first anyway. He had skills and was actually fairly good at it if you didn't mind the hyperventilating.

"That's correct," said the Monarch softly. The silence was deafening inside the tube of the wreck. Maybe all you could hear was the black smoke boiling up from the gargantuan engines high above us. A dull kind of puffing bass rumbling that seemed to come from somewhere deep within. Her voice was monotone, like the voice of someone almost hypnotized by what she was seeing. A fully intact generational starship. Something out of Earth's distant colonization past. Here, mostly intact, inside a deep canyon that seemed to fall away into an unknowable darkness to our left and down below. Where the ancient vessel had driven itself into this world long ago.

The whole scene played with your sanity.

"It almost looks familiar..." muttered the captain, who rarely said much beyond orders or questions on company biz. I could tell he too was taken aback by what we were seeing. The wreck was almost as much of a mystery as was his fabled past with the Ultras if that were to be believed.

"I thought it was a crash," I said to her again. Staring at her now. Accusing her and not hating myself for doing it. Dismissing her otherworldly beauty and the pheromones that seemed to fall from her whether she liked it or not. Starting to feel angry at her. I wanted answers. I needed answers and I was beginning to feel we were being lied to. That a lot of people had gotten killed for nothing except deceptions designed by someone to make someone else rich. Except this was something else. This was stunning and amazing. This was bigger than petty power games even if those games were played by Monarchs. This shook the foundations.

What had Stinkeye said? Shake the pillars of the galaxy stuff?

Was the war on Crash, or Astralon, nothing but a pretense to get this ship under Monarch control finally? Had we fought for nine months for nothing but a lie? I felt the world begin to spin just a little and I had no idea whether that was from the insanity of what I was looking at, or the narratives raging inside my head.

Ah, Sergeant Orion, I whispered to myself. *You never fought for anything other than money.* And money is the biggest lie of all, ain't it?

My emotions were getting out of control. I grabbed a piece of my own skin and twisted, causing as much pain as I could. Getting myself centered.

I felt my hand creep toward my sidearm. I felt wild and dangerous regardless of the self-inflicted discipline I was forcing myself to endure. I knew I'd blow her brains out if she'd lied to us. If everything, all the universe and the lies about Crash... were just that. Nothing but lies.

I turned to look at the ship in utter amazement one more time. Wondering what ancient race had made such a thing that could hard crash itself into a world and survive.

I whispered something. I think I was muttering that I didn't want the Monarch to say what she'd been saying all along. If she said *You gotta believe in something, Sergeant Orion...* Well, then... Boom. I do her right here and let the captain decide what to do with me on the other side of it. I was cool with the judgment.

But she didn't do that.

"The primary ship was destroyed during reentry and the crash," she said. "What you are seeing is... the lifeboat. This is how the ship crashed. Much of the larger ship exploded across the desert up there and created the crust fractures after her primary pulse shields overloaded and softened the landing by creating the continental crater to brake for impact. They were still going too fast and so the main superstructure detonated to save the lifeboat. We theorize some kind of superweapon fired and created the tube down into the core at the last second, allowing the lifeboat to enter with maximum armor, using something we think is called a 'Repulse Ram' and of course braking engines in full reverse. Farther down, the entire front end of the ship is smashed. The crew there were killed instantly. We've only been down that far externally and with drones. The damage is very bad there. Most of the technology is unrecoverable from those sections. But most of the ship beyond the bow survived."

"That's not possible," said Punch. "That ship is bigger than a damned Ultra Battle Spire. The original ship would have to be… huge. Enormous. Gigantic even. Ain't nothing like that ever been built in the galaxy, lady."

"This ship isn't from this galaxy. Not in its current form." She came out of her trance and looked at the rest of us. Her eyes landing on me. Then the captain. "But…"

She looked at me again. Like maybe she'd said something she hadn't meant to. And now she wanted to take it all back.

"We're running out of time," she said. "They'll be directing more guards to react to us. We've got to cross now and enter the ship. We'll be safer in there."

"Safer from who?" asked Choker.

The captain, still cradling the shotgun, turned toward the Seeker. His voice was cold as the grave. Monarch or no Monarch.

"My sergeant has questions. I think you should answer them, ma'am."

The Monarch must've sensed we'd all kill her right there. The company thinks as one. We may fight and gamble and play tricks on each other as much as we do on any enemy. But when the captain has made it clear he's not happy with someone, well then, the company isn't happy with that particular someone.

"Okay," she said. Taking her hands off her wicked high-speed little machine gun. It dangled by the two-point sling. I was waiting for her to pop one of her dangerous grenades and do something freaky to us. Stun us. Gas us. Make us disappear to the ninth dimension. Heck, maybe she'd just turn into bats and fly away. Things felt tense and uneasy. Dark. Dangerous even. "But let's get an advance team across the gap, Captain. We'll be safer in there. I'll explain as we go."

"Safer from who?" mumbled Choker again.

"The apes," she answered softly. "They'll be back. In greater numbers next time. They're the guardians of the wreck."

The captain waited, staring at her. Not liking the deal. But knowing she was still our employer. I could see him thinking there are some deals you just don't make. Shouldn't make. Deals with the devil. And him thinking we'd made just that.

I didn't think it. Didn't need to. I knew it. Knew the kind of deal we'd made. Later I'd tell myself we had no choice. That we'd had to make the deal as the Ultras started their first pass. That we'd had no other real option.

But that's a cop-out. You've always got choices. Some are just easier than others.

"I assume we're using the cables to swing across," said the captain. Allowing the bargain. Allowing the story of our tragedy to progress.

She nodded.

The Old Man turned to me. His eyes as hard as those nails in that cold coffin grave.

"Sergeant Orion, get a team across and secure a breach point."

CHAPTER FORTY-TWO

The company worked mountaineering skills whenever we had a chance. We'd found combat climbing skills came in handy when you didn't want to fight fair. And as a rule, our SOP was all about never actually fighting fair.

Fighting fair is for amateurs. Plus, we didn't have the manpower, guns, and best tech to do so. Sometimes I was glad we didn't. It made us work harder knowing we were lacking. If we'd had those things, maybe we would have gotten lazy. Then where would we have been?

The galaxy is filled with the graves of dead mercenaries who got lazy. But there are also graves for the pros who have to do it the hard way. I have to be honest about that because it's best to. I've found that graveyards are sometimes the least discriminatory places you'll ever go.

Death is the great equalizer. That's for sure. Right, Orion? So get it on.

I slammed into the alien ship's cold hull after following Punch and Jacks across on the first vines. Her voice was in my ear. In all of our comms. She was telling us what she knew. Why we were here. What was so important about this wreck. The whole show. The ticket to the ride if we were willing to buy it. And take it.

We'd established an entry point on the alien hull and selected vines that would take us roughly near that spot we'd selected, as she lectured us about exactly how weird the galaxy could get.

Now we were crawling down a couple of decks to reach what looked like some kind of docking port for small craft. The hull doors had been left open here. We opted for no access points in the damaged areas as the hull was too ragged.

Getting cut up trying to go through hull breaches filled with jagged hull plating, possible live currents, and twenty other dangers was a great way to end up dead. Or wounded and useless. A drain on the little of which we had none to spare. Plus, the company had enough experience with breaching operations to know such maneuvers took time. Lots of time to do right. Explosives. Even in deep space. And time was a luxury we currently did not have. And an underground bottomless pit, clinging to an immense alien starship, seemed like a bad place to play with high-ex. The lack of forgiveness was stunning.

I crawled down toward the docking port, never minding the vertigo of the cyclopean dark tube the ship had created when it slammed itself in long ago.

"… the entire ship sacrificed itself to save the lifeboat," continued the Monarch over our comm. This had happened at least ten thousand years ago. Long before Earth's first moon landing.

Okay, I thought. So the engines are still lit ten thousand years later? Power?

I concentrated on not falling as I worked my way down the slick hull, looking for handholds where I could find them. Getting a weird feeling about all of this. Why was it weird? I didn't know. Not then. But I put it down now because it was the first time I had begun to feel it. As I crawled across the hull trying to get to the breaching point two decks below where we'd landed.

Punch was silent as he worked along behind me. Choker was hyperventilating behind Punch. But that was just SOP for him.

"How do you know all this?" he asked, gasping and struggling with the vertigo of the fantastic cyclopean surroundings and what it did to small minds like ours.

"As a Monarch," she answered across the ether of our comms, "I've had access to the science team and their reports. Most of that comes from up near the engines. In the hundred years since the teams first arrived at the colony and started working the wreck, we've only managed to make it through main engineering up near the surface and down into the mass tanks. And a few decks below that, which is nothing more than some sort of empty stores section that's been held by the apes. That's the best we've been able to do. Other teams have spelunked and tried breach points farther down the hull, but we've lost contact with them. We even sent in a combat cyborg extermination team. The best we'd ever developed. Omega Six models. Lost contact once inside the hull and never recovered them. Officially."

"How come the ship is still burning?" asked Choker.

He thinks for us all, I muttered to myself as I slowly inched closer to the top of the cargo port. I was crawling down laterally at close to a fifteen-degree angle to reach the entry point. It felt like crawling down a cliff. If I let go now, I'd tumble and bounce off the hull for miles. I'd find the bottom eventually. But I'd be dead by then.

I took a deep breath and studied our position. Scanning up-hull back toward the engines. Going up-hull would be like going uphill all day long. Down-hull, toward the bow, once we were inside, would be like running down a steep hill real fast and probably braining yourself. Our muscles were already at the edge. They'd turn to jelly in just a few decks of humping uphill with plates, weapons, and a combat load. Plus whatever she'd sent us in to recover.

But of course, that's how an NCO thinks. He thinks about his knees.

"The ship's reactor, it's like nothing we've ever seen, and still burning mass," she said calmly in our ears as we studied the next bit of hull we needed to navigate. Clinging where we were clinging like our lives depended on it. Because they did. "It boils out of the main fissure. The science team tunneled in from a few kilometers away just under the surface. Then they set up the base alongside the fissure and established a rail line into the ship under the engineering decks behind the engines. We'll exit there once we retrieve what I came for."

I made the lip of the port bay and peeked over, hanging upside down as I did. I didn't know what I was expecting to see in there. But what I saw I wasn't prepared for. The bay was dark. And with a ship, hull down at this inclination within atmo, or on a world, everything not secured would be clumped into a corner forward in the space. Smashed and destroyed by such an impact. Gravity was unforgiving to anything inside starships once the grav-decking had failed.

What I saw was a normal human starship-looking docking bay with most everything where it should be. Though much of it looked pretty rough and broken. Mounts had broken loose and some things hung at odd angles from the impact.

There was even some kind of shuttlecraft anchored into the docking slots. The anchors had warped as they tried to maintain hold long ago during the crash. They'd held. But the shuttle was ruined.

"Here goes nothing," I grunted and heaved myself down and over, and then in. Keeping my core tight and preparing to land on the canted tilt of the deck. But then something wonderful and comforting washed over me as I got that momentary disorientation and stomach drop of being under the influence of grav-decking.

I landed on the bay floor.

Though the ship was tilted bow down at the steep angle of fifteen degrees, I was standing straight up. My thighs and leg muscles rejoiced that we wouldn't have to climb out of here if we did get the chance to make it through. The grav-decking was still on. In whatever form this ship operated such technology, it was still working. That would make life a lot easier.

Then I saw the writing on the wall.

I could read it all. It was in Old Numerican, the original of what we all spoke, but I'd seen enough of it to get by. In rough strokes of dried blood, written across the back wall of the docking port, were three words.

"We rule now."

And underneath was a crude cave art painting of an ape, like the ones who had attacked us, holding a torch in one hand. And a rifle in the other.

CHAPTER FORTY-THREE

Things started to happen fast from there. The clock was on fire, as they say. We began to get everyone across the gap from canyon wall to wreck of the alien starship. I checked my watch, going over the timetable of events. In three hours Dog and Ghost Platoons would start their hit on the bank. In three and thirty we'd pop out of the tube station and try to take our ship.

Margin for error: none.

Systems were smashed here inside the dark docking bay aboard the Crash. Even though it was alien, I was getting a very bad feeling about all of this. This felt…

"Sarge…" It was Punch, who'd been working with Jacks as we took a brief ten to get everyone ready to go deeper into the ship. They were working on a computer terminal that seemed to handle the maintenance for the bay. Pulling it apart and looking at its guts. Like I said, something about this was tickling the back of my scalp. Like it was familiar in some taunting memory of a song kind of way. But I'd never been on any kind of starship even remotely approaching this level of tech. Or size.

"System don't work. But look at this…"

I crossed the bay, feeling and hearing the crunch of eons-old grit. Sand from the world. Broken glass and plastic fragments done to death by an unimaginable stellar impact. Like I said. Starships never survive crashes.

Why had this one?

Punch was pointing toward something near the terminal. Something that looked a lot like the battle boards we used. Except older and clunkier. A tablet of some kind. Like any starship crewman would use to perform duties.

"It don't work. But look at what's on the cover."

He handed it over to me. I studied the cover and saw the outline of a ship that didn't look anything like the one we were on. This was the silhouette of one of the old ring-drive warp ships that had been early colonization explorers. Fast ships using quantum destabilization to reach incredible speeds. Even by today's standards. But that was the ship history nerd in me talking. Still, holding it was like holding a historical relic that had no place being where it was.

"That's an old..." I was just about to say as the ancient Numerican printed across the back of the tablet organized itself in my mind and I was able to translate.

U.S.S. Enterprise.

Then...

Engineering something something *protocols*. Some of the old words had no modern translation.

I turned to the Monarch and held this out.

"What's this mean?" As in, *Why is this here?*

The *Enterprise* was one of the most famous explorer ships from those early days of stellar exploration. I didn't know much about it. Hadn't interested me for some reason I couldn't quite remember. But here it was. On board the most infamous wreck of alien origin in the galaxy.

There're others. The Malkinar Hull on Hobart. The debris fields of Gnay. Others... Starships from undiscovered cultures that ruined themselves all over the face of some distant world during their arc of final descent. Often there was so little left of the ships as to be unrecognizable. But in the case of the Malkinar Hull you can still see much of it rising out of the stormy waves of that world. The sea and the salt have gutted the rest and carried it off into ocean canyons.

And we've never found the origin civilizations that built those ships. They must have come from far away across the galactic lens. Or even farther.

The Monarch crossed and took the battle board thing from me. Ran one of her slender hands over it like it was some sacred object. Some memory of a thing she hadn't touched in years. An old photograph. A lost book found again. A memory. Yeah, I had those thoughts then as I watched her response to it.

She looked up and around, studying the structure of the ship.

"It's starting to come together," she said to herself. Almost a whispered mumble to no one else.

"What?" I asked her. "What's starting to come together? Why is this important?"

She seemed to want to say something. Then didn't. Then remembered who she was dealing with and decided it was best to give us something. Give me something.

She cleared her throat in the silence of the wreck.

"*Enterprise* was lost early on during the First Expansion. The official story is… she disappeared somewhere in the Orion Nebula. But knowing how we Monarchs do things, that was probably just the 'truth' we wanted known. I had suspected back then it was another ship that ultimately got used for the experiment, but… this pretty much confirms the *Enterprise* was the ship they used to go forward for Operation Zephyr. So…"

She stopped. I could see her eyes roving over data none of us could see. She must've had some kind of cloud operating system. She shifted her hand around like she was gesture-sifting through the data.

"None of that means anything to us," I said. "So, from the top. Why is this important?"

I was tired of this. I wanted answers. Monarch or not, I was tired of the games. Even though I had a feeling this was everything but.

I felt the captain step close.

Over her shoulder, behind her and in my direct line of sight, Chief Cook raised his eyes. They had a mischievous glint to them. Like he was suggesting he could make her talk. Just say the word. No one had ever interrogated a Monarch before. This was his big chance.

She read the room. I could tell as her eyes came back to me. Like she was suddenly figuring out she was dangerously close to some edge with us. I watched the realization dawn in her pretty face.

A face I could have lived lifetimes with and still not gotten tired of.

"The official story about this whole thing is a bigger lie than the one I've already uncovered for you. This wreck, the Crash, is not alien. Not totally. There's definitely some alien technology at play here. This ship went faster and farther than any ship ever will. Trust me on that one. What you're looking at is a ship, manufactured by us, but about ten thousand years in the future from now. As near as I can estimate. That's where we were sending the *Enterprise*. That was what Operation Zephyr was looking to accomplish. So… this must be it. This ship… is what they found."

No one said anything. Then we heard the horns and the drums. Tribal. Erupting and ululating outside along the hull. *Uroooooo UrUrUrooooo*.

It froze your blood to hear them shrieking alarm. You knew it wasn't good. Knew they were coming for you.

Choker swore. He was near the edge of the docking port we'd come through, staring out into its vastness like some kind of psychopath endlessly fascinated with all the oblivion it implied. And yes, the record notes he's a sociopath and there's a difference.

"Orion, we got big problems."

I raced over, my battle rattle feeling heavier than usual. Heavier than it should. Already tired that some new thing was about to ruin my already no-room-to-be-ruined schedule. I was wondering how much more one man could take.

Choker was looking down-hull, toward the black gaping chasm the starship, or lifeboat, had plowed itself into long ago. Down into the crust of the dark subterranean world. The hull down there was alive and moving. Alive with movement sweeping up along its ancient and fantastic cylinder. Like a sea of dark locusts swarming up the hull. Suddenly torches, hundreds if not thousands of them, sprang to life as the locusts surged up along the hull toward us.

Except they weren't locusts.

I irised in with my combat lens and tagged incoming monkey soldiers. Apes too. But smaller and faster than the ones that had gone up and down the cliffs during our first encounter. They had weapons. Some even had firearms.

But it didn't matter whether they did or didn't. We didn't have enough ammunition for the numbers coming at us even if they were unarmed. This was at least brigade-sized. Making the word *outnumbered* a laughable representation of our current situation.

The captain got us busy doing the survival game.

"Time to move, Sergeant. Let's go. Now."

CHAPTER FORTY-FOUR

Hustling and moving deeper into the ship revealed two things to us as we scrambled to put distance between us and the apes. Maybe we could find some kind of chokepoint to fight them off for as long as we could. Regardless of the lack of ammunition we had left. But as we moved, yeah, once you saw it... saw it was a human-designed ship in its basic DNA of design, you couldn't unsee it. Even though there were fantastic differences, there were similarities that must be the music of all ships of the stars made by humans. All the things you'd expect in a starship of this size. Things you'd only seen in spectacuthrillers, of course, about ships no non-Monarch citizen of the galaxy would ever have the privilege of riding on. But human at first light and the more you looked. Scanning the darkness for exactly the way conduits and piping would be laid out. Where the interface panels were. How the hatches operated. The feel of the floor in this section. Different because of usage type than it would be in another section.

The second thing revealed was that the wreck had become a madhouse. Everything had been rage-ruined. Walls scrawled and gouged with nonsense writing like we'd seen in the docking bay. Except more often some kind of ape/monkey hieroglyph system had taken over in long and more orderly strings. Here and there splash pages of pidgin Numerican slogans proclaimed ape supremacy and never-ending death to "hooma" which seemed to indicate humanity.

Man. Mankind. Hooma.

Only good hooma is dead hooma!

"Sergeant Orion," ordered the Old Man as we moved fast into what looked to be a quarters section of the vast ship. Lifeboat, she called it. "Take the lead element. I'll take Team Two. Get her to take us toward the Node. We're still on mission. Things just got more interesting. That's all."

"Copy that, sir." I slithered along the column in the darkness of the madhouse tight corridor and linked up with the Monarch.

"How far to target?"

"We can be there in twenty minutes if the way is clear, according to my map."

I nodded, hearing my own ragged breathing. "Show Punch the way. I'll keep up the rear of Team One and stay in visual of the captain. Let's move."

"On it, Sarge," said Punch, and we were off.

Eighty meters later, the apes hit our rear at a T-intersection. I could hear the successive booms of the Old Man's combat shotgun working to keep them back as we moved forward as fast as possible. Then Hauser picked up the fire support to our rear, both men talking their guns to keep the dark shapes down-corridor from overrunning us as we moved fast along our new course track. The staccato ring of gunfire reverberated across the dark passages as we hustled forward.

The comm was chaos.

"Two from the left." Jacks.

"Engaging." Hauser.

"Got one!" shouted the Kid. "More coming in!"

"Fall back by twos. Hauser, you're with me." The captain.

"Watch out!" Jacks.

Suddenly my combat lens got an airdrop and I could see the route into the ship. It was an incomplete map. But it was fascinating. The ship, as we already knew, was huge, but it seemed even more so from the inside. There were many strange and interesting things on the map I didn't have time to study.

"Ever been here before?" I asked the Monarch in a sub-channel over the comm.

"No. Believe it or not I'm learning and developing as much as you are right now, Orion. I gathered data, as much as I could during my incarceration. Then what I could while I was rogue from the Monarchy. Accessing the Library was difficult with my restricted status. But not impossible."

Okay, so that's new information. She was in Monarch jail. Oh and there's such a thing as Monarch jail.

"So what happened? Why are we here?"

We broke out of quarters and entered some kind of giant tube.

"Hang on..." said the Monarch. "Picking up a signal."

I told everyone to halt and ran back into the darkness. The captain hustled up out of it, flipping around to walk backward as he thumbed more shells into his shotgun. Hauser and Jacks behind him. The Kid just behind the captain.

I tapped the Kid as he passed.

He looked at me and I could see the fear was gone. He was on point. He was Company now. Grim. Determined. And willing to do just about anything to make sure we all got through.

"Doing good?" I asked him.

He smiled. "Good enough, Sar'nt." Then... "Where ya want me?"

"Go forward and link up with Chief Cook."

The captain turned toward me in the darkness. Suddenly light went on forward of us in the tube we'd just encountered. Bright white light.

"There's a lot of them back there, Sergeant," said the Old Man. "Give 'em enough room and they'd break out. We're down to half on ammunition. If so, we'll switch Pigs and leave the cyborg to hold our rear. Copy?"

I didn't like it. But I did copy.

It wasn't quiet to our rear. You could hear animal screeching. Howls. More rude drums and those horns echoing off distant and unseen corridors throughout the corpse of a ship. I could only imagine horror-show dark passages with torches and the strange hieroglyphs that told the madhouse stories of the apes. And of course, their propaganda that didn't bode too well for us hooma.

Comm from the Monarch.

"I have access to systems deeper in. The science team was able to tap in and jury-rig some access. There are a couple of defendable science stations this far forward. The Node is one. My Monarch credentials get recognized instantly. Should we move now, Orion?"

I told her to start out. I waited and then led Team Two toward the big tube. Suppressive fire from Hauser was able to keep the ape-monkey swarms back despite stray incoming that whistled past us and slapped interior hull.

The giant tube that ran through this section was now illuminated. And it was empty. A seamless hatch, molded to the curve of the wall, had been opened inward on the opposite side of the tube. The Kid popped out there, signaling that Team One went that way.

Another thing I hadn't spotted on the first visual recon of the big tube was now apparent in the brilliant white light. Someone in a spacesuit. Someone giant. At least nine feet tall. He was lying in the center of tube, near the hatch. His upper torso leaning against the rising curve of the tube wall.

I led Team Two forward and into the hatch. Passing the skeleton looking out from the shattered mask of the spacesuit. It was an old spacesuit. Something from the early days of extra-solar exploration. The first systems. Alpha Centauri. All the usual safety seals and breathing gear. But we don't have nine-foot-tall humans now, and we didn't have them then.

I only had a moment to glance at it. The skeleton inside the spacesuit behind the smashed faceplate. The horns and drums behind us had switched to down-tube by the time we reached the hatch. The apes and monkeys had decided to come at us from a new direction and the tube was telegraphing their move. The captain went past me, barrel of the shotgun leading the way. Then Hauser who was linking another belt effortlessly to the big Pig he carried. Then Jacks with his ruck full of claymores.

The skeleton… I stopped and stared in amazement at it for the brief second I had before we moved on. It was human-ish. Desiccated. And it had three eyes. Or rather three empty eye sockets staring out at me where there should have been eyes in the long ago of life.

I wondered who it was in that way I do when I pass such corpses. But then remembered mercenaries don't have to wonder. They just have to stay alive to the next gig. It's what we do.

It's the private military contractor version of not my monkeys, not my circus.

Speaking of…

The first of the leaping monkeys, almost running on all fours, came out of the darkness down-tube, racing and madhouse screaming for hooma flesh and blood. Spears and gunshots too.

Time to go.

I ducked into the hatch and was grateful it could be closed and locked down manually. Hauser took over and dogged it tight as we watched the panels running alongside it indicate lockdown mode, electronic locks in place.

The monkeys began to beat on it almost instantly, thundering a hundred paws and claws at once. Enraged at its presence. The sound is something I'll never forget. The screeching. The hammering. The spine-scratch of claws dragging mindlessly mad along its length.

There was no doubt once I ran out of ammo there wasn't even the option to fight it out. Those things would tear us to shreds. Then, as Punch signaled me they'd found the last passageway to the Node and we were proceeding in, the red lights that ringed the hatch switched over to yellow. Indicating the locks were being disabled. Then green. A moment later dozens of claws reached in and through the appearing seam, beginning to tear and heave at the hatch to move faster.

"They're just animals!" shouted Jacks. "How are animals gonna disable complex systems?"

I had no idea.

"*Pull back now!*" ordered the captain.

None of us needed to be told twice. We'd made it fifty meters down the electronics-filled maintenance passage when the hatch came open and a tidal wave of killer monkeys flooded in and came screeching and gnashing for us. Swarming along every surface. Deck. Walls. Ceiling.

There's no way we're getting out of this, that background app in my mind kept screaming as I told it to shut up and get moving. Sometimes you just keep fighting even when it looks like you're gonna lose.

That's what conflict is.

Everyone wants a fight to go the way they first plan it all out in their fantasies. In the spectacuthriller the mind sees them being the hero of. But those are just fantasies. Plan meets reality on crack is usually how these things turn out.

Sometimes you're not even sure you know you won. You just keep swinging even though you're tired enough to stop and take whatever beating is getting handed out. Not sure if you're gonna win and pretty sure you've lost. You just keep doing it. Keep swinging. Keep fighting. Stabbing even if you've been done fatally.

The captain's shotgun boomed, echoing across the passage and comm. Then again. Again. And again. He was holding the line.

All of this competing with short staccato bursts from the Pig as we fell back, burned brass, and gave ground as little as we could afford. I knew Hauser would do whatever it took. Everyone wanted him to lay down his life, except they didn't think of it like that. Just spend all the runtime he had on our behalf. And he'd do it. He considered us the only friends and family a combat cyborg could have.

How'd he put it? His life was stopped at one second to end of runtime. If he chose, he could activate that internal clock and det on our behalf. A small and very dirty nuclear yield. He'd buy what time he could for his friends.

He even thought he was lucky to have someone like me, someone who knew what he could do in a pinch to save my butt, as a friend.

I felt like the opposite of a friend as the thought crossed my survival mind. I swapped mags and turned and burned a couple of targets, like that would do something against the sea of madness swarming our rear. This was what hopeless looked like.

"Jacks!" I shouted because I had no time to do anything else. "Heads up! Left flank!"

We'd reached a four-way. Down-ship, a second element of murder monkeys was coming straight up a wide passage that looked like some kind of ancient comm and stellargraphy section. Huge map-glass installations and ruined plot tables pulled from their foundations and tossed over carelessly. The monkeys came through this on every side of the passage. Including the ceiling. They were cutting us off.

We were about to get crushed from two sides.

"Heads down!" shouted Jacks as he pulled his ruck off his back and deployed it out in front of us.

I knew this play. I'd seen it before. Things had reached *Desperate* before. I dove on the Kid who hadn't and was standing there, rifle up and ready to engage even though everything looked absolutely hopeless.

He hadn't been around long enough to realize how bad things had gotten. The luxury of youth.

I tackled the Kid as my squad leader wirelessly detted anti-personnel mines all over the passage the new monkey attack was trying. The blast was deafening even with hearing protection. Tungsten-steel balls scattered, exploding violently in every direction. According to specs, the claymores were smart explosives with signature recognition. They were supposed to detonate away from friendlies.

Supposed to is the operative phrase.

Plus, we'd gotten the smart mines from a weapons bazaar and I was pretty sure Chungo, our Voodoo indirect specialist, had picked them up. He'd let us cross a lot of broken glass for a cheap arms deal. But even that is Company SOP. So, you never knew.

I felt the wind get knocked out of me from multiple blasts and hoped I was gonna get to my feet without a serious wound. Or even a minor one.

Just wasn't room. Sorry, reality, my hands are currently real full. I'd like to pass, pay a small fine, or just ask the dealer for mercy on this one. I seriously can't afford to be hit if I'm gonna get everyone out of here.

I pushed off the Kid and dragged him up as the smoke cleared. I didn't feel hit.

But mines do strange things.

"Injured, sound off!" I bellowed in the smoky confusion. Ship's emergency red lighting had suddenly switched on to react to the damage. Probably on some kind of backup battery still hardwired into the old systems. I got everyone. The captain had taken a metal ball straight through his hand but there wasn't a lot of blood loss. We had about thirty seconds to assess and move. The anti-personnel explosions had ruined the second monkey element, but we still had the originals flooding up our back trail. Hauser had stayed upright, returning fire through the explosion. More synthetic flesh ripped away from the almost human side of his body. He taken shrap from the blast and gone on relentlessly killing.

"Time to move!" I roared. If only just for motivation.

On the run, we picked up Team One's back trail and raced up the last corridor for the Node that was our target. Ahead, our feet pounding down the slotted walk where piping and wiring ran beneath, I saw shield barriers and modern auto-gun sentries that had been installed recently. Lighting rigs faced outward.

The science team's defenses.

I was guessing their security forces had set these up to keep the apes and monkeys back from the areas of the ship they'd reclaimed.

The Kid was there, waving for us to hustle through. We made it as more of the simian killers raced out onto the walk behind us, swarmed, careened, and surged forward with pure hot murder in their screeching howls.

That was the part that was the worst. The madhouse shrieking they made constantly.

Then the auto-gun sentries, huge tripod snout-barreled death machines, opened up and began to spray hot fire in short *braaaaps* at the animals trying to tear us to pieces, their low-grade sentry-gun AIs tagging, targeting, and allotting as much lead as needed to bring about ends to hostile behavior. The monkeys disregarded their comrades' sudden rag-dolling death and kept on coming despite it all.

On the other side of the initial defensive ring, we passed through a heavy-duty reinforced security door. Another install, no doubt from the science and security teams as they unlocked the secrets of the buried ship.

And then the Monarch.

"Good news or bad news, Orion?"

Bad news. Always take the bad news first.

"Those drone guns are gonna give us about six minutes before they run dry. Then they'll use the heavier apes to come and get us."

"And the good news?" If there was any.

"I've already started the hack on the dig computer that discovered what I need. What we came here to recover. Eight minutes and change and it'll crack the locks. Ten seconds for me to access the core operating instructions and then we can go."

"So… that would be bad news too then?"

Two minutes to hold in position, while already running low on ammo, wasn't going to be any kind of picnic. Not by any stretch of the imagination.

Outside beyond the security door the monkeys screeched, died, and kept on coming. It made no sense. It was a madhouse.

No. It wouldn't be any kind of picnic at all.

But it was the picnic I'd arrived at. And it was all you can eat, brother.

Perfect.

Bring it.

CHAPTER FORTY-FIVE

For six minutes those killer monkeys threw themselves straight into the guns. Mindlessly screeching as they died violently. The guns didn't stop. They just kept relentlessly burping out ammo in the correct and efficient doses to annihilate each predator. Never stopping. Never hesitating. Never tiring. And I knew when they did, when they ran dry on ammo, that was going to be it.

The captain ran our defense beyond the security door.

There wasn't much to our location. The Node was nothing more than a field science base set up inside the derelict starship. Gathering and initial recovery was done from here. Field computers processed and scanned recovered tech. Clamshells stood by for transport of all sizes. No superweapons. Just the guns to keep the monkeys back and maybe a security team with some serious firepower when needed. Mines probably. But the science station had been abandoned, or at least it wasn't in use. And the monkeys and apes seemed to have been dealt with in the past. Had been driven off by the local defenses. Something though, this time, had caused them to push all their chips in.

They were going for it come hell or high water.

If that didn't make ya nervous I don't what would. I'd been part of at least two last stands. Both swung my way. This one was worse than the other two and Punch, who'd been on those other two, kept muttering, "Third time's the charm, Sarge."

So there's that.

This ship. The one from ten thousand years in our future. Or rather, the one that had gone there, taken a look around, and then tried to come back and missed its timeline exit by about another ten thousand years, this ship was looking like a tomb right about now. Our tomb.

Who knew? Maybe it had been all along.

Yeah. That was the story I got from the Monarch in the last minutes before the guns ran dry. Six minutes as we topped off our magazines. Layered out what we needed. Took cover or arranged cover. She talked in my ear, telling me what she knew. Confessing was what it felt like because it felt just like what they all do when they come and tell me their stories. For the log. For the official record of the Strange Company.

"The *Enterprise*," she began. "I never knew the name of the ship, but now from what I've seen here inside their data cloud, and the item we recovered here, I'm convinced that was it. The *Enterprise* was sent forward in time using a new engine system we'd developed in the labs on Ganymede. Monarch super-science at the time had experimented with small time leaps forward and back. Back is much more difficult, Orion. Days. Weeks. A couple of years at best was the safest we could do reliably. Even that gave us some edge in shaping the future the way we wanted it to go. But with interstellar distances, these brief looks at the future by a starship crew didn't do much for us in the grand scheme. Events happened we couldn't control. And control is the basis of Monarch culture. Also, there was one more effect. These explorer ships sometimes came back with compromised data banks. No idea how it happened. But often the basic information we had and knew to be true, came back changed when the ship came back in time to the anchor point. Their data corrupted *our* data and so containments had to be put in place. I know that's a lot of information, Orion. But it's important.

"So. The Monarchy needed to know what would happen to us as we expanded our control and influence over human culture. We were seeing some disturbing images and data that made no sense with regard to our current operations then. It was as though we had ceased to exist at some sudden undetectable point. I knew a ship was being used for an operation we called Project Zephyr. I had no idea it was the *Enterprise*, specifically. It's down inside a central hangar several decks in from here. When they went forward in time, they found this larger ship, or the future interacted with them in some way, or something, and the *Enterprise* tried to come home with a much bigger and better starship surrounding it. This ship. The maximum of what they thought they could pull off. Technically, according to the official Monarch science data, it never returned. But it did. I suspected it had. I thought there was a chance the Crash was actually the Project Zephyr starship."

She paused.

The auto-guns spooled up to critical levels out beyond the security door our own guns were trained on. Smoke drifted through cracks around the installation of the tight security door. Then gun one went down.

"Thirty seconds on gun two," the Seeker announced over comm. Apparently her operating systems could take control of local devices and hardware. She was in communication with the guns. Monarchs can do that stuff, or so I've been told.

She looked back at me. We were crouched on the right flank. The Kid was near us. I checked my elements. Everyone was set up for interlocking fire with the two Pigs on both flanks.

We'd do what we could.

"That's all you can do?" I whispered to myself as I made eye contact with Hauser. He smiled grimly and gave me a thumbs-up.

"What?" she asked, snatched away from her narrative. I could tell she was talking as much to hear it as to put the pieces together. Or maybe she knew our chances weren't good, and she was downloading on me. A virus? An SOS?

It was hard to tell which.

"Nothing," I said. "This is it now. Tell me. I don't care about lost starships or whatever Monarch games the better half wants to play. I just need to get Reaper through this. Tell me what's so important about what we came here for. What you're here to get if we survive the next two minutes."

"Fifteen seconds," said Hauser, whose onboard clock had managed to sync the calc to *weapons dry* on both guns.

At ten he began to count down our doom.

"Freedom," she said breathlessly. Nervous. Worried. But steel and fire in her resolve. She was a Monarch after all. The best of us, that was what the constant media whispered in our ears, day and night. Our heroes. Our benevolent providers. Our avengers. "Real freedom for everyone who wants it."

But she definitely could have been Strange Company. She was dumb enough not to quit when the night was dark and the odds were real bad.

"The operating file for the device is still deep inside the ship's secure memory banks. The deep storage systems that were designed to regulate against the unintended effect of time travel."

We were under five.

"The pure data. Uncorrupted."

I stabilized my Bastard and set up my sight picture to dispense death. Front sight forward now, Orion.

The last gun ran dry and instantly the monkeys were beating at the doors with tools. And something larger, large, something very large in fact, was coming up the walkway we'd used to access the Node. It sounded titanic compared to the monkey-lings scrabbling to break in here.

"And what is it?" I said. My voice calm. The storm imminent. "What is this device that does freedom for all of us?"

"It's the last chance at that freedom. It'll destroy the entire mem-currency system the Monarchs control everyone with. It's the weapon that ends the Monarchs two thousand years from now. Gave rise to the Simia who rule the future. Those things out there are the Simia. They came back with the ship as far as I can tell. From the future. Ten thousand years from now. I'm trawling the science logs as fast as I can. This was all site-restricted to the Monarchs with the highest of clearances. In the future of the galaxy, the Simia, they rule absolutely. What's left of us are the animals. No Monarchs. No humanity. Just animals hunted to extinction. The crew of the *Enterprise* recovered the data and the device that destroyed Monarch culture from the Doomsday Vault on Cygni Nine. It's a Monarch updating time capsule where even we don't play with the truth. It's where we hide all the secrets, including the truth. We protect it with all our lies."

The giant thing outside began to rip the door from its hinges. Whatever it was, it was coming through soon.

"And if it destroyed the Monarchs. Humanity… then why do you want it now?"

"Because, Orion…" The door began to groan as it was pulled from its frame. Rending metal screeched. Massive hinges screamed. "Freedom is our only hope to prevent what happens. That weapon, the Deletion Drive, it will, in time, collapse the Monarchs' rule and allow humanity a chance to get ready to meet the Simia with some shot at winning this time. Releasing the device now, two thousand years ahead of schedule… gives us a chance, Sergeant. We need that chance. Because the Monarchs… they would rather try other means. Means that allow them to remain in control. Even if the chances aren't good. Even if it means the eradication of humanity."

CHAPTER FORTY-SIX

The giant behemoth that opened up the vault doors to the Node was the largest ape I'd ever seen. Technically speaking, I hadn't seen a lot of apes. None before today. But today... I'd seen a lot of them. And this thing was easily twice as large as the ape the captain had killed atop the rock with his Hardballer shot to the head. Blowing its brains out all over rock and sky. Their war leader for the assault to wipe us out in the canyon.

"Get it on!" I shouted as Reaper opened fire. As the thing heaved the door aside and swept a great gargantuan paw in at us. Dead monkeys and one of the auto-gun sentries came flying in right at us.

Both Pigs drew bright lines of sudden automatic fire across the thing's broad chest.

Nothing. It didn't seem to mind 7.62 moving at twenty-four-hundred feet per second.

It roared and pounded its chest. Lowering its jaw-heavy skull and baring its immense fangs at us as it roared death right into our faces.

It bled. Yes. But it didn't stop its attack. It squeezed itself into the tiny room that would be our tomb for sure, a mass of other apes howling and gibbering to get past it. These were big too. Not *as* big. But things you wouldn't want to meet ever.

The captain fired six concussive booms, adding shotgun slugs to the damage, blowing out one huge malevolent eye in the giant ape's immense skull. The thing roared, dragged a bloody claw at its devastated eye, and heaved another paw across our line. The captain and Hauser went flying as the tree trunk arm batted them into the wall of the science station.

I stood, dumped a mag, ejected, and got tackled by a flying monkey. The spider-quick thing was arms, claws, and fangs all at once. It smelled bad and tried to rip through my chest rig as it fought to tear my face off. I let go of my rifle, pulled my karambit, and rammed the blade into its skull as it was the only chance I had with the second and a half left to me. I pulled the blade out and rammed it home five more times to get the thing to stop mindlessly flailing at me. The Monarch was blazing away above, standing over my body, spent brass hitting me in my blood-covered face as I struggled with the feral predator.

The Kid pulled the monkey off my body.

I was still holding the magazine I was going to insert when I got to my feet and watched as the team brought down the big ape with more fire. Hauser was back up and spent the last belt walking forward and spraying the goliath everywhere he could with a cone of lead death that washed over the beast. Portions and chunks of its flesh came away in great sprays as the hail of gunfire ruined its massive frame. Monkeys and apes moving past their dying god streaked in at the combat cyborg and tore away more of his own synthetic flesh.

The captain pulled them off with his bad hand and shot them with his good hand wielding the Hardballer.

More monkeys were flooding in. More by the second. We were going to get overrun now that our line had lost cohesion and integrity.

"We can do this!" shouted Punch over full-auto blare from his shorty. "Hold the line, Strange!"

He'd make a good platoon leader, I thought as I watched the battle from some distant part of my mind. If we survived. But there were so many of them coming through the security door now, over the dead giant and straight at us, that it seemed impossible the flood would ever end, or that we would survive more than another minute at best.

"Thirty seconds!" shouted the Monarch. "Once I have it, we can fall back through to the next security station. More guns there will buy us time to reach the transport lift to the science base. Hang in there, Reapers."

I burned another mag on six of them, unsure if I'd killed any or just shot them a bunch. It was like a lunatic asylum had turned into a carnival shooting gallery. It was madness. Blood spray. And monkey guts. Hard to know what was true in the bloody darkness.

I've fought battles. But nothing like this. And I never wanted to again if any of them were ever going to be like this one. It wasn't human. It wasn't sane. And if these were somehow the Simia from a future with no humanity, forced back in time with a lost starship that couldn't make its way back to when it was supposed to be, then I could see why humanity wasn't the apex predator in the future. The Simia were relentless when enraged.

Last mag.

I called it.

"Black on magazines!"

It had been a long day. A very long day.

"Grenades, Sar'nt!"

"Negative," I yelled at the Kid. The quarters were too tight for explosives. We'd kill ourselves.

"I know!" he shouted over the madness. "Cover me. I'm going to throw 'em out the door."

I saw what the Kid was saying. If he could wade through and chuck them out into the main passage, maybe he could buy us some space. But it was a bad idea. A real bad idea. Ridiculous even. The kind a kid who joined up to become a mercenary and really needing to be a hero would think of. Trying to right some wrong no one would ever find out about. And... I didn't have enough confidence in him to get those tossed grenades through the door under pressure.

I pulled my sidearm.

"Pull your sidearm!" I yelled at him. A monkey came flying in. The Monarch shot it, and blood splashed across our faces as the thing thrashed and died. "Follow me!"

I pulled my first fragmentary grenade. It would be easier to deploy while just working the sidearm. Easier to get the grenades in play. The Bastard dangled uselessly on its two-point sling as I waded out, blazing away at screaming monkeys, splashing skulls with rounds. Screaming for no reason I can remember.

"Captain!" I yelled as I surged stupidly forward into everyone's field of fire. "Keep 'em off us now!"

I'll take fun last words before fratricide for a thousand.

I had no idea if that was even possible. To keep them off of us with supporting fire. Gunfire was wild. Emotions and adrenaline high. Survival instinct kicking in above all else. It was here, at the intersection of these points that people got good and killed by their own actions and friends. And not just by the enemy.

But what other way did we have?

We needed time to reach the next science station and the protection of its guns. When in doubt, grenades out.

I shot one point-blank, blowing it back with the force of my weapon. It screamed and staggered away, its monkey claws still reaching to do harm. Another came in and I just pressed the muzzle of my sidearm to its skull and pulled the trigger in one motion, pivoting to engage as I waded through guts and bodies to get close to the door. Monkey brains spraying everywhere in slow motion as I felt my mind begin to fracture. Of course, the Kid was right behind me. Firing and picking up what targets he could.

I only have shadowy images of what happened next. It's like my mind doesn't want to remember what I saw as I pushed past the big dead ape and looked out into the darkness of the rest of the doom ship down a dark passage filled with the future's monsters. I have images. Impressions. Nightmares. A sea of something so angry and hateful it makes being human seem like a weak and scared thing.

I was popping the grenades and flinging them out… I felt numb. My fingers were numb and bloody. I got the grenades off my chest rig. The Kid's too. And I flung them into the angry monkeys crouching and crouch-running forward to do us in. Coming from the darkness like the monsters they were. Are. Screaming and shrieking. Words I could almost understand…

I think that's where my mind broke.

The Kid blazing away behind me because this is the stuff heroes are made of. That's what we all tell ourselves, right? That's what the dead were thinking before they went down.

Gains. Boom Boom. All the others.

The Monarch in my ear telling me she had what we'd come for. But that might as well have been from far away and not right now.

The Kid pulling me away as the captain gave the order to pull back to the next station.

I didn't come to myself until we were away from the Node. There was another firefight. Another element of monkeys and apes tried to intercept us. It wasn't until the lift out of the starship, crossing through a glass tube toward the hive-like science base that had been built in the rock wall of the canyon, that I came to myself. Sort of.

I looked down at my chest rig.

The claw of a dead monkey was still hanging there. Clutching in death and its removal from whomever it had belonged to.

Had I done that?

Things were hazy.

The Little Girl was looking at me the way she always did.

"He's coming soon," she whispered. Just to me. I don't know that anyone else heard it. We weren't out of this just yet. Her friend was coming to play.

"Three Ultra Marine Raptor-class dropships inserting onto the station, Captain," announced Hauser. I looked up and saw their shadows cross over the opening of the canyon above the Crash. We were inside a lift moving from the ruins of the ship to the wall of the tube where a new science lab had been established by the science teams.

"Well," said Choker. "That's just great."

I did the reloading work. Wiping away the blood. New magazine in sidearm. The Bastard was dry, and no one had any spare ammo.

Last mags for everyone else.

The captain handed me his shotgun. The legendary Beretta 1301 Tactical. A relic from when man was free and made great weapons to keep it that way.

Freedom. She, the Monarch, was gonna set everyone free with a superweapon that made the mem the Monarchs controlled us with good and useless. Sure. And all that mem Amarcus and Dog Platoon was recovering, it would be worthless too.

And wasn't that our deal? Her deal with us. All the mem we could carry away to get paid enough to fix the ship on Blackrock?

I wanted to tell the captain. But I didn't. And I had no idea why I didn't. I just didn't.

Choker was wrapping the captain's wounded hand as the elevator climbed up along the canyon wall. Raging about Ultras and this being a real gyp-job on the company. Boy, I thought, he didn't know the half of it. We weren't even gonna get paid. I had no idea what to do with that info. But as I looked around, everyone was alive. Banged up. Even the Monarch had caught damage from a claw that had dragged itself across her fancy suit. Cutting through armor that should have resisted mere monkey claws. I saw the rage evident in the white flesh and blood there where she'd been caught by the slash.

Down below us, just as we reached the science base hive along the far canyon wall, I looked back at the ship one last time. It was crawling with apes and monkeys, surging along its length. They looked like demons in the darkness racing for souls.

Our souls.

And I heard the Little Girl whisper again, "He's coming soon, Sergeant."

I smelled fall leaves. Fall leaves burning.

He was coming.

The Wild Thing.

CHAPTER FORTY-SEVEN

"I am currently tapped into the station's motion detection systems," stated Hauser as we moved through the upper decks of the science station built near the Crash. "Tracking three Ultra teams moving into the base now. Combat posture alpha."

We were in a wedge and we looked rough. At best. Even Hauser was limping from a badly articulating leg joint. His combat chassis had taken a lot of abuse. Abuse meaning heavy damage. A lot more than the rest of us. But he was still carrying the Pig and scanning for targets. We were low on ammo and had to make the terminal for the high-speed tube to the airfield. The problem for us right now was the Ultra Marine Raptor dropships. High-speed hunter-killer variants, down in the main plaza between the terminal and the hive-like science base full of windows and levels looking out at the big wreck of a starship disappearing off into the tunnel darkness.

The drops had come in and landed their teams. Now the teams were hunting for us and the drops were on ground standby.

The science labs we were currently moving slowly through were quiet and heavy in that way deeply reinforced data-gathering stations feel. The soft lighting and carpet. The heavy processors quietly humming their number-crunching titterings. The opposite of what we did. Here was order and knowledge. We were chaos and survival. Not just opposites. But aliens.

The quiet. The massive holographic displays endlessly churning their meaningless, to me, data. Tables spread with the drives and papers. Even empty coffee cups waiting to be filled.

I was thinking if we passed a machine that could churn some out, then I was gonna hit it and hit it hard. I was thinking about coffee. Not lost starships from the past and the future. Or a race of killer apes called the Simia that are somehow responsible for the end of humanity. My pay grade did not care. My pay grade needed coffee to keep putting one foot in front of the other in this insane asylum of a contract.

Now we were on the third level, Science Operations, behind tinted reinforced invisi-steel windows, with eyes on the drops in the courtyard below. Punch was doing recon while the Monarch hacked a display and downloaded our situation into a tactical format. Updating it with data from Punch's feed off of Boom Boom's rifle.

I turned to the Little Girl and gave her a look. Asking without words how much longer we had until her friend showed up. I wasn't opposed to it. I just needed to know. Sending that thing in to wipe out the Ultras blocking our exit would really make all our collective days right about now.

She nodded her head and silently mouthed the word "soon."

I raised my eyes.

"When," I whispered impatiently.

She gave me a look indicating she had no idea. But soon. The way our luck was running it would be at the worst possible time. But I tend to think positively that way. That's me.

"We got three crews. Two pilots each. Two door gunners each. One of whom is probably the crew chief. Tagging twelve tangos." Punch then ran through the weapons he was seeing. We assumed they had full combat loads.

So, there's that.

Our number was currently eleven plus a kid. A little girl.

Me, Punch, Choker, Jacks, Hauser, Hustle, and Hoser. The captain. The Monarch. Cook and the Little Girl. And the Kid.

The winds were picking up outside the station. Coming off the desert floor above and sending sand down through the shafts of light. Racing down the orange rock canyon walls and blowing that skirling sand and light debris here and there. It was a high-tech ghost town, and we didn't have time to wonder what had happened to the science team.

Either the monkeys had gotten them, or they'd been pulled out now that the Monarchs had begun their final conquest of the world.

The scene would have been almost beautiful if not for the twelve killers between us and a way out. And I couldn't find any coffee.

I checked my watch. Time. There was none to spare.

One hour to the hit on the airfield. Dog would be storming the bank now after fighting its way through the outskirts of the small town surrounding the desert starport. According to the schedule.

And we sergeants are all about our schedules.

Ghost in sniper support. The First Sergeant running the whole show. Our situation looked bad, but I didn't know who had it worse. The guys taking the bank. Or us.

Twelve Ultras, even though they were aircrew, were still Ultras. Every one a killer. That's their motto, according to Chief Cook. Every one a graduate of their most advanced infantry schools. The average Ultra carries sixteen weapons. MX battle rifle. Savage Rampage model short-barreled shotgun. Stuka 9mm sidearm. Six frags. One banger. One Ultra combat knife. Two arms. Two legs. One bucket. Head smashes are their favorite. Supposedly they keep tallies on the sides of their helmets. But I've never been close enough to verify.

Nor do I want to be.

The captain took a drag on his cigarette and lowered his smoke-stained finger still holding the smoke to the table the Monarch was updating.

"Base of fire here with the cyborg and myself. The rest of you move here along this rock garden area off to their left. Our right. If they're distracted you can make it to the tube station. Board and go. We have to take that ship, Sergeant Orion, once you get there. That is No Fail. The rest of Strange is counting on us, so get it done."

The unspoken part of his plan was evident. The cyborg was expendable. And the captain was a real leader. They'd buy us an exit window. Few of us, and especially those who had served in other Monarch support military units, had ever had the privilege of having that kind of leader. Someone who led by example, instead of special privilege. Of course, he was gonna make sure he paid the price for a shot at the company's freedom. He and "the cyborg" would buy us time to reach the tube station. The rest was up to us.

The Monarch seemed satisfied with the plan. It got the job done. She drew on the plans an axis of movement for both elements in broad blue holographic strokes. Who was going where. Who was staying behind to die.

It was possible. The captain's plan. But the Ultras would ruin us across fifty meters of open ground if we got spotted. The plan could go from *maybe* to *wrecked* in about five seconds from what I was looking at. But NCOs are optimists that way.

"Permission to tag along, sir." Punch of course. If just for the fight. But also because he was that kind of guy. Reaper would be in good hands with him someday.

Chief Cook cleared his throat and stepped up to the table.

"Uh, sir," he said in his pseudo-officious voice like he was addressing the judges who enforced the laws and revenges of the Monarchs. "Perhaps we could do this another way."

The Old Man was silent, pulling his smoldering cigarette away from the table and taking a drag. His way of saying our Voodoo chief had the floor. Any good commander gives warrant officers a lot of room and credibility. Especially when it comes to their areas of expertise. Because they have a practical wisdom about how to get things done the smart way instead of the military way.

"Sir, the way I see it is, uh, we can do this the easy way, or the hard way."

"Which is the violent way?" asked Punch. "For the record, I'm extremely comfortable with violence."

Chief Cook gave him a quick brothers-from-another-mother smile and continued.

"Ah. Then that would be the easy way. Hard way was the captain's plan. So, here's how we could really crash their mental hard drives…"

Ten minutes later, me, Chief Cook, and Hauser walked out into the courtyard. Hauser was carrying the Old Man's combat shotgun hooked to the back of his carrier. What was left of the ammo from both Pigs had been linked to make one and a half belts. Enough to ruin some days with.

We'd each had a pull from the flask Stinkeye had loaded up for us. Chief Cook was the first.

"Well, if the old bastard was trying to kill me, he certainly arranged the right set of circumstances to make his dreams come true. Here's to ya, you old fraud. Hope yer already dead somewhere."

He studied it for a brief second, then hit it. He winced. Coughed.

"Ain't bad. In fact... I feel... purty good, for the record. Like I could take on the whole galaxy and not really care much who won or lost."

We each had a shot. Even the captain.

Hauser mimed a pull and passed it on. I loved him for that.

All it did was make you feel invincible. Like you could pull something just about as crazy as we were about to pull and get away with it.

"We're gonna shake the pillars of the universe," whispered Chief Cook as we walked out into the Ultra door gunner's kill zone. Ready to pull our last trick.

So there's that.

What the Ultra aircrews were seeing, or so we hoped, as the three of us strode into the courtyard, was three things.

A Monarch spec ops intel officer. That was Chief Cook, who always kept his old green beret handy in his ruck, according to him as he quickly walked us through the skullduggery he had planned.

A combat cyborg model trained for asymmetrical urban warfare. Spec ops worked with them often. That was Hauser.

And a prisoner.

That was me.

Because hey, why not?

Chief Cook had even put a cyber collar around my skull. If it worked properly, the cyber collar, I'd be rendered little more than a walking zombie taking orders from the command voice authenticated for the collar.

I could play the part. I was pretty sure I could act dead on my feet. I'd been infantry long enough.

"So," muttered Chief Cook as we walked out into the orange sunlight to begin the show. "Like I always say. Just because it's dangerous doesn't mean it's not fun. Be cool and don't start shooting until I do the crew chief. That's the signal for *get it on* time, boys and girls."

Girls made me think of the Little Girl. Her friend showing up right now would be downright awful. Yeah it would kill the Ultras, but we were a little too close for comfort. It would be like playing tag with a tornado.

It made me nervous the chief was repeating our plan. Like he didn't trust it and was trying to find some last-minute weakness in it so that we'd know exactly how we got killed even as we had no time to correct the deficiency.

"Copy," said Hauser, sotto voce. "The simians are engaged with the Ultras at the lift on deck six of the science station. Cliffside. There are casualties already. Acting cool now, Chief Warrant Officer Cook."

"Not you, Hause. You just act like you. Orion. You act dumb. Me. I'll do the cool part. Ready…"

Guns came out fast. The door gunners drew a bead on us and a crew chief carrying a short automatic carbine came out, weapon aimed right at us.

"Hold on, boys," croaked Chief Cook in the dry desert air. Then, "Warrant Officer Foster, Two-Twenty-Second Tactical Com Operations. We've been planetside for weeks now. Me and the Tin Man bagged us a high-value target and I need to turn him over to your commander for transport if you're heading back into Centcom."

The Ultras were all business. They weren't stupid. You had to score high on intelligence tests to join or so the rumors say. Every Ultra was highly trained in all protocols and procedures. They're highly efficient killers trained to combat cyborg levels of competency. They are the very definition of *razor-sharp* and if the plan had involved any edge being gained by our hopefully clever deception, I would have had no hopes as I stood there and looked brain dead.

Mouth open.

Drooling a little. Chief Cook said it would help.

But that wasn't our plan.

Suddenly the lead dropship started her turbines. The lead pilot whirled his hand giving the mount-up signal. The main engines, bulbous cylinders along the aft fuselage above the cargo deck, began to spin up to their idling howl. Drops two and three started seconds later, the pilots working through their start-up sequences, as the crew chief approached. Weapon pointed at Cook. Obviously the commander on the ground while the Ultra infantry were out sweeping the facility, probably looking for us.

"Intercepting packet bursts on their comm. It's encrypted," said Hauser. "Running decode now but my combat probability assessment indicates the Marines are in trouble and falling back to their ships for immediate evacuation. Estimate arrival in six minutes. The simians will be in close pursuit."

"We only need two, Hause," muttered Cook from the edge of his perma-grin. Then to the Marine he said, "All on the same side, Sergeant…" as the high-speed low-drag Ultra in combat armor came forward fast. Short carbine ready to dust us all if he smelled anything he didn't like. And this was when he made the mistake he made.

Combat cyborgs are fearsome predators. For other people. When you're Ultras you regularly work with them. Maybe like an aircrew might, dropping them well behind enemy lines among a civilian populace to go cause their particular brand of mayhem and harm. Then you tend to see them as just other military tools. Weapon systems. The crew chief wasn't totally convinced Chief Cook was on the up-and-up. Maybe seventy percent. Cook was going to give him some bogus authentication codes that would have bought us another five meters closer to being covered by only one of the door gunners on the three drops. Five meters closer to the one in the drop we wanted.

But the sergeant stopped like a pro at just the right distance to keep us covered by at least one other gunner on another drop. Like it was SOP and Ultra DNA at the same time.

"Get down!" thundered Hauser, lowering the Pig and greasing the Ultra Marine sergeant at close range with a sudden burst of automatic fire.

While the sergeant was still stumbling backward, his chest armor ruined by smoking holes left from high-power AP 7.62, I faded behind Hauser, clearly not zombified by the bogus cyber collar, and dragged the shotgun off Hauser's chest rig as incoming fire from the door gunner, depleted uranium incendiary, smacked into our combat cyborg and erupted across the dirt of the garden courtyard. Hauser absorbed the fire as best he could even though this stuff was perfectly good at jacking him up. Rounds came in hot, smashed into his metal frame, and began to melt it.

Without flinching, Hauser returned fire with the Pig and dusted the door gunner at twenty meters.

Chief Cook was doing some kind of awkward combat roll on the ground to get away from the door gunner's fire. When he came up with his sidearm, lying on his belly in the dust, he screamed and unloaded on the door gunner facing us from the other drop on his flank.

I had no time to see if he got hits.

I was coming around Hauser, watching pieces of his metal frame and synthetic flesh fly away from the dying door gunner's last burst as I dragged the combat shotgun up, loaded with slugs, and unloaded on the pilot through the glass canopy of the drop we were gonna take.

Surprise, super-soldiers!

The first two slugs smashed safety glass, and the third tore off his jaw, blowing brain matter and blood all over the front windshield. I could see pilot number two pulling his sidearm, but he had no shot on me. I raced for the cargo deck trying to get an angle on him for my last three shells.

He came out onto the cargo deck. But he was slow with the draw and I only needed to shoot him once, blowing him out onto the plaza on the far side of the drop.

Hauser pivoted and unloaded on the drop crew Chief Cook was targeting. Raking the aircrew with his particular brand of highly accurate and efficient fire.

The third aircrew was reacting and failed to see Punch, Jacks, Choker, Hustle and Hoser with the captain dragging the Kid out into the sunlight, while the Monarch picked up targets and engaged with her wicked little submachine gun, come at them from an opposite angle. Leaving the shadows of the data relay comm tower they'd come out of. They moved fast, using carbines and sidearms to sweep past the ship while Jacks tossed in his last explosive. Not a big one. A door charge he'd packed with tape after wrapping lots of fragments he'd found in the science lab. Steel screws he'd found boxes of.

The improvised explosive devastated the aircrew as flying metal fragments tore through armor and skin. Ruining instruments and hydraulics. One of the engines ingested something and exploded a second later, sending more debris across the courtyard. A fire started onboard that drop and by the time we were aboard the one we were taking, Chief Cook sliding into the pilot's seat and running through the startup sequence, flipping switches and tapping contacts, that one was fully engulfed in black smoke.

"You know how to fly one of these?" I asked as we strapped in. The engines beginning to howl.

"Every Monarch intel operator knows how to jack a vehicle," bragged Cook in a voice I'd seen him straight-up lie to people in. "Got five whole hours of stick time on one of these babies. Did an op on Venemah. Part of the train-up."

At the same moment the Ultra teams, or what was left of them, appeared from the main hive of the station, running fast. Behind them were all the monkeys and apes in the world. Raving and racing to drag them down. Animal eyes murderous. Fangs working.

I watched as a sergeant, covering their rear, turned to unload with the squad automatic weapon. A storm of monkeys jumped him and dragged him down. Pulling the weapon out of his gauntlets as they tore at his armor.

Then he detted one of his grenades and blew a cluster of them in every direction. Including himself.

"Hang on to your butts!" shouted the chief as the Monarch slid into the blood-and-bone-matter-caked co-pilot's seat next to him and started helping to get us ready for lift. "Combat takeoff in effect."

Then we were airborne and turning away over the top of the station. Engines straining for lift. Orange daylight washing the cargo deck.

Some of the Ultras stopped to fire at us, assessing the situation. Seeing the carnage. Angry they were about to get the short end of the stick for once.

Those Marines got flying-tackled by more swarms of monkeys with guns, spears, and knives. Ripped apart by the larger apes bounding and racing for a piece of the action.

Hustle turned the Little Girl's face away as we climbed. "Don't look, honey," he murmured over the comm.

The sun flashed through the blood-washed windows of the drop's cockpit as the engines howled and we lifted away and over the desert, picking up our course track. Flying through the black billowing smoke of the forever engines of the Crash. And then the desert beyond and below. The wide white endless desert sands here at the bottom of this world.

"ETA fifteen to starport."

The captain leaned back against the seat in the rear cargo deck opposite me. He looked tired as he gave me a thumbs-up.

We'd made it this far. Just a bit more to go.

CHAPTER FORTY-EIGHT

The Kid told me his story during the last flight out of Dodgeistan. The last view of the science station near the Crash site was nothing but a sea of predators overwhelming everything like some grim foreshadowing of everything the Monarch had told me so far. Now I watched the clean desert pass beneath our hijacked Ultra dropship. Not even the best of the Ultras could have survived back there.

I watched Hoser put a found flight helmet on the Little Girl. Comically too bulky for her already giant head compared to her tiny, lithe, lollipop body.

We've never bought her a lollipop. Like you should for little girls whenever you have the chance. Girls love sugar. It's a stand-in for love in the time of no love. Or at least the love they crave and cannot have or that will not give back. But then again, we've never passed a place that sold lollipops. We were too busy doing what we did. Which is war. And maybe those two don't mix but I'd bet Choker would tell me they did.

I heard the captain making our plan to take the armored transport on the field once we hit the LZ. The Monarch would fly that one. Chief Cook, along with Hustle and Hoser, would stay aboard this one and make gun runs until Strange Company was aboard the larger transport and clear to depart. Choker was trying to fix the damage to Hauser, suffocating the burning white phosphorus incendiary rounds with packing gel. Some of the fragments were still smoldering in his synthetic flesh and metal frame. The medic was watching with ghoulish fascination as he did his work.

But that's Choker. A war crime to the rest of the galaxy. A brother to the company. Bullets and lollipops.

"My story ain't nothin' special to anyone else, Sergeant."

But it's important to me, I could hear, reading his mind. It is, Kid. Even though the galaxy conspires every day to tell us all our stories aren't important to the big turn of the wheel of the galaxy spinning about the hot central core. But I don't say that. Best to listen. Too tired to do anything else. More to do in just a few minutes.

Listening to the chatter of the comm that the LZ we're about to hit is gonna be lit.

"Just thought you should know it," continues the Kid. "I've heard some others. From guys since I've been part of the company. But…"

He said nothing after that for a few seconds.

The dull hum of the comm waited between us. I was monitoring the captain's orders. We were getting reports from the First Sergeant on the ground at the objective. Things were bad. Real bad. Bank hit went rough. Wounded. Sergeant Hannibal fighting a retreat to the airfield. Package in hand though. The Ultras have shown up and are dropping indirect fire all over the route as assault teams hit the perimeter from air cav.

One of the Ghost snipers has eyes on the armored transport we need to get the whole unit off-planet. "She looks like she's getting ready for dustoff."

This could be hopeless. If it leaves we're gonna have a lot of explaining to do to people who are interested in explanations.

"Stay on mission," said the captain over the comm like he was reading all of our thoughts. "We'll find a way." Pause. Dull hum of ether. Distant howl of the engines as Chief Cook pushes it to max throttle.

I smell the burning leaves of autumn on all the worlds I've ever been on. One in particular though. Or is that just the engines? The draft washing across the cargo and flight deck. And not the Wild Thing coming soon.

"There's a way," finishes the captain as we get ready to go.

I tap the Kid and give the hand signal to continue. Twirling two fingers tiredly. Old as time. Veteran to Kid. Old man getting older and taking the time to listen to the so real problems of the young. So important. So damn important back then when everything was life or death. The reasons you wanna die. The stands you make. The things you're gonna have to live with whether you like it or not.

No one cares, Kid. But you don't tell him the truth of that. You just listen. Old men listen.

Soldiers live and wonder why, right?

"So..." continued the Kid. "There's a girl. I was straight crazy about her. I think she was crazy about me. Once. We were both at different schools. I'd already been in the local military. No combat. Now in university. We were... we were gonna get married. We had plans. Y'know, stuff you say when you're in love and it's like a secret no one else can know because it's so good. See the galaxy together and do all that adventure stuff."

Casualty report coming in from Dog. It's not good.

I can see the sky and desert past the Kid. His face is haunted and blackened by smoke and gunfire. He's different now. Different from whoever she thought he'd ever be. I think to myself, *If she could see him now, would it matter?* But I don't know who she is. Haven't heard the whole story. Then again, I've probably heard it before.

"Five minutes," shouts Cook over the comm. Hustle stands and goes to the swing-mounted door gun. Hoser pats the Little Girl's flight helmet and makes sure she's good and strapped in. Then he goes to the other door gun. Checks it. Racks a round and runs through the traversing motion like he's already looking for targets. He nods at the captain with a big smile. *Get it on,* he mouths silently. The Ma Deuce is always a privilege to fire. Has been ever since there were soldiers to fire it.

"One night I drive over to her college to pick her up. We were gonna see a spectacuthriller. *Lethal Monarch.* Ever see that one, Sar'nt?"

I hadn't.

"She ain't there. At her dorm. Friend tells me she's at this guy's. So... I go over, knock on the door, and he answers. Shirtless. Smile on his face like he knows what's up is up. Real Jodie type. Know what I mean?"

I do. I really do.

"I ask for her. Sinda here? He says no. But I hear her, and she says yes she is. Like someone else was coming to look for her not me. He disappears, and she opens the door a crack and I'm just standing there, and the look on her face is..."

Two minutes to LZ. I check my weapon. I can see the airfield out there on the desert floor. There's already black smoke rising from across the city of low buildings around it. It's clear we're flying into a battle. But like all battles it looks peaceful from above. Almost lazy. I'm betting it's a real different story down there right about now with Amarcus and company fighting a street battle to take the airfield. Ghost shooting down as many as they can while moving from position to position. The First Sergeant running the whole show with his particular brand of relentless good humor.

There were dead. I knew that already from the comm chatter.

I look at the Kid as I get ready. We've got some ammo and weapons. I'll be going with the captain to take the armored transport once we're down.

I look at the Little Girl. She's watching me and I swear an autumn leaf dances into the open cabin of the cargo deck, swirls around, and we both watch it knowingly. Her, a child watching a leaf play, never minding all the death and chaos about to go down. Me, freaked out but numb. Thinking... *This might as well happen*. It's probably for the best. The Wild Thing might not even be enough considering the mounting odds and growing casualty reports we're getting.

Besides. Her friend is showing up whether we like it or not.

It's *get it on* time. And then some.

I take a deep breath. This might as well happen.

I've got two mags now. And some beat-up dudes to take to the transport. Hauser is ruined. But he's going anyway. Of course he is. The captain is shot but he's hard as nails so that don't matter. Jacks and Punch and Choker look like three killers ready to do what they do best. The Monarch slithers out of the co-pilot's chair as we make our approach. Fresh mag, chambers a round, and flips the safety to off. The airfield grows wide ahead and below. Tracer fire and explosions all across the city. The taxi aprons and clamshell hangars down there are silent. Other ships are departing fast, rocketing off into the upper atmosphere and the burning daylight. One ship is on fire in the late-day desert sunlight down there on the tarmac. It explodes suddenly sending hull plating and debris in every direction.

I spot the company crawler making the airfield. Under heavy fire. Dog soldiers are falling back in squads. Firing and covering. Carrying their wounded to the crawler, or around the crawler, for cover. Local security forces are pursuing in armored technicals and teams on foot. Someone fires AT and it smokes off and smashes into a building. Blowing debris out the back.

I can't believe we've made it this far.

I can't believe we'll make it any farther. I can't believe that at all.

That seems impossible as I see Monarch Ultra Marine death squads sweeping in from all points of the compass now. Like this was some kind of trap they knew we'd arrive at eventually. Nice try, Strange Company. But the dice were loaded the whole time. Whether you listened to the ghost of John Strange in the Bar at the End of the Universe or not. Don't believe in anything, Orion. Not ever. It'll just get you killed like it's about to.

"She just looked at me and said, *It's over*." The Kid is watching it all too out his side of the aircraft as he finishes his story of who he was before the Company of Strange. "Maybe for her, Sar'nt. Maybe. I love her though. Still do even though she doesn't anymore. Maybe sometimes, she'll think of me and wonder what happened to me. Ya think? Wonder if I bought it in some battle no one remembers but that made a difference for someone I'll never know, y'know. That's all I guess I wanted. That's my story, Sar'nt. And it ain't much of one. But… it's mine. That's why I'm here. That's why I joined. I loved a beautiful girl, and she didn't love me anymore. Dumb, huh? I thought I'd just do something dumb because…"

Someone's shooting at us. Rounds smack into the fuselage. He doesn't finish. We're in it now.

Nothing after that because we were down and clear. Door gunners laying the hate in every direction because the environment was absolutely target-rich. We hustled out into a firefight we didn't start, with every intention of finishing it. 'Cause that's all we had. All we ever had. Strange Company gets paid to finish the fights other people start.

I think John Strange would be proud of that. He was that kind of dude. I only met him once, and he was a ghost then, but I think he'd proud of how we hung together even when the odds were against us

But I'd heard the Kid. Heard his story that was the same as all of our stories though the details and reasons are often different. You should hear Choker's. It's really messed up.

I knew the parts the Kid didn't know. Not yet. You gotta live longer to know those parts. That you can love someone even if they don't love you back. Nothing wrong with that. Maybe if more of us did that the galaxy might change and be something better without superweapons and ideological concepts to kill one another over. Wars would become obsolete and Strange Company would sit in bars and tell stories growing old. And I knew that… sometimes… sometimes you go do dumb stuff trying to become a hero like that'll make a difference in the choices that were made. Like you'll prove something to those who dismissed you. Or you'll do dumb stuff trying to prove something to yourself. Even though you lie and tell yourself you're trying to prove something to everyone else except yourself.

I didn't have the heart to tell him she doesn't care anymore. And that no, she never thinks of him.

Sometimes, you do make a difference. Just not where you expect. And what you do on a bad LZ, echoes in eternity.

CHAPTER FORTY-NINE

Everything went wrong from the start. We hustled away from the idle-roaring dropship not taking fire yet. But there was lots of flying lead and bright tracers going in every direction. Both gunners were bleeding brass and Chief Cook was shouting "Go go go!" over the comm as the hijacked drop made ready to go back into action and buy us some airborne covering fire.

A rocket smacked into one of the distant hangars and exploded the thin roof in every direction.

"Just in time for the party, Sarge," yelled Punch as he took the tip of the spear for our hijacking ground force to secure the armored transport dropship that would get us back onto the *Spider*.

Once we were clear I heard both door gunners, Hustle and Hoser, give the "down and clear," signaling we were far away enough from the drop for it to take off again. We were fifty meters away from our target moving in a combat wedge to intercept. Both gunners opened fire as the drop climbed above our heads and out over the battle.

The captain, with his Hardballer out, gave the signal for his three killers, Punch, Choker, and Jacks, to light up the ground crew as we approached. They made short work of them and took the rear boarding ramp, dusting the crew chief as they did so.

Jacks grabbed the dude and tossed him off the back ramp.

The captain ordered the next phase of the takeover as we hit our first snag. The Little Girl had come with us. Everyone had just assumed she'd stay on the Ultra drop we'd hijacked. The one that was gonna go and do gun runs over the top of a citywide firefight. Because we're good with children like that. Now she was crouching low and keeping behind me, and Hauser was bringing up rear security. Hauser there only because he was moving slow with a limp on the bad articulating joint in his shot-to-hell leg.

"Take her!" I shouted at the combat cyborg once we reached the deck.

"Negative," shouted the Old Man over the rage and thunder of the battle in all directions. Hauser, myself, and the Monarch were Team Two. We'd be clearing the forward compartments and the flight deck of the armored transport the company needed if we were to make the rendezvous with the *Spider*. Hauser because he could still take more damage. And he had the combat shotgun which was perfect for that kind of close-quarters work now that the Pig was bone-dry on ammo.

"Message from XO," shouted the First Sergeant over the company comm. "*Spider* entering outer atmosphere now for rendezvous. He's got interceptors inbound and we are to get the hustle on, Strange Company. Ain't no time to dally."

The Old Man looked at all of us with disgust as he tried to figure out what to do with the Little Girl.

"Come here!" he snapped at her and held out one wounded hand.

Jacks got shot at that point by a sniper somewhere among the terminals. He was on the rear deck, holding the perimeter there with Punch and Choker. Punch, who'd grabbed the deck gun, a thirty-millimeter eight-barreled rotating minigun, opened up on the sniper team that had nailed Jacks. They disappeared in a hail of outgoing angry black wasp bullets as Punch worked over the hangar they were firing from. Something deep inside exploded a second later and sent flaming jet fuel across the floor over there.

"That'll give 'em something to think about!"

Choker was on Jacks and stabilizing him immediately. He was hit bad and I helped drag him onto the aft cargo deck, leaving a bloody trail. The Kid was returning fire from behind the massive portside landing gear as we started to get pushed by a four-man team of Ultras who were inside the perimeter now and trying to shut down our escape. One of them had an anti-ship launcher and was getting ready to deploy.

Punch saw the attack, swung the long deck gun, and opened up with everything he had in a sudden blur of violent fire. No short bursts. The gun killed them all as they scattered, and Punch carefully murdered them with traversing fire.

The Old Man was in my face, dragging the Little Girl.

"Need you to organize the load. Crawler's broke down out there on the departure apron. Took a direct hit from AT. Dog is coming in under fire, but they're pinned down. Ghost is working counter-sniper but running low. They have vehicles to come in at the last second. See what you can do, Sergeant. Take the cyborg. The Monarch and I will clear the ship."

"On it, sir!"

Which is all you can say when everyone is stretched thin.

The captain bent down to the Little Girl.

"Go sit over there in that jump seat. We're leaving soon." And then he added "Honey" like it was the most alien and least likely thing he'd ever utter.

She did, and leaves only I could see lay on the cargo deck. She buckled in and waited, watching me with her big dark eyes. She swallowed hard and nodded.

I knew what she was telling me.

But why me?

He's coming now, Orion. The Wild Thing. He's coming… now.

The captain and the Monarch nodded to each other, topped off on mags, and moved inside the ship to clear it. Seconds later there was the thunder of gunfire in the tight spaces forward.

"Time to go," said Hauser flatly. "Dog Platoon is pinned down. They need our assistance immediately, Sergeant Orion."

I looked at Choker for an update on Jacks, who didn't look so hot.

"Good to go, Sergeant," said our medic, putting all his weight on a pressure bandage. "He's gonna make it."

Jacks was gray.

I nodded at Hauser and we made the ramp. I commed with the Kid as we hustle-crouched along the dropship's flat and wide hill going forward to intercept the men coming from the wounded crawler.

"It's all on you and Punch, Kid," I said. "You gotta hold that ramp or there's nothing for anyone to come back to."

"We got this, Sergeant," interrupted Punch. "Did I mention I was comfortable with extreme amounts of violence?"

The Kid just gave me two clicks on his comm as he engaged more targets pushing the hijacked drop. We were getting hit now from three directions back there.

He was Strange Company now.

We depended on him.

And he knew that.

CHAPTER FIFTY

The wind was beginning to howl, and the leaves of autumn were sweeping across the desert starport airfield like dancing whirling dervishes on sudden end-of-summer sciroccos. Moving from ship to ship, under fire, we linked up with the first elements of Dog in retreat. In the distance, we could see the hit crawler. Smoke was billowing out of the side in great big black oily huffs and bursts. What remained of Dog Platoon was fighting a fixed defense from every side they could hold out there.

Monarch Ultra Marine infantry were moving in swiftly from our southwest as a blank space in the universe began to open up. Music like sizzling acid you could never remember playing on the keys of the brain as you watched the horror that came next become real. There were other Ultra death squads coming in. Coming at us. From all points of the compass. But these were the reinforcements that were here to stop us. That was clear. Like they'd known we would always try to exit here at the starport by hijack, and now they were going to put a stop to that.

I heard that unholy music begin to thunder from that other place in the universe that I didn't ever want to know. It was happening now. He was coming. The Wild Thing. I could smell fall. Autumn. And it smelled of the end of all things good and the coming of the winter of the universe. Maybe that was where he came from. The Wild Thing. Like the ship we'd crossed through deep down in that dark crevice made thousands of years ago. The ship from tomorrow and yesterday. Things way above my pay grade. Maybe the Wild Thing was a doomsday weapon from the future. Made as humanity's last stand against an unquenchable force that had finally come to take our place on the galactic scene. The Simia. I had no idea.

But after everything the Monarch had told me, maybe that was the explanation for the unexplainable.

If there can be one.

And the Little Girl? War's orphan. Maybe she was just some gift from the universe that took pity on humanity and knew that we'd need some help. Placing its use in the most vulnerable of hands.

Like there was some new order coming to the universe and we would be governed in a new way. A way foreign to us. A way of mercy.

The Wild Thing came on, running at them, our enemies, as he began to fire. That fantastic weapon of his opening up and creating a cone of shadowy death that was like a hail of speeding bullet ravens ruining everything in their outbound path. A human carrying a GAU weapon. Which was impossible now. But who knew when and where this Wild Thing came from. What was possible in the future, or the other. Or what could be imagined when death came knocking at humanity's collective door. I bet we got real creative ten thousand years, or whenever, from now. When it's desperate you can get up to all kinds of tricks. As anyone in Strange Company knows.

In seconds out there as I watched in fascination and horror, that enemy assault team was ruined and the Wild Thing was already engaging another Ultra death squad. They reacted faster, sending man-portable rockets at him. He weaved, ducked, seemed to accelerate into their midst, and began firing. Smoking missile trails threaded past him as he shot them down. Grenades detonated and he moved closer, drawn to the slaughter like a moth to a flame.

Someone detonated an explosive, and the Wild Thing was rocked by the shock wave. He'd bought us time by destabilizing their attack. We could get ours pulled back now that they were reacting to our unknown superweapon loose and in their midst. Killing spree in effect.

I scanned the crawler.

There were dead. Theirs and ours there.

"The magazines have been hit. Fire suppression systems are struggling to contain the damage," reported Hauser, who was assessing with his combat scanners and matching data with comm chatter and various telemetry feeds he could pick up off Strange Company members' equipment.

Overhead, Chief Cook, Hustle, and Hoser in the Ultra dropship lumbered across the battlefield murdering Ultras trying to push from the city onto the airfield. Heavy fifty-cal fire, incendiary mixed with tracers, ruined an assault team who'd just breached the high concrete wall ringing the starport. I saw Hustle shouting inside the drop, telling the chief to shift position so he could engage new targets.

We were covering behind the bulk of an inter-system ore hauler that had been parted out and hadn't seen a run upwell in twenty years. The patchwork ship was a ghost of itself, but it was cover in the middle of a battlefield. An island of defense in a sea of gunfire and explosions. I knew we had to leave it, and I wasn't crazy about that coming moment.

I caught sight of the Wild Thing again, heard the bark and blur of his terrible weapon as he went after the Ultra indirect and sniper teams on the far side of the airfield like some untamed and vicious dog that couldn't be stopped. Explosions daisy-chained there in fiery apocalyptic bloom as they sought to defend themselves from his horrific and relentless onslaught.

I comm-linked with the First Sergeant, who was supervising the retreat from the wounded crawler ahead of us at our nine o'clock. Dog machine-gun teams were laying down suppressive fire there as the wounded were pulled back and toward our hijacked armored transport and commandeered LZ.

Our *hopefully* hijacked armored transport by now.

"Reaper Six to Doghouse. We have cover secured. Marking now for your teams. Point your casevacs this way."

I turned to Hauser.

"Trade me," I said, indicating the captain's shotgun he was carrying. He did so immediately. Because that's how he is. He trusts me. I'm his combat leader. Even damaged, he was much better with any weapon than I could ever be. The Bastard and her two mags would give him some range to cover me as I went forward. And I needed to move fast and he was too wounded to keep up.

"Defend here," I ordered.

I grabbed the shotgun and dashed toward the crawler through the teams even now reorienting toward our cover position. Hauser didn't need to be told what to do. Single-shot fire, he began engaging anyone shooting at our retreating company members. He'd hold there better than anyone. He'd make sure everyone got the best chance for survival his combat computer could give them.

Across the airfield I heard the bark of the Wild Thing's doomsday weapon again and there was a huge explosion that rocked that side of the fight. Terrible orange flames leapt into the air as a hot blast washed across the field. After that I didn't hear it anymore and I wondered if the Ultras had succeeded in doing what no one ever had. Killing the Wild Thing. Whoever he was.

What would become of the Little Girl now?

"Orion." It was the Monarch on our private channel. I passed Scooch fireman-carrying Duffy, two Dog soldiers, as I ran forward toward the wounded crawler. "You absolutely need to make sure I get the contents of Box 88. Otherwise, all this was for nothing."

"Goin' the wrong way, Sergeant Orion!" said Duffy, who seemed to have been shot in both legs. I ignored and kept moving, passing more wounded evac-carrying teams. Cradling the shotgun as I ran.

Overhead Cook's dropship was coming in to stabilize the line of battle to the rear of our advance onto the airfield, hovering and taking fire, both gunners dumping all they had to keep the Ultras back for just a few more minutes. A missile streaked up from across the starport, and Chief Cook popped flares. Smoking star clusters rocketed out from the aft fuselage of the drop as the rocket lost tracking and ran off into the sky, detonating just above the battlefield seconds later.

Ahead, I saw the First Sergeant on this side of the crawler, pistol out, moving low and getting the carry teams staggered for evac under fire away from the wounded crawler.

One machine-gun team went black on ammo. Commotion there as the Ultras pushed hard. The other team over-cycled their weapon despite needing a barrel change, the gunner just picking it up and shifting his cone of fire almost onto the first team as he cut down more Ultras when they tried to surge. Rounds smacked tarmac and exploded across the Ultra attack wedge. Some were down. Some were continuing to move forward under fire and engage. Both sides were just throwing everything they had at each other now. Someone in the black-on-ammo team lobbed a grenade out there. It erupted, blowing debris and bodies across the tarmac. Still the Ultra Marines continued to close through withering fire.

Chief Cook swiveled the drop above as Hoser drew a bead on that force and unloaded. Someone had popped smoke to cover the retreat but the drop was blowing it everywhere.

Twenty meters to go and I sprinted hard, rounds whistling through the air past my head. I saw Chungo on top of the crawler, working a robomortar and dropping rounds everywhere as fast as he could heave them into the tube.

One round went up, divided into eight and hung there, then ignited burst rockets and showered the line forward of our position with shrapnel.

I didn't know how much that would do against Ultra armor, but every bit helps.

"First Sergeant…" I'm gasping for air as I come up on him and hunker down next to the crawler.

Chief Cook was in my ear. "Sitrep. We got inbound monkeys coming from the tube station and within the city. Streakers moving in among the Ultras. This looks bad, kids."

"Copy that, Voodoo Two," said the First Sergeant.

I could see that the First Sergeant had been hit in the chest armor. It was fractured through the rig. No blood. His teeth were bloody though, as he smiled at me and said, "Bad day, Sergeant Orion. But hey, that's why they pay us the big bucks, eh?"

There weren't many wounded left. But there were dead we'd be leaving behind. I counted the faces I recognized.

"First Sergeant, where's the package?"

"Sergeant Hannibal's got it, son. Pinned down with Team Three that way. His comm went bad. He took a frag in the bank and I think that did it. We're gonna lose him out there if I don't do somethin'."

He knife-handed toward our nine o'clock. I could see another Dog team out there fighting from a small maintenance hub they'd turned into a bunker. I irised in and saw my worst enemy directing fire there. Keeping us from being overwhelmed and overrun to the rear. There were only three of them out there.

"First Sergeant, you need to pull back to Hauser. I'll go get them."

He looked at me with a look of pure hatred. I'd committed the mortal sin of indicating I was better suited to do what needed to be done. That I was young and a warrior. And that he was just an old man.

"Sorry, First Sergeant. Company needs you more."

He hissed and swore.

"Nah, they don't, Sergeant Orion. I need 'em more'n they need me. But you're right, son. I'll get Chungo to drop IR smoke all over that area and you go pull 'em back. Dodgeistan no longer seems all that interesting."

Then he turned and bellowed to both machine-gun teams and the remaining riflemen. Ignoring the dead, for these problems were no longer theirs.

"We are leaving, Strange! Pull back by twos now and get a hustle on. This show's about to be over."

Chungo dropped smoke rounds that would make it easier for me, and harder for enemy targeting. Thirty seconds later I raced out through the fog to get Hannibal and his team back to our lines.

And to get the package.

The package that would ruin all our plans if she was right. A package I hadn't told anyone about. If she was right it would save the galaxy. And Strange would be broke.

I reached Amarcus Hannibal, sliding into the bunker. Hannibal looked like a bloody mess. His Frankenstein patchwork face was even more ruined by viscous blood. He was crouched down and holding his shorty, pointing where he wanted fire. As I assessed the fight from his perspective it was clear he was keeping the Ultras back and off the company. Without this team we would have been flanked and murdered easily. All his men were hit.

He was a great soldier. A lousy human being.

"First Sergeant says pull back, Amarcus. We got cover from the smoke rounds and the drop is on orbit clearing the way. Time to move."

Hannibal looked at me, clearly surprised to see me here. Some light going on in his eyes about the reality of the situation. He nodded to his men, made them grab the heavy gun, and then the four of us were running back to the wounded crawler. Chungo had leapt down off the top, ahead of us, and now the chubby indirect specialist was waddle-running for all he was worth to reach Hauser at the cover behind the ore hauler.

I let myself believe for a second that we were almost out of this.

Overhead Chief Cook's hijacked drop came in hard, both guns rattling lead in every direction. Another rocket streaked up, bounced off the hull, and exploded. The ship went sideways as one engine went offline. Chief Cook fought the spin and had it under control a second later, its engine bellowing like a wounded prehistoric beast.

"We're hit," he grunted over the channel. "Gotta pull out now or we won't make it to the rendezvous. Sorry, Strange!"

I heard the captain over the comm.

"Cleared to depart, Voodoo Three. We have the transport under control. Loading finals and waiting on stragglers. Liftoff in the next five."

Amarcus sent the two men toward Hauser. Then he dashed into the wreck of the crawler.

"Orion!" he shouted, like he'd just remembered a secret. "We got the high-bit mem in a clamshell from the bank. This stuff is worth millions. Help me."

And now, later, I realize he was smart to stack his shorty near the entrance to the burning crawler before going in to get the high-bit mem that would make the company rich if the Monarch didn't use her doomsday delete-all-the-currency weapon. Signaling to me he was unarmed. Deceiving me.

I ran after him. I would tell him the mem was worthless. Once the Seeker, she, the Monarch, got that package he had, she was going to do something that would make everything, all that mem, meaningless. All across the galaxy.

If you believe that, Amarcus.

If you believe. That.

Do you believe it, Sergeant Orion?

Believe things can be different? Believe in freedom.

But it was too late. I was just inside the crawler when he jumped me. Smashing me in the back of the head with something heavy. I never saw what. I broke out into a cold sweat as I stumbled forward knowing with cold-water clarity Amarcus had chosen this moment for his revenge. To murder me. That I was about to die after coming through all this. To be free of me so he could take over the company someday. Make it something petty and small. A band of thugs terrorizing his own perfect little fiefdom on the edge somewhere. An homage unto his own brutal self.

Which is why I'd always known I'd need to kill him fast when the time came.

Someday.

If just to save the company.

If just to save even myself.

I let go of the shotgun because I couldn't get it around and on him in those tight smoky quarters of the burning crawler. He was coming after me now with whatever he was going to crush my skull with a second later.

I pivoted, index finger going into my karambit's ring as natural as the thousand or more times I'd done it. Practicing for this moment. Knowing it was coming all along.

I got my feet under me.

If that hadn't happened nothing would've in what came next. I dragged the pop-knife, felt the blade lock open. Wrapped my hand around the hilt and threw a savage swipe at his throat. Low and away from the carotid arteries as I then dragged it up across one of them.

He was dead then.

Maybe he knew it. But he kept coming, slamming into me and bleeding more than he already had been. I gave two steps as my right knife-holding hand drew back over my left shoulder. Then jackhammered into his xiphoid process just beneath his plate carrier.

To save me.

To save the company.

Twice was enough. The third time I hit plate and broke the blade because my hands were shaking so bad and the funnel was consuming my vision. Like I was gonna have a heart attack. Everything was going dark. Real dark.

He was on his knees, grabbing his upper stomach and trying to breathe as I tried to realize what I'd done. I knew where he'd keep the package. Inside his carrier. I reached around the webbing, found a memory device, and pulled it out. It said something about *Project Zephyr Recover*. And some numbers. I stumbled over him, picking up the shotgun and leaving the vehicle. Stumbling across the airfield, through the smoke and gunfire.

I saw the Wild Thing one last time. In the smoke and the mist. Going from Ultra to Ultra like some angel of death, standing over them and passing by as he shot the ones still left alive. I paused to watch him, even though there was the sound of other gunfire coming from all around. Elements not us were still fighting. And he turned, standing over a dead Ultra, and stared back at me. The faceplate of his future armor was a dark mirrored lake and distantly I thought I saw a face in there. I shivered like something had just walked over my grave.

Then he turned and walked off into the mist, disappearing into what remained of the battle once more.

The ghosts came next. Apes like wraiths were racing through the smoke that smelled of cordite and chemicals, tackling the Ultras and dragging them down as more racing monkeys and apes swarmed the field all around. I didn't care in that moment. Knowing I was kind of invisible to them. Hoping I was, really. Too tired to care anymore as I stumbled forward. Satisfied with accepting a lie that let me keep picking my feet up and putting them down to get a little closer to salvation.

I missed Hauser, but he found me in the smoke.

"Sergeant Amarcus?" he asked. His computers needed to reconcile the numbers.

I just stared at him as we trotted for the looming armored security transport ship somewhere ahead. I felt hollow. Empty.

And like the galaxy was going to be a better place now.

"I understand, Orion," he said.

The monkeys came now. Like fast missiles. I drew a bead and fired. Clearing our left flank. I could see the ghost image of our rescue dropship ahead. Landing lights on. Engines spinning up. The Monarch in the cockpit. Hauser fired on the right. We weren't gonna make it. The monkeys were everywhere now.

Ahead of us was a downed Ultra. Struggling on the ground. Wounded. The apes would take him.

I stopped.

"Help me, Hauser."

We picked him up and carried him to our ship.

Why?

Because he was a human too. Just like us.

And the galaxy was different now.

The game had changed.

Humanity was becoming rare. Best to hold on to what we had.

CHAPTER FIFTY-ONE

I made the flight deck. We were climbing through high atmosphere by then. Gears up, engines to full. We'd departed the starport battle turning into a slaughter of apes. The world below growing calm and peaceful as the details of its ruin lost all meaning up here among the clouds. Alarms ringing.

"Interceptors coming in!" someone shouted from the nav station.

I pushed forward toward the pilot's station.

Handed her the memory device from Box 88.

She was flying the ship for the rendezvous with the *Spider*. We still had a few minutes to intercept. High above I could see some of the larger Monarch starships coming down through the atmo to cut us off.

She watched me. The Monarch. The Seeker who ruined the galaxy by making meaning meaningless. By bringing back truth. By making us believe if even just in ourselves.

She turned to the comm panel, inserted the memory device, and tapped in the docking signals array for the *Spider*. I watched her fingers moving across the number pad display, entering some secure login for something called *Motherlode*.

She turned to me.

"That's the bank ship. *Motherlode*. They're currently receiving all uploaded mem for transfer."

I nodded. The algorithm she'd recovered from the ship would transmit in the packet. Then it would infect the upload. And in time, ruin the galaxy. And destroy the Monarchs.

If just to give humanity a chance against a new enemy.

Ahead I could see the *Spider* screaming through upper atmosphere ready to make the intercept. She's a big beautiful ancient destroyer from when ships were made to stand up to fleet combat at broadsides. We got her for a song because she was derelict. Fighters were swarming but her point defenses were old-school good. Avengers were going down in smoke and flames at ten thousand feet.

She was from back in the days of the big carrier battles. Escalon. Darru Reef. Suntokur.

"This changes everything," she whispered to me without words. Or whispered words in my head now. "No more safety net, Orion. No more Monarchs. But that doesn't mean anything if no one believes."

"I know," I said. "I know that now."

The sky was big and beautiful. We'd make the hard dock. Flee for the other side of the world. And then boost for deep space. They'd never find us in the interstellar dark. Not for twenty-five years. Things would be different then. I had a feeling, much different.

I believe.

Life. Liberty. The pursuit of happiness. Old words. Old words that never should have died, been taken away, or been traded for the lie of a sure thing. Human words that embodied humanity. Despite everything the Monarchs had done to us. If this was the way back... then I was cool with that now. I guess.

I nodded and walked off the flight deck. I had to find out who was left alive. Who'd made it.

"Who was he?" Preacher asked when I found the Kid's body on the cargo deck just after departure off the hot LZ. We were nearing the *Spider* now.

"Just a kid," I mumbled and closed his eyes. Watching that beautiful face. All that wasted youth. He would always be that way now. Whenever I thought about him, and I think about all of them, he would always be this young and not some old ruined merc getting older and more ruined. Always.

"Who was he, Orion?" Preacher asked a second time. Knowing. Demanding the answer I was supposed to give. The Strange Company answer.

Stinkeye came to stand over the boy and drink from his flask. He said nothing and then turned away, muttering, "Damn shame. Damn, damn, damn shame."

But I couldn't because I was choking. Couldn't say the words that needed to be said. I knew if I said another word, then...

Being a bastard about the truth. That was Preacher, who only showed up when they were dead. Our dead. We. Us. Always the truth when no one else cared to listen anymore. No one cared about the truth, I wanted to scream. The Monarchs got rid of that or we gave it all up a long time ago.

We don't believe in it anymore.

"Who was he, Sergeant Orion?"

"Just some kid!" I shouted at our company holy man. Beginning to sob because I didn't care anymore. "Just a boy. A boy who loved a girl who didn't love him anymore so he became a soldier because he thought... hell, he thought he might make a difference like all the young who don't know nothing about it. Like that might mean something to someone who doesn't care anymore."

In the distance the guns of the *Spider* could be heard echoing titanically through the atmosphere. Thundering out against those who would try to stop the company from reaching another world as we departed atmo. They didn't stop. And neither did death.

"Who was he, Sergeant Orion?" asked our holy man, gently. And I could hear how tired and old he really was. As old as the galaxy. As old as war itself.

I hated Preacher. Hated the universe and hated the whole damn mess we'd become.

But Preacher was right.

And I hated him for it all the same. Because this is what we do when we die. When one of ours goes down on some foreign world in a fight no one's ever gonna remember.

"I just looked over and some bullet had caught him near the landing gear," Punch had said, beginning to cry. And then gone away, slamming his hand into a bulkhead because that was all he could do. Grieving. The Kid had held his position when it got close. Too close. We needed him there. And he did what needed to be done. Died next to a landing gear on a bad LZ so the company could go on and fight other wars for the Monarchs on other worlds.

Or maybe that would change now. Who knew.

"Who remembers him, Sergeant?" whispered Preacher in the red-lit cargo deck of a hijacked ship. Docking connectors coming online as we approached our salvation, the *Spider*.

We do. We will remember who he was. Who they were. Even if no one ever does. Even if some young girl doesn't care if you died both bravely, and badly, on a foreign world. For your brothers. Even if you were brave at the last, when it was most needed.

Who was he, Sergeant? asked Preacher for the last time.

"He was Strange Company. He was one of us."

THE END

EPILOGUE

Two weeks out from Crash, we're heading into the coffins aboard the *Spider* for the long cryosleep to Blackrock. The Monarch took the dropship after we docked. Disengaging in the middle of a running fight with Monarch interceptors swarming all quarters. Her job was done.

She took the Little Girl.

On purpose? I don't know.

Or just because everyone had forgotten our youngest and tiniest company member in the mad dash to disembark and get the wounded onto the *Spider* during hard dock.

I guess she, the Seeker, didn't want to stick around and find out how disappointed we'd be when it turned out our mem was worthless now that she'd uploaded the doomsday algo that had destroyed the Monarchs two thousand years from now. Decided to get it done sooner than later. For freedom, or something…

Or maybe she had other things to do.

We'd find out in twenty-five years.

We already knew our mem was worthless. The markets were collapsing while we were still under boost thrust away from war-torn Crash.

I got a letter while I was planetside during the whole war on Crash. Came to me, but I usually don't forward mail down-planet so I can focus on what needs to be done while we're operating.

It was a reply to one I had written before we were planetside. A letter I had written and sent before the war.

I'd written the Falmorian party girl I'd spent the evening with. The one who had asked me if there were regrets.

I told her my answer because I'd been thinking about it ever since.

Told her yes, there were regrets. And that somehow, she was a regret to me. That I wished I'd stayed. Gotten to know her. I told her I knew I was being silly.

And I understood if she didn't even remember me. I was no one. Just some tired soldier who had felt something that evening. Something missing. Something much needed.

She wrote back.

One line from across the stars.

Yes. I remember you, estrangier.